# Finding Sara

## Nancy DeMarco

*Raven's Wing Books*
Peterborough, NH

# FINDING SARA
## By
## Nancy DeMarco

Softcover:  ISBN-13 9781618070203
Hardcover:  ISBN-13 9781618070210
Kindle (mobi):  ISBN-13 9781618070227
ePub (Nook, Sony Reader, iPad): ISBN-13 9781618070234
Generic (PDF): ISBN-13 9781618070241

Library of Congress Control Number (LOC): 2012933196

Cover and Interior Design:
Pamela Marin-Kingsley, Far-Angel Design

Photo Credits:
Cover photo courtesy of Ann Everett and Nancy DeMarco, with special thanks to Reese Ball.
Author photo: Tammy McCracken

Raven's Wing Books

Ravens' Wing Books
an imprint of Briona Glen Publishing LLC
ATTN: Customer Service
PO Box 3285
Peterborough, NH 03458-3285
Email: customerservice@brionaglen.com
Web site: www.brionaglen.com

*This book is dedicated to*
*Sandi Nason,*
*the bravest person I know.*

# Acknowledgements

Thank you to Tammy McCracken, who sat in my kitchen and listened while I read the entire novel to her, twice.

To Phyl Manning for her line edits, and for her encouragement and guidance.

To my number one cheering section, the members of Writers United, for their kindness and support.

To J.E. Nissley, Ann Everett, Wayne Zurl, John VanCott, jlmo, Patti A. Yaeger, Linda Ulleseit, Madison Ready, Joy Campbell, Susan Stec, LeeAnn Mackey, Caroline Kellems, and all my other friends at thenextbigwriter.com, who told me the truth and made me a better writer.

To my dear friend Connie Lee, and to my sister Sandi Nason, for reading the whole thing and pretending to like it.

To Briona Glen Publishing, for taking chances, and for making so many dreams come true.

Finally, thank you to my ever-patient, eternally supportive husband Jim, without whom I would never have had the opportunity to write.

# Prologue

*One dream is enough.* That's what Sara Morgan told herself as she calmed her injured horse and tried not to panic. *Just one dream.* The others were long dead and had never been possible anyway, not for someone like her.

She cradled Harlee's big black head while Dr. Harris sedated the mare and stained the bloated eye. Tears the color of grass ran down Harlee's cheek, dripped to her white knees, and spattered the pine shavings at her feet. The veterinarian shined a light between the lids, his breath sounding hollow in the darkened stall. Sara told herself Harlee would be fine and her dream was safe. But she knew better. The injury was serious, and luck was rarely on her side.

Finally Dr. Harris put the light away and tousled the mare's forelock. Sara's stomach pinched as he turned toward her, his face grim. "It's a good thing you called when you did, Sara. Another day and she might have lost the eye."

Sara winced as he turned back to Harlee and squeezed antibiotics beneath the swollen lid. The mare stood motionless for the procedure, head slung in Sara's arms, lips stretched toward the fragrant timothy beneath her feed tub. Dr. Harris gave her a final caress and cleared his throat. "I think she'll recover, but you should be aware an injury like this is often caused by a whip."

Sara's heart beat harder. *He wouldn't.*
*-He hits you.*
*Shut up.*

"Could she have banged it on something?"

-*Worthless freak.*

-*Freak, freak, freak, freak-*

*Be quiet,* she pleaded. *Just let me get through this.* She smoothed her features and built a wall around the voices in her head. They'd been impossible to silence for months, drowning her thoughts, chanting until she wished she could fall unconscious, quiet only when she slept.

Frustration flashed in the veterinarian's eyes, but he shrugged and turned back to the horse. "It looks as if someone whipped her over the head, and the end of the lash punctured her eye." He glanced at Sara and sighed. "But anything's possible. She could have banged it."

-*After he hit her.*

*It might have been an accident.*

-*Stupid, stupid, stupid, stupid-*

Dr. Harris gave Harlee a shot of banamine for pain and swelling while Sara stroked the snow white neck and spoke to the mare in soothing tones. Then he packed his things and wrote up an invoice. "Keep her out of the sun until that pupil returns to normal," he said as he handed Sara the bill. "Call me if anything changes."

"I will, and thank you." Sara cringed at the amount; Mark wouldn't be happy. She waved goodbye and pulled her hood up against the chill. Then she sprinted across the gravel driveway toward the house, shivering with thoughts of her husband's escalating temper.

*He wouldn't hit Harlee, would he?*

-*Of course he would.*

-*Stupid, stupid, stupid, stupid-*

Mark didn't look up when she slipped through the door, hung her coat on the hook by the wood stove and placed her boots in the tray on the floor. Instead he ripped through the drawers and cabinets, flung the neatly organized contents on the floor and kicked them with filthy boots.

She opened her mouth to ask what he was looking for this time, but the familiar scent of alcohol told her it was useless. As always she would wait for him to finish, and then she would clean up the mess. *Much like sex.*

Guilt washed over her as the voices took up the chant. -*Sex, sex, sex, sex-*

Her hand went to her forehead, and she pressed her thumb into the space between her eyes. "Harlee has a corneal ulcer," she said to the walls. "Dr. Harris thinks she'll be okay, but another bill is the last thing we need."

She caught herself a moment too late. Mark was on a tear. She was stupid to mention money. Reprimanding herself with a sharp pinch to the thigh, she turned and hurried toward the door. A few minutes outside on the steps should be enough. Maybe he hadn't heard.

-*Stupid, stupid, stupid, stupid-*

In the space of a breath he slammed her against the wall, yanked her from her feet, and wrapped his hands around her throat. Spit spattered her face as red-rimmed eyes met her own.

"It's always money, you fucking frigid bitch! Nothing is ever good enough for you."

Sara pushed hard against him as her chest squeezed and lungs screamed for air. He choked her longer than usual, and she fought panic as a voice came to her in a whisper. -*Play dead.*

Eyes closed, she allowed her body to sag like a rag doll, chest convulsing against the increasing grip on her throat. Mark let go with one hand and roared as he punched a hole in the wall beside her. Then he released her, let her tumble to the floor, and kicked her aside like a pile of dirty laundry.

Air burned past her throat as he screamed, "If you don't fucking like it, leave!"

A lesser voice answered, -*Okay*. But she dared not say it aloud.

"See what you made me do! Bitch!" He picked up a chair and threw it past her as she closed her eyes and peeked through her lashes, pretending to be more dazed than she was. The door was eight steps away and he was twice her size. She'd never make it.

Crouching, she crab-walked to the bathroom, slammed the door, locked it behind her and hunched in the corner beneath the window. Her gaze landed on a shriveled deer fly suspended in an abandoned spider web, wings bound to its desiccated body. Deep within a sneering voice snickered and said, -*Do you see yourself?*

The door shuddered beneath a sharp crack punctuated by a scream of rage. "Open the door or I'll fucking kill you!" She hugged herself, flinched with each crash, closed her eyes, covered her ears—

*He'll calm down in a minute. I'll be okay.*

-*Run!*

-*Run! Run! Run! Run!*

The voices shot through her like electricity, propelling her to the window. Rain cooled her face and the scent of sodden earth calmed her as she pushed up the sash and crawled through the narrow opening. For once she was glad to be tiny, wiry as a child. She hung from her fingertips, gathered her courage and let go. As the ground rose to meet her she tucked and rolled, heedless of the mud that seeped through her clothes and plastered dark curls across her eyes. A coat and shoes would be welcome, but she couldn't risk going back. Not now.

A dozen horses nickered as she crept past the shed row, and her heart turned her feet in their direction. She paused under the overhang outside Harlee's stall and let the sound of contented munching and the intoxicating smell of horses and hay wash over her. The pinto's breath touched her cheek, and the unexpected warmth made her shiver as she closed her eyes and whispered, "I'll get my dad. We'll come right back for you."

*What if he hurts her again?*

*-She's worth more than you.*

*-Hurry!*

Sara lifted the spare keys from the hook beside the water spigot and crept up the driveway to the hill behind the barn. Her mind raced, and everything around her slowed. The wind stilled and fat drops of rain floated toward the ground like snowflakes, peaceful and unhurried. She glided forward, no longer connected to her feet, recognizing the subtle change in perception that preceded a blackout. As she slipped inside the rusted truck, the door creaked; the sound echoed in the hush.

*Fifty yards to the house, another seventy-five to the road.* A sense of purpose enveloped her like mist. *I can do this.*

*-You'll pass out again.*

*No, I won't.*

*-You always do.*

*Not this time.*

With shaking hands she turned the key and released the brake, waited for the truck to roll, popped the clutch. The old heap choked and jerked. She held her breath, silently chanting, *Please, please, please, please* until the engine sputtered to life.

The front door crashed open. Mark thundered down the steps and ran for the driveway.

She hit the gas.

# Chapter One

## Six Months Later

In a cottage at the edge of a sprawling estate, Sara woke crying. Her cotton nightgown clung to clammy skin as she hugged knees to chest and sobbed herself awake. Six months had passed since Mark choked her for the last time. But the nightmare had followed her.

*You'd think I could get over this already.*

*-Useless, stupid girl. Die before you hurt someone else.*

*-Die, die, die, die, die-*

Angry at herself and sickened by the voices, she rolled onto her back and tried to remember the dream. *Mark.* It must have been about her ex-husband. She pressed her eyes shut and tried to block memories of his face in the headlights, of her mother's shock and her father's disgust over what she'd done. The fragments of memory seemed unreal, as if another person's nightmare had attached itself to the space behind her eyes.

*How could I have hit him and kept going?*

*-Crazy, crazy, crazy, crazy-*

*Why can't I remember?*

She told herself it didn't matter. Mark's injuries had been minor; he deserved worse. And now she had a new job and a new life. A flicker of excitement rolled her out of bed, bare toes searching the floor for yesterday's clothes. Moments later, dressed in lumpy sweats with her usual cotton socks and muck boots, she stepped out into the bracing air of a

New Hampshire dawn.

"Morning, everyone!" Sara called out as she entered a spacious stable. Warm, moist air laden with the scent of hay and pine shavings enveloped her. Eight horses reached over Dutch doors and nickered in unison. Sara made her way down the aisle and poured pre-measured supplements into each bucket.

The horses stepped back in response to her soft commands, then dove into breakfast with abandon. Once the feed tubs were licked clean, she opened the doors to a twenty-acre pasture, and the little herd shook off the night's confinement with enthusiastic leaps and bucks. Harlee led the way, her elastic stride carrying her forward at a pace that made the others look like nags.

"Anything to report?" Janet's voice startled her, and Sara spun around to face her new employer. Tall and lanky, Janet embodied the calm exterior and relaxed manner of a lifelong horsewoman. She was a welcome, yet worrisome, distraction.

"Everything's fine," Sara replied. The familiar feeling of being on trial made her tongue thick and dry, and she worked hard to form thoughts into words. "I have vaccinations set up for next week, and the farrier's due tomorrow."

Janet flashed a smile. "Thank you for keeping on top of things. We're lucky to have someone of your caliber looking after our little family operation."

Sara flushed at the unaccustomed praise. "You and Marty have been so generous," she said, tripping over her words. "The cottage is wonderful, and the gym membership is a big help."

Janet fixed her with a dissecting gaze. "I can't believe you want to exercise after slaving away here all day. Careful you don't disappear."

"But I have to work out," Sara insisted. "I have to be

super fit if I'm going to make it to Rolex."

"Still on the three-year plan?" Janet's grin held a subtle dare.

Excitement spilled into Sara's voice, but she stammered in embarrassment. "It's, it's been my *dream* to compete at Rolex, since I was little. And Harlee is amazing. If anyone can do it, she can."

"How is your lovely mare? Still enjoying the pasture?" Janet shaded her eyes, and Sara followed her gaze across the fields. A knot of horses searched a south-facing rise for the first sprigs of grass. At the base of the hill, an appaloosa rolled in loose granular snow. The drifts were still knee-high in the valleys, deeper in the shady areas beneath mature pines.

Sara nodded, one quick dip of her head. "Harlee loves it here. I'll have to be careful she doesn't get too fat once the grass comes in."

"She's like you," Janet chuckled. "She could use a little meat on her bones." As Sara opened her mouth to protest, Janet held up a hand. "I know. I know. You eventing people are insane, racing like madmen over those gigantic jumps. You don't want to be carrying extra pounds."

Sara's confidence dimmed at Janet's tone and the word *insane*. Her love of the sport was sometimes difficult to justify to others. Eventing had its dangers, yes, but there was so much more.

"I guess maybe we do enjoy the thrill," she said, trying to answer as candidly as possible. "But it's not all speed. It's a triathlon. Three phases. The dressage portion is about precision and harmony, and the show jumping is—"

"Not my thing," Janet said. "I prefer a nice trail ride. We go places on horseback most people never dream of." She paused, eyes twinkling. "Speaking of distance rides, we're taking the kids and horses to Vermont for the month of October. So you'll only have Frosty to look after, and Harlee, of course."

Seriously?" It was months away, but the thought of having only two horses to care for was intoxicating. She barely recognized the excited squeak of her own voice. "The whole month?"

"Yup. The whole month. That's the beauty of home schooling."

Feeling guilty for taking an unscheduled break, Sara lifted a dirty water bucket off Frosty's wall and emptied it out the back door. "Wow," she said as she picked up a long-handled brush and began to scrub. "Maybe I can find someone to look after the horses for a week so I can take a real vacation."

Janet shot her a furtive look. "With anyone special?"

*-No one wants you.*

*-Crazy, crazy, crazy, crazy-*

Sara scrubbed harder. "No, there's no one special. Maybe Cassie can get some time off."

"Is that your old friend from college?"

"Mmm hmm." Sara rinsed the bucket with a short length of hose and returned it to Frosty's stall. "We're meeting for lunch later today."

"That's great! I'm glad you're getting out and starting to see people." Janet touched her shoulder and Sara stiffened without meaning to. Janet withdrew her hand and stepped back. "I need to go. The kids will be up by now, driving Marty crazy. Talk later?"

Sara nodded and reached for a second bucket, relieved her employer hadn't asked more questions. Janet knew about the voices, knew Sara had been confined to a mental hospital, twice. Yet she treated her like a normal person, even let her play with the kids. But Sara knew she was always on trial. Her job could end in a heartbeat if she appeared different or strange. And then she'd be back in Lubec with arguing parents and a very short leash.

Suddenly in need of comfort, she set aside her chores and whistled for Harlee. The mare arrived at a gallop, patchwork coat gleaming, eyes sparkling with curiosity. The pinto's eagerness always lifted Sara's spirits. Following a few minutes of preparation, she slid gratefully into the saddle, still amazed she'd been able to keep the valuable mare. Mark had fought for her, hard. But for reasons known only to him, he'd abruptly backed down.

She breathed in time with Harlee's strides as the voices fell away. The pinto was filled with enthusiasm. Eyes bright, her feet tapped a delighted rhythm as they bounded over miles of snow-packed trails.

They paused in a sunny meadow surrounded by white pine. The footing was unusually firm for mid-March, and Sara took the opportunity to sneak in a practice session. Her dressage test, a series of choreographed movements at the walk, trot and canter, would be evaluated by a judge and awarded points based on accuracy and beauty. Dressage was the first phase of the triathlon known as eventing.

Harlee floated over the ground as Sara asked her to lengthen her stride. She danced sideways in response to Sara's subtle shift in weight and a whisper of pressure against the horse's lively barrel. Sara breathed Harlee's breath, felt her horse's muscles ripple in harmony with her own. Their union was intimate and absolute. Harlee's movements reflected Sara's thoughts and brought her spirit to life.

Insistent ringing ruined the magic of the moment. With a sigh of resignation, Sara fished her phone from her vest pocket. Bits of hay and pine shavings came with it, powdering Harlee's clean mane and drifting on the breeze.

"Hello, Sara." Her father's tone was clipped and impatient, as if he had a lot of calls to make. As Chief Medical Officer at the Machias Psychiatric Hospital, he undoubtedly did.

"Hi, Dad." Sara slipped her reins and allowed Harlee to walk back along the trail. Cell service was spotty at best, and she hoped perhaps the signal would be lost.

"Have you contacted my referral?" Her father was all business, as usual.

Sara closed her eyes and willed herself calm. "Yes, Dad, I met with her when I got here last week."

"And your next appointment is?"

"I haven't made one yet. I don't like her. I want to stay with Dr. Franklin." Sara steeled herself for her father's disapproval.

"He's here in Machias and you're eight hours away. If you want to live on your own, you have to stay in weekly therapy. That's the deal."

*-The deal sucks.*

*-Ass, ass, ass, ass-*

"But I feel like I'm getting somewhere with Dr. Franklin." Sara's voice cracked. She swallowed and tried again. "He said he'd be willing to work with me by phone."

"That's not good enough."

*-Tell him to fuck off.*

*I can't. I'm still his ward.*

*-Run away.*

*No.*

Sara's shoulders drooped. She knew her father had a point. His idea of supervision was *in person,* and Dr. Franklin worked at the Machias Psychiatric Hospital, too far away for weekly visits. Her doctor's final words to her were a comfort, and she went to them often: "I'm a phone call away. You won't be alone."

"I'll call her today," she said through growing misgiving. "But, Dad."

"Yes?"

"Please don't ask her to put me on medications. You know that doesn't work for me."

The silence that followed seemed to stretch between them, tension building until her heart yanked at her chest. When her father finally spoke, his voice sounded as if it came through clenched teeth.

"Sara, there have been advances, new drugs, new therapies. If one doesn't work, we can try others. Don't write off medicine so quickly."

Sara hooked her fingers in Harlee's mane and took three deep, steadying breaths before she answered. "But I'm doing really well."

"You hear voices in your head and you're mucking stalls for minimum wage," he shot back. "I'd hardly call that doing well."

*-Fucktard!*

*-Dick, dick, dick, dick-*

Sara stopped breathing. She struggled to shake off her father's words and the growing shame that accompanied them. *Baby steps*, she reminded herself, remembering Dr. Franklin's advice. *Start small and keep going forward.* She began the new breathing exercise he'd taught her, and when she spoke again, her voice was calm.

"My job may not be much, but it's a start. It gives me time to ride Harlee and enough money to compete." Still counting her breaths, she searched for a better argument. "Medications make me clumsy. I'm not safe on a horse, certainly not at speed."

Again there was a pause. She could hear her father's fingertips drumming his desk a moment before he spoke. Her calves inadvertently hugged Harlee's sides, and the mare burst forward before Sara could soothe her. Harlee danced sideways and threw her head before she settled into a ground-eating walk.

"Of course," her father said. "That's why I'm sending you to Sylvia Green. No drugs, no hospital, as long as you continue to do well. Happy?"

"Relieved, I guess." Sara realized she'd been holding her breath. She relaxed her belly and let air fill her lungs to bursting. Gaining her father's permission to remain medication-free was no small victory. "Don't send her my records, okay? I want to start from scratch."

She heard her father's exasperated sigh followed by, "Fine. Just make sure you go in with a good attitude. Sylvia is intimately familiar with conditions like yours. We're lucky she relocated and agreed to take you on."

"Yes, lucky." Sara spoke so softly she wondered if her father had heard the sarcasm. She changed the subject.

"I'm looking forward to seeing you and Mom next month."

"Your mother is excited, too. Make sure you call her." Her father sounded more relaxed.

"I will, Dad. I'll call her today."

As Sara said goodbye and slipped the phone back into her pocket, she let her mind wander to the rugged beauty of Lubec, Maine. Despite her father's ongoing criticism and control, her heart rose at the prospect of visiting her home town. Maybe that was the answer to all life's twists and turns. Maybe you had to go back to the beginning and get your bearings before going forward.

# Chapter Two

Dressed in jeans and a sweater too nice to live on her bedroom floor, Sara watched as Cassie ran her fingers over a cropped cashmere hoodie on the sale rack outside JCPenney. Malls made Sara itch. Crowds were as good a place as any in which to hide, but she felt pressured, pushed to buy things she couldn't afford, compelled to fit in. Shopping was supposed to be fun, wasn't it? She probably ought to smile.

Her friend's flawless lips pursed in concentration as she asked, "So, what have you been doing for fun?"

Sara's embarrassment quickly grew to shame. Bad enough Cassie was tall and willowy, her hair sleek and golden and never in need of brushing. When Sara stood on tip-toes, her eyes met Cassie's chin. And her hair exploded around her, its kinks and corkscrews refusing to be cowed by her admittedly cursory attempts at grooming. She ignored the sick feeling in her stomach and pretended to look at a down jacket.

"This."

"Don't you go out? Socialize?"

"What do you think I'm doing now?" Sara looked toward the food court and bit down on her frustration. "You know I'm not good at meeting people."

"It takes practice." Cassie replaced the hoodie and moved on to a silk blouse.

"I suppose, but why bother? Who wants to hang out with someone like me?"

Cassie didn't answer. Sara kept her head down as the silence stretched between them and inadequacy swelled inside her. Cassie was right. If she wanted to be more normal, she'd have to try harder. With a tentative sigh she looked up, ready to meet Cassie's inevitable reproach. Instead there was a sly smile on her friend's face, one Sara hadn't seen since college.

"We could play the game."

Sara's tongue glued itself to the roof of her mouth. "No."

*-The game! The game! The game! The game!*
*Shut up! You're not helping.*

With manicured hands on perfect hips, Cassie jerked her chin toward the food court. "Number seventeen. First guy you see sitting alone."

"You've got to be kidding." Sara swallowed back the anxiety that threatened to become panic. "We haven't played that stupid game since college."

"But it got you out of your shell."

"It's humiliating." Sara broke out in a sweat.

*-Play the game!*
*I don't want to.*
*-The game! The game! The game! The game!*
*No!*

"It's a great game, and it helped before," Cassie said. "Number seventeen. Two-point grip, three-point peck. Meet at the Panda Palace when it's over." Her lips were set in a determined line. Sara recognized the expression. Cassie wouldn't back down.

"Fine. Spot me." Sara had no intention of going through with the dare, but if she headed for the food court, perhaps she could distract Cassie with lunch. Legs turning to rubber, eyes blurred, she pushed her way into the crowd. Mall mothers, intent on herding tired children, bobbed against her. Texting teenagers blocked her path while checkout clerks grabbed quick meals and gulped sugared caffeine.

At a table near the exit a man sat alone. Short and balding, face buried in a comic book, he bit into a double cheeseburger from the dollar menu. A ratty tee shirt with a *Far Side* cartoon depicting an old woman with a squashed cat on her ass completed the picture.

*Aw, shit.*

*-Nerd, nerd, nerd, nerd-*

*Maybe Cassie didn't see him.*

Her eyes leapt from the bald man to Cassie. Panic swept through her when she realized her friend was looking right at the man with the burger. Sara shook her head and mouthed no. *She'll give in. She has to.* But Cassie didn't budge. From halfway across the mall, she pointed a polished fingernail at the rumpled backside of the doughy little man with the burger.

*-Dork, dork, dork, dork,* changed to *-Nerd, nerd, nerd, nerd-*

*Not now,* Sara hissed in what she hoped was a commanding tone. She slipped into a chair and fought queasiness as the room revolved around her. *Maybe I can do this. I can pretend to be someone else, someone normal.*

*-Never normal.*

*-Sick, sick, sick, sick-*

Anger pushed Sara to her feet, and she tried to remember what it was like to pretend to be someone else – someone brave. Cassie had been a big sister, helping her feel as if she belonged. But that was before Mark pounded the hope out of her, before she *broke* and woke up in restraints at the Machias Psychiatric Hospital.

*Can I?*

*-No.*

*I can try.*

*-The game! The game! The game! The game!*

The chanting faded as Sara smoothed her hair, slipped her glasses into her purse and closed the distance between herself and her mark. With a silent prayer to no one, she forced herself forward.

"Pretend you know me!" She dropped into the seat across from the man and fixed him with an anxious look. Her heart leaped like a cricket in the hands of a small boy, but quitting now was unthinkable. Cassie would never let her hear the end of it.

"Uh, what?" The man tore his eyes from *The Tick* and knocked over his dollar fries. His glasses slipped down his nose, and he pushed them in place. Sara lowered her lashes and moistened her lips.

*-Slut, slut, slut, slut-*

*-Stupid, stupid, stupid, stupid-*

"Just act like we're a couple, like we've been dating." Sara darted a look to her left and to her right, trying to create just the right amount of tension. Too little and he might ask questions. Too much and he would bolt.

"Please say something, anything." An over-deep breath caused Sara's breasts to lift and jiggle beneath her best V-neck sweater. Burger Man's discreet glance told her she had his full attention, and she struggled to invent a believable lie. "Talk to me. My life may depend on it."

*Youch. Too much. Man, I'm out of practice.*

*-Stupid, stupid, stupid, stupid-*

The man's eyes met hers with a mixture of amusement, concern, and distrust. His hand moved to protect his wallet. He might be nerdy, but he was no dummy. Sara fought off the embarrassment of her last statement, steadied herself and tried harder.

"Oh, shit! He's right over there by Mrs. Fields." She pointed at a tall, beefy man in a bomber jacket. Then she bent forward to give Burger Man a good look at her far-from-disappointing cleavage. Heart pounding in her ears, she took his hand, the one that wasn't on his wallet. *Two points*, she told herself as she whispered, "Is he still there?"

"Um, yes, he is."

"Damn it. Does he see me?"

Burger Man looked past her and frowned. "I don't think so."

"Thank God. Can you tell me when his back is turned?"

He didn't answer. He stared into Sara's eyes while distrust edged out concern. Unless she engaged him quickly, he would walk away. She screwed up her face like a small child begging for candy. "Pleeease?"

*-Please, please, please, please-*

Burger Man's skepticism melted, replaced by kindness and support. "Um, okay. Hold on." He squeezed her hand. The warmth was unexpected and comforting, and she peeked up. Round cheeks and a gentle smile sent a tingle down her spine, and the corners of her lips tugged upward. A tide of guilt surged through her. She looked away.

"Now! He's turned around now." Burger Man was getting into it.

Sara jumped to her feet, poised to dash away. Instead she swallowed hard, leaned across the table and touched her lips to the balding forehead. *Three points. Five total. Cassie owes me a drink.*

*-Drink, drink, drink, drink-*

"Thank you." She paused long enough to grab a fry and suck it between her lips. Burger Man's eyes locked with hers. They were rich brown, the color of good earth.

*-Run!*

Startled, she broke the gaze and bolted to the hallway. She ran straight down the mall, past Niemen Marcus, and ducked into the Panda Palace. As the double doors closed behind her and she caught her breath, she felt a glimmer of courage rise to the surface.

Heads turned in her direction. Eyes cut through her pretense, saw the cripple behind the disguise. She slid to a stop and backed toward the door. Cassie would be right behind her. They could enter together.

Fingers wrapped around the door handle, she paused. *Can I?*

*-No.*

*-Coward, coward, coward, coward-*

Weak and trembling, Sara steadied her breath and leaned against the door. Maybe she could pretend a little longer. She ground her teeth, held her arms rigid at her sides and turned around.

"Table for two, please." Her voice was faint but audible, adequate, she realized, for the purpose. Giddy with a sense of accomplishment, she followed the host to a booth near the back. It was a small thing, walking into a restaurant alone and asking for a table. Something a child might do without a thought.

*But I'm twenty-five, and this is my first time since they let me out.*

*-Crazy, crazy, crazy, crazy-*

The thought reminded Sara that she was defective, but she clung tight to Dr. Franklin's words. *Baby steps,* she told herself as she took her seat and glanced at the buffet. A mound of shrimp fried rice caught her eye and she got to her feet, shaking less violently than she'd expected.

She watched to see how other people removed covers, used serving utensils, and moved from one item to another. Then she did her best to copy them, to blend, to fit in, to put her doctor's advice into action.

*Play the part. Practice being the person you want to be, and in time you become that person.*

Plate piled high, she made her way back to the table. Dr. Franklin might be hundreds of miles away, but his words had followed her. He was right. She wasn't alone.

# Chapter Three

Cassie swept through the door of the Panda Palace ten minutes later with a smug smile and a bag from JCPenney. Sara looked up from her half-eaten shrimp fried rice and waved.

"You got a table!" Cassie seemed oblivious to the amused looks of diners and wait staff drawn by her bold entrance. She plopped onto the stuffed vinyl bench and returned Sara's grin. "Sorry to keep you waiting, but after you pulled off a seventeen, I had to try a twelve." She tugged the cashmere hoodie from her bag and pointed to a small stain that matched her lips. "Half off."

Torn between laughter and reproach, Sara snorted. "You're not a struggling college student anymore. That's stealing."

"So it would be okay if I were broke?" Cassie stole a crab Rangoon from Sara's plate and bit off the end.

"That's not what I meant."

"I know, lighten up. You've been such a downer since your divorce." Cassie popped the last bite of pastry into her mouth and ran her tongue over her lips. "You really need to get laid."

*-Laid, laid, laid, laid-*

A man at a nearby table turned and wiggled his eyebrows. Sara slid lower in her seat, her skin prickling. "I don't see you with anyone special."

"Who said anything about special?" Cassie leaned toward the buffet and sniffed. "Don't be such a prude."

*-Dirty girl, filthy. No one wants you.*

*-Sex, sex, sex, sex. . . .*

"That's enough!" Sara flinched when she realized she'd spoken out loud.

"Enough what?" Cassie reached for a spring roll and Sara pulled her plate closer.

"Don't you get it, Cassie? I'm not like you."

*-Broken, broken, broken, broken-*

Cassie looked confused, and Sara sucked in a calming breath and focused on the ceiling. The decorative dragon hanging above her head reminded her of a gift from her father when she was a little girl; a papier-mâché pony from Mexico. She focused on the memory of smacking the piñata with a plastic bat until candy rained down on her head.

Gradually her shoulders dropped away from her ears, and she let her eyes wander. The buffet line had dwindled with the end of the midday rush. A knot of kids elbowed for position, making ice cream sundaes beneath the tip of the dragon's tail. In a booth near the buffet an elderly gentleman sat alone.

*-Turnabout's fair play!*

*-The game! The game! The game! The game!*

Sara turned back to Cassie with her best innocent smile. "Old guy in the booth at twelve o'clock. Number thirteen."

"Piece of cake." Cassie slid from her seat and strolled toward the buffet. Her sleek blond hair swept across the tramp stamp peeking out above her True Religion jeans, and the effortless sway of her hips attracted envious glances from women and furtive looks from men. As she drew alongside the older man, Cassie feigned a trip, grabbed him, and buried his face between her breasts. Then she pulled herself to her feet with a practiced yelp.

"Sorry, sir. I'm *so* embarrassed." She backed toward the buffet with a smirk only Sara could see, turned and headed for the shrimp and salmon. Once her plate was full she sauntered back to the table and slipped into her seat. "How's he look?"

"The old guy? I doubt he'll wash his face for a week." They both laughed, and Sara felt a weight lifting from her shoulders. She let herself sink into the feeling of release. *It's good to be free.*

"So tell me," Cassie said. "What's up with your folks these days? Does Daddy Dearest still have you on a leash?"

*-Never free.*

Her ribs constricted, squeezing her lungs, but Sara tried for a breezy tone. "Well, legally he's my guardian. But he mostly stays out of my life."

Cassie raised an eyebrow. "Why are you still his ward? You're living on your own, holding a job. Why don't you get a lawyer and contest the guardianship?" She took a bite of salmon and sighed. "Don't let it drag on for four years like you did the last time."

"That was for my protection." Sara hated to state the obvious, but Cassie seemed to forget how dangerous her illness could be. "I jumped out a window. I could have killed myself."

"That was forever ago. You went through four years of college with no problems."

"And then I broke again." Unable to meet her friend's gaze, Sara picked at the paper placemat poking out from under her plate. "It's too soon. I've only been out of the hospital for three months, and this is my first time living alone. My dad is afraid I'll have another episode."

"He could help you in other ways, without being such a control freak."

Shame settled into the empty places as the last of Sara's confidence fled. She tensed and relaxed, tensed and relaxed, counted her breaths, and felt a failure when her shoulders bunched and her throat closed. She gave up and dug her thumb into the opposite thigh until it hurt. "I cost my parents a lot of money. They had to pay Mark not to go to the police after I ran over him."

"Mark deserved it." Cassie stabbed at a spring roll before she pushed her plate away. "He attacked you. How could he go to the police?"

"That's not the way it works, Cassie. I left the scene of an accident." Sara closed her eyes and hunched as her mind filled with images of that night. "I guess I should have stopped and let him choke me some more."

"What?" Cassie shook her head. "That's insane, Sara. You did what you had to do."

Sara glanced at her friend and tried to keep the whine from her voice. "I still don't remember what happened. According to my dad, after I ran over Mark I ended up in Lubec village. I was out of my mind. I attacked a police officer."

Eyes closed, she tried to remember something, anything from that night. But there was only racing the old truck down the driveway, swerving, hitting the brakes. Then nothing. "They brought me to the hospital in handcuffs. I'm told I was crackers for six weeks."

Cassie's expression was difficult to read as she opened her mouth to speak, closed it, and squashed her napkin in her hands. "It must have been horrible waking up in that place again. You've been doing so well for such a long time."

Sara's throat plugged as she tried to answer, and she only nodded in reply. With a swallow and a deep breath, she managed a whisper. "I guess I'm lucky Daddy's a psychiatrist." She shoved rice into her mouth and pretended to enjoy it, but the taste was gone. If only she could spit it into her napkin without being rude.

"Is it okay for you to hang out with me?"

"I didn't ask." Sara twirled lo mein on the end of her

fork and avoided Cassie's eyes. "My mom likes you, but my father still thinks you're a bad influence."

"The feeling's mutual." Cassie said nothing for a moment, but Sara listened to her friend's regular breathing and wished she could be so calm. "What rights did they take away from you this time?"

"Pretty much the same as before." Sara swallowed her lo mein and forced another bite. "My father decides who I see and where I live, and anything I own is under his control." Frustration had her stomach cramping, but she forced a laugh. "It sucks, but at least I don't own much. My clothes, an old truck and horse trailer, and Harlee." She peeked up and met Cassie's encouraging smile.

"I'm sorry." Cassie spoke in a much more sympathetic tone. "I just hate that he has so much control over you. It's not right. You're fine now."

"I'm never fine, Cassie. I'm coping."

Cassie flinched and stared at the table. "Sometimes I forget about the voices. You hide them so well."

Sara risked a smile. Her friend's honesty was always a challenge. Most people treated her like a toddler, using sing-song voices, saying what they thought she wanted to hear. But with Cassie, she always knew where she stood.

"I try to fit in, but you're the only real friend I have." Sara pressed down on the disappointment that threatened to erupt into anger. "When we were in college I did my best to make friends. I met new people and spent months getting to know them. But everyone panicked and ran the moment I told them I hear voices in my head."

"Their loss." Cassie's shrug was dismissive, but there was empathy in her eyes. "You should tell people right away, you know. Weed 'em out before you invest a lot of time and effort."

Sara snorted and covered her mouth. "I can see it now. 'Hi, I'm Sara, and I hear voices. Wanna be friends with us?'" She laughed, but it sounded fake, even to her.

Cassie's response surprised her. "Yup, that's exactly what I mean. Be bold. That way you'll know when you finally meet someone worth keeping around."

Sara pasted a smile and mumbled thanks as a server refilled her water glass. Cassie's advice worsened the pain in her stomach, but it also made sense. "Doubt I'll be meeting anyone at the barn," she said. "Besides, I'm not sure I'm allowed to date."

"Your father?"

Sara nodded. *Of course, my father.*

"Don't ask. What he doesn't know won't hurt you."

*-Liar! Deceitful, devious girl with sex on her mind. Shut up!*

Sara shot Cassie a quelling look. "I shouldn't lie to my father. He's trying to do what's best for me."

"You didn't tell him about seeing me. Besides, your mom would take your side." Cassie lowered her voice to a gentle purr. "Wanna meet me at the gym tomorrow after work? It's wall-to-wall guys. Ripped guys, doughy guys trying to get ripped; fat, bald guys—whatever you want."

"Maybe whatever *you* want." Sara scrunched up her face and shook her head. "I'm planning to work out, but I'm not ready to meet anyone. And don't try to set me up again. You don't have the best track record." Cassie looked mystified, and Sara shot her a withering look. "Oh, please, remember Paul Cooper?"

Cassie went blank for a moment, then giggled. "Okay, he was a loser. But don't quit. Just swear off Pauls." She swiped the corners of her mouth with a paper napkin. "There will be countless frogs between you and your prince. But if you don't look, you don't find."

Sara chewed on the inside of her lip; the sharp sting brought tears to her eyes. Cassie didn't get it. How could she? Confident and gorgeous, Cassie could have any guy she wanted. "Who in his right mind would want me?" she blurted. "Someone like Mark? I'm better off alone." She shot Cassie a defiant glare. "There's no point in dating. Even if someone looks past my problems, what then?"

Cassie shrugged. "Look, I know you have more than your fair share to deal with, and it sucks. But don't give up. I met a great guy there last week. Maybe he'll show up and I can introduce you."

"Don't bother." The words came out louder than Sara had intended, but for once she didn't care.

*It wouldn't work out anyway.*

*-Broken, broken, broken, broken-*

Cassie's cheeks turned red. "Sorry, sweetie. You can't have this one."

The chanting faded as Sara caught her friend's meaning. "You *like* this guy? You? The woman who says men are playthings?"

Cassie looked so completely flustered, Sara had to stifle a laugh. Cassie covered her face with her hands and peeked through her fingers. "He invited me back to his house on Thursday, and I stayed over."

"You didn't! A guy you just met? What were you thinking?"

*-Slut, slut, slut, slut-*

"I was thinking, *Wow*." Cassie cleared her throat and sat up straighter. "Look, tomorrow is St. Patrick's Day and I want to celebrate. So meet me at the club. We'll work out and have dinner afterwards."

Sara folded her arms across her chest and set her jaw. "Fine, but just you and me. No setups."

"Whatever, Sara." Cassie stole the last spring roll from Sara's plate and bit it in half. "Suit yourself."

# Chapter Four

Paul Emerson frowned at his computer screen and scanned line after line of code. Normally he'd have no trouble spotting the error, but today was different.

*Who was she?* He'd been enjoying a cheap burger and fries at the mall, reading a classic *The Tick* comic book, when out of nowhere a pretty woman dropped into the seat across from him. Obviously involved in a role-playing game, she'd pretended to be in trouble. Then she stole a French fry, kissed his forehead, and pelted away.

*She was like a fairy.* He closed his eyes and rocked his chair back. The woman was tiny, even shorter than he, and that was saying something. At a mere five feet four inches, he found himself eye-to-eye or looking up at most women. But this girl—

*I could probably kiss her forehead without standing on the stairs.*

He squinted at the screen, but his thoughts filled with startling blue eyes framed by a mane of dark curls. *What was she up to?* The game was nothing he recognized.

"How's it going?" Adam, Paul's housemate and coworker, startled him back to reality.

"Could be better." Paul glanced at his watch. "Five already?"

"Just after. Heading out soon?"

"Naw." Paul returned his attention to the code. "I need to find this error. It's probably right under my nose."

Adam leaned across him and pointed. "Here it is," he

said, indicating a comma where a semi-colon should be. "Can you leave now?"

Paul looked at the ceiling. "I'm an idiot. Let me fix this and make sure it works. I won't be long."

"Okay. Couple hours." Adam chuckled as he walked away. "Steak around eight—"

"—if you don't pick up a girl," Paul finished.

Once the simple mistake was fixed and tested, Paul crossed it off his bug list. The last one out, he flicked off the lights and walked to the only car in the parking lot. It was a Honda Accord Coupe, and his eyes lit up at the sight of his one extravagance.

But even this was meticulously researched and found to be unfailingly reliable, a sensible choice for New Hampshire winters, destined to last until either he or the car died of old age. He paused to rub out a tiny surface scratch with the square of polishing cloth he always carried in his back pocket. Then he wiped his feet and climbed inside.

The twenty-minute drive passed quickly with New Hampshire Public Radio, and as he stepped from the car the smell of grilled sirloin made his mouth water. Adam was cooking, so he must not have a date.

"Try this." Adam blocked the doorway, ceramic bowl and fork in hand. "A pasta thing I threw together. Whaddaya think?"

Paul pushed past him into the kitchen. "Jeezus, Adam, can I get inside first? The neighbors already think we're gay."

"So?"

"So, maybe they have sisters." He set his laptop on the counter and tried to hang on to his annoyance. But Adam looked like a kid with a brand new PlayStation, and Paul gave in and reached for the fork. "Fine, lay it on me." Eyes closed, he dutifully tasted his friend's latest creation.

"This is awesome!" Paul helped himself to another fork-ful, then took the bowl. "It's even better than that potato thing you made last night."

Adam's face lit up. "Great. I made a lot. You better be hungry."

"When am I not hungry? I've been trying to lose the same thirty pounds for six years now. It's impossible with you for a roommate." Paul sniffed the cream-cheese brownies cooling on the stove. "Tell me again why you don't cook for a living."

Adam grabbed a bowl of marinade and rushed outside to brush the sizzling meat. "Cooking is fun. Programming pays the bills."

"I dunno, Adam. Much as I appreciate getting your rent check on time, sometimes I wonder why you don't quit your job and open a restaurant."

"Restaurants are risky," Adam replied. "Besides, thanks in part to my rent, you almost have this place paid off."

"True, but I haven't had much fun." Paul's thoughts strayed to the girl from the mall. *She* wasn't afraid to take risks and have fun. Why hadn't he introduced himself, asked her name? *Outta my league.* He heaved an exaggerated sigh as he took a seat at the round oak table. "You bring home a new girl every week and I work late."

Adam slid the steaks onto a platter, retrieved the pasta bowl, and sat across from Paul. "You could try harder, you know. Hit the gym. It's a great place to meet girls."

Paul cut into the sirloin, seared to perfection on the outside, moist and pink on the inside. When he took a bite, the combination of seasonings brought tears to his eyes. "God, this is good," he moaned. "I guess if I'm gonna keep eating like this, I should get some exercise."

"That's the spirit." Adam leaned across the table and

cuffed Paul's shoulder. "Maybe I'll come with you and check out the offerings."

Paul studied his friend. Tall and blond, with a muscular physique and handsome features, Adam could have any girl he wanted. Near as Paul could tell, he wanted them all.

"With you for a wingman, no one will look twice at me."

"You have other things to offer. Don't sell yourself short." Adam doubled over and coughed until his face turned red.

Paul passed him a glass of water. "Short. Very funny. You deserve to choke." But he laughed to himself even as he thought, *Life isn't fair.*


On the following evening Paul checked into the Tamarack Athletic Club and presented himself to Dan, the personal trainer. The man reminded him of Adam, lean and fit with a handsome face and a full head of luxurious hair.

"Don't overdo it on your first visit," Dan cautioned as Paul started his second mile on what he now referred to as the treadmill of doom. "Just finish up at a walk and treat yourself to the hot tub."

"Sounds good." Paul was proud when his voice sounded normal even though he was panting hard enough to inhale his tongue. As he struggled through his second mile, he let his mind wander. To his dismay, thoughts of the blue-eyed fairy returned. There she was, looking straight at him. And it wasn't a gratuitous *let's throw the short bald man a bone* smile while looking over the top of his head for something better. It was an honest smile.

He shook the vision away as he stepped from the treadmill to solid ground. After a quick shower he walked to the hot tub on wobbly legs and stuck his big toe into the water. Soapy foam covered the surface, and he couldn't help wondering what it was made of. The possibilities weren't pleasant, but the temperature was perfect. He slid into a molded seat and breathed a contented sigh.

*Heaven,* he thought. *Why didn't I do this sooner?* He wiggled his toes in the currents, enjoying the warm, tickling sensation and the rush of jets against tired shoulders.

Two women slid into the seats across from him. At least, he thought they were women. They were nothing more than indistinct blurs with his glasses in his locker rather than on his face. Paul smiled in their general direction and said hello, not expecting an answer. He thought perhaps they smiled back.

Then the impossible happened. The tall one stood up, looked straight at him, and said, "You! I know you!"

# Chapter Five

At five minutes before six, Sara drove into the parking lot of the Tamarack Athletic Club. She went straight to the ladies' workout room, where she could avoid the social atmosphere of the main gym while using a variety of exercise equipment constructed with a feminine frame in mind. Even here she had to reach for handles and footholds made for someone of average size.

Cassie found her there, drenched in sweat. "Slow down before you have a stroke," she said, eyes crinkled in amusement. "Your face is redder than sunburn."

"Hello to you, too," Sara replied, still doing inverted crunches at a rapid pace. "Not everyone can look like you by sitting around eating bon bons."

"Good genes," Cassie grinned. "And designer jeans." She patted her thigh. "I have an early meeting. Wanna take a rain check on dinner and hit the hot tub?"

"Sounds wonderful." As Cassie turned to go, Sara stopped her. "Wait! Did you bump into that guy again?"

Cassie answered in a breezy tone. "Nope. He never called, and he's not here tonight."

"Ass."

Cassie returned an awkward smile. "Even I make mistakes. C'mon. Keep me company, and don't let me pick up another jerk in the hot tub."

Sara showered quickly, yanked her bathing suit over damp skin, and ran fingers through a tangle of chocolate curls. "Hey, you," she called out when she spotted

Cassie's backside heading toward the pool. "Wait up."
She stood before the full-length mirror and twisted,
reaching for a strap just south of her shoulder blades. Used
to seeing herself through Mark's eyes, puny and plain with
frizzy hair and glasses, she stared.

*I've changed.*
*-You look like a slut.*
*-Slut, slut, slut, slut-*
*Shut up!*

Flushed with embarrassment, Sara twisted her hair into
a matronly knot and wrapped herself in a towel. Shoulders rounded, she jogged after Cassie, relieved she would
go unnoticed as long as she stuck close to the long-legged
blonde.

They walked past the pool into a small windowed area,
heavy with steam and the smell of sweat and chlorine.
Together they slipped into the bubbling water. Sara's skin
burned for an instant, and she returned a less-than-enthusi-
astic smile to the man who sat across from them. He looked
familiar, but without her glasses she couldn't be sure.

The next thing she knew, Cassie was on her feet. She
pointed straight at the man, voice hissing with accusation
and said, "You! I know you."

Sara squinted and tried to place him. Cassie stammered,
"You're, you're Adam's roommate. You're—"

"Paul," he finished for her, "Paul Emerson."

Still unable to get a good look at him between her lack
of glasses and the heavy steam, Sara startled at the sound of
his voice.

"Shit, Cassie. He sounds like Burger Man."

"Burger Man?" asked Paul.

"Burger Man?" repeated Cassie.

"From the mall," Sara stammered as she slipped from
the molded seat and crouched lower in the water. "Number
seventeen."

"Seventeen?" asked Paul.

"Seventeen!" Cassie dropped back into the water. "Oh, shit."

"Shit! Crap! Frick!" Sara peeked nearsightedly through her fingers.

"Seventeen?" Paul asked again.

"I'm so sorry. It's a game." Cassie sounded nervous, and Sara glanced at the exit.

"Role playing?" Paul's voice rose an octave as he sat up straight and squinted through the steam.

"Sort of," Sara admitted, not willing to look in his direction. Instead she slipped toward the steps and planned her escape. The hallway was thirty-seven steps away.

*He must think I'm insane.*

*-You are insane.*

*Shut up.*

*-Stupid, stupid, stupid, stupid-*

Paul spoke again, and she cringed at the sound of his voice. "I trust milady was not captured by the mysterious man in the bomber jacket."

Hardly daring to breathe, she sat on the bottom step, scrunched down, and peeked over the foam.

*Isn't he angry?*

*-Answer him.*

Sara thought fast. "Um, I got away, thanks to the kindness of a gentleman of the Burger clan." Eyes closed, she waited for the yelling to start. She had it coming.

Paul chuckled. Sara glanced at Cassie and whispered, "He seems nice." Cassie flicked water at her.

"His roommate is an ass." She sent a splash in Paul's direction. "And did you catch his name? It's *Paul*."

"So?" Paul and Sara asked together.

Cassie sent another splash in Sara's direction. "You swore off Pauls last night."

"That's a new one." Paul shot Cassie a teasing grin. "Usually the infinite forehead and vertical challenge are reason enough to look elsewhere."

Sara snorted and covered her mouth. Cassie stared for a moment before she relaxed into the water and nudged Sara's foot with a practiced toe. "I'm thirsty. How 'bout the three of us go get something to drink? Maybe a bite to eat?"

"I thought you had an early meeting." Sara retreated to the seat farthest away from Paul.

"No problem. You up for it?" Cassie was looking at Paul.

"Sure." He answered without hesitation, and Sara's heart gave a jerk. "There's an Irish pub about a mile down the road," he said with a grin that had her recounting the number of steps to her truck. "Drinks and dinner. I'm buying."

"Perfect." Cassie poked Sara and raised an eyebrow.

-She's using Paul to get back at his roommate.

Cassie's not like that.

-Run while you can!

Sara felt as if an invisible band tightened around her chest, squeezing her breath away, inch by inch. But Paul and Cassie were waiting for an answer. She closed her eyes and pretended to be someone brave enough to mean it when she said, "Okay."

An hour later, Paul feasted on bangers and mash while the girls sat across from him and split shepherd's pie. Green beer and live music added to the mood of celebration. With two Harp Lagers straining his belt, Paul had a comfortable buzz, and the company of not one but two pretty women made the evening magnitudes better.

Cassie was a knockout. At first glance, she appeared a bit too put-together, definitely high-maintenance. But her discreet efforts to support her less-outgoing friend told Paul she was special. *Adam's a jerk. Why didn't he call her?*

And then there was Sara. She was exquisitely petite with a rare but beautiful smile. A scattering of freckles dusted her nose and cheeks, and a mass of unruly curls tumbled past her shoulders, halfway to the small of her back. On the surface, she seemed uncertain, her vivid blue eyes more often on the tablecloth than turned toward him. But then, he wasn't the sort of person a pretty girl would look at.

"So tell me about this game you play," Paul said, trying not to stare. "It's nothing I've ever seen before." A waiter dressed as a leprechaun set a grasshopper cocktail in front of Cassie. She thanked him and took an appraising sip.

"It started in college," Cassie said, licking whipped cream from her lips. "We were roommates, and Sara was sort of a wallflower. I wanted to build her confidence."

They both turned to Sara, but she bit her lip and said nothing.

Cassie winked at Paul, took another sip, and continued. "I dragged her to a party and introduced her to some friends. It wasn't long before this jackass, Dick Sloan, tried to hit on her."

"Uh-huh." Paul imagined someone tall and fit, handing Sara a practiced pick-up line. His appetite faded.

"And here's Sara with no idea this guy's trying to get into her pants." Cassie nudged Sara, and she jumped and looked up.

"I was really stupid," she said.

Paul tried to catch Sara's eye. *Why is she so shy? Doesn't she know how adorable she is?*

Sara's head tilted forward and curls fell across her face. "He told me he'd been wounded in the war, and he asked if I wanted to see his scar." Her voice was hesitant. She seemed guarded and wary, far less assured than the part she'd played at the mall.

Cassie shot Paul a see-what-I-mean look.

"And I felt sorry for him," Sara said. "I didn't want to see his scar, but I hugged him. He was trying to pull my hand lower when Cassie came to my rescue."

"I could see she was going to need a den mother." Cassie looked affectionately at her friend. "So I dragged her off to the ladies' room and explained things." Cassie took a bite of potato, and Paul hid his impatience behind a smile.

"I grew up in Boston," Cassie said. "I wasn't exactly worldly, but compared to Sara, I'd been around the block."

"And so a friendship was born." Sara looked up for an instant. "Cassie taught me a sixteen, and she sent me back to even the score with the war hero."

"And a sixteen is?" Paul waited. *This should be good.*

"Advanced," mumbled Cassie. "Sara was a quick study."

"Do I want to know?" Paul turned to Sara and tried to coax her with an encouraging smile.

"Probably not," Sara replied. "Basically, I let him think I wanted to see his scars, and I *accidentally* spilled my soda in his lap."

"We made sure it had plenty of ice in it," Cassie added.

"And then I pantsed him." Sara looked at the table.

"You pulled his pants down?" Paul was stunned. Perhaps Sara wasn't as shy as she appeared.

"I did." She put her hands over her face and peeked between her fingers. "You are aware of the effects of cold on," her face turned red, "you know."

Paul crossed his legs. "Turtled, was he?"

"Yup," Cassie answered as Sara clamped her mouth shut. "His name went from Dick to Dickless that night."

Paul doubled over, laughing harder than he had in years. He caught Sara's eye, saw cautious restraint.

"It was probably worse than he deserved," she said.

"Nope." Cassie cut her off. "He was a predator. Predators deserve no mercy."

Paul laughed so hard his breath came out in cartoon-dog wheezes. "Remind me to stay on your good side," he said. Both girls giggled. It felt good.

"So what were you doing in the mall yesterday?" Paul asked as he wiped his eyes.

"Well," Cassie looked sideways at her friend. "Sara's been a little down lately, and I was trying to cheer her up." She poked Sara in the arm, and Sara swatted her hand away.

"I was married," Sara said, "and it didn't work out very well." She looked at the table again. "The divorce was final a month ago, and Cassie was trying to get me out of my funk by daring me to do a seventeen."

"And a seventeen is?" Paul wanted to ask about the jerk Sara had been married to. Was that why she seemed so apprehensive?

"That's when you pretend you're in trouble, and you get a random guy," Sara gestured to Paul, "to help you."

"So I was in the right place at the right time?" Paul worked to keep his voice smooth. Sara reminded him of the wild birds that came to his feeder—beautiful, delicate, and easily spooked.

"I guess so." Sara looked up. A hint of panic flashed through her eyes before she went back to pushing her food around. "Cassie put restrictions on it. You had to be sitting alone, and I got points for a grip—holding your hand, and a peck—kissing your cheek or forehead."

"Isn't that risky?" The thought of Sara messing with the wrong guy made Paul queasy.

"Cassie spotted me," Sara hurried to explain. "She watched to make sure I didn't get in trouble." Sara's gaze met his, and he saw a hint of a smile before she looked away.

"Wait. Cassie was there?" Paul caught Cassie's eye. "Didn't you recognize me?"

Cassie shrugged. "I was halfway across the mall and I only saw your back." She grinned at Sara. "It's just as well, though. If I'd introduced you, Sara would have run the other way."

"I would not." Sara's denial only lasted a moment. "On the other hand, you don't always have the best taste in men."

Cassie looked hurt. Paul thought of Adam and changed the subject.

"What's number one?" He felt the need to fill in missing numbers starting at the beginning. He supposed it was a character flaw, but it made him good at his job.

"Oh, number one? That's just bending over and showing cleavage," Cassie said in a dismissive tone.

"And two is bending over the other way, showing panties," Sara added. "You have to make sure you're wearing public panties, nothing baggy or faded."

"I always wear public panties," Cassie said. "You never know."

Paul's beer went up his nose. He pitched forward, red-faced and coughing. Cassie giggled.

"And three is?" he asked, trying not to choke again.

Cassie glanced at Sara. "Three is lifting your shirt."

"You get bonus points for every second." Sara peeked at Cassie, holding her breath. Her face contorted, and both girls burst into laughter.

"What?" Paul started to feel left out.

"It's nothing." They waved his question away. "Just a restaurant we can never go to again."

Paul closed his mouth with an effort. "Oh, man. I wish I'd been there."

"Glad you weren't!" Sara's cheeks turned pink, and she hid her face behind her hands.

"Anyway, a four is just blowing a kiss to a guy and saying, 'Call me,'" Cassie began.

"That seems pretty tame," Paul said, confused.

"Yabbut, the guy has to be with a girl," Cassie explained. "And you have to make it look as if you know him *well*, if you know what I mean." Cassie looked at Sara. "That one's cruel. We only did it once, and only because he had it coming."

"Yup." Sara's curls danced around her face as she nodded. "He was cheating. We did that girl a solid."

The waiter brought dessert, and they drank coffee and shared Flan Eireann. Paul was lost in Sara's dimples, aching to get to know her better. Her smile lifted his spirits, reminded him of the dreams he had of marriage and family.

*You just met her. Don't be pathetic.* He tried not to get his hopes up, but every so often he caught her looking at him as if she didn't know what to make of him. *Oh well. At least she's looking.*

Paul walked the girls to the parking lot. First he said goodnight to Cassie. Then he held the door of Sara's pickup as she jumped up into the cab. His heart raced.

"Do you think maybe you'd like to go out sometime?" Paul's voice cracked when he spoke, and he hoped it wasn't too obvious how much her answer meant to him.

For a moment she looked as if she might bolt. But the fear vanished as quickly as it appeared, replaced with a slow smile. She pulled a scrap of paper from a pile of loose trash in the console beside her seat, scribbled something, and handed the note out the window as she said goodnight.

Paul watched until the old truck left the parking lot and vanished at a bend in the road. He stopped breathing as he held the note to his keychain light. Then he let out a whoop, punched the air and danced in a circle.

# Chapter Six

Humming to himself, Paul bounded up the steps to his four-bedroom Colonial. He let himself into the kitchen, set his laptop on the table, and poked his head into the living room. Adam sat in a leather recliner, sock feet on a hassock, nursing a beer.

Adam looked up from a crossword puzzle. "How'd it go?"

"Great. I did two miles on the treadmill, and I met a girl." Paul tried to keep his tone light, but Adam snapped to attention.

"Name?"

"Sara."

"Phone number?"

"Yes."

"Yes?" Adam sat upright. "You? You got a phone number?"

Paul tried to feign nonchalance, but Adam's surprise was justified. They'd been roommates for six years, and not once had Paul come home with a girl's phone number. He dangled the yellow sticky note from his fingertips. Adam lunged for it, but Paul snatched it away.

Adam settled back into the recliner and smirked. "What's she like, besides blind as a bat and completely lacking in taste?"

"She has a smile that can make the sun shine on a cloudy day." Paul mugged an expression of rapture. He was rewarded by a theatrical eye roll from Adam.

"Spare me."

"She was there with Cassie," Paul added.

"Cassie?"

"Yup. She asked about you." Remembering the hurt in Cassie's eyes, Paul frowned. "The three of us went out for dinner. You missed a good time."

Adam stared at his beer.

"What's wrong with you?" Adam's gloomy expression, combined with a beer and a crossword puzzle, was disconcerting. "I know you like to play the field, but I like Sara. Don't screw with her friend."

Adam sipped his beer. "I like Cassie, too," he admitted. "And I don't want to talk about it."

"Well, maybe you should."

"Nope."

"Jerk."

"Yup."

Paul groaned and turned away. "Are you at least gonna call her?"

"I don't know. She's not really my type." Adam's tone pronounced the subject off limits.

"Not your type? She's gorgeous."

"Look." Adam glared over his beer. "I'm not up for anything serious, and that girl is most definitely not a one-night stand."

"Do you even hear yourself?"

"I said I didn't want to discuss it."

"Aw, come on, Adam. Grow a pair." Paul walked to the kitchen and stuck his note to the refrigerator. "Mine," he said, pointing to Sara's phone number. "Don't touch."


The following evening, Paul bolted out of the office at one minute past five and drove straight to the club. Not wanting to appear overeager or desperate, he hadn't called Sara. She seemed shy, and he wanted to avoid crowding her and scaring her away.

That was what he'd told Adam. To himself he acknowledged a nagging fear that she would come to her senses, realize a cute girl could do a whole lot better, and send his short, balding self packing. So, he had a plan.

He commandeered a stationary bike that gave him an unobstructed view of the check-in counter. He would pedal until Sara arrived. Then he'd wait twenty minutes before heading to the hot tub. With luck, perhaps he could talk her into dinner.

Ninety minutes later, Paul began to question his plan. His quads ached long before the first ten minutes were up. They transitioned to burning, then screaming, and now lapsed into a state of trembling numbness. He shook with fatigue, sweat drenched his shirt, and only a combination of stupidity and willpower kept him going.

Not sure he'd be able to walk if Sara did show up, Paul decided to try a different machine. Stepping from the exercise bicycle, he limped to the Stair Climber. Immediately, he wished he hadn't. He clutched the padded handles and swayed like a Boy Scout singing *Kumbaya*.

*This is stupid.* Paul clutched the safety rail and pulled himself upright. *I should go home and call her.* But the blow of being turned down would be lessened if he disguised their meeting as a chance encounter. So he ground his teeth and pushed on. Just when he thought he couldn't take another step, Sara walked through the door.

Almost crying in relief, Paul waved, digging deep and marching up the steps with renewed vigor. Sara waved back and vanished into the women's locker room. He let the machine coast to a stop. Sweat ran down his face, dripped from his chin, and pooled in his sneakers as he hobbled toward the men's locker room, grinning. His plan might work after all.

Sara's workout was brief, and before long she and Paul shared dinner at McDonald's. He carried burgers and fries on an orange tray. She filled paper soda cups and collected napkins and ketchup packets from the self-serve counter.

"Are you sure I can't take you someplace nicer?" Paul asked again. "I don't want you to think I'm cheap."

-*Cheap, cheap, cheap, cheap*-

"Nope, it's my turn to pay." She settled herself into a booth by the exit and glanced at her truck, seventeen steps away. "I already know you don't mind the dollar menu."

Paul laughed and Sara tried to relax. What was it Cassie told her years ago? *Look up, make eye contact and breathe.* She sucked in a lungful, felt her breath catch in her throat, and exhaled slowly.

"True," he agreed. "I'll eat anything. But I thought you were a little more health-conscious."

Sara's insides squirmed when she tried to meet his eyes. Instead she unwrapped her double cheeseburger and feigned interest in the word puzzles on the tray liner. "Why do you say that?"

"Look at you!" he blurted. "You look like you've never seen a donut. I look like I've never seen a donut I didn't like."

-*Fat, fat, fat, fat*-

Sara forced a bite of burger, embarrassed for him and unsure how to respond. Would he be offended if she laughed?

-*Ask him something.*

*What?*

-*About him.*

Her heart raced, her vision clouded, and she spoke in a rush. "Tell me about yourself."

*-Idiot.*

*-Vapid, warmed-over, uninspired, cliché-*

*-Stupid, stupid, stupid, stupid-*

Eyes closed, she focused on her words. "What I mean is, I think Cassie and I did all the talking last night. You didn't get a chance to say much."

Paul's voice was soothing, and her eyes opened as he spoke. "There's not much to tell. I'm a software engineer. I work a lot. And when I get home I usually work some more." He looked uncomfortably apologetic.

*He's embarrassed.*

*-Pitiful. Like you.*

Sara ignored the voices and reached for a French fry. It was silly, but the small action made her feel bolder. "Do you like your job?"

Paul's eyes lit up. Sara let out her breath in a whoosh as his words tumbled over one another in a lively cascade. "You know, yes, I really do. I like the work, and I like the people I work with." A wide grin lit his face and Sara caught herself smiling back. "A bunch of us have dinner together each week. We're like family." He looked at Sara with a hopeful expression. "Maybe you can come along sometime."

*-It's a trap!*

*-Don't trust him!*

*-Run!*

"I'd like that." Sara blocked the warning voices and worked to stay calm. "I don't know many people here. My family is eight hours away in Maine."

She hadn't noticed the loneliness until she voiced it out loud. In most ways, she was better off away from her parents' immediate control. Here, at least, she could meet a nice guy and share a cheap lunch without Daddy's interference.

"I'm heading up for a visit soon," she said, "the first since I moved here."

"Are you from Maine?" Paul asked between bites.

"Yes. I grew up in Lubec. It's the easternmost point in the USA," she said with a trace of pride. "It's beautiful there." Her mind unfocused as she pictured the fog rolling in off the ocean and smelled the salty air.

"How'd you come to be here?" Paul had a spot of ketchup on his chin, and Sara found her smile growing wider.

"Well, when Mark and I split up, I couldn't afford to buy or rent." Memories pounded against her. How to explain without revealing too much? "I stayed with my folks for a few months. Then I started looking for live-in jobs with horses. Riding is the only thing I've ever wanted to do."

Sara felt like a popped balloon as she waited for Paul's reply. He wouldn't understand her dedication to riding and competing. No one did. Horses were as much a part of her as breathing. But working in barns meant she would always be broke, and she'd spend her life dirty and smelly and swatting flies.

"So, do you like your job?" Paul wore a crooked smile as he handed back the question she'd asked him.

"I love it. Only—"

"What?"

"Well—" Sara thought about her words, not wanting to appear ungrateful to Janet and Marty. But the job, she hoped, would be temporary, a stepping stone to something better. "I do spend most of my time shoveling and grooming and making repairs," she said. "I can't do as much riding and training as I'd like." Embarrassed, she shrank into her seat.

*Now I sound spoiled.*
*-Lazy ungrateful cosseted bitch!*
*-Spoiled, spoiled, spoiled, spoiled-*

"I don't mind hard work," she insisted, speaking as much to the voices as to Paul. "But my dream is to buy my own place. I want to teach riding and coach students at shows and events. To attract good students, I need to win at the upper levels, and so far I've only won at Preliminary, the mid level of the sport."

Paul listened as if he were interested, and Sara was surprised to see a look of understanding rather than tolerance on his face.

*-He only wants one thing.*
*Shut up!*

"I would guess money is part of what's holding you back?"

"I suppose." Sara stared at him, wondering whether to trust him or listen to the voices. "If I could put all my attention into preparing for competition, I could move Harlee up through the levels more quickly. My goal is to run her at Rolex in three years."

"Rolex? What's that?"

Determination and longing welled inside her and spilled into her voice. "In the sport of eventing, it's the biggest, most prestigious competition in the U.S. People come from all over the world." Sara envisioned herself and Harlee traveling to Lexington, Kentucky, riding shoulder-to-shoulder with the very best. "It's a very challenging, tough triathlon," she explained. "We'll be up against the big names, the very best international competitors. Just to finish would be amazing."

Part of her was overcome by misgivings. Competing was expensive, her salary tiny. But she sat straighter and spoke with a conviction she didn't feel. "Others have made it on the cheap. I can too. It might take longer, but I have to keep at it and give it my all."

Paul still stared at her, admiration and disbelief overtaking his face. "It's nice to meet someone working toward a dream," he said. "It seems most people wait around for things to be handed to them."

Sara flushed at the compliment. *He really is a nice guy,* she told herself with a trace of surprise.

*-He pretends.*

*I don't think so.*

Is there anything else I should know about you?" Paul's smile joked while his eyes remained serious. "Do you have any children, jealous boyfriends, deadly diseases, that sort of thing?"

Sara laughed at his directness. "No, no boyfriend, and no children," she said, "and nothing worse than a completely non-contagious heart murmur." But her moment of happiness died as she thought about the rest.

*-Don't tell him.*

*-Tell him.*

*Maybe he won't mind.*

*-Of course he will.*

*It doesn't matter. I'm better off alone.*

"Are you okay? You look like you're gonna faint." Paul reached across the table and touched her hand. She watched his face. His initial concern was tinged with dread, and her heart quivered like something dying.

*If I tell him the truth, it will end here. I'll never see him again.*

*-Do it now.*

*-It's worse later.*

*I know. It always is.*

She squared her shoulders. "Paul." She drove her thumb into her thigh as she spoke, barely aware of the pain.

Already her vision dimmed, and she hoped she wouldn't have to put her head between her knees.

"I'm in weekly therapy." She watched his expression, saw only concern and interest, and pushed herself to go on.

"It's open-ended, maybe for the rest of my life, because. . ." Sara looked straight into his eyes, ready to see the disappointment and fear, ready to see him turn away.

But she stopped. Maybe Cassie was wrong. She didn't need to tell him everything yet. She'd just met him, and lots of people were in therapy these days. Maybe part of the truth was enough.

*-Lying cunt!*

*-Tell him now!*

*-Liar, liar, liar, liar-*

Her throat closed. She couldn't stop shaking as she shut her eyes and whispered the words. "I've been in a mental hospital. Twice." Her heart pounded in her ears, nearly drowning the chanting. "And I hear voices."

She couldn't bring herself to look at his face. The shock, the revulsion; it would all be there. Next would come the transparent excuse, the rapid departure, and the relief that he'd found the truth before she'd wasted his time.

"You're very brave." Paul's voice was soft and supple, and his hand held hers in a firm, reassuring grasp. She hardly dared breathe.

*Why is he still here?*

*-Desperate.*

*-Short and bald.*

*-Hard of hearing?*

She peeked up. She could see surprise at the edges of his face, but there was more. Deep in his eyes was something that looked like respect.

She lowered her gaze to his button-down shirt and spoke into the air between them. "Why are you still here?" When he didn't answer she looked up again. It was hard to keep suspicion from her eyes.

He popped a French fry into his mouth and squeezed her hand. She thought maybe his voice hitched when he said, "Why not?"

# Chapter Seven

*Why didn't he run?*

Sara crouched in the saddle and coaxed Harlee from a rhythmic canter to a heart-stopping gallop. As they tore past the first distance marker, she set her watch. Eyes squinted against a stinging wind, chin brushing her horse's flying mane, Sara bridged the reins in the little hollow just ahead of the mare's withers. Harlee bore into the bridle, an upsurge of raw power and enthusiasm. Sara reprimanded herself for thinking of Paul; this was no time to lose focus.

The ground fell away as the pair topped the hill and tore down the opposite side. Sara tightened her core and shifted her weight, balancing her horse as they flew down a steep embankment at speeds normally reserved for level ground. As they blew past the second marker, she stopped her watch and allowed the reins to slip through her fingers. Harlee coasted to a walk and thrust her neck forward and down, nostrils flared, feet dancing. Three more sets at this speed, and they'd be done for the day.

The pinto's shoulders were slick as a wet seal, and Sara threw her arms around the sweaty neck, buoyed by her horse's eagerness. As they walked back along the galloping lane she tried to focus on her conditioning regimen, but her thoughts ran irresistibly back to Paul. The question repeated itself.

*Why didn't he run?*

His reaction to her revelation made no sense. Paul had just met her. It wasn't as if he had an investment in the relationship. A sensible man would have thanked her for dinner, even if it was only McDonald's, and then he would have run screaming the moment she was out of earshot.

Instead he held her hand, and said she was *brave*. And when he walked her to her truck, he asked when he might see her again.

*Why does he want to see me again?*

*-Desperate. Like you.*

Sara ignored the voice and dragged her attention back to Harlee. The first event of the season was still two months away, and the pinto was coming along beautifully. They had schooled endless ring figures, practiced over big, imposing jumps, and galloped for miles, building strength and endurance. The horse was eager and fit, and Sara was in the best shape of her life.

But it would be her first competition without Mark, and while he hadn't been much of a husband, he was a gifted rider and coach. Moving up to the more demanding Intermediate level without a more experienced horseman to offer guidance was risky. Horses and riders made mistakes at events, sometimes fatal. It wasn't common, but she'd be a fool to believe it couldn't happen to her or to Harlee.

The thought of anything hurting Harlee always caused Sara to feel as if she were falling. She steadied herself against the mare's neck and spoke to her softly. "We just have to make sure we're ready. We have to train hard, and not let anything get in our way."

Harlee's ears swiveled, and Sara frowned as her thoughts returned to Paul. He could become a distraction. He was different from the few men she'd known, and it wasn't just his humor and wit. He seemed unguarded in a way that almost made her feel safe. Almost.

She scratched Harlee's favorite itchy spot, giggling as the mare leaned into her hand and lopped her ears. "I told him about the voices, and he still wants to see me. Now what do I do?" Her smile faded, and for a moment she forgot to breathe. "What if he wants something serious?"

-*He'll be disappointed.*

-*Hate you.*

-*Hit you.*

A little whimper escaped. Sara took a shallow breath and held it. *He's just got a crush*, she reassured herself. *When he stops to think about it, he'll realize I'm not worth it.*

The disappointment that accompanied the thought was way out of proportion. She'd known him a few days. So what if he moved on? But part of her hoped she was wrong. She hadn't enjoyed being close to a man, *ever*. But Paul—

*Maybe this time.*

-*Idiot. Men have needs.*

Sick with humiliation, Sara hid behind an often-used defense. *I'm too busy for more than friendship. He'll give up soon enough.* She knew a serious relationship wasn't an option, and Paul would figure that out in time. Then he'd be gone, and with him would go the constant reminder that she was broken.


Once home, Sara brushed the last of the sweat from Harlee's coat. The rich sheen and dark dapples bore testament to the quality of the horse's care, and Sara allowed herself a moment of pride. Her phone interrupted the grooming. Torn between bewilderment and unease, she stared at Paul's name across the display. She walked to the bench at the edge of the barn aisle, sat, and calmed herself before answering. Harlee stood on the crossties, ears pricked in interest.

"Hi, Paul! It's great to hear from you." Paul's dogged persistence was unnerving, but Sara was even more dismayed by the bubbly quality of her voice.

*What's wrong with me? I sound like an idiot.*

*-Foolish hope.*

*-Setting yourself up for a fall.*

"It's Paul, Paul Emerson."

"I know." Sara frowned at the phone. She'd already spoken to him by name. Why did he feel the need to introduce himself again?

"Can't be too careful," Paul said, his voice warm and buttery. "You mentioned there was another Paul, and I don't think I want to be confused with him."

Paul, it seemed, had doubts of his own. Knowing this, she found him more approachable, safer, more like . . . her. She tried to keep her tone casual. "I won't be hearing from *that* Paul again, and just to be clear, I'm not seeing anyone."

Paul's voice was distant, shouting, "Yes! Yes!"

*He has his hand cupped over the phone.*

*-He's a loon.*

*-No wonder he likes you.*

"Anyway," Paul said, his voice back to its rich baritone, "I wondered if you might like to come to dinner tomorrow night."

*-He'll hurt you.*

Sara spoke in a small voice. "I'd love to come to dinner."

"With me?"

"Yes, of course with you." Sara burst into laughter. "Are you always this weird?"

"It saves misunderstandings." There was another pause and then a sigh. "Is it annoying?"

*-Yes.*

*-Dork, dork, dork, dork-*

"No, of course not." Sara marveled at the comfort she found in his words. There seemed to be nothing hidden, no dark ambush lurking beneath the geeky surface. With him, perhaps she would know where she stood.

*-Fool! Everyone lies.*

*I know.*

"It's at my house, and Adam is cooking." Paul's tone was uncertain. "A couple friends from work will be there. Is that okay with you?"

*Mark would never have asked that question.*

*-Ass, ass, ass, ass-*

"Sure. That sounds like fun." Her hands trembled even before she finished speaking.

*What if his friends hate me?*

*-Of course they'll hate you.*

As if reading her mind, Paul added, "Cassie is coming, so you'll have a friend there."

Sara breathed a sigh of relief. "Can I bring anything? A dessert, maybe?"

"Adam has it covered," Paul laughed. "Is six too early?"

"That'll be fine. See you then." She tingled with excitement as she wrote his address on the barn's whiteboard and said goodbye. *With Cassie along, I'll be fine.* She dropped the phone into her pocket, picked up a towel and scrubbed at the last bits of dirt peppering Harlee's white stockings. *Cassie always has my back.*

*-So do we, and you're late.*

Sara checked her watch. How could she have lost track of time?

"Shit! My father's gonna kill me!" She ran with Harlee to the pasture, turned her loose, latched the gate, and bolted for her truck. As she backed out of the driveway and headed for the main road, Sara held a lock of hair to her nose and sniffed. The scent of sweat and manure clung to her like campfire smoke. Her nails were broken and filthy, her sweatshirt covered with black and white hairs from Harlee's patchwork coat.

*Great*, she thought. *I hope Dr. Green doesn't mind the smell of horses.*

-*Reeking, dirty girl.*

-*Worthless, worthless, worthless, worthless*-

She rolled her window down and let the wind pound against her, hoping some of the stink might blow away.

# Chapter Eight

Twenty minutes after bolting from the barn, Sara perched at the edge of Sylvia Green's couch. With a surreptitious glance, she traced a path to the door and silently counted. She visualized each step, felt every shift of balance as she mentally skirted the coffee table, sprinted over the beige carpet, and lunged for the door.

Once the all-important escape route was assessed, she gave the rest of the room a visual once-over. Pale blue walls held a single landscape painting. A fountain gurgled from a decorative table tucked into a far corner. The only window was curtained against afternoon sun, and a massage table, folded up, leaned against the wall.

Sara moved to the corner of the couch and eased back until her shoulders touched the cushion. Knees pressed together, hands folded in her lap, she darted a glance at her new therapist.

Sylvia Green relaxed into the office chair across from her, chestnut hair pulled up in a neat bun, tailored business suit hugging a figure uncluttered by muscle or fat. Sara tugged her sleeves over her own muscular arms, feeling less feminine, clunky.

"Please call me Sylvia. That doctor thing is way too formal." Sylvia wore the usual professional smile, the kind that never showed teeth. Her voice had the soothing quality of an FM radio host. "Where would you like to begin this week?"

Sara shrugged. At their first meeting, Sylvia had asked a string of questions from a standard intake form. The interview was designed, Sara knew, to pigeon-hole her into a neat box with its own set of rules. With seventeen years of therapy under her belt, Sara had sidestepped the questions easily, leaving her new doctor with nothing definitive and no reason to recommend curtailing Sara's freedom. *So far, so good.*

She put on her sweetest smile and looked Sylvia in the eye. "I dunno. Where do you want me to start?"

*I could run this session.*

*-Tell her something.*

*There's nothing I want to tell her.*

*-Say something positive.*

Sara nodded and lifted her chin. "I met a nice guy, and he asked me out today." The words were out before she thought to edit them. It was too late to snatch them back.

*What if I'm not allowed to date?*

*-Stupid, stupid, stupid, stupid-*

"That's wonderful news." Sylvia appeared genuinely pleased, and Sara breathed a tentative sigh of relief.

*-Don't trust her.*

*-She spies for him.*

*I know.*

"Where did you meet him?"

"In the hot tub at Tamarack." Sara cringed. *That didn't sound good.*

*-Slut, slut, slut, slut-*

"How unusual." Sylvia drew the words out. A wrinkle formed in the smooth skin between her perfectly arched eyebrows. For a moment Sara felt like a teenager shocking a parent for the first time, off balance, but a little bit pleased.

"So, tell me about him. Tell me what you like about him."

Sara started to say he made her laugh, but she hesitated. There was something more important.

"He's honest," she said, trying to be candid. "When he laughs, he wheezes a little. I think he's not holding back. He isn't hiding anything."

Sylvia beamed at her. "That's very perceptive. What else?"

"He didn't run away." Again Sara wished she could suck back her words. She hadn't told Dr. Green about the voices or the hospital. Those questions, the ones that hinted at schizophrenia, she'd answered with a blank stare.

*-Pretending you'd never heard voices coming from inside you.*

*-Liar!*

*She doesn't need to know.*

"Why did you think he might run away?"

"I told him something private." Sara avoided Sylvia's gaze. "It didn't seem to scare him."

Sylvia rocked forward. "What did you say to him?"

*-Don't tell her!*

*-Hospital, drugs, try to jump again.*

*But he promised. No drugs.*

*-He lies.*

Sara scrunched backwards until her head sank into the overstuffed cushion. "I'm not ready to tell you that yet."

"So, I'm not as trustworthy as this guy you just met."

Guilt washed over her, and Sara stammered, trying to make amends. "It's not you. It's my father. And it's the rules you have to follow."

"What rules?" Sylvia seemed to look right through her. The voices laughed as Sara scrambled to explain.

"He's my guardian. He decides my treatment. You have to do as he says." Sara tried to manage her breathing, but already it was quick and shallow, and sweat broke out between her breasts. Her words sounded more desperate than she'd intended. "I won't take drugs again. They don't work for me."

The confusion drained from Sylvia's face, replaced by understanding. "Calm down, Sara. None of this is a problem, not here." She picked up a notepad from the table beside her and wrote, bearing down hard enough to crease the paper. When she spoke again there was a sharp edge to her voice.

"I don't know what happened in the past, but I want to make one thing clear. I do not report to your father. He may ask questions and offer advice, but I am under no obligation to answer him or to do as he says." Sylvia leaned closer. "Your father will know you showed up for your appointment. Nothing more. Okay?"

Sara was unconvinced. "But what about medications? What if you want to put me on a bunch of drugs that make me clumsy and slow?" She allowed accusation to cover her fear like a mask, and she hid behind a reproachful glare.

"Your father is a psychiatrist," Sylvia replied. "He can prescribe medications. I'm not. I can't give you drugs."

Sara felt as if the couch tilted as her world shifted to accommodate the new information. Sylvia must be a psychologist, and Sara had never worked with a psychologist before. Immensely relieved, she felt her nose plug as an ache thrust itself behind her eyes. She crumpled forward, fighting back tears.

"But Dr. Franklin was helping me." She reached for the box of tissues on the coffee table. "Every time I get comfortable with a therapist, my father finds a reason to send me to someone else. I trust Dr. Franklin. I don't know anything about you."

"Well—" Sylvia spoke softly as she set down her notebook and rested her hands on the arms of her chair. "What would you like to know?"

Sara's mind went blank. It had never occurred to her to want to know anything about a therapist. She looked warily at Sylvia and tried to slow her breathing. "How old are you?" she finally asked.

Sylvia answered without hesitation. "Thirty-two."

"Married?"

"No."

"Ever?"

"No, never."

"Huh."

Sylvia laughed. "Why the huh?"

"Well, where I come from, if you're not married by twenty-five, you're an old maid."

"Huh."

Sara huffed and rolled her eyes, suddenly feeling like a bug in a jar. "Okay, I get it. Why the huh?"

"Is that why you married Mark?"

A wave of humiliation rushed through her. Sara broke eye contact and began her relaxation ritual. *Tense, breathe, relax, tense, breathe, relax. . . .*

*-Be careful.*

*-She's tricky.*

Sara caught her breath and glared. Why not tell Dr. Green the truth? Discussing her marriage to Mark was better than exposing the voices in her head. "If you really want to know, I married him because I didn't think I had a choice."

Sylvia's smile vanished, and she looked on with an expression of detached interest. Sara swatted tears from her cheeks and searched for words.

"I had just graduated college. I was living at home, my parents were fighting, and it always seemed to be about me." She looked at the floor, letting her hair hide her face. "My dad was my legal guardian, and he wouldn't let me live alone. He insisted I stay under some sort of supervision."

"Marriage isn't about supervision."

"It was to my father." Sara caught the frustration in her voice and clamped her mouth shut. It wouldn't do to express anger. She flexed and relaxed her toes, then slowed her breaths until she could speak in a more reasonable tone. "Mark was my riding instructor and my coach. His stable was the only place where I felt like I belonged. Besides, no one else wanted either of us. Mark was an ass, and I'm—"

"You're what?"

Sara shrank into the cushions and tried to disappear. "I'm a mental patient."

"And why is that?"

Sara pushed the hair from her face and scowled as humiliation turned to anger. "They tell me I've had two psychotic episodes." She spat the words and tried to picture herself safe behind a door, swinging shut in Sylvia's face. But Dr. Green's gaze pushed for more, and Sara looked past her to the opposite wall. *Oh, why not just tell her?*

-*Locks and bars.*

-*Needles and restraints.*

-*Crazy, crazy, crazy, crazy-*

"And I hear voices." Sara closed her eyes, mortified.

"I know. That wasn't so hard, was it?"

"Yes, it was hard," Sara shot back, annoyed and nauseated. "And what do you mean, you *know?* Did my father tell you?"

"He didn't have to." Sylvia looked a little bit smug. "I've spent much of my life with schizophrenics and voice hearers. I notice things. Your attention is directed inward, and you gesture when it has nothing to do with our conversation." Sylvia folded her hands and crossed her legs at the ankle. "It's easy to tell. You count, too. How many steps are there to the door?"

"Fifteen." Sara clamped down on the fright in her voice. "Can everyone tell?" The thought of being unmasked, naked and exposed, had Sara's heart pounding and fresh tears burning their way past her eyes.

Sylvia seemed oblivious to Sara's panic. "I doubt it," she said. "You hide it well, better than most. Is this the secret you told Paul? The voices?"

Some of Sara's tension faded, replaced by the question she'd been asking herself all day. "I told him I'd been in a mental hospital, too. And he still wants to see me. I don't understand why."

"Ask him. You're off to an honest start. Don't chicken out now." Sylvia set the notebook face-down on the table beside her. "Is there anything else you'd like to know?"

Sara hesitated. There was something else. Perhaps she hadn't heard correctly. "I probably misunderstood," she said, careful to say one word at a time so none of them would be lost. "But did you say you had experience with schizophrenics, and *voice hearers?*"

"Yes, I did."

"Is there a difference?"

Sylvia settled more comfortably in her chair, as if she planned to be there a while. "I forget you've only been seen by psychiatrists rather than psychologists and other counselors." She picked up her notebook and flipped through the pages, then stopped and read while Sara fidgeted. "In answer to your question, voice hearers have only the one symptom, hearing voices. Schizophrenics generally have a much more distorted perception of reality."

"But isn't hearing voices a delusion?"

"A hallucination."

Sara fought the urge to discount Dr. Green's explanation. It didn't sound anything like what her father had told her. She stammered in confusion. "But. . . well. . . I *hear* them, *out loud,* and I know they aren't real."

"Well, there ya go. You know they aren't real." Sylvia's

expression of patient tolerance caused Sara to shrivel inside. It was a look she saw frequently. People pasted it on when they saw her as feeble-minded and spoke to her as if she were three years old.

*She thinks I'm crazy.*

*-She's right.*

Sara stared at the floor, unwilling to meet Sylvia's gaze. The words weren't at all what she expected.

"When you hear voices, you use the same part of your brain that everyone uses when they talk to themselves. But you hear your internal dialogue out loud rather than as thoughts, and your thoughts take on distinct personalities." Sylvia paused. Sara listened for her to continue. She didn't.

*-She's waiting.*

*For what?*

Finally Sara looked up. Sylvia was beaming. "Many experts consider voice hearing to be a normal variation, rather than an illness. As many as one in twenty people hear voices at one time or another throughout their lives."

A little thrill of excitement rose all the way to Sara's voice. She stared, open-mouthed. "Are you saying I might not be schizophrenic?"

Sylvia's open expression vanished behind a more clinical veneer, and Sara's hopes dimmed. "If hearing voices were your only symptom, then yes, I would consider you to be mentally healthy. But you've also had those two psychotic episodes, and while you don't necessarily come across as schizophrenic, that does point to some sort of disorder."

The disappointment only lasted a moment. Sara's mind was spinning with all the things Sylvia didn't know. "But usually the voices *are* the only symptom. The episodes, it's only happened twice. And both times, I was under a great deal of stress."

*-You're broken.*
*Shut up! I want to hear what she has to say.*

"Let's forego labels for now." Sylvia's voice was gentle, but Sara still felt the sting of judgment. She did her best to shake off the shame of having a mental illness, and she gave Sylvia her full attention.

"Since the voices are currently your only symptom, how 'bout we focus on coping with them? We can try to figure out where they originated, and perhaps we can integrate them into your thoughts. But first and foremost, we want to make it easier for you to live with them." Sylvia's eyes sparkled as she spoke, and Sara felt new interest struggling to the surface.

"Dr. Franklin told me to talk with them," Sara said. "Before that, I tried to block them out. It didn't work very well."

Sylvia picked up her notebook. Sara resisted the urge to peek.

"I remember Dr. Franklin." Sylvia chuckled, and Sara was pleased to see that her laughter didn't seem fake or forced at all. "He's quite a character, and he's absolutely right. Blocking them rarely works." Sylvia looked over her glasses, pen hovering above the page. "Have you ever tried rapid age regression? Therapeutic hypnosis?"

"I don't think so." Sara's skin prickled at the thought of giving up control.

*-She'll make you think you're a talking chicken.*
*-And leave you that way.*
*Shut up.*

"I just wondered." Sylvia tapped her pen against the arm of her chair, her lips pressed tightly together. "Often hearing voices is the result of some sort of trauma. Do you remember anything? An accident? A bad experience?"

Sara shook her head. "My folks don't get along very

well. They've always fought a lot, but there was never anything specific."

"Do you remember when the voices began?"

Sara nodded and flopped back against the cushion. She'd told this part of her story to countless therapists, and the reaction was always the same: initial shock quickly covered.

"My father figured out there was something wrong with me when I was seven. My grandfather died, and I started having nightmares." A familiar pain hooked into her gut, and she worked to keep her tone casual. "My father had me admitted for observation, and that's when he discovered the voices."

"You were hospitalized as a child? That could be traumatic." Sara waited for the stunned surprise, but Sylvia seemed to take the information in stride, calm as an old lesson horse. "So you've lived with this for most of your life."

Sara managed a dismissive shrug. "Yup. I've been the crazy girl of Lubec for as long as I can remember." With a pasted-on grin reserved for therapists, she recited her usual line. "I'm used to it."

"But you do want to get better." It was a statement, but Sylvia's eyes asked the question. Sara stared at her, not sure what to say.

"Of course. But—"

"But what?"

"I've been in therapy for eighteen years, and I'm still sick. There's no point getting my hopes up." Sara realized she was repeating her father's words. He believed in managing her illness, not foolishly dreaming of cures.

"Not trying is the absolute best way to fail. Is that what you want?" Sylvia's question sounded more like a challenge. Sara nearly choked.

"Of course not."

"Then would you allow me to try hypnosis? There's no guarantee. It might not work at all. But if we can uncover the source of the voices, it would help to develop a treatment plan." Sylvia sat back expectantly. "Does this sound like a reasonable approach?"

"I guess so." Ignoring her father's advice was scary, new. "It's just that, I don't think my father believes I can get better."

"What do you believe?"

Sara's eyes began to blur. Dr. Green was asking things no one had ever asked before, and she had no answers prepared. She counted her breaths, pulled them all the way to her belly and searched for a truthful reply.

"I don't know. Everyone says my father is a good doctor." The edges of her vision swirled black, and a dull hum invaded her ears. She gave up the pretense of composure and put her head between her knees.

Dr Green's voice returned to its usual calm. "Is fainting a problem for you?"

Sara nodded and pressed her eyes shut.

"That's what the couch is for. You can lie down, you know." Sylvia's chair squeaked as she got up, and her shoes padded softly past the low table. Sara didn't resist as Sylvia lifted her feet up onto the cushion and pillowed her head. All the while, she spoke in a soothing timbre.

"Your father is a wonderful doctor; I worked with him for many years. But perhaps he's too close to you to be objective." She paused, and Sara relaxed against the pillow. "Comfy?"

"Yes, thank you."

"How 'bout that hypnotherapy?"

Sara opened one eye and tried to identify her therapist's expression. There seemed to be nothing there beyond honest optimism. "You aren't going to make me think I'm a goat, are you?"

Sylvia chuckled. "That's stage hypnosis. This is different."

"Then what are you planning to do?" Sara relaxed as Sylvia returned to her chair and the space between them widened.

"You do seem to have issues with trust," Sylvia said. "Maybe we'll start by looking for a memory of betrayal. It could be something very small. But even little things can leave a lasting impression." She paused, and Sara peeked through her lashes at her therapist's expectant face, eyebrows arched in a quiet dare. "Willing to take a risk?"

*-Run!*

*It might help.*

*-You won't like what you find.*

*-Say no!*

"Yes." Sara set her jaw and hushed the voices with a silent hiss. A flicker of hope took root inside her, and she latched on to it with all the determination she could gather. Something very much like excitement caused her to grin as she asked, "When do we start?"

# Chapter Nine

With her lungs filled to bursting, Sara pulled her shoulders to her ears, then let them fall on a slow exhale. Paul's leather couch felt cold through her jeans, and she crossed and uncrossed her legs, wishing she were tall enough to rest her head against the cushions while placing her feet flat on the floor.

Cassie lounged at her side, seeming completely at ease. Sara felt measly beside her, like a child. Furniture fit Cassie as if it were custom made.

*It's just dinner with Paul's friends,* Sara reminded herself, *and it's not as if I'm here by myself.*

Paul crawled on hands and knees behind the widescreen TV while Adam and someone named Douglass ran speaker wires to the far corners of the house. Caitlin, a plump redhead not much taller than Sara, sipped a diet soda and shouted encouragement. Wineglass in one hand, lobster-filled creampuff in the other, Cassie nudged Sara's toe, gestured to Adam and whispered, "Isn't he dreamy?"

Giggling, Sara returned the nudge and pointed to Paul's chubby butt sticking out from behind the TV. "Isn't he dreamy?"

Cassie looked as if she'd eaten a pickle. Sara hid her face and snorted.

Caitlin flopped down in an armchair and leaned across a glass-topped table to wipe up a spilled drink. "It's been tough being the only girl in this group," she said as she popped a cream puff into her mouth. "I'm so glad you two decided to join us."

"I was nervous about meeting you," Sara admitted. "You're all close, and I didn't know if I'd fit in at all." She looked gratefully at Cassie, relieved that she and Adam seemed to be getting along. "But you're so normal. I feel like I've known you my whole life."

"You think we're normal?" Caitlin gestured to Adam. He stood on the kitchen table, wrapping speaker wire over the curtain rod. "You're crazier than I thought."

Sara let the *crazy* comment slide and threw a don't-get-started warning at the voices. "Well, you all have real jobs," she said, struggling to meet Caitlin's friendly gaze.

"So, what do you do for a living?" Caitlin settled back in the overstuffed chair and flopped one leg over the armrest.

Sara hesitated. "Um, I'm a caretaker on an estate in Amherst. I look after the horses and oversee property maintenance." She looked away, knowing she didn't measure up. "That's a fancy way of saying I shovel a lot of manure."

Caitlin laughed, her tone warm and accepting. "We just shovel a different kind of shit. Deadlines and changes, screaming customers. It's insane."

"That's what I keep telling her," Cassie said. "I'm in marketing, and most of the time it's a circus. It only looks glamorous from the outside."

"But you travel," Sara insisted, "wear heels, go to business dinners."

"Sleep in cheap motels, sit in airports, get pawed by drunken company reps." Cassie made check marks in the air as she spoke. "Like I said, it's just work. There's nothing special about it."

"Just ask Paul." Caitlin gestured toward the television and raised her voice. "He's always the last one out at the end of the day. Until lately, that is. He's developed a sudden interest in going to the gym."

Caitlin stifled a chuckle, and Paul shot her a thanks-a-lot look. A buzzer went off on the kitchen stove, and Adam jumped down from the table and hurried to the oven. He and Paul ferried serving platters from the kitchen to the dining room, arguing like an old married couple. Adam finally appeared in the doorway and announced that dinner was served.

Sara stared in disbelief when she walked through the dining room doorway. The table was set with a linen tablecloth, and white napkins were folded to look like swans. Fresh flowers adorned every place setting. And the food...

"What *is* that?" She pointed to an oblong platter holding a golden pastry.

"Beef Wellington." Adam shrugged as if he made gourmet dinners every day. "It's a tenderloin with mushroom stuffing wrapped in phyllo dough."

Sara stopped breathing as her gaze swept over buttered asparagus, stuffed baked potatoes and an elaborate garden salad. Cups of fresh fruit sat atop each plate. As she watched, Adam placed warm homemade bread in a basket and covered it with a cotton cloth.

"Crap, Adam, did you do all this?" Sara waved a hand toward the table. "I figured we'd have spaghetti, maybe meatballs if we were lucky." She paused, wondering if she'd overstepped.

Caitlin giggled in her ear. "He's not just a hot guy—he's a hell of a cook."

"I'll say!" Sara smiled at Caitlin, grateful for her help. Paul dropped his gaze and Sara's stomach pinched in regret. "I meant the cooking part," she added.

"It's okay. We all know Adam's hot," Paul said with a tight laugh. "Just ask his last dozen girlfriends."

Paul cringed, and Sara could feel his regret. In the silence that followed, everyone stared at Cassie.

But Cassie seemed not to notice. "It's not like I haven't had my share of men," she said as she took a seat. "Don't give it another thought, Paul."

Paul mouthed a silent "thank you" to Cassie before holding Sara's chair and sitting down to eat. They polished off their fruit cups and passed plates to Adam, who carved and served the Wellington.

"This is so good," Sara said, still stunned by the elaborate meal. "Where'd you learn to cook like this?"

"My father was a chef," Adam said. "He passed away a long time ago, but when he was living we used to whip up meals together. Cooking reminds me of him, sort of keeps him with me."

Sara smiled, touched by the trace of color that migrated across Adam's cheeks.

"I thought after dinner we'd have chocolate mousse and coffee in front of a movie," Adam said. "The speakers are all set up."

Paul turned to Sara and explained, "Douglass doesn't want to have to pause the movie when people leave the room. So we set up speakers everywhere, even the bathroom." He bit into a chunk of warm bread, then bent closer and whispered, "In case you haven't noticed, we're geeks."

Douglass smiled proudly, his cheeks swollen with an enormous slice of beef. Sara swallowed another giggle.

Caitlin nudged Sara's elbow. "Tonight is stupid movie night, you know. It's Douglass's turn to rent something, so there's no telling what we'll be watching."

"I brought *Orgasmo*!" Douglass announced.

Paul groaned. "I thought you were bringing *The Meaning of Life*."

"That's not stupid," Douglass replied. "It's a classic."

"But *Orgasmo* is…" Paul looked as if he wanted to die.

"Hilarious." Douglass shoved potato into his mouth and shrugged. "What's the problem?"

Paul turned to Sara, panic in his eyes. "I'm so sorry. I asked him to bring something appropriate for normal people."

"Me? Normal? You think I'm normal?" She stared at him, dumbfounded. "I think that's the nicest thing anyone ever said to me." Chuckling she turned to Douglass. "Bring on *Orgasmo*. How bad can it be?"

For the next hour and fifteen minutes, not including previews, Sara sat next to Paul and peeked through her fingers at the plight of a young Mormon thrust into the world of filming pornographic movies.

"Want to go for a walk?" Paul's voice was soft in her ear.

"Could we?"

Paul took Sara's hand. They ducked past the others, pulled on jackets, and slipped out into the cool night air. As they walked in silence, Sara took in the expensive houses lining the quiet street, and once again she felt defective and out of place. They rounded a corner and continued into a park with a playground and picnic tables. Paul cleared his throat.

"I wondered if we could talk." His grip on her hand tensed. She knew without looking that his face would be full of regret, and his words would be a version of, "I thought I could handle it. It's not you. It's me."

*Shit.*

*-Here it comes.*

Sara twisted her hand from his and walked faster. Paul's rejection was inevitable; she wondered why he'd waited this long. Still, it stung. She thought dinner had gone well. Paul even said he thought of her as normal.

*-Liar!*

*-Fucktard!*

*-Ass, ass, ass, ass-*

She stopped, turned, and faced him. "Look, Paul, I'll make it easy for you." She managed to keep her voice calm while her hopes crumbled away. "You don't owe me a thing. It's okay if you'd rather not see me again." There. The words were out. All that remained was the walk back to her truck.

"What? No!" Paul reached for her hand. "I really like you. I want to see you again." He looked even more distressed than Sara felt. What else could he possibly want to talk about? She turned her attention inward and listened for advice. When none came, she looked at her feet.

"I'm confused." She left out the part about being afraid. That seemed childish.

Paul was silent for a moment, and when he spoke his voice was uncertain. "I know it's none of my business, and you don't have to tell me. It's just, I can't help but wonder what it's like for you."

Her heart beat erratically as Paul paused. *Not that question.* She didn't talk about the voices to anyone. Even her therapist had only a cursory explanation, and she certainly hadn't described them to her father or even to Cassie. Why would he shine a light on everything that made her defective, incapable of being loved? If only he would dump her rather than expose her. A dull roar began deep in her mind. She pressed her elbows to her sides to keep her hands from flying to her ears.

*Please don't ask me that.*

"I wondered if you might, maybe, be willing to talk to me about the voices."

She shattered inside, closed her eyes tight and focused on breathing. "Oh."

"Like I said, it's none of my business. I just want to get to know you better." Paul's hand was sweaty as he stroked

her fingers. She pulled free and walked a few steps before a
wave of dizziness caused her to stumble.

His arms were around her in an instant, guiding her to
a bench where she sat and put her head between her knees.

*-Pathetic.*

"I'm so sorry. I shouldn't have asked. It's okay if it's not
something you want to talk about. Really." The anguish
in Paul's voice only deepened Sara's guilt. He obviously
hadn't realized his question would upset her so.

*What do I tell him?*

*-Nothing.*

*He deserves something.*

Prickling sensations swept over her skin and settled as
an ache in her stomach. "I don't know how to explain."

*I'll sound crazy.*

*-You are crazy.*

*Dr. Green says voices are a normal variation.*

*-So, tell him.*

Sara lifted her head and glanced at Paul's face. There
wasn't a trace of ridicule, but he did look worried. Unable
to hold his gaze for more than an instant, she settled for
tracing patterns in the dirt at her feet. Maybe, if she tried,
she could make him understand.

"Have you ever gone to a movie with someone who
whispers in your ear," she began, hesitant, "someone who
talks nonstop during all the good scenes and ruins it for
you?"

"Yup. That would be Caitlin."

Paul's answer surprised her, and she smiled briefly before
plunging on. "It's sort of like that. I can hear them, lots of
them, like they're right here with us. Sometimes they whisper, and sometimes they shout. Sometimes they're helpful,
and sometimes, they're really, really cruel. Sometimes they
band together and sing songs, or they chant one word over

and over until I want to scream." Sara realized she must sound completely crazy, yet when she looked up, Paul listened attentively without visible signs of judgment.

"They have personalities," she explained. "There's one who's always trying to help, and one who cracks jokes. And there's one who scares me a little. He, well, he's vicious, and he says terrible, cruel things. But they all usually shut up when I'm really, really focused, like when I gallop my horse over jumps. I think maybe they're afraid they'll get us killed if they distract me."

"Is that why you like to ride so much?"

"I guess. But horses are part of me. I was miserable without Harlee. It took me months to pry her away from Mark."

"Mark is your ex?"

Sara looked away, not wanting Paul to see the pain in her eyes. "Yes."

Paul touched her hand again. She tucked it under her arm, out of reach.

"I take it he didn't treat you very well."

Sara looked at her lap and let her hair shield her face. "No, he didn't. But it wasn't just him. I wasn't much of a wife." She rubbed her eyes as guilt pricked at her.

Paul touched her shoulder. She let him, too exhausted to pull away. "Look," he said, "I wasn't trying to upset you. It's just, you seem so sad sometimes." He reached forward and traced his finger along her cheek. "I just want you to know, if you need someone to talk to, I'm here."

*Is he saying he wants to be my friend?*

*-Like Cassie, only shorter.*

*That's all I can manage anyway.*

Sara's head started to clear, but when she tried to stand, dizziness overcame her. She folded into a ball, head down, knees pulled up. Paul gathered her close and held her in a soft embrace. A feeling of peace and belonging stole over her, and she allowed herself to lean against him. She knew she was defective and incapable of a normal relationship, lucky he wanted to be her friend, lucky he wasn't foolishly expecting more.

# Chapter Ten

The movie was over when Sara and Paul returned to the house. Paul excused himself and ducked into the bathroom, and Sara peeked into the dining room where Cassie and Caitlin chatted as if they'd known each other for years. Adam carried dishes to the kitchen while Douglass spread out on the couch, laptop balanced across his thighs.

"Good walk?" Adam hurried past her as he spoke. He set a coffee pot on the ceramic stovetop and turned to face her.

Sara nodded and swallowed, hoping her face wasn't as blotchy as it felt. She glanced at the door, just six steps to her left.

"So, what do you think of Paul?" There was something teasing in Adam's tone, and Sara wondered if she were missing a joke.

"I've only just met him," she answered with a cautious smile. "But I'd like to get to know him better."

Adam snorted. "What's to know? He's not very deep."

Sara's mouth fell open. "That's mean. He's really nice."

"That he is," Adam said, laughing. "What I mean is, what you see is what you get. Don't look for his evil twin. He doesn't have one."

Sara followed Adam back to the dining room where he held a hand out to Cassie. "How 'bout we go for a walk and work off some of that dinner?"

Cassie darted a glance at Sara before accepting the invitation. Caitlin and Douglass looked up as Paul entered the room. They shared a glance and jumped to their feet.

"It's late. We really should be going." Caitlin spoke so quickly she was almost babbling. "It was great meeting you, Sara. Hope to see you again."

Amid a flurry of activity everyone bolted to the door. Cassie paused to squeeze Sara's shoulder, and Sara shot her a wide-eyed silent *don't go.* "Back in half an hour," Cassie said. "Don't do anything I wouldn't do." The door closed behind them, leaving behind a thick silence.

Paul stood awkwardly in the living room doorway while Sara peered at him from behind the kitchen table. He seemed nervous as he asked, "Would you like to go upstairs?"

"What?" Sara's mouth went dry and every muscle stiffened. She looked at the door. How could she have forgotten to count her steps?

*-Run!*

"No, not that. I just thought—" Paul pinched the bridge of his nose between thumb and forefinger, groaning. "I'm sorry. It's just that I'd love for you to see—Adam and Cassie will be back soon. We won't be alone long, and I won't, I don't expect, I just want to show you the house."

Sara's heart was beating so hard she could hear it. *I'm so stupid. He's a nice guy.*

*-Nice guys have needs, too.*

*It's only our first date.*

*-You're an idiot.*

"Sure, I'd love to see your house." Sara's voice came out in a squeak.

Paul grinned. "Follow me, then. It'll only take a few minutes."

He seemed giddy with excitement as he guided her up the stairs to the master bedroom. "This is Adam's room now," he said. "But in a year, when the house is paid off, it'll be mine."

He showed her his room at the end of the hall. She was oddly comforted at the sight of a twin mattress on the floor. The room was bright and clean, but it was clear Paul was a man of simple needs.

-*Simple, simple, simple, simple*-

Two additional bedrooms were used for storage. One was filled with rows and rows of identical plastic shelving units from the Home Depot. Each shelf was covered in matching boxes from the post office, neatly stacked and labeled with meticulous printing.

Sara leaned through the doorway. "What's in the boxes?"

"Um, well, lots of them are comic books. And there's some great stuff from flea markets."

-*He's crackers.*

-*He keeps everything.*

-*Is that a Flowbee?*

-*Hoarder, hoarder, hoarder, hoarder*-

*Stop it!*

The other bedroom had built-in shelves tucked within the walls, and sitting neatly on top of them were stacks of folded pants. Every pair of slacks, jeans and sweats was crisply ironed and accurately folded to the same length. Every stack was the same height as the one next to it. Each pile was marked with an identical label with neatly printed letters that said, "Slightly Tight, Very Tight, Very Loose, Slightly Loose," or "Just Right."

-*Slightly tight, slightly tight, slightly tight, slightly tight*-

Sara giggled to herself as she followed Paul back down the stairs and through the kitchen. He may not be mentally ill, but Paul had a few quirks of his own.

The two-car garage was neat and tidy. Evenly-spaced tools hung on pegboard walls within carefully drawn outlines of themselves. At the end of one wall sat a stack of yogurt cups, and next to them, a gigantic mound of neatly folded plastic grocery bags.

Faced with the mountain of bags, Sara dissolved into giggles, no longer able to hold back amusement and relief. "Plastic bags and yogurt cups? You collect plastic bags and yogurt cups?"

Paul returned a bewildered expression bordering on hurt. "But you never know when you might need a bag. And these yogurt cups are great for storing nails and screws and nuts and washers. Look how nice and tight the covers fit."

Paul's embarrassment brought Sara up short. He'd been completely supportive of her problems, yet here she was making fun of a little idiosyncrasy. Guilt surrounded her as she hurried to make amends. "You're absolutely right," she said, ducking her head in apology. "You never know."

Another thought came to her as she took in Paul's collections. He never parted with anything that might, possibly, someday be useful. *If he can't throw away a plastic bag, maybe he'll hold on to me.*

*-In a box.*

*-With a label.*

*-Several boxes.*

*Cut it out!*

She followed Paul back into the house and watched as he scooped the last of the dessert onto two plates. He offered her the larger portion, and his eyes lit up when she reached for the smaller of the two. Maybe Adam was right. Maybe everything she needed to know about Paul was right there on the surface. And maybe, just maybe, there was a chance for her after all.

# Chapter Eleven

Thoughts of Paul were Sara's traveling companions as she drove toward the coast of Maine and her childhood home. His growing friendship meant more than she could put into words. As the miles flew by, she savored memories of resting with her head against his shoulder, the sound of his heartbeat blending with her own.

*If only.*

*-Don't get your hopes up.*

*I know.*

The granite outcroppings of New Hampshire were gradually replaced by meadows of soft grass. Sara rolled the windows down and drank in the Christmas scent of balsam and spruce. The sky opened up and stretched as mountains surrendered to gentle hills.

There was a subtle change in landscape when she crossed into Lubec. Scrubby trees hunched against the wind. Slender grasses grew wiry and tough, and the scent of seaweed drifted on wet air.

Her parents' house hadn't changed in the time she'd been gone. She was told it hadn't changed all that much since her great-grandfather built it three quarters of a century before. It rose resolute from the rough land. Weathered pastel shingles and curtained windows reflected a reluctant spring light. The first crocuses bloomed against the stone foundation, huddled together in a smear of sunshine.

As she walked up the three brick steps to the two wooden ones, Sara felt a vague sense of unease. She knocked twice, then twisted the glass knob and let herself inside.

"Mom? Dad? I'm here." Shivering, she crossed the narrow sitting room to the kitchen. Its floor sloped perpetually east and creaked hollow beneath her feet. The smell of fresh bread and smoked pollock made her mouth water.

Goose tongue greens soaked in the soapstone sink, bringing back memories of exploring clam flats with her father, riding his shoulders and laughing as he bounced her up and down. She tried to hang on to the vision, but it crumbled away. Everything had changed when the voices took root in her mind. The father she'd loved as a little girl was gone, replaced by the doctor who tried to cure her and failed.

Peering through the back door, she spied her mother. Camera in hand, Joanie Morgan focused on the base of a cracked wooden post at the edge of the dormant garden. "Hey Mom! What'cha got there?" Sara called as she ran down the back steps.

"Sara!" Her mother turned to greet her, a smile stretching her lips. Dark curls with the first tinges of gray formed a wild cloud around her face. "Come see! It's a spotted salamander. I've never seen one this early."

Sara bent down to look at the little creature with its bright yellow polka dots glowing like stars against a dusky blue hide. Her mother snapped a picture before wrapping her daughter in a welcoming hug. "It's so good to finally see you. How was the drive?"

"Long." Sara closed her eyes and stretched, happy to be on her feet after the eight-hour trip. "Wanna take a walk? It's been months since I've been down to Sail Rock. And there's no fog today. I'll bet you can see all the way to Grand Manan."

Her mother's smile faded, and she turned toward the house. "How 'bout we talk for a while first. Maybe your father will take that walk with you later." Sara followed her mother up the back steps into the kitchen, wondering at the lack of spring in her stride. Joanie had recently been diagnosed with diabetes and Sara knew she was resisting her doctor's treatment recommendations.

"Are you okay, Ma?"

"I'm fine." Joanie's closed expression forbade additional questions related to her health. Sara changed the subject.

"Where's Daddy? I didn't see his car when I came in." She watched her mother's face, knowing it would say more than her words.

"He went into Machias to check on a patient, and I think he's taking her out shopping." Joanie's face was nonchalant, but Sara flinched at the edge in her voice. "He gets more like his father every day."

Sara burst out laughing. "He isn't jumping out of closets and tickling you, is he?"

"No, not that bad," her mother answered with a rueful smile. "But, like your grandfather, he does seem to be drawn to pretty girls."

The mention of her grandfather always chafed at an old wound. Sara rubbed gooseflesh from her arms and reminded herself, even now, to make allowances for the old man.

"C'mon, Mom," she said. "Even when I was little, I knew Grampie didn't mean any harm. He just wasn't right in the head, like me."

"Stop that, Sara. He had dementia, not schizophrenia. Your problems have nothing to do with him." Her mother opened the refrigerator door and bent to look inside. "Can we drop the subject? Your father will be home soon, and you know how talk about his father upsets him."

A sense of loss surrounded Sara like sea smoke. The old man had made her uneasy when she was a child. But she'd loved him, too, and his death had hit the family hard. Her father, she knew, blamed himself for not keeping a closer eye on the befuddled old man.

"I don't remember anything about him drowning," Sara mused. "Just the sadness. Everyone was so quiet and pale."

Her mother set a bowl of clams on the counter next to the sink, then scooped the goose tongue greens into a colander. "You were little. I doubt you picked up on what was happening." She handed the greens to Sara and chuckled. "You were always off by yourself, anyway. I swear, the way you snuck out before sunrise, we hardly ever knew where you were."

"I liked being alone." Sara rinsed the greens and turned on the tap to refill the sink. The delicate leaves grew in sea water, and they'd be too salty if not soaked and rinsed several times.

"His death affected you, whether you remember it or not." Sara's mother returned to the refrigerator, took out a bowl of hard-boiled eggs and set it on the counter. She cracked one and began to peel.

"I know, Ma. The nightmares." Sara picked up an egg, expertly cracked it, ran it under water and slipped the shell off in one piece. Her mother nodded approval.

"Your father carries a lot of guilt, you know." Joanie left the eggs to Sara and whisked cream into melted butter. "He still thinks he should have known you were sick, should have done more. But he was so preoccupied with your grandfather, you didn't get the attention you needed until it was too late."

Sara peeled another egg and shrugged off her mother's excuses. "I'm doing fine, Ma, but it sucks. Daddy treats me like one of his patients. Always has."

Her mother nodded, lips pursed in disapproval. "He has been more of a doctor than a father to you. And now you're his ward again, thanks to Mark." Joanie's jaw tightened as she peeked into the oven. The smell of baking bread wafted forth in a cloud of steam, and Sara's stomach growled.

"Don't worry." Her mother closed the oven door, picked up a skillet, and set it on the stove. She poured the butter and cream mixture into the pan and stirred it. The iron surface hissed with each pass of the wooden spatula.

"When it comes time for your father to file the annual court documents," she said, "I'll make sure he has the guardianship dismissed. And until then I'm on your side as far as those medications go, too."

"Thanks, Mom."

"No need to thank me. He's being overprotective and I'm sure he knows it. I'll make sure this guardianship doesn't drag on like the last one." Sara's mother fixed her with a stern expression. "You're just different. There's nothing wrong with that."

Sara winced. *Different* didn't begin to cover it. "But I went off the deep end, Mom. I still don't remember a thing about that night."

"After what Mark did to you?" Her mother's eyes filled with anger and hurt. "Sara, even someone completely normal might have come apart under the stress. Don't look back. Just move on."

"All I've ever wanted is to be normal."

"Normal doesn't make a person happy."

"Like you and Daddy?"

Joanie stiffened, turned her back to Sara, and began adding chunks of smoked pollock to the simmering butter and cream. "You know I'm not gonna talk to you about that."

"Why do you stay together?" Sara asked the question she always asked, even though she knew she was on dangerous ground. "You both seem so unhappy."

"At my age," her mother muttered, "where else would I go?"

"You're only forty-seven. You could do anything."

Her mother said nothing for a moment, but in time her tone brightened. "I was head over heels in love once, but it didn't work out." Joanie's voice returned to its usual stoicism. "Your father is a good man, and I have my church, my charities. I'm as happy as most people. You just worry about yourself."

Joanie walked to the cupboard and set out flour and milk for batter. Her industry rose between them like a wall. "Slice those eggs for the finnan haddie, will you? I'll get these clams fried up. I hear your father's car in the drive."

Sara's head began to throb. One parent, she could handle. But facing the two together never went well. She closed her eyes and mentally prepared.

*Be Switzerland. Be the buffer.*

*-Idiot! Say what you mean!*

*No!*

Her mother composed her face and dipped clams into thick batter. She kept her back turned as Carl Morgan strode through the door. Tall and imposing, the man seemed to own the room. He stopped at the closet and shed his suit jacket before walking toward the kitchen, loosening his tie.

Sara crossed the room to give her father a respectful hug, but her mother spoke to the hot oil in the fryer. "Well, look who decided to show up."

Her father's embrace was stiff and short, his smile tolerant as he turned to his wife. "Always a pleasure to come home, Joanie." He turned back to Sara. "It's good to see you. How are things going with Doctor Green?"

*-Short answers.*

*-Don't give him enough to analyze.*

"Fine."

"And how was your patient?" Joanie's voice was cool, her seething palpable.

"Excellent." Carl was upbeat, as if he had no clue he was being accused. "She did well today. I think we can move her to outpatient status."

"She must be very pretty to warrant so much of your personal attention." Joanie threw Sara a pained expression, and Sara worked hard to maintain her mask of neutrality. Her stomach turned, and she felt rather than heard the familiar chatter growing in her head.

Carl dropped a sheaf of papers onto the kitchen table. Glancing toward his wife, he ran a hand through thick brown hair. "I spoke to a travel agent on the way home. I booked a psychiatric conference for myself in Mexico next month, and…"

"Mexico, again?" Joanie spun around, looking as if she might scream. "Don't they have conferences anywhere I'd like to go? You know I hate the heat." She kept her back turned, and Sara couldn't tell if she was angry or hurt.

Carl sorted through his papers. "I was about to say, I think we finally have a date for our cruise."

"Did you book it yet?" Joanie's voice softened, and excitement played beneath the fierce expression. Sara knew her mother was looking forward to this vacation. It was half a year away, but she was already clothes shopping and taking off a few extra pounds.

"It looks like I'll be able to get away at the beginning of October." Carl pulled a sheet of paper from the pile. "I brought back a sample itinerary." He pushed the paper across the table, and Joanie turned away from the fryer long enough to pick it up. "It's still a bit off season," he added, "so the fares are lower."

Joanie's scowl returned. "It's a trip of a lifetime and we're hardly poor. Do we have to go when it's cheaper? Can't you for once just splurge?"

Carl looked expectantly at Sara. The voices nudged her into action.

*-Say something.*

*He's playing me against her.*

*-And vice versa.*

*-Bitch! Bitch! Bitch! Bitch!*

*-Ass! Ass! Ass! Ass!*

*Shut up!*

Sara's hands flew to her head, and she rubbed ineffectively at her temples. "If you'd rather go another time, I could kick in money for the difference." She knew her offer wouldn't be accepted, but it might break the tension.

Her father shot her a furtive wink and turned to his wife with a look of hope and anticipation.

*He's good. Even I almost believe him.*

*-He's a liar.*

*Everyone lies.*

Her mother gave in. "No, Sara, that's silly. October will be fine." Her face hardened, signifying there would be no further discussion.

"Great!" Carl pounded the table and Sara jumped. "It's settled. Can't wait."

Sara set out plates and silverware, ashamed for taking part in her parents' games. With a lifetime of practice, she played her role well, but she felt dirty. It was no wonder she avoided visiting.

Grinding her teeth in frustration, she sat down to finnan haddie, fresh oatmeal bread and goose tongue greens with buttered red potatoes from Prince Edward Island. Her mother placed the clams, crispy and golden brown, in a flowered ceramic bowl close to Sara's elbow.

"I know they're your favorite," Joanie said. "Take what you want before your father hogs them all."

Sara tossed her father a look of apology, then helped herself to the home-cooked meal. "You've no idea how much I miss your cooking, Mom. I eat out of cans most of the time."

"What?" Her mother looked at her in dismay. "But you're such a good cook."

"It's not worth the trouble for just me, and I don't have friends over. Cassie and I meet for lunch once in a while and—" She looked at her plate, wondering if she should mention Paul.

*-Don't.*

*Why?*

*-They'll make you feel bad.*

*No, they won't.*

"I met a nice guy. Maybe I should ask him over for dinner someday."

Both parents stopped in mid-chew. Carl shot his wife a worried glance and Joanie returned a warning glare.

Her father spoke first. "You met someone? Does he need to borrow money?"

"Dad." Sara drew the word out to two syllables.

*What the hell?*

*-Mark took money.*

*-Deadbeat!*

"What's he do?" This time it was her mother asking.

"He's a software engineer."

"Ah, a nerd." Her father chuckled, but it sounded forced.

Sara peeked up. Her parents continued to exchange ambiguous glances. "We're just friends," Sara said with a deliberate sigh. "Don't get all worried on me."

Her father's eyes crinkled in amusement, but his mouth was frozen in a rigid line. "Is he gay?"

"What? I don't think so."

"Then you can't be just friends. You'll either move on to romance, or you'll break up." He squashed his potato in melted butter and took a bite. "That's the way it is."

"Or maybe we'll stay friends." Sara did her best to radiate defiance.

"Don't be silly." Her father rolled his eyes. "You don't believe that any more than I do."

*-He's right.*

*Shut up.*

Sara stared miserably at her plate, no longer hungry.

*-Told you so, told you so, told you so, told you so-*

"But I really like him."

Her father smiled, and for an instant she saw a trace of compassion behind his clinical façade. "Work hard with Sylvia Green. Maybe she can help."

*-Broken, broken, broken, broken-*

Sara picked at her food, wishing she could disappear. *Why did I say anything?*

*-Stupid, stupid, stupid, stupid-*

"He's really nice." Sara folded her hands, hoping the shaking would be less visible. "I told him about the voices, and he, well, he didn't head for the hills screaming or anything. I think he's willing to take things at my pace. Really, really slow."

She looked up to find her parents staring at their plates. Accusation crept into her voice. "You know, Dr. Green says maybe I'm not even schizophrenic. She says hearing voices is considered a normal variation by some."

Her father snorted. "That's a bunch of claptrap from those InterVoice people. They want us to believe they hear spirits, or angels, and they're not delusional. Don't go buying into that nonsense." He glared as he bit into a chunk of smoked pollock. "Sylvia should know better. I'll have a word with her."

"Don't," Sara pleaded. "Stay out of it for once."

"I won't have her filling your head with false hope." Carl set down his fork and fixed Sara with his usual look of exasperation. "You're sick. You need to face facts and deal with your illness. Learn to manage the symptoms better."

*-Broken, broken, broken, broken-*

Sara ducked her head and played with her food. Her mother heaved a sigh, glared at Carl and began clearing the table. Sara breathed herself calm, rose to her feet, and headed for the door.

"I'm walking to West Quoddy Head. Wanna come?" She looked expectantly at both parents. Her mom shook her head and turned back to the dishes, but her father followed her to the hallway and shrugged into his coat.

Together they walked the short distance to Lubec's rustic state park. Sara took her time climbing down the rough path. She paused on a small outcropping and drank in the ragged beauty of the black cliffs plunging into the Bay of Fundy. In cheerful contrast, the candy-striped lighthouse sat atop the precipice, its beacon flashing dependably into the mist.

"Is Mom doing okay?" She didn't look at her father as she spoke. "The light is perfect today. I'm surprised she didn't come along to take pictures."

Her father moved beside her and rested his hand on her shoulder. "She's fine. Her legs are bothering her. This path is a bit steep for her now."

Sara peered through the rising mist to Sail Rock, the easternmost bit of land in the United States and the pride of Lubec. "So I shouldn't worry?"

Carl squeezed her shoulder. "She'll be around a long while yet."

"You'll call me if she gets worse? I can't help but worry, being so far away."

"I'll look after her whether she wants me to or not, and I'll let you know if there's cause for concern."

Sara wrapped her arms around him. It was a spontaneous gesture of gratitude, and she was surprised by the ferocity of his return hug. He'd always been distant, guarded, beyond her reach. But sometimes she caught a glimpse of the father she'd once known. In those moments she wondered if it might be possible to build a new relationship from the ashes of the old.

They walked back to the house in silence. Sara sat with her mother and looked through photo albums. Then she packed up her few things and prepared for the drive home.

"It's a long way to come for a few hours' visit," her father scolded as she hesitated on the steps.

Sara nodded, knowing she couldn't share the real reason she had to leave. "I know. But I can't skip riding Harlee for more than a day, not if I want to get to Rolex."

"Same old pipe dream, huh?" Her father's disappointment weighed against her as she hugged him goodbye. She didn't have the strength to tell him it was more than a dream. It was a goal. One she intended to reach.

Her mother took her hand and walked her to the truck. "Don't you listen to him. Anything's possible. You just have to want it bad enough and work hard enough."

Sara flung her arms around her mother and squeezed her hard. "Thank you for believing in me."

"I've always believed in you. Just don't make my mistakes. Don't settle for less than you deserve." Joanie glanced back at the house as she handed Sara a letter and twenty dollars. "Would you mind mailing something for me on your way home?"

"Mom, you don't need to give me money. I'm doing fine."

"It's just in case." Joanie tossed the money onto the dash of Sara's truck. "It's a long drive, and you never know what could happen on the road."

Sara slid behind the wheel and tucked the money into her ashtray, knowing it was easier than arguing. "Thanks, Mom. I'll try to come back soon. I miss you."

As she drove away, Sara's thoughts returned to Paul.

She wondered, *Is there a chance?*

*-No.*

She scowled at the road. *Broken things can be mended.*

Feeling a little less miserable she picked up the letter and read the address. Samuel A. Randall, P.O Box 2037, Boxford, Massachusetts. She placed the letter on the seat beside her and returned her attention to the road. "Never heard of him."

The long drive stretched before her, and she knew her father was right. She was silly to drive such a long way for a short visit. But she wanted her life back, wanted the guardianship set aside. The smallest hint of anything *abnormal* would sway him, and if she stayed the night, he would know.

The nightmares were getting worse.

# Chapter Twelve

Weeks passed, spring spread over Hillsborough County, and Paul eased his way into Sara's life. Like an overstuffed couch or waffles for breakfast, he was comforting and supportive. *A good friend*, she told herself. *Someone I can count on.* She hoped someday he might count on her, as well.

Double dates with Cassie and Adam were now the norm, but today's early-morning outing had Sara's teeth chattering. Overwhelmed by the bustling activity of the Hillsborough fairgrounds, she stood on tippy-toes to shout in Cassie's ear. "Whose idea was this?"

Cassie grinned down at her. "Mine. It's *my* birthday. Pretend you're enjoying yourself."

All around her, people drew vast expanses of brightly colored fabric across the grass and held it aloft. Whirring fans blew cold air toward hoop-shaped mouths. Like paper dragons, one by one, giant balloons undulated over the ground and stretched toward the sky.

Burners belched flame. Hot air rippled beneath nylon skins and breathed them to life. As she stared at the woven gondolas where passengers would ride, Sara tried to take charge of the desperate pace of her heart.

"You do know I'm afraid of heights, right?" She leaned into Cassie, as if her friend's courage might somehow be passed to her.

"You'll be fine." Cassie swatted her away. "I'll be right there with you."

Sara's toes prickled as a wave of apprehension swept from her hair to her feet. "Aren't you scared?"

"Hell, no." Cassie grabbed Sara's shoulders and shook her. "Paul and Adam spent a fortune on this. Suck it up. Face your fears."

Cassie grabbed Sara's hand and pulled her across the grassy expanse toward Adam. He jumped up and down and waved, pointing to a rainbow-colored balloon. "This is ours!" he shouted above the roar of the burners.

Sara's stomach twisted as the deafening roar reverberated like the Atlantic under hurricane winds. Her voice seemed too small to be heard. "Where's Paul?"

"I'm right here!" Paul ran up behind them with clipboards and release forms. "I have them all filled out. Just sign the bottom and we're good to go."

Sara stepped back, shaking so hard she thought her legs might give out. She stared at the tiny basket hovering a few inches above the ground, straining against the four members of the balloon crew who fought to keep it earthbound. She tilted her face up at the five-story balloon towering above her head.

*Shit.*

She looked at Paul, saw anticipation and excitement in his eyes. Swallowing hard, she turned and scribbled her name. *Shit, shit, shit, shit!*

"Now what?"

Sara barely heard the safety lecture. All around her balloons lifted off. People cheered, and music set a festive rhythm that clashed with the thrashing of her heart. Looking around, she realized she was the only one shaking.

*-Coward!*

*-Chicken shit!*

*I know.*

Dizzy and weak, she pulled herself up into the gondola. Her fingers turned white as she gripped a rigid vertical support and backed away from the edge. She was glad to be only five feet tall, easily hidden behind the others, shielded from the rail.

-*Gutless quitter!*

*I'm here, aren't I?*

A wave of fright swept through her when the pilot swung over the rail and the basket bounced sideways. He flipped a lever. Flames hissed. The ground crew backed away. Someone tossed a rope to the pilot, and he caught it one-handed.

Suddenly Sara felt as if she were floating, like standing in a row boat, feeling the ocean rock and buffet a small craft. Her knees bent without her permission, absorbing the motion. She took a deep breath and peeked tentatively past Paul's shoulder. The ground plunged away. A new bolt of fear surged through her and she buried her face in his shirt.

"Hey!" Paul turned and wrapped his arms around her. "Are you okay?"

She nodded, pasting a smile on her face. "Great! I'm, um, just a little bit, uh, afraid of heights."

"What?" Paul glared at Cassie. "You told me she's always wanted to try ballooning!"

"I lied." Cassie wound her arms around Adam's neck and pressed herself against him. "Her therapist told her to face her fears. She's facing her fears."

Paul hugged Sara and looked in horror at Cassie. "Crap, Cassie. We could have started with a ladder."

"I'm fine," Sara said. "Cassie's right. I, uh, have to learn to take risks."

"You're afraid of heights?" The pilot turned to her, a little tic causing his eyelid to twitch. "What exactly are you afraid of?"

"Seriously?" Sara thought hard, trying to find an honest answer. "I'm afraid I'll panic and jump out."

The pilot paled. He reached for a cable hanging from the very top of the balloon and pulled. They began to sink. When the basket leveled off just above the trees, the shorter treetops looked like a meadow as the taller trees brushed past.

*It looks like I could step out and walk on them.* The illusion of earth so close below let Sara begin to relax. Even the floating sensation felt less threatening. "Can I touch them?"

"As long as you hold on with one hand." The pilot motioned to the sturdy uprights. Then he pulled a second cable, twirling the balloon so it brushed gently alongside a white pine. Paul wrapped his arms around Sara's waist, and she reached out, her fingers grazing the needles. "This is awesome," she admitted as her fear lessened.

"Ready to go a bit higher? I'd like to follow the riverbed. The air currents down here are going the wrong way."

Sara nodded, not sure she was ready but willing to try. "So, the currents go in different directions at different altitudes? That's so cool."

The pilot flicked the burners to life, and the balloon continued to sink.

Sara's stomach clenched. "Why are we still going down?"

"It takes a moment for the heat to reach the top of the balloon. Hang on." As the words left the pilot's mouth, the basket was pulled skyward. Sara buried her head against Paul and closed her eyes. When she found the courage to look, they hovered above a river, the balloon lazily drifting along its course. Sara marveled as the last of her fear fell away and they hung weightless, floating through the air like dandelion seeds.

"This is—it's amazing. I've never done anything like this." A smile crept across Sara's face. She leaned into Paul and surrendered to the feeling of release. "I feel like I could do anything. It's magic."

"Told ya." Cassie stuck her tongue out before turning back to Adam. Sara grinned up at Paul and saw her own smile mirrored on his face.

Her heart seemed to expand. She flung her arms wide and stared in wonder at the world spread out beneath her feet. The feeling of abandon was impossible to describe but too big to keep inside. "I know it sounds corny," she said, "but this is so uplifting. I think it's the most free I've ever felt."

"Really? Even better than galloping and jumping?" Paul's expression was teasing, and Sara's laughter rippled up and spilled into her voice.

"It's a tie," she admitted as she snuggled into Paul's shirt and inhaled the fragrance of scented dryer sheets. "You sure are full of surprises."

"I hope that's a good thing." Paul brushed a kiss across the top of her head.

Sara wound her arms around his neck, tipped her face up to his gentle eyes and honest smile, and without stopping to think, she kissed him. As warm tingles cascaded over her, she ducked her head, once again resting her face against his shirt.

-*That didn't suck.*

*No, it didn't suck at all.*

Still in awe, Sara turned to face the sunrise and cautiously allowed herself to dream.

# Chapter Thirteen

Wednesday was couch day. Sara sat in Sylvia Green's modest office, still bubbling over her balloon ride. Sylvia lounged across from her, feet stretched beneath the coffee table, amusement lighting her features. She picked up her notepad and ran her finger down the page. Sara latched on to the fading sense of freedom and steeled herself for the coming scrutiny.

"You've been seeing Paul for over two months now. Are you still just friends?"

Sara bristled, hearing her father's judgment. "Why do you say *just* friends? Does there have to be sex for it to mean something?" The last of her euphoria spilled away, leaving behind the usual feelings of frustration and defeat.

*What's wrong with me?*

*-Cock tease, cock tease, cock tease, cock tease-*

Feeling raw and exposed, Sara glanced at the door. "I don't need this."

"Sara, wait. That's not what I meant." Sylvia looked apologetic, but her contrition did nothing to lighten Sara's mood. Her worst fears were out in the open now, laid bare for Sylvia to poke at and dissect. Sara shrunk into the couch and tried to disappear, barely aware of her therapist's words.

"In answer to your question, friendship is very important. I think it's wonderful you have both Cassie and Paul." Sylvia's tone didn't sound patronizing, but Sara still leaned toward the exit. Just fifteen steps and she wouldn't have to listen, wouldn't have to admit she was still as broken as ever. No amount of therapy could make her whole.

"Two friendships. Yay. Good for me." Sara forced the words, her voice as flattened as her hopes. "But somehow I doubt it will be good enough for Paul."

"Give him a chance. Give yourself a chance too." Sylvia assumed a more formal posture. Back straight, hands folded, she indicated the session was about to start in earnest.

Eager to dive deeper into hypnotherapy and hoping to learn something useful, Sara adjusted her pillow and tried to ignore her growing apprehension. They'd found nothing off-putting thus far, nothing to justify her unease. Yet her feelings of dread increased with every halting step into her past.

Sylvia's words cut through her concerns. "I wondered if you might tell me a bit more about the voices before we get started with hypnosis."

Sara froze. She dropped the pillow and turned to face her therapist. "Why? What do you want to know?"

"Well, can you tell me how many there are?"

The question was unexpected and Sara fumbled for an answer. "I don't know."

*-Stupid, stupid, stupid, stupid-*

"Are there more than five?"

"Yes, definitely. I think. I'm not sure." Sara closed her eyes and fought down a whimper. *I'm such an idiot. How many of you are there?*

*-Stupid, stupid, stupid, stupid-*

The taunting was no worse than usual, but Sara's patience was at an end. "Most of them are part of a collective. They chant like a bunch of idiots."

*Go ahead. Tell me I'm wrong.*

"So, you have a chorus of voices who make noise."

"It's not just noise," Sara said. "It's a comment, like calling me names or making fun of someone, like you."

*-Mind fuck, mind fuck, mind fuck, mind fuck-*

The chanting was louder than usual. Even though she knew it would do no good, Sara covered her ears. Sylvia's voice sounded far away.

"Are they all part of the chorus, or are there distinct personalities as well?"

"Both." Sara tried to shut out the voices as she focused on her thoughts. "There are three distinct voices apart from the chorus."

"Let's start with those. Do they have names?"

"No." The chanting began to fade, and Sara returned her hands to her lap. "Dr. Franklin tried to name them, but they didn't like it."

"And it was Dr. Franklin who recommended you talk with them?"

"Yes. Before I met him I tried to shut them out, to block them. But he told me to try to get to know them and reason with them, as if they were . . . people."

Dr. Green nodded her approval. "How did that work?"

"Better." Sara dropped her chin to her hand, lost in thought. "The chorus didn't change much. But one of the main voices turned into, I don't know, almost like a friend."

"Is this voice male or female?"

"Female. I think she's based on my mom." Sara smiled. The thought carried with it feelings of warmth and support. "She's sort of like an advisor. She suggests things to say, gives me a shove when I'm nervous. To be completely honest, she's helpful, even if she does talk to me when I'd rather she not."

Sylvia's voice softened to a compassionate tone. "It sounds as if you aren't in a hurry to let her go. What about the others?"

"One tells jokes." Sara shrugged, half smiling. "He's funny, but the jokes are always at someone's expense. It's nothing I could repeat out loud."

"Seriously?" Sylvia snorted a little when she laughed. "I've never heard of that before. Most people who hear voices have a terrible time with foul language, abuse."

"That would be the third one." Hopelessness sickened her stomach, and Sara fought the urge to cry.

"When does he appear?"

"Always." She hadn't meant for the word to sound so hopeless.

*-Stupid girl with sex on her mind, wishing she could be dirty-*

"What's he saying now?"

*-Teasing men with perky breasts and tight little-*

"You want me to repeat what he says?"

"It's okay. Let me hear it."

"It's stuff I'd never say." Sara glanced at the door and pressed her feet into the carpet.

"Try."

"No."

Dr. Green made another notation on her pad, her lips nearly disappearing between her teeth. "If you can say the words, you can take away his power. He has way too much sway in your life, and he's nothing more than a part of you."

Sara put a few more inches between herself and Dr. Green. "He's not part of me."

"He's made of your fears, your anger, the things you'd rather not face. If you want to be well, you'll need to look closer." Sylvia softened her tone. "He may also be the key to your strength."

Sara bowed her head, knowing she was a failure. "What if I'm never ready to face him?"

"Then we'll find another way. Give yourself a break." Sylvia checked her watch. "Ready for a hypnosis session?"

"I guess so. We didn't get far last week."

"Just relax and let it happen." Sylvia set down her notebook and smiled. "We got through the induction phase and you experienced a memory. You did well."

"Not well enough." Sara molded her head against the pillow and closed her eyes to the apprehension clawing at her chest. "So, shall I pretend I'm on a beach again?"

"I was thinking we'd try Round Lake."

"Why?" Sara sat up, puzzled. The sick feeling hooked into her throat.

"Well, when we focused on your feelings of distrust, you went to a memory at Round Lake." Sylvia smiled encouragingly. "Your cousins made fun of you for having imaginary friends. Remember?"

"So what? Lots of kids get teased. They don't hear voices."

"True." Sylvia chuckled and Sara smiled back. In spite of her ingrained mistrust, she found herself liking Dr. Green far more than she'd expected.

"Let's focus again on your feelings of distrust. As we go through the induction phase, picture yourself at the lake, happy, playing with your imaginary friends."

Sara let her muscles turn to jelly. She sagged against the cushions, pictured the dark water, imagined the pebbled shore. The breeze would feel wonderful against her skin, seated in her favorite sunny spot at the end of the wooden dock, feet dangling, toes flirting with the waves. She barely heard Sylvia's voice leading her through the initial relaxation, allowing her to sink deeper into the vision. Her eyelids fluttered, and she smiled up at a blue sky.

*She was seven years old, camping with her parents in a four-man tent outside her grandfather's hunting cabin. In the pre-dawn light, she slipped from her sleeping bag and crept past other tents occupied by her cousins, aunts and uncles. Silent as mist she climbed down steep wooden steps to the edge of Round Lake.*

*She walked on tippy-toes lest she step on the myriad tiny toads scrambling among pebbles at the water's edge. When she waded into the shallows goose bumps rose on her thighs. Her calves cut through the water like oars, leaving tiny whirlpools in her wake. The rhythmic swishing of her feet merged with sounds of lapping water against the shore, and a steady bump, bump, bump of a canoe upon a distant mooring.*

*Laughing, Sara herded minnows across the sandy bottom, captured pollywogs and cradled them in her hands. The water was clear and she was at peace until her eyes were drawn to a phantom shape rippling toward her, followed by another, and another.*

*"Bloodsuckers!"*

*The glassy surface exploded as Sara burst from the shallows, whipped her head back and forth, scanned every inch of her slim body—*

*She screamed. A two-inch leach wrapped half-way around her ankle. She threw herself to the ground, tore at it with fingernails she'd bitten to the quick. It clung to her, and she flung her hands in panic until finally it broke free.*

*Sobbing, she got to her feet and turned for home, head down, blinded by tears. She kept the lake to her left and the forest to her right, knowing the shore would lead her back to the cabin. Instead she came upon a still lagoon with a sandy bottom. A birch canoe, loosely tethered to a submerged branch, bumped steadily against its mooring. The hairs on her neck rose in creeping fear, and she came abruptly to a stop.*

*Which way was home? Had she passed the cabin? Or was it still ahead? She tried to stay calm, but terror took over, and she threw herself to the ground shrieking, "Help me! I'm lost!"* Why had she forgotten her whistle? All the children had whistles, and blowing hers would bring instant help from one of her uncles.

Then she looked down. Streaks of crimson trickled from her ankle to her foot and pooled in the sand. She pulled knees to chest, hugged herself with bony arms and tried to stop shaking.

Someone walked out of the woods and asked, "Are you okay?"

Sara opened her mouth to answer, but no words came out. He lifted her from the sand, kissed her wet forehead and stroked clumps of hair from her eyes. She leaned against him. A sharp pinch made her wince and squeeze her eyes shut. He hugged her and kissed her, and pulled her panties down.

Sara snapped upright on the couch, her mouth wide open, screaming. She heard the screams, but they seemed to come from outside her, deafening, beyond her control. She screamed until her throat was sore, and still she couldn't reach her own voice, couldn't stop the screaming.

She clamped her eyes shut as her body rocked in the frantic rhythm of her heart. A voice chanted, *All your fault, all your fault, all your fault,* in endless rhythm while she tried to remember the man's face. It was a blur, nothing tangible, nothing distinct. Perhaps it hadn't happened at all.

"What did you see?" Sara had almost forgotten Dr. Green, her voice barely audible above the roaring in her ears.

-*Tell her nothing.*

-*She'll report it.*

*But I don't even know if it's real.*

-*Then say nothing.*

Sara was too shattered to argue. "Blood," she answered in a hoarse whisper. "I was seven. I cut my ankle. The blood made me pass out."

"Are you sure?"

Sara nodded.

*-Coward!*

*-Tell her.*

*No.*

*-Tell her, tell her, tell her, tell her-*

*-Don't, don't, don't, don't-*

"Shut up!" Sara didn't care that she'd shouted out loud.

Sylvia touched her shoulder, and Sara shrank away. "What don't they want you to tell me?"

"Nothing." Sara focused on breathing in and breathing out. She blocked the voices as best she could and tried to make sense of the dream. Sylvia's breath was slow and steady. Sara hugged her knees and rocked, forward and back, forward and back. Her own voice was distant and faint, and she heard the words before she realized she'd spoken out loud.

She dug a fingernail into her thigh and whispered, "I think I was raped."

# Chapter Fourteen

Sara squatted beside Harlee, hose in hand, washing away the mud that caked the pinto's legs and spattered her belly. The mare fidgeted in the cold water, splashing Sara's jeans and tee-shirt with bits of wet muck. Sara grabbed a towel and scrubbed at her clothes just as Cassie strolled through the wide aisle door.

Her friend's periwinkle-blue drawstring capris were immaculate, her hair sleek and glistening beneath the warm May sun. Of course, Sara had mucked eight stalls, stacked a hundred bales of hay and groomed four horses while Cassie sat in a lawn chair and read a romance novel. The comparison was hardly fair.

"I'm beat," Cassie whined as she gave Sara's butt a nudge with the toe of her pristine white sandal. "How 'bout we go out for ice cream?"

"You can't be serious." Sara straightened up slowly and stretched against a dull ache in the small of her back. "You've hardly done anything."

"It's not my job," Cassie said with a smirk. "This is why I live in a condo and work in an office."

Sara curried Harlee's neck, leaning into the work and laughing as the horse wiggled her upper lip in pleasure. "I could never live in the city. Where would I put Harlee?"

"Oh, the pool, the sauna, the living room. I'm sure you could stuff her in somewhere." Cassie giggled, but then her expression grew thoughtful. With a casual flick of her hair she asked, "What would you think of running an inn?"

"Me?" Sara shrugged. "Not something I'd want to do." Her mind filled with the practical aspects, and she prattled on without pausing to think. "It would be a heck of a lot of work. Meals to cook and serve, dishes to do and beds to make." She picked up a body brush and rhythmically flicked away the dirt churned up by her currying. "Bathrooms to scrub, piles of linens and towels to wash. The house would always have to be immaculate."

Sara dropped the brush into a plastic caddy, picked up a damp rag, and began polishing Harlee's coat to a brilliant shine. "And it would need gardens for people to walk in, places for them to hang out, probably a library and a fireplace. So there'd be weeding, wood to cut and stack, fires to tend—"

"Okay! Okay! I'm sorry I asked!" Cassie covered her ears and chanted, "I can't hear you. La la la la la."

Sara giggled. "What's this about? Is it something you're thinking of doing?"

*Cassie would never.*

*-She'll break a nail.*

*-All her nails.*

"Not really." Cassie picked at a strand of hay that had somehow found its way to her sleeve and spoke in a dismissive tone. "It's just something Adam mentioned."

"Do you think he's serious?" Sara's stomach began to ache. The thought of Cassie moving away . . . she shook the thought from her mind and focused. "I know he loves to cook, but does he want to live in a house full of strangers? It's a lot to think about." As she spoke, Sara's anxiety faded. Adam would realize an inn was a terrible idea. But Cassie looked deflated.

*-You're such a buzzkill.*

*-Try being helpful.*

Sara started to nod, caught herself, and checked to be

sure Cassie hadn't seen. "Well, what do you think? Is it something you might want to try?"

Cassie scrunched up her face. "I don't know. Adam has this crazy idea of creating a gourmet getaway in Vermont." Cassie's wide-eyed expression said *Help me*, and Sara's stomach cramped. Cassie was usually the one dispensing advice, and the reversed roles felt awkward. She turned back to Harlee.

"Well, your marketing skills would come in handy." She tried to sound encouraging, still hoping the whole idea would blow over. "It would be a heck of a lot of work at first. But if you attract a wealthy clientele, it might really take off." Sara ran a soft brush over Harlee's face and smiled as the horse lowered her big black head and closed her eyes. "Would you miss working in Boston? It would be a big change for both of you."

Cassie's dismissive shrug was at odds with her expression. "I guess I am conflicted," she admitted. "I like my job, and it certainly pays well. But it's just a job. It's not something I'd do for fun."

The two friends' eyes met, and this time it was Cassie who looked away. She pushed a stray lock of hair in place and said, "I envy you."

Contemptuous laughter cut across Sara's mind. She stared in disbelief. "What? Me? Why?"

*How could Cassie envy someone like me?*

*-She meant Harlee.*

*Shut up.*

"You're following your dreams," Cassie said. "You aren't prostituting yourself for a paycheck." She met Sara's bewildered gaze and smiled. "That takes more courage than I have."

For a moment Sara stood with her mouth open. But a flood of shame swept over her, and she turned away to hide her embarrassment.

*Cassie doesn't know me as well as she thinks she does.*
*-Coward!*
*I know.*
"I'm the biggest chicken there is, Cassie. Look at me. I've been dating this great guy for what? Over two months? And I haven't even—" The last of her boldness dissolved. She turned her back to Cassie and wiped flecks of dirt from Harlee's nostrils. "Never mind."
*-Sex, sex, sex, sex-*
*Shut up!*
But Cassie was back in her element, taking charge. "No way, Sara. You can't toss out a teaser like that and leave me hanging." Her usual poise returned, and she rolled her eyes in exasperation. "You haven't even what? Done page a hundred ninety-seven of the *Kama Sutra?*"
*-Sutra, Sutra, Sutra, Sutra-*
"What? I've never even seen the *Kama Sutra.*" Sara managed to look affronted before her resolve crumbled. "You're not far off though," she admitted, still holding on to a hint of reproach.
"So, this is about sex?" Cassie snorted. "Is everyone from Maine such a prude? Have you even kissed him?"
Sara hung her head. "Just that one time in the balloon. I think about it, and to be honest, it scares the hell out of me." She wrung her hands together with so much force, her fingers turned white. "I don't know what to do, Cassie. I'm going to lose him, aren't I?" Sara steeled herself for a lecture. But when she looked up, Cassie's expression was unexpectedly sympathetic. She swallowed the thickness in her throat and managed a smile.
"Why are you afraid?" Cassie asked gently. "Is it because of what Mark did to you?"
The question set off a chain reaction of fear and revulsion. Sara clipped a lead rope to Harlee's halter and led her

to a stall. Then she grabbed a broom and attacked the dirty aisle, ignoring the tears that pressed behind her eyes.

"I think it started long before Mark," she said. Her hands shook as she swept hair and dirt toward the open door. Already her vision clouded and the world shifted to slow-motion. A crackling hum in her ears promised she'd be flat on her face if she didn't heed the warning.

Cassie blocked her path, took the broom, and led her to the bench at the edge of the aisle. "You're white as death," she said. "Sit. Talk. Now."

Sara collapsed onto the hard wooden surface, put her head between her knees and gulped a lungful of air. Cassie settled beside her and placed a warm hand against her back. "What's going on?"

Sara felt as if her heart were crushed and bleeding. She stared at the rubber-matted floor beneath her feet and whispered, "I think I was raped."

Cassie gasped. "Mark?"

"No." Sara wound her fingers into the hair at the base of her skull and pulled the words out. "It happened when I was little, maybe seven years old. I don't know who it was." She squeezed her eyes shut as the fragment of memory came back to her. Terror and helplessness squashed her like a bug while her own shattered screams ripped through her mind.

"Oh, Sara," Cassie murmured. "I'm so sorry."

Sara tried to look up. The walls rippled as if through heat waves. "It's weird," she said on a shuddering breath. "I can't remember what happened, but I'm so afraid. The thought of being intimate is terrifying. It's like it just happened yesterday." She rubbed at her eyes, as if she might scrub the fear away. "I don't get it. You'd think after all this time I could get over it already."

"That's not the way it works," Cassie said gently.

119

"Something like that is a part of you forever. You don't get over it. You find a way to walk around it."

"How? I don't even know where to start."

"You just did." Cassie leaned closer, a grounding presence. "I'm sure Dr. Green can help, and Paul would do anything for you. Have you talked to him yet?"

"God, no. I only just remembered." Sara's newly regained composure threatened to abandon her, and she huddled against Cassie, trying not to cry. "I really like Paul. But I'm so broken. Who'd want me?"

Cassie pushed Sara away and forced her face upward. "I want you," she said with a tight laugh. "And I'm a mighty picky bitch."

Sara sniffled and whispered, "That you are."

"And if a picky bitch like me wants you, don't you think a nice guy like Paul might hang in as well?" Cassie's smile faded as Sara burst into tears.

"I don't want him to have to *hang in* with some poor, damaged thing. I want him to be happy with someone free to love him the way he deserves.

"That would be you," Cassie said solemnly.

Sara opened her mouth to protest, but Cassie didn't give her a chance.

"So get off your butt and get better." She grabbed Sara's shoulders and shook her. "Look. You finally know what happened to you. This is huge. You understand why you don't trust people, so now you can fix it, right?"

"That's what Dr. Green said, but do you really think it's possible?"

"Of course." Cassie jumped to her feet. "You've always been a fighter, and now you have even more reason to fight. And you have friends. You don't have to do this alone."

Sara made a half-hearted attempt at laughter, ending in a sniff. "I'm not sure what I ever did to deserve you, Cassie, but I'm sure glad you're on my side."

"You should be. I'm a class act."

"Do you really think I should tell Paul?" Sara sucked on her lip.

"I would." Cassie shrugged. "He needs to know how much you care for him, and he needs to understand he's not doing anything wrong." As Sara's heart filled with dread, Cassie draped an arm over her shoulders. "Just make him dinner, and while he's eating, tell him the truth. He'll be okay. I promise."

Sara laughed. "Everything's okay as long as he has food, huh?"

"Exactly." Cassie pulled Sara to her feet. "Look, he'll be okay anyway, but food never hurts."

Still shrinking at the thought of discussing something so intimate with a man, Sara took a step back. "Maybe I should ask Dr. Green first."

"You could, but go with your instincts. Shrinks don't know everything."

"But I trust Dr. Green." Sara laughed, surprised to hear those words coming from her mouth. "I've learned more in two months with her than I did in eighteen years with other therapists. It's like she's been living in my head."

"That's great. It's about time you found someone who can help you." Cassie paused, frowning. "But try not to get too dependent on her."

"I know," Sara said. "But honestly, Cassie, you worry too much. Dr. Green is on my side."

"Probably," Cassie agreed with a sheepish smile. "So am I. And don't forget," she said, poking a finger at Sara's nose, "so is Paul."

"I know." Sara swallowed and leaned into Cassie's embrace. "But it doesn't make telling him any easier."

# Chapter Fifteen

Paul pitched forward, grabbed the front of the saddle and stared at Frosty's shaggy mane. Heaving a sigh, he pushed himself upright and tried to remember all the things Sara had told him.

*Look straight ahead, sit up, open my hips, let my legs hang like noodles, keep my heels down and toes up, and breathe, all at the same time.*

*Is she nuts?*

Frosty moved into a jog so slow it reminded him of dial-up Internet. Paul doubled over and wrapped his arms around the horse's bony old neck.

"What am I doing wrong?" he called out, yelping as his balls whacked the saddle.

"Maybe you're trying too hard." Amusement bubbled in Sara's voice. Paul began to regret asking her to teach him to ride.

"How do I try less hard and still stay on?"

"Um, how 'bout we just work on walking today." Sara's cheeks turned pink and she looked at her feet. "I think Frosty's back and your, um, private parts will all thank me."

Paul blew out a grateful sigh and leaned over to pat Frosty's shoulder. "Does that sound as good to you as it does to me, Frosty, old pal?"

The horse snorted, more to blow dust from his nose than to express an opinion, but Paul still laughed. "Frosty agrees," he said. "Walk it is." Frosty continued his stiff-legged meander around Sara. The quiet appaloosa, Sara had assured him, was the elder statesman of the barn. Safe as a couch and gentle as they come, Frosty taught everyone to ride.

Paul glanced at Sara. Her smile warmed him, made him feel special. His life had changed the day they'd met; he'd become part of something more than boring Paul, the software engineer.

His throat bunched up when her expression went blank. Hurt and irritation flicked across her face, followed by firm resolve. *The voices.* He couldn't imagine what it would be like having his mind invaded, and he doubted he could be so strong.

"Earth to Sara. Having a private conversation with your friends?" He made certain to keep amusement in his voice. Her illness wasn't funny, but Sara might interpret concern as judgment. Best to keep things light.

"Yes, sorry." She grinned back, but worry pinched the corners of her eyes and reduced her lips to a thin line. "Wanna call it a day? You did great."

Paul snorted. "If that was great, I'd hate to see someone beyond hope." He flashed a grin and was rewarded by an almost imperceptible loosening of her shoulders. "But I accept your praise and hereby invite you to dinner. My treat. I'd invite Frosty if I thought he could stomach Wendy's."

Sara giggled, but the sound was no more than a murmur. She was struggling.

*Whatever it is, she'll tell me when she's ready.*

"I have a better idea," she said. "How 'bout we eat leftovers at my place?"

Paul stroked Frosty's neck to hide his surprise. Sara rarely risked being alone with him, not indoors where, he guessed, she couldn't run if she needed to. He gave her the sort of smile that said, *No big deal.* "Works for me."

He carried Frosty's saddle and bridle to the tack room while Sara led the horse back to the pasture. When she returned, she linked arms and tugged him toward the cottage. Her hand was clammy, and she walked without a word. Whatever was bothering her, it was big.

"Are you all ready for this weekend?" He hoped asking about Harlee's first Intermediate competition might break through her fears, put her in her element, but Sara only nodded in reply. Her silent dread stretched all the way across the lawn and into the neat kitchen. "I'll be there with you," he tried again. "I don't know what I'm doing, but I can maybe carry your saddle or hold your horse or something."

Sara seemed not to hear him, so he lapsed into silence and waited. She turned her back to him and opened the refrigerator door.

"I need to talk to you about something." Her voice quavered, and Paul did his best to radiate encouragement. Sara's honesty was one of the things he loved about her, but each new revelation seemed to terrify her, and he wondered if she'd ever believe he wasn't going to run away.

"Lay it on me."

She didn't reply. Instead she placed a pot on the back burner, removed the cover, and sniffed.

Paul peered over her shoulder, careful not to touch her without warning. "Is that beef stew?"

Sara nodded and Paul's stomach rumbled. He could handle anything if it came with a bowl of beef stew. "So? What do you want to talk about?"

Her voice still shook as she stirred the pot. "It's something I remembered in therapy, something that happened a long time ago. But it affects me, and maybe us."

She turned and faced him. On impulse he reached out, touched her shoulder. When she didn't duck from his hand he drew her close, careful to keep his hold light. Her heart pounded against his.

"Take your time," he said. "I'm not going anywhere."

"You sure about that?"

The plaintive quality of her voice made Paul wish he could smooth her doubts away. Instead he kissed the top of her head, careful to make it tender, but quick and platonic. Anything that could be taken as forceful or sexual would send her running. That she allowed his embrace was a tremendous show of trust on her part, but he was never sure if she enjoyed or merely tolerated his cautious displays of affection.

"Positive."

She leaned against him, and for a moment she seemed to relax. Her body softened and settled against his, and her heartbeat seemed less frantic as she spoke into his shirt.

"Can we try something?"

"Sure." He shifted to an A-frame hug, careful not to touch her from the waist down. "What is it?"

"Kiss me?"

"Um, okay." Paul bent forward and kissed her forehead. Soft curls tickled his nose and made him smile.

"I meant a real kiss."

"Are you sure?" Paul took an involuntary step back. "You don't have to prove anything to me." His eyes wandered down her face and paused at her lips. His stomach clenched. To overstep with someone as reticent as Sara could be a mistake impossible to repair. She looked so worried, so vulnerable...

She nodded, "I'm sure," but she seemed to shake even harder.

He moved closer and cradled her as if she were a wounded bird, kept the hold feather-light, and waited until her breaths became even and her heartbeat slowed. "Ready?"

"Mmm hmm." It didn't take a genius to see Sara had been treated badly. Paul had promised himself to be patient, to wait until she was comfortable enough to make the first move.

"You tell me the moment you feel uncomfortable, okay?" He couldn't stop staring at her dimples, her lips, the soft curve of her throat sloping to the valley of her breasts. She tipped her head back and closed her eyes.

Paul bent down and lightly brushed a kiss. Her lips were soft, and she smelled of peppermint and timothy hay.

Sara moved closer, her body soft against his, mouth slightly open. With a little groan of surrender Paul reached for her again. Her breath caught as her mouth molded to his.

For a moment they remained pressed together, neither moving. Finally Sara stepped back, and Paul released her, dropping his arms to his sides. She reached for his hand, lifted it up and touched it to her cheek.

"Kiss me again, please."

"Um, are you . . . never mind." He gathered her close and kissed her forehead, the tip of her nose, her cheeks, and finally her mouth. Cautiously he teased with his tongue. To his surprise, she allowed the intrusion and met his tongue with her own. She playfully explored his mouth and sent little tingles of pleasure cascading over his skin. They remained locked together until the sound of simmering beef stew caught Paul's attention. He tried to ignore it, but...

"Um, is that going to burn?"

"Let it." Sara's fingers inched over his shoulders, tentative. Her eyes, vivid blue behind a brush of lashes, were uncertain as the length of her body shifted to accommodate his.

Paul felt himself harden as her mouth closed over his. Not wanting to scare her, he shifted his hips away from hers and filled his mind with the one thought that always brought him back to earth. *Margaret Thatcher, Margaret Thatcher, Margaret Thatcher. . . .*

Chanting silently, Paul guided Sara around the kitchen chairs to the stove. He disentangled one arm and turned off the stew while Sara giggled, still kissing him. She broke free of his mouth and trailed little caresses across his cheeks, down his neck to the tangle of hair curling above his button-down shirt. She looked up at him, shyness giving way to a touch of daring. "May I?"

Paul only hesitated an instant. "Sure."

She pulled his shirt free of his jeans, slipped her hands beneath the soft cotton and tousled his curly belly hair. Paul's head was spinning as she unbuttoned his shirt and nibbled his already hard nipples. His knees went weak. He added baseball to his thoughts. *World Series, 2004, Red Sox versus Cardinals.*

Beginning to trust the change in Sara, Paul traced his fingers down her cheek to the curve of her throat. Fear flashed through her eyes before she squeezed them shut. A moment later she whimpered, slipped her arms around his neck and pressed against him. Margaret and baseball were losing fast.

Her breath came out in little catches as she took his hand and tugged him toward the hallway. He followed her to the next room, staring in disbelief as she pulled her shirt over her head, stepped out of her jeans and discarded them on the floor. Her eyes locked with his as she slipped onto her bed and removed the last of her clothing, blushing, but holding his gaze. She was stunning, more beautiful than he'd imagined, and he had a damn good imagination.

He had to ask once more. "Are you sure?" She nodded once and held out her arms.

"You sure do make it hard for a guy to be a gentleman." He gulped the words as he lowered himself beside her, kissed her forehead and allowed his hands to wander downward from her shoulders until he touched her breasts. They were perfect, soft and warm, and so much larger than his own.

"I'm going to take advantage of you," he said, "just a little." He kissed her mouth, her throat, her shoulders, thrilling to the sound of her little gasps and moans. She pulled him closer, and he gathered her against him, overwhelmed by a need to surround and protect her.

She exhaled slowly and deepened her kiss, deftly removing his already unbuttoned shirt and turning her attention to his jeans. Even with the zipper down, they were snug. She slipped her hand over the bulge in his Fruit of the Looms and closed her fingers around him. A deep groan escaped as he tried to control his all-too-enthusiastic response.

Holding her eyes, he rested his palm over her belly button, then cautiously inched fingers down through the tangle of curls. Her face twisted as she wriggled against him, opening her thighs as he closed his mouth over hers and stroked, slow and deliberate.

She pressed against him, tugged at his jeans and said, "Please, Paul. I'm sure."

"Really sure?"

"Really sure."

Paul pawed his way into his pocket and withdrew a baggie containing two packets of sample-size antibiotic lotion, an adhesive bandage, one safety pin and one foil-wrapped condom. He slipped out of his jeans, took a moment to prepare, rolled onto all fours and lowered himself over her. She was tiny, almost nothing beneath him, and he thought once again how easily he might hurt her. But she rose up to meet him, wrapped her legs around his waist and guided him inside. He bit down hard as shivers cascaded over him, and a slow burn ignited everywhere her body touched his. Kissing her and stroking her, he began to move inside her, slow and careful, watching for signs of pain or fear. She wound her arms around him, pulled him close and whimpered as if she might dissolve into sobs.

"Are you okay?"

She answered by clutching him with her fists and driving him high inside her. Her body convulsed around him, while his responded with an intensity beyond his control. Gasping, he buried his face in the soft curve of her neck, and gave himself over, wanting nothing but her, nothing but Sara. She clung to him, her cheeks moist against his chest, soft breath warming his neck.

She was silent for a long time, holding him close as if unwilling to let the moment end. Her voice was husky when finally she said, "That was amazing."

Paul bent down and kissed the tip of her nose, and she shuddered and pulled him closer, burrowing into the crook of his shoulder.

"It's the first time I ever..." Sara lifted her head, curls spiraling past flushed cheeks. She stared at him with a look of awe that made him feel like the most special guy on earth. "It's the first time—" She swallowed and whispered, "The first time I liked it."

Then she started to giggle, and Paul felt a little less special.

"What's so funny?"

Sara was in stitches, barely able to speak. Paul waited patiently until her words finally found their way out. "I brought you here to tell you..." She dissolved into throaty chuckles, ending with a loud snort. "I wanted to tell you how much I hate sex. Always have. It's horrible."

She nearly choked then, laughing so hard she couldn't catch her breath. Paul wrapped his arms around her and nuzzled her ear.

"Wow," he said, reveling in the feel of her, warm and vibrant against his skin. "You sure do hide it well."

# Chapter Sixteen

The sun rode high in the sky at the fifteenth annual Cedardale Horse Trials. The dressage and show jumping portions of the competition had come to an end. Points had been tallied, scoring disputes resolved, and the Intermediate division began their cross-country rounds. Sara and Harlee stood in third place following a stunning dressage test and a clean show jumping round.

Harlee was wild with excitement, and Sara worked hard to keep her on the ground as she entered the start box and waited for the final countdown. The big mare crouched beneath her, coiled like a jack-in-the-box, eager to burst forward the moment the time keeper gave the signal. Sara waited, breathless, suspended in the final seconds before surrendering herself to speed and adrenalin.

"Five, four, three, two, one . . . good luck."

Sara started her watch, closed her legs and softened her fingers against the reins. The mare came up beneath her. Sara's heart beat hard. Her breath caught in her throat as the black and white mare exploded from the start box in a rush of galloping feet.

With her attention focused on Harlee, wind whipping past her ears, Sara barely heard the voice of the announcer, "Now on course, Harlequin Romance, ridden by Sara Morgan."

Harlee pressed into the bridle, nostrils flared, eyes bright. She closed the distance to her first fence, a gigantic roll top shaped like a half barrel. Sara bridged her reins and fractionally braced her back, rocking Harlee's balance rearward before sending her forward, bouncing like a rubber ball. With an air of defiance, the talented mare launched herself into the air, sailed over the inviting fence and landed cat-like. She burst forward, searching for her next jump.

"Easy, Harlee," Sara cautioned her horse. "We have a long way to go." She crouched in the saddle and steadied the exuberant mare before allowing her body to follow the motion, to blend and become one. They galloped effortlessly to the second fence, a log nearly four feet high with a spray of soft pine boughs above it. Harlee was breathing fire, and she cleared the fence, brush and all. It felt like flying.

Sara guided the mare onto a grassy expanse and Harlee hit her stride, galloping at a speed that left Sara gasping. The mare's ears locked on to the massive *Trakehner* half a field away, its red and white penalty flags winking in the wind. Constructed from a telephone pole suspended above a wide and spooky ditch, the fence was a test of the horse's courage and trust. Harlee sailed over it without a look. She pulled hard against Sara's hands, sending great clods of earth skyward in her wake.

The fourth fence was a bank followed by a *skinny*. Almost four feet high, with a face only two feet wide, the second fence was easily missed. To the horse, it appeared to be something to gallop past rather than jump. Its placement, perpendicular to the bank, increased the difficulty.

Harlee bounded up the bank and launched herself off the six-foot drop. Sara contained the mare within the boundaries formed by her legs and hands, sat her down and spun her around the sharp turn. They arrived at the base of the fence in perfect rhythm and sailed over the *skinny* as if it were nothing.

They entered a wooded trail, and Sara let Harlee fly. Time seemed to slow as they tore down a wide trail flanked by maple and pine. Harlee made short work of a series of massive jumps with a joyful abandon that had Sara's heart bursting. All too soon they made a sharp turn and descended a steep embankment with a simple post-and-rail fence at the bottom. The challenge here was to keep the mare balanced, not allow her weight to shift to her shoulders as she slithered down the hill. Keeping Harlee up in front was critical in avoiding a somersault over the deceptively difficult little fence.

Harlee jumped the vertical in tidy fashion and again galloped on, moving out, making up lost time. Another combination beckoned; three birch fences in a row with only a stride between them, enormous in size and placed at odd angles to one another. Sara chose a path right through the middle, jumping the first fence dead-on and the following two almost sideways. The combination rode like a dream, and horse and rider burst from the trees onto a wide mown path alongside a cornfield.

The following fences were big, substantial jumps, but they were meant to be galloped at speed and posed no technical questions. At the halfway point, with seventeen fences behind them and fifteen to go, Sara checked her watch. Relief and elation swept through her. They were a few seconds ahead of time.

She reminded herself not to be overconfident. The remaining jumps would all be maximum height, and many were shared with the Advanced horses, the highest level in eventing. They still had a long way to go.

A handful of easy fences gave them a chance to gallop on and make good time, but the next combination was the much feared *coffin*. This group of imposing fences took advantage of a natural swale where two steep hills came together. It was a challenging jump, requiring both courage and accuracy. Sara had seen a horse somersault over the third element earlier in the day. The horse escaped with a few bumps and bruises, but the rider had left in an ambulance.

Sara closed her legs, caressed her horse's neck and pushed on. She and Harlee would be the ones to make it look easy.

The first element was an *oxer*, constructed of parallel logs suspended almost four feet high. This would be simple, but the landing was steep and slick, much like the side of a gravel pit. At the bottom was a seven-foot-wide ditch with a three-and-a-half-foot wall on either side, and the landing was on a steep incline. Harlee would have to dig in and thrust upward with all her might, jumping out over a third obstacle once she reached the top.

Sara had ridden the fence in her mind a hundred times. The first two elements always rode well. But she'd been told that landing on the uphill side was like slamming into a brick wall. She had to attack the first two obstacles, ride them boldly in a controlled but bouncy *coffin canter*, if she hoped to have enough power to successfully make it up and over the other side.

Harlee galloped over the *oxer*, sat and slid downward, her eyes on the ditch at the bottom. Sara drove her forward, confident she had enough energy to make the jump and blast up the opposite side. Harlee gathered herself and leaped. They flew up and forward, for a moment seeming to hang in the air. Then everything crashed to a stop.

Sara smacked into Harlee's neck, her breath knocked out in a whoosh. Her feet flew out of the stirrups, and she had an awful look at the ground rushing up to meet her.

She grabbed mane and hung on. For an instant she dangled over Harlee's shoulder. But she yanked herself upright and pressed the mare forward. Harlee dug in and powered herself up the sheer face of the hill. Sara stopped breathing.

The pinto launched herself over the last element, her

enormous effort tossing Sara out of the saddle. Harlee scraped the rail with her belly as she scrambled to the opposite side. Sara pushed herself back into the tack and regained her stirrups, thrilled to still be on board. But she knew she'd lost precious seconds. They'd have to run the rest of the course as if Harlee's tail were on fire.

The water complex loomed ahead, and Sara couldn't help but grin. Harlee loved water. At this point in the course, with the mare hot and sweaty, she had no doubt the jumps would be met with enthusiasm.

True to form, Harlee leaped off the cliff-like edge and landed with a gigantic splash. Two tethered canoes had to be jumped. The water's drag and soft movement of the boats increased the difficulty, but Harlee made it look like a game. Soon they made the turn toward home, finally galloping toward the finish.

The final fences were imposing but straightforward. Sara had only to adjust Harlee's stride such that each obstacle was met and jumped with a minimum of effort. As they tore through the finish flags, she stopped her watch, slipped the reins and let the mare coast to a walk.

Wiping sweat from her eyes, Sara checked her watch and let out a whoop. They were one second ahead of the optimum time. If there were no penalties at the coffin, they would finish no worse than third, a very good showing for Harlee's first Intermediate outing.

Sara dismounted, loosened her girth, and headed for the wash area. Surrounding horses were attended to by grooms while their riders relaxed with a cold drink. Normally Sara took care of Harlee herself, but today Paul waited for her. He held a halter, lead rope, water bucket and sponge, and his face was ashen. He smiled as she approached, but she could see panic in his eyes.

*I knew I shouldn't have let him come. He probably saw us at the coffin.*

*-You blew it.*

*I know.*

She halted next to the buckets, gave Paul a quick kiss and smiled back. "I take it you saw us at the coffin?"

His face fell. "Someone next to me yelled, 'She's gonna die!' I don't know what's going on, so I, well..." He peeked at her through squinted eyes. "It scared the crap out of me."

Sara gave Paul's shoulder a playful cuff. With a deliberately carefree smile, she removed Harlee's saddle and bridle. "I won't lie, Paul. People do get hurt at these things, and I did underestimate that fence." She turned to face him, making sure her manner revealed not an ounce of concern. "But we're fine. I think we finished in the top three."

Sara offered Harlee a drink. The mare played with the cool water, exuberantly flipping it into the air with her lower lip before she buried her muzzle in the bucket. Sara methodically hosed the sweat from the black and white coat, and the pinto closed her eyes and leaned into the cool shower.

"Can I help?" Paul stood just beyond the spray, watching, but obviously unsure what to do.

"You already helped just by having everything ready for me," Sara laughed as she unbuckled her helmet and pulled it from her head. The cool air felt glorious against her sweaty forehead. "I'm used to doing all of this alone. But someday, I'll be somebody. And Harlee will have her own entourage."

"You already are somebody," Paul said. "You just don't know it yet."

Sara caught his eye and a warm flush spread through her as she turned away and replaced the hose. As she tugged Harlee toward the parking lot, she called back, "Wanna carry my tack? That would be a big help."

Paul followed behind, struggling to balance the saddle, bridle and bucket. Once back at the trailer, he put Sara's things away. Then he held Harlee while Sara brushed her dry. Finally finished, Sara tied Harlee to the trailer and hung a net of fragrant hay in easy reach. The mare cocked a hip and relaxed in the shade, a cool breeze fluttering her mane and forelock.

Only then did Sara grab a bottle of water from the cooler. With a grateful sigh she hopped up onto the truck's tailgate and drank it down. Gingerly, she reached up and removed her glasses. They were loose and crooked, but not cracked, and she smiled in relief.

"I thought I might have broken them at the coffin," she said. "I kinda smacked my face on Harlee's neck."

Paul held out his hand. "Let me take a look." He checked both lenses, wiggled the loose temple, then fished a small leather pouch from his pocket. "It's just a loose screw," he said as he reached into the pouch and withdrew a tiny Phillips head. "I'll have it fixed in a jiffy.

He chewed on his lip as he worked, and his words came out shaky. "Those jumps are really big," he said. "They're bigger than my car."

Sara inhaled her water and burst into laughter. "Your car isn't all that big," she said. "Harlee could jump it easy."

"No need to demonstrate." He shot her a look of mock dread as he cleaned her glasses with a small scrap of chamois. "I believe you."

Sara giggled and Paul laughed along with her as he gently slipped her glasses onto her head and checked the fit. She thought of the many times Mark screamed at her for mistakes she'd made in competitions. A shudder ran through her. *It's so easy being here with Paul. Mark would have ripped my head off for that mistake. Paul is just concerned.*

*-You could have been hurt.*
*I know.*
*-Harlee could have been hurt.*

Sara winced. *I know that, too.*

She was vaguely aware of a man walking toward them.

He looked familiar, handsome, she supposed, and he had a confident stride. Sara's stomach did a flip-flop when he stopped in front of her and held out his hand.

*Oh, shit. Look who it is.*

"Are you Sara Morgan?" The man's eyes were friendly, but his attitude was all business. "I'm Brett Foster, and I wanted to tell you what a great job you did." He nodded to Paul, then smiled warmly at Sara. His gaze wandered to Harlee and traveled quickly over her feet and legs. "Hell of a ride," he said. "Your first Intermediate?"

"Yes," was all Sara could manage to say. Brett was an internationally acclaimed competitor and trainer, one of the best. A compliment from him meant something. But she frowned as he continued to study her horse.

"Lovely mare. What's her breeding?"

"She's by Aberdeen." Sara was always proud to discuss Harlee's lineage. "Her mum was my first event horse, a race-bred paint with a hell of a jump." Sara grinned, remembering the game little mare who barely tolerated dressage, but came alive over fences. "She was the best starter horse ever, but she didn't have the scope for the upper levels. So we bred her to an International horse and crossed our fingers."

Brett nodded. "I wondered—" His eyes finally came to rest on hers. "Might you consider parting with this mare? I have a student who would pay six figures."

"A hundred thousand?" Paul gasped as Sara's mouth fell open. That kind of money would make a tremendous difference in her life. She could afford lessons and coaching, could spend more time training and competing. But what good would it do her without Harlee?

"Quite a bit more than a hundred thousand." Brett grinned back. "Are you interested?"

Sara shook her head, hardly daring to believe she was being so foolish. Horses are deceptively delicate creatures, *eggs on legs* a familiar euphemism. Harlee's career could end tomorrow if she stepped on a nail or twisted an ankle. But replacing her with a horse of equal talent and temperament would be a daunting task. A partnership like theirs was something rare.

"Harlee is special to me," she said. "I'm not sure I'll ever find another like her."

Brett didn't stop smiling, despite a hint of disappointment. "I wouldn't sell this mare either," he said. "And between you and me, she wouldn't do as well with my student as she does with you. You're a great team."

The compliment washed over Sara, making her forget all about her exhaustion. She straightened up, giddy with a sense of accomplishment. "Thank you," she said. "That's really nice of you to say."

Brett chuckled, and Sara couldn't help but notice how his eyes crinkled when he laughed. "I don't give praise where it's not deserved," he said. "So you can believe what I..."

His words were drowned by the blare of the announcer, calling Sara's division to the awards pavilion. Brett turned and jogged away. "Sorry to run," he called over his shoulder. "I have to get back to present the ribbons."

Sara rushed to tack up Harlee, and then made her way to the judge's stand where she lined up with her fellow competitors and waited for her name to be called. She expected to finish in third place, but secretly hoped one of the horses ahead of her had incurred penalties.

*It would be amazing to finish second.*

*-Pfffttt! It's enough to finish.*

*True.*

But the announcer called both the third place and the second place horses, and neither was Harlee. Sara's heart plunged to her boots.

*Did I go off course? Or did I get penalties for the near fall at the coffin? I'm such an idiot.*

She hunched in the saddle, wishing she could disappear.

*-Stupid, stupid, stupid, stupid-*

Sick with humiliation, she grabbed a hunk of Harlee's mane and steadied herself. She'd been foolish to try to compete at this level on her own. Now she'd be a laughingstock. She caught sight of Paul on the sidelines. He was jumping up and down. Was he crazy? The announcer sounded distant and garbled when he shouted, "In first place is Harlequin Romance, with Sara Morgan aboard."

Tears stung her eyes as the crowd cheered. Brett Foster walked up to Harlee and pinned the blue ribbon to her headstall. "Congratulations!" He reached up and shook Sara's hand. "You earned it."

Sara stared at him, not daring to believe. "Three years to Rolex," she said, her voice barely a whisper. Laughing dismissively, she looked down at Harlee's mane.

Brett grinned at her. "I don't doubt it for a minute." He reached up a second time and slipped her a business card. "I could use a good working student. If you'd like my help, give me a call."

Sara stuffed the card into her breeches, her heart racing. With a last look at Brett Foster's wide grin, she turned to the other riders.

"Ready?"

In unison they nodded assent. Sara gathered her reins, sat tall, and urged Harlee forward to lead the victory gallop.

# Chapter Seventeen

Sara thought she might burst with excitement as she and Paul shared dinner at a restaurant Cassie had recommended. Soft lighting surrounded them in a warm glow while a musician played classical guitar. Their waiter was friendly and attentive, and the food tasted a whole lot better than the dollar menu.

"Harlee was amazing," she said, still tingling and flushed. "She didn't bat an eye at anything on the course." Paul's face mirrored her enthusiasm. His grin spread wider as he gave her his complete attention.

"Can you believe Brett Foster wanted to buy her? And he asked me to be his working student. Me! Working with Brett Foster!"

Paul sat across from her, chin cupped in his hand, reflecting her joy. "Tell me again who Brett Foster is?"

Sara rolled her eyes in mock exasperation as she cut into chicken cordon bleu. "Brett's been to the Olympics twice. He won the individual silver and the team gold. He's like a god."

"Is he nearby? Or do you need to travel?"

"He's about two hours away," Sara admitted, "just over the line in Vermont." She ducked her head and played with her rice pilaf, wondering if Paul would explode when he realized the time commitment involved in working for Brett.

-*He'll be angry.*
*Maybe not.*

She wasn't sure, but she thought she saw disappointment on Paul's face. It vanished quickly behind a smile, and she tried to relax.

"Is this as exciting an opportunity as it sounds?" He cut a sizable chunk from a gigantic slab of prime rib and stuffed it into his mouth.

"It's huge," Sara said, giggling as juice ran down Paul's chin. "But I'd have to drive up there with Harlee every Friday as soon as I'm done at the barn. I'd work all weekend, and I wouldn't be home until Sunday night." She watched Paul for signs of disapproval, saw none and raced on. "He'd help me school Harlee, and he'd coach me at events. That would give me an edge." Sara sipped her water and waited for Paul to digest the information.

"Can you handle the workload? It sounds like you'll be spreading yourself pretty thin." His smile had vanished, but his concerns appeared to be for her rather than for himself.

*-Luring you into a false sense of security.*

*-And then he'll make you pay.*

*Shut up.*

"I'd like to try. It's an incredible opportunity. But I couldn't see you as often as I'd like, not until November when the season ends." She held her breath. *Any minute now—*

Paul took a bite of tenderloin and closed his eyes. "This is awesome. Want to try a piece?"

Sara shook her head.

"When would you start? Would it be right away?"

"My folks asked me to help them clean out the garage next weekend." Sara spoke in a rush, wanting to get everything said before the inevitable repercussions. "It's an excuse to check up on me, so I need to go. I'd start working for Brett the week after." She twisted her napkin in her lap and waited.

"You do realize you don't need my permission." Paul quirked a smile, and it looked real, but Sara still worried. He reached across the table and squeezed her hand. "We'll make it work. Do what you want to do."

*-He lies.*

Sara stared at him, wishing she could erase the mistrust from her eyes. "Why do you always make everything so easy for me?" The question was out before she thought to stop it.

"Why do you think?" The intensity of his gaze hinted at a devotion she'd never seen before. She ducked her head under the weight of emotion in Paul's eyes.

"Because I'm great in bed?" She peeked though her lashes.

Paul's water went up his nose. He sputtered and coughed into his napkin, and the serious moment came to an end. "Yup. That's it exactly," he finally wheezed, no longer looking at her.

Sara went back to pushing food from one side of her plate to the other, wishing she could bring herself to hear what he'd wanted to say.


On the following evening, Sara bustled about the kitchen while Cassie lounged on the sofa, an amused smile on her face.

"I can't believe how well things are going." Sara bounded across the living room, handed Cassie a steaming mug of raspberry tea and plopped down beside her. "Harlee and I are doing great, I start working for Brett Foster in ten days, and Paul is amazing. No matter what I throw at him, he rolls with it."

Cassie nestled in the corner of the couch, chin in hand, lips curved in an indulgent smile. Sara pulled bare feet onto the cushions and hugged her knees. "He's incredible, Cassie. I feel safe with him. I trust him. Me! Trusting someone! Can you believe it? And I feel completely free to make my own decisions and live my own life. He's not clingy or needy or resentful. He's a grownup."

Sara flopped back against the cushions and planted her feet on the coffee table. Cassie held up a hand, but Sara brushed it aside. "Even the voices have toned down. It's as if they're starting to blend with my thoughts, not so intrusive, almost a part of me. Dr. Green says they're nothing more than an *inconvenience*. She thinks I have a good chance of beating this thing, being normal, having a life."

Sara's thoughts darkened, but only for a moment. "My dad says not to get my hopes up. But I'm not listening. My hopes are up. And I'm gonna take back everything that should have been mine all along."

She grinned at Cassie, suddenly realizing she was being rude. "I'm sorry. It's just that I can't remember ever being this happy. I didn't think it was possible, not for me. Did you want to say something?"

Cassie sipped her tea, making odd little gestures with her hand. Amusement crinkled her eyes while her lips pursed in frustration. Finally she flung her arms in the air and huffed. "Okay, Sara, I've been sitting here listening to you ramble, waiting for you to notice. But subtlety is lost on you." With a flourish, Cassie held her hand inches from Sara's nose and wiggled her fingers. "Notice anything different?"

Sara squinted for an instant before her gaze landed on the diamond.

"Crap! When did that happen?" She slapped her hand over her mouth and took a moment to compose herself. "Um, I mean, congratulations! I'm so happy for you!"

Cassie's face was glowing, and Sara continued to stare

and stammer. "But, but, it's all happening so fast. I figured this day was months away."

"That makes two of us," Cassie said, beaming. "But why wait? I can't imagine my life without Adam. He's the one." Cassie wrinkled her nose. "Yuck! I sound like one of those insipid girls from college, the ones who prattled on and on about their boyfriend-of-the-month until we both wanted to vomit."

"But this is different. The good behavior has worn off and you two are still together." Sara struggled to keep a straight face. "Although, I can't quite picture you pretending. As you once told me, you're a class act."

"True." Cassie held the diamond to the light, and little rainbows skittered across the surface of the coffee table. "And yet here I am, ready to do just about anything to make Adam happy."

"Even if it means running an inn in Vermont?" Sara gave Cassie a playful shove.

"Even then." Cassie swatted Sara's hand. "We've been looking at properties, you know. We made an offer."

"Seriously? You might really move away?" Sara's heart clutched at the thought of losing her best friend. "I had no idea things were that far along." Shame enveloped her. Cassie radiated happiness, and here she was, thinking only of herself.

*-Do better.*

*I'll try.*

"Tell me about this place in Vermont." Sara tried to hang an expression of burning interest over her worry. "I'd really like to know."

Cassie's eyes lit up as, somewhat shyly, she began to describe her future home. "It's huge, Sara. It has twenty-three rooms with sixteen bedrooms. Each bedroom has its own half bathroom, and each floor has a gigantic bathroom with a steam shower and one of those really deep whirlpool tubs."

Sara almost commented on the enormous amount of cleaning needed for that many bathrooms, but she held her tongue. "What about the kitchen? Is it up to Adam's standards?"

Cassie nodded. "He loves it. He was like a little kid. I've never seen him so excited."

"What else?"

Cassie's voice took on a dreamlike quality, her words carried over a contented sigh. "Oh, Sara, you'd love it. There's a big dining room and a really cozy living room with a huge fieldstone fireplace. It has a library and a parlor. It rambles on and on." Cassie's face grew even brighter. "And the stables are to die for."

"Stables?"

Cassie laughed. "I thought that might get your attention. There's stabling for twenty-two horses with over thirty acres of fenced pasture. It has an indoor riding ring, jumps, trails, and a pond."

Sara gaped as disappointment settled across Cassie's face, momentarily blocking her sun. "Unfortunately, it's outside our price range. But we're looking for a business partner or an investor. The stable is on a separate lot, and it has a cute little house of its own. So we have the option of buying the whole property and selling that part off. But then we can't control what happens with it. A badly-run horse farm next door could ruin us."

Sara's eyes stung, and she held on to her smile with difficulty. *If only I'd been normal.*

*-Silly pipedream.*

*-Impossible for someone like you.*

Sara pinched herself for her selfish thoughts and pulled her attention back to Cassie. "Have you considered leasing it?"

Cassie shrugged. "Maybe, but if we get a bad tenant it could blow up in our faces."

"I wish I could do it." Sara's thoughts darted to Brett Foster's interest in Harlee. "If I sold my horse..." She stopped and swallowed. "But without her, I'll never be anything." She stared at her lap, determined to be sensible and strong.

"I just have to be patient, work hard, and make a name for myself. Then I can coach riders as they come up through the levels, and I'll finally be able to make enough money to build something of my own."

Cassie smiled apologetically, but almost immediately her expression turned thoughtful. She stood and walked to the window, keeping her back to Sara as she spoke. "I shouldn't ask, and I'd need to discuss it with Adam, of course." She was silent for a moment, the drumming of her fingertips against the windowsill the only sound. "Do you think you could make a go of something like this? Could you bring in an income to help with the mortgage payments, and still keep up with your competition schedule?" Her voice trailed off.

Sara looked up. A jolt of hope and excitement nudged her forward. "I don't see why not. And it would be fun, wouldn't it? Working together?"

-*They need money.*

*I can make money.*

-*You'll fail.*

*No I won't.*

-*What if you do?*

The question landed like a fist to the gut. What if she did fail? What if the inn went belly up because of her? Cassie deserved better. Sara sat straighter and managed a smile. "But if you find someone with money in hand, you should take it. Because let's face it, that someone isn't me."

*Broke mental patients aren't high on anyone's list of potential business partners.*

*-She's not stupid.*

"I'd love it if you'd move there with us and run the stable," Cassie mused. "You never know. We might find a partner who has no interest in living there or taking part in running the place. It could be someone who looks at it as an investment and nothing more."

Cassie ditched the serious face. "It would be so much fun, wouldn't it? And you're so good at what you do, I'm sure you could manage it with your eyes closed."

"It would be wonderful," Sara agreed, still doubtful, but allowing herself to hope. But another thought intruded. *What about Paul?*

*-Don't settle for less than you deserve.*

*But we're a couple now. Shouldn't we compromise?*

As the thought faded, Sara realized she and Paul hadn't talked about the future. What did he want? Was he looking ahead, or was he happy the way things were? Sara wasn't certain of much in her life, but she knew she wanted Paul to be a part of it. And realizing this, she turned to Cassie. "There's one more thing."

"What?"

"I have to talk to Paul."

Cassie's radiance dimmed. "I keep forgetting we're not free anymore." She smiled, but there was regret in her eyes. "Of course. You need to talk it over with Paul, and I need to ask Adam. Even then there's the money issue. Just let me know what you decide. If you're interested, maybe we can work something out."

Sara nodded, but her stomach panged in protest. What if this job with Cassie worked out, but further separated her from Paul? He'd been endlessly supportive, but even he must have a limit.

But now wasn't the time to think negative thoughts. She walled off the worry and doubt and focused on Cassie's happiness. Her own problems could be sorted out later.

"So tell me more about this inn. What's the master bedroom like?"

"Oh! It's enormous, with wide pine floors and a private sauna." Cassie's words tumbled out, and she giggled, her face flushed.

"Crap, Cassie, are you blushing? You really are in love."

"Sickening, isn't it?" Cassie rolled her eyes and looked away.

"Not sickening at all," Sara said, surprised by the yearning inside her. "Nope, not sickening at all."

# Chapter Eighteen

$P$aul leaned into the couch cushions and lifted his toes toward the ceiling, trying to soothe a leg cramp that wouldn't quit. *Is there a rule?* he wondered. *When a girl falls asleep with her head in your lap, do you have to sit through the entire movie? Even if it's* Hope Floats?

He listened to Sara's steady breathing and chuckled as she shifted to a gentle snore. In a few short months she'd come a long way in daring to give her trust. But as the credits rolled, the cramp spread to his thigh. So he slipped his hands under her head, lifted just high enough to wiggle free, and carefully slid a pillow beneath her cheek. She shifted in her sleep with a soft moan, and Paul couldn't resist kissing her forehead. Soft curls scented with vanilla shampoo brushed his nose, and he closed his eyes and inhaled her scent before tucking a fleece throw around her and sneaking away.

Moments later, he sat at the kitchen table devouring a plate of mac and cheese. This, he told himself, was the way things should be. Adam was spending the night at Cassie's, and Sara was here. Add macaroni and cheese topped with buttered cracker crumbs, and life was perfect. With his attention focused on his food, he only gradually became aware of sounds beyond the rhythm of his steady chewing.

Low murmurs drifted from the living room, and he realized Sara must be awake and looking for him. "I'm right here," he called as he gulped the last of his macaroni and hurried through the door.

But her eyes were shut tight. Careful not to disturb

her, Paul crept across the carpet and lowered himself to the floor beside the couch. Sara mumbled something he couldn't make out. Her face, twisted in profound sadness, took away the warmth of the mac and cheese in his belly. As he reached for her hand, she murmured again, so softly he could barely hear the words. He stopped breathing and strained to hear.

"Please, no, not the needle. I hate the needle. Please."

"Are you okay?" His hand hovered an inch above hers. *Should I wake her?*

She'd warned him of her nightmares, told him not to be alarmed if she woke crying. But this was something else. He felt a surge of guilt, as if he were reading her diary or searching through her closet, running his fingers over things he had no business touching.

Sara's voice rose, frightened and incredibly sad, high-pitched like a child. "It's not my fault," she whimpered. "I didn't mean to scream." Tears rolled down her cheeks as she hugged the pillow tighter.

He touched her hand, and she snatched it away, her face distorted with fierce loathing. Paul's stomach lurched as her voice dropped to a menacing hiss, and she began to chant. "Evil, stupid, wicked girl, all your fault, all your fault, all your fault, all your fault. . . ."

Paul cleared his throat, his hand moving away from hers, seeking her shoulder. The chanting continued, louder. "All your fault, all your fault, all your fault, just die, die, die, die. . . ."

He spoke as softly as he could. "Sara? Please wake up."

She screamed. It was a frantic, painful keening that seemed to reach inside him and hook into fears he didn't know he had. Unsure what to do he said, "Shhhhhhhh," and stroked her hair with trembling fingers. She struck out. A solid punch landed on his left cheek.

"Ouch! Okay, bad move." He backed away, tripped over the coffee table, sprawled onto the floor, and yelled, "Sara! Wake up now!"

To his relief, the screaming stopped, and she sat up. Her eyes met his briefly before she closed them tight and bit down on her lip. "What happened? What did I do?"

"I think you had a nightmare." Paul flinched as she dug a fingernail into her thigh and winced at the pain. He rubbed his cheek. "You pack a nasty right hook."

"Oh, God, I'm so sorry!" She looked as if she might cry, eyes already puffed and reddened, lips vanishing between her teeth.

Paul got to his feet, stepped around the coffee table, and slipped cautiously onto the couch beside her. "Is it okay to hug you? Or are you still out for blood?"

Chin quivering, Sara nodded.

"Which one?" Paul did his best to find a bit of humor in the situation, but he was dismayed by the suspicion in his voice.

Sara held out her hands. Paul slid closer and slipped his arms around her. She crumpled against him, shuddering. Cheek throbbing, he rolled her words around in his head. *What the hell?*

"Do you remember what it was about?"

She shook her head, face pressed against his chest.

"You sounded like a little girl." Suspicion colored his voice. Even he could hear it. Sara went rigid beneath his hands. She pushed away, scooted to the opposite end of the couch and fixed him with a look that conveyed a lifetime of disappointment.

"What exactly did I say?"

Paul wished he could turn back the clock, be more supportive, handle his shock without suspicion or doubt. But it was too late. Besides, given what he'd heard, he wanted answers. Was this a nightmare or a memory? *What happened to her? What could she possibly have done?*

"You said something about a needle," he began, "like someone was giving you a shot? And then I think you were apologizing for screaming." He paused and waited for Sara to say something. When she remained mute, he cleared his throat and tried to speak in a lighter tone. "Then you screamed." A shudder swept through him. He swallowed. "Before that, you were chanting."

"'All your fault,' over and over again?" Sara rattled the words as if they were completely normal and expected.

Paul nodded, surprised she could be so matter-of-fact. "You were using a creepy voice."

"Same dream as college. It woke Cassie up a lot, and she told me what I said." Sara shrugged as if it didn't matter, but her face lost its color. "I've been having that dream since I was a little girl. It's the reason my dad put me in the hospital when I was seven." She got to her feet and walked toward the kitchen. "I'll get my things. Still want to come with me to Lubec tomorrow?"

"Of course." Paul silently kicked himself. "Why would you even ask?"

"Well, let's see, I chanted like a mental patient, I screamed, and I slugged you. I thought maybe you'd had enough."

"No. I was hoping you'd stay over." Paul scrambled to his feet and followed Sara to the kitchen. She pulled on her sandals, her face set in determination. But when she reached for the door, she seemed to shrink, as if all the air left her at once. She leaned against the wall. Her sadness made him hurt inside.

"I'm sorry I scared you," she said, "and so, so sorry I hit you." The rest of her words came out slowly, as if it hurt to say them. "I thought you understood. I'm not normal. This stuff happens. It's part of the package."

Without a word Paul wrapped his arms around her and lifted her up, her weight nothing. She hugged his neck and sobbed into his shoulder. "You don't owe me anything. I can go away. It's okay."

He kissed her all the up the stairs to Adam's room. "Please stay," he said as he lowered her to the bed. "We can drive straight from here to Lubec. It'll save time."

Sara nodded assent, but her breathing was rough and wet. Wiping her eyes with the back of her hand, she looked past him and asked, "Where are you sleeping?" She didn't hint at a preference.

"That's up to you." Paul slid her sandals from her feet, placed them neatly on the floor, and waited, unsure whether to ask.

"Here?"

Relief flooded through him. He crawled in beside her and drew her close. She snuggled against him, shuddering.

"I'm sorry I upset you," he whispered, kissing her forehead. She flattened herself against him and clung like a frightened kitten, as if longing to be closer than skin allowed.

Her fears made him ache inside. If only he'd been less kneejerk in his response. *I'm such an idiot. It's not like she didn't warn me.*

In time she relaxed against him, her trembling lessened, and her breaths became steady and slow. Paul marveled at the way their bodies molded together, as if they really had been made for one another. Once again he drifted into the fantasy he'd enjoyed only minutes before. Sara, the girl of his dreams, was here in his arms, and her shampoo smelled like sugar cookies.

But the nightmare reminded him there had been times in Sara's past when she wasn't entirely competent. The gentle spirit he held in his arms had run over a man with a truck, had assaulted a police officer, had even jumped from a second-story window. What else might she have done during those times of madness?

He told himself none of it mattered. The past was over, and a bright future spread out before them. As Sara's soft curls touched his chin and she smiled in her sleep, Paul fervently hoped he was right.

# Chapter Nineteen

Most men, Sara assumed, would try to make a good first impression on his girlfriend's parents. But Paul was not most men. As he opened the passenger-side door for her, she ducked past him and tried not to stare. Once inside, she clapped her hand over her mouth and held her breath, shaking with concealed laughter.

As he walked past the windshield she darted a glance at his lime green sweat pants. They clung like a sack overfilled with potatoes, every lump and bulge in bas relief. He had undoubtedly taken them from the slightly tight stack of pants, and she could only assume he wore them because he wouldn't care if they were ruined. His matching sweatshirt was equally snug, accentuating his spare tire.

As Paul climbed into the car beside her, she studied his face. The way he looked at her made her feel safe, cherished, like someone special. Despite his obvious concern over her nightmare, he'd been completely supportive, and she wondered how many people found such comfort in the closeness of another.

*Is this what it's like to be normal?*

*-You'll never be normal.*

Her conversation with Cassie still occupied her thoughts, and her mind traveled to the inn in Vermont. What would it be like spending her days managing a stable as she saw fit?

*-Mucking stalls until your arms fall off.*

*At first.*

*-No time for Paul.*
*That part sucks.*
*-He'll leave you.*

She sucked in a breath. "Can I talk to you about something?"

"Sure. What's on your mind?" Paul's face tightened as his eyes dropped to his lumpy sweats. "Adam told me I should wear something nice, but we're going there to work. It seemed silly to ruin good clothes."

Sara stared at her hands and bit her lip, willing herself not to laugh. "It's about the inn," she said, not sure how to explain what the possibility meant to her. "Cassie asked if I might be interested in running the stable, that is, if they buy the place. It's all up in the air right now." She pinched herself, letting the sharp pain distract her from worry. *Will he understand?*

*-No.*

"Would this give you the freedom to ride and compete and make a name for yourself?" Paul's tone was patient and matter-of-fact, and Sara nodded in reply.

"Not immediately, but in time, yes, I think so." Her heart gave a little tug as she thought back to the day she'd told Paul her dream of running her own stable. It was the same day she'd told him about the voices and the hospital. Months had passed, yet he remembered.

*No one ever listened to me the way he does.*
*-And yet you leave him.*
*I'm not leaving him. We can make it work.*
*-Stupid, stupid, stupid, stupid-*

"Is it near Brett Foster?"

Sara nodded. "He's only fifteen minutes from the inn. I googled it."

Paul's face was strained, but he glanced sideways and gave her an encouraging smile. "I think you should go for it. Maybe I could drive up on weekends and give Adam and Cassie a hand while you work for Brett. We'd at least have evenings together." His smile spread to a broad grin. "That is, of course, if you wouldn't mind."

Sara leaned her head against his shoulder and sighed in relief. "I would love that. But they still need an investor, so there's really no point getting my hopes up. It probably won't even happen."

Paul was quiet for a long moment. Sara remained silent, hoping she hadn't asked too much, afraid he was disappointed in her. Nestled against him, she listened to his even breathing and the steady beat of his heart.

In time, his usual humor returned. "Well, I do hate the idea of being separated from you, but seriously, I hope it works out. You deserve a chance to make your dreams come true."

"Even if my dreams take me farther from you?" She sat up and watched Paul's face, needing to see if his expression matched his words.

Paul kept his eyes on the road, but a smile tugged at his lips. "I don't expect you to compromise your dreams in order to simplify my life," he said. "I expect you to do the things that make you happy." He reached across the seat and placed his hand over hers.

"But I'm so busy. How can we be together if we never see each other?"

Paul hesitated before speaking. "Sara, I love the time I spend with you. And of course I'd love to see even more of you. But you don't need to change your life to accommodate mine." He laughed, as if a funny thought had just struck him. "In case you hadn't noticed, I'm an independent guy. I want to be with you, but if you're not available, I'll read a comic book."

Sara stared at him. "A comic book? You'd replace me with a comic book?"

"Not *just* a comic book. I'd go to a book store, or a flea market. Or I might see what's on sale at Best Buy." He took his eyes off the road for an instant and caught her eye. "I'm good at amusing myself. You don't need to tap dance for me."

Sara sat back and allowed Paul's words to come to rest. With them came a sense of freedom she'd never known existed.

*-He lies.*

"Are you for real?" She hated that disbelief slipped into her voice. "I've never had anything like this. I'm not sure what to do with it."

"Me neither," Paul said, suddenly serious. "I'm new at this whole relationship thing, too, and I don't have all the answers. But I do know one thing."

"What?"

Paul's serious look vanished, and he grinned at the open road before them. "It'll be a blast figuring it out together."


Carl and Joanie Morgan blanched when Paul stepped from the car. Sara's mom snickered, hid her face behind her hand and whispered to Carl. He returned a tight smile before striding across the driveway, soles crunching the gravel with military precision.

Sara's mom ducked past her husband and met her daughter halfway to the front walk. "Does Paul always dress like this?" She whispered, but her voice carried.

*-Dork, dork, dork, dork-*

"Pretty much." Sara worried her lip and glanced at Paul, hoping he hadn't heard. "He doesn't try to impress anyone."

"He does make an impression," her mother replied, giggling. "And it's not a very good one."

*-Bitch!*

Sara drew herself up to her full five feet, one half inch, and said, "I think he's adorable."

"You never did have the best taste in men." Her mother grinned, but her smile faded as her eyes met Sara's. "Oh, for goodness sake, I'm just kidding. Introduce me to this vision in green."

Paul and Carl were already deep in conversation. Paul had the driver's side door open, and Carl settled into the leather seat with a look of surprise. Sara snorted. "Daddy's relieved I haven't brought home another loser who needs a loan."

Her mother raised an eyebrow. "Can you blame him?"

*-User!*

*-Bloodsucker! Leech! Parasite!*

Sara shook her head, trying to dispel the familiar weight of guilt. Her father had given Mark a lot of money to keep the farm afloat. Add that to the payoff for his silence, and... "I suppose not."

Paul was at her side in an instant. "Is everything okay? You look like you ate liver."

Sara looked up and giggled. Even bad memories had no hold over her when Paul was at her side. She gestured to her mother. "Paul, this is my mom, Joanie Morgan."

A smile brightened Paul's face as he shook Joanie's hand, his boyish charm evident even though he looked an awful lot like Kermit the Frog. "I see where Sara gets her looks," he said with a sincerity that transcended his clothing. "I hear you're a photographer. I'd love to see your work."

*-Manipulator. Liar.*

Joanie's eyes lit up. She led Paul through the front door and began showing off the framed photographs covering every wall. Paul praised them all, using terms Sara figured he must have googled in preparation, like *cropping* and *vignetting.* Before long Joanie wore the same foolish grin that Sara so often found plastered across her own face.

"I like him," Joanie admitted with a trace of apology. "He's a nice guy, isn't he?"

*-He lies.*

"That he is," Sara agreed.


They made short work of the garage. Paul filled the trunk of his car with items he thought might be useful: an old hoe, a weed whacker that hadn't started in years, and a wooden cigar box with a broken hinge. They loaded the pickup with things even Paul found useless, and he and Carl headed off to the local salvage yard, determined to get a few dollars rather than paying to drop off junk at the dump. While they were gone, Sara and her mother cooked dinner.

"You seem to be feeling a lot better," Sara observed, taking note of her mother's improved energy level and enthusiasm.

"I have a new doctor." Joanie busied herself beating egg whites to soft peaks. "I finally gave in and started taking medication for the diabetes, and I can't believe I'm saying this, but it's helping a lot."

Sara knew how difficult it must have been for her mother to come to this decision. Like her daughter, Joanie believed medications did more harm than good.

"Too bad you're such a stubborn old bat," Sara teased. "You could have felt better months ago."

Joanie shushed her with a look, but she laughed as she turned away. "Your father has been helping me. I can't bring myself to prick my finger." For once there was not a trace of deprecation in her voice, and the omission made Sara more uneasy than relieved. It was as if her world had come unbalanced.

Her mother prattled on, seeming oblivious to Sara's confusion. "He's been testing my blood sugar for me and giving me insulin shots. I don't know what I'd do without him."

Sara stared, wishing she could feel comforted by her mother's change in attitude. Instead a dull pain pinched her stomach.

*-They hate each other.*

*-She lies.*

*Maybe. I can't tell.*

"Wow. Maybe I don't have to worry so much if you and Daddy are getting along for a change." She looked away, breathing against the hurt in her belly and pretending to be immersed in shelling peas. "I know it's none of my business, but I can't help but wonder what changed."

"We talked." Her mother rummaged through the junk drawer and withdrew a wooden spoon. "We settled a few things that have been eating at both of us for a long time." Joanie folded stiff egg whites into a thick chocolate batter, her expression betraying mild disbelief. "I probably shouldn't tell you this, but I told him a secret I've kept from him for decades. If I'd had any idea he'd take it so well, I would have let it out a long time ago." There was a catch in Joanie's voice, and Sara looked up to find tears in her mother's eyes.

"It just goes to show you, Sara. Don't hold things inside. Look at all the years your father and I wasted being angry at one another. Look at what we put you through, having to listen to us fight all the time. It didn't have to be that way."

"What was the secret?" Sara's heart beat harder, and she realized she wasn't sure she wanted to know.

"It doesn't concern you."

*-Liar!*

Sara let the matter drop and set the table. Paul and Carl returned home, triumphantly waving twelve dollars and bragging of their haggling abilities. Sara hadn't seen her father so happy in years. It was as if a great weight had been lifted. She looked from one parent to the other and wished she could let go of her suspicions.

*They've always been at each other's throats. How can it get better overnight?*

*-It can't.*

Dinner was fried lobster tails and fresh summer vegetables. Paul kept everyone laughing, first asking Joanie if she'd like to photograph his head as a bald-scape. Then he moved on to suggestions of nerd studies. Everyone begged him to stop so they could swallow. There was not a hint of the tension Sara had expected.

"You hang on to this one," Joanie said, her voice light and free. "He's a keeper." Her dad winked at her, and his smile appeared genuine.

"How are things going with Sylvia Green?" her father asked.

*-Careful!*

Sara was so caught up in her parents' happiness, she didn't bother to edit her answer down to one word. "Really well, Dad. We've been doing hypnosis, and she thinks we're getting close to figuring out what caused the voices." She grinned at her father, and his answering smile was unnaturally wide. "There's a memory I can't quite reach, but we'll get it. Dr. Green doesn't give up."

For a moment her father's face was more brooding than thoughtful, but he followed up with a toothy grin. "I told you she was good. I'm glad everything is working out so well for you."

Astonished, Sara dropped her eyes. "Thanks, Dad. She's been great."

*Where is my real father?*

Both parents hugged Paul as he and Sara prepared to leave. Heartfelt words followed them out the door and into the car, and Sara felt more and more as if she'd landed on another planet.

"I thought you said your parents didn't get along," Paul said as he drove down the driveway.

"My mom says they've worked things out." Sara stared back at the house, still not believing. "It's weird."

"Well, good for them," Paul said. "I hope it sticks."

When they reached the mailbox, Sara put a hand on Paul's arm. "Wait, maybe I'll run back and ask my dad about Vermont. I should talk to him while he's in such a good mood." She jumped out the door and jogged back toward the house. "I'll just be a minute," she called over her shoulder.

Joanie was still in the yard, pulling a few stray weeds from the round poppy garden beneath the bird bath. She looked up at Sara's approach. "Did you forget something?"

Sara nodded. "Where'd Daddy go? I want to ask him something."

Her mother glanced around and wiped her hands on her jeans. "He may have ducked into his study. I think he wanted to make a call, maybe check on a patient." She stood and waved to Paul as he backed the car up the driveway.

"Thanks." Sara hurried into the house and down the hallway to her father's study. The door was open a crack, and his forceful voice carried into the hallway. He was arguing with someone. She stepped back, not wanting to eavesdrop, but it was difficult not to overhear.

"You should never have let things get this far," he said. "I want you to put a stop to it."

There was a pause, and Sara looked furtively down the hallway to see if her mother or Paul had followed. She held her breath as her father continued.

"No, you listen to me. Let her think it's her idea. Take care of it." He slammed the handset down and swore. Sara took a deep breath before she knocked. Her father spun around, a look of stunned surprise on his face.

"I thought you and Paul had already left."

"We did, but I wanted to ask you something, so we came back." Sara's eyes darted from Carl's face to the phone and back. "Sorry. It sounded like you were having a serious conversation, so I waited."

Carl raked his fingers through his hair and cleared his throat. His smile, so genuine earlier, now appeared forced. "No problem, sweetie. What did you want to ask?"

"Well, nothing is decided yet, but I might have a chance to run a stable in Vermont. I wondered if you would have any objections." Sara clamped her jaw shut, hating to have to ask permission. But as her guardian, he had the right to approve where she lived.

As she waited for an answer, she felt, as always, as if she were under a microscope. "So," he said, drawing out the word until her throat closed. "Would you leave your current situation and move to another state? What about Paul?"

"I'd have to move to Vermont, and seeing Paul would be tough," Sara admitted. She tipped her head forward to avoid her father's gaze. "I'd hardly be able to see him at all."

Her father sighed and turned away. "That would be a shame, Sara. I think he's very good for you."

"I think so too." Sara shifted her feet and focused on deep breaths. "But it would be a great opportunity. I could be my own boss."

Her father turned back to look at her, and again she squirmed. "I'd have to find you a new therapist."

Sara shook her head. This argument was one she'd expected and planned for. "I really like Dr. Green," she insisted. "I could easily drive down to see her on a weekly basis. It's only a couple hours."

Her father's face lit up. "Really? That would make things much easier. In that case, I say go for it. It sounds as if you have your bases covered."

Sara sighed in relief and gave her father a heartfelt hug. "Thanks, Daddy. I'll talk to you soon." She jogged down the hallway and out the door. Paul waited in the driveway, laughing with her mother. Sara's heart lifted at the sight.

*He really is special, isn't he?*

*-You have to ask?*

As they made the long drive home, Sara dozed. Her mind wandered to her conversation with her mother. What secret could she possibly have kept hidden all these years? And how did the telling magically lift the pall from her parents' marriage?

"Um, Sara?" Paul's hesitant voice made its way into her thoughts.

"Mmm?" His face was oddly strained, and she sat up quickly. "What is it?"

Paul's Adam's apple bounced as he cleared his throat and swallowed. "I'm having dinner with my folks Thursday, and I wondered if you might like to come along." Eyes fixed on the road, shoulders rigid, he added, "You don't have to if you'd rather not. I know you don't have a lot of free time."

Sara came wide awake. "Your family? Why wouldn't I want to meet them?"

"Well, let's just say my mom can be overwhelming." Only his lips moved. Sara stared at him, holding back a nervous laugh. Aside from the nightmare, this was the first time she'd ever seen him worried.

"Gee, Paul, chill out. I'd love to meet your family." Although doubt niggled at the back of her mind, Sara did her best to exude calm.

Paul's jaw softened. "Really? That would be great."

"It's a date." Sara grinned unabashedly. "I can't wait."

# Chapter Twenty

"She speaks Italian with family, but her English is passable," Paul assured Sara as they walked up the steps to his parents' front door. "She's, well, she's..." The apprehension in his voice made Sara's stomach squirm. Paul had been jumpy as a squirrel ever since she'd agreed to meet his parents, and she was at a loss to understand why.

"Do you mean she's from Italy, or she has ancestors from Italy?"

"Born and raised in Italy. She's a typical Italian mamma." In response to Sara's blank stare he explained further. "You know, Italian. Compared to your folks, she can be emotional, pushy, but not in a bad way. *Italian.*"

As Sara tried to make sense of Paul's explanation, the door burst open. Luisa Emerson descended on her son with a flood of Italian, delivered with a vehemence that had the blood vessels of Paul's forehead visibly throbbing. She seized him and hugged him, chattering far too quickly for Sara to make use of the smattering of Italian she'd learned in high school. An animated exchange ping-ponged between mother and son before the woman's wide brown eyes settled on Sara, still frozen on the steps, mouth slightly open.

"Sono tette grande!" Louisa pinched Paul's arm, eyes gleaming.

"Ma!" Paul pulled his arm away.

"È un bel sorriso." Luisa added, laughing.

Paul beamed at Sara and translated, "She loves your smile."

Sara stared at Paul, trying to ask with her eyes, *Did she just say I have big tits?* In response to Paul's pleading expression she bit back the question and held out a hand to his mother, saying, "Thank you. It's so nice to meet you."

Paul's round little father Richard stood just behind Luisa. He bobbed a bald head, fringed in hair so fine it was nearly transparent. "Paul told us you were beautiful," he said in a rich baritone that rivaled his son's. "But he didn't do you justice."

Paul's earnest, friendly eyes peered out from beneath his dad's bushy eyebrows, and Sara felt instantly close to his father. She reached out to shake his hand, but he pulled her into an embrace, hugged her flat against a well-padded belly, and exuberantly kissed both cheeks.

"Um, my family kisses a lot," Paul said with a trace of apology.

"Not a problem, Paul. Your father is adorable."

In response, Richard wrapped his arms around her and squeezed until she could barely breathe. When he finally let go, Paul's mother pulled her close and added a few cheek kisses of her own. Then Luisa pushed Sara aside and cast a look of maternal reproach on her only son.

"So, Paul, why you no dress nice for visit you family? You look like a gypsy." Luisa's thick accent was hard to follow, but her disapproval was clear.

Paul's jaw muscles stood out, and Sara interceded. "I think he looks wonderful. His socks even match." Paul shot her a look that warned she might be mistaken. Luisa's frown deepened and her voice rose as she looked Paul over from sneakers to skull.

"You are still bald, I see," she said, frowning. "Why you no use the Viagra like I tell you?"

Sara shot Paul a questioning look, and he leaned close and whispered, "She means Rogaine, to grow my hair back."

"Oh." Sara began to protest, but Luisa ignored her and rounded on Paul, her voice rising to a barely controlled shriek.

"You bring home a nice girl, and you dress like a street person? Come. I fix." Luisa waved her arms and muttered in Italian as she bolted to the hallway.

Paul mouthed, *Sorry!* as he was whisked from the doorway, leaving Sara alone with Richard.

"Come on in," Richard said, his voice an oasis of calm. "We're excited to finally meet you." Paul's father led Sara through the hallway into a small sitting room stuffed with couches, chairs, and display tables topped in lacy fabric and crammed with family photos. The room was dimly lit, every window buried beneath layers of thick privacy curtains. Feeling restless and uncertain, Sara prowled the small space and pretended to study the framed family portraits that covered every wall.

*It's a little claustrophobic in here.*

*-Run!*

*No.*

"So, what do you think of my son?" Richard grinned, and his chest seemed to swell with pride. "Paul's a nice boy, isn't he?"

"Very nice." Sara glanced down the hallway. Luisa's piercing voice, speaking rapidly in Italian, joined Paul's, also in Italian, equally loud and equally incomprehensible. The clock ticked on the wall, marking the lag in conversation. Searching for something to say, she reached for one of the many pictures of Paul and smiled at the full head of hair. "Is this high school graduation?"

Richard nodded. "First in his class. He looked so handsome in his cap and gown. I think his mother took a hundred pictures, maybe more." He leaned toward Sara and whispered, "Don't let Luisa get to you. She means well, but she can be intimidating."

Sara was about to respond, but she was interrupted by the return of Paul and his mother. Paul still spoke Italian in a whiney voice, waving his arms to ward off his mother. She fussed with his collar and took stabs at his remaining hair with a plastic comb. At the sight of Sara, she pocketed the comb and shifted the conversation back to English.

"Sara! Tell him, please," Luisa wailed. "He must do something about his hair. Are almost gone. I see on television, are treatment. He would look so much better, no?"

Sara tried to keep a straight face. But the sight of Paul wearing freshly creased dress pants, dress shirt and tie, with his mother combing his hair and pinching color into his cheeks, was too much. She burst out laughing.

"You look wonderful, Paul," she said, trying not to giggle. "Those clothes really suit you." Sara was used to running interference with her own parents, and she used an inflection that Luisa would hear as serious while Paul would understand as joking.

*This, I can do. I've spent my whole life practicing.*

*-Lying.*

*Yup. Pretty much.*

Luisa beamed at her. "You like? I buy cheap on sale. Eighty percent off."

Paul dropped his chin to his chest and slowly shook his head. "Are my cheap suit and I presentable enough to have some dinner?" He headed toward the dining room and Sara hurried after him, not wanting to be left alone with his parents.

As they moved past the dining room table, Sara counted sixteen place settings. She clutched at Paul's arm. "Who else is coming? I thought it was just going to be your parents."

Paul sighed. "Could be anyone. Family, friends, clergy. I expect my mother's been bragging that I have a girlfriend, and Italians are..." Paul hesitated, again searching for the right words. "Italians are nosy," he finally said with a tentative smile. "Be happy my dad is American, or we'd have to rent a hall."

Sara laughed, but her hands began to shake and her eyes darted to the door. It was nine steps away. "Mind if I hold the keys?" she asked. "It would calm my nerves."

Without a word, Paul handed her the keys to his treasured Honda. "It's okay, really." He squeezed her hand. "They'll love you."

The words hardly left his mouth when guests arrived all at once. They crowded through the doorway, boisterous and friendly, laughing and shouting. A dozen strangers converged on Sara in a great wave and welcomed her with wide smiles, bear hugs, and endless kisses.

"Am I supposed to kiss them back?" She felt very much out of her element and unexpectedly giddy.

"Up to you." Paul was obviously working hard to keep from laughing. "Normally, yes. But don't worry. They realize you aren't used to this."

Sara settled for hugging, but occasionally she managed to bump her nose against a fast-moving cheek. In less than a minute she met four aunts, six uncles, the dry cleaner, and the woman who ran the convenience store at the end of the street.

"When you gonna learn Italian?" Luisa asked, beaming. "Now we all must speak English. Better you learn our language."

Sara managed a weak smile. "I learned Italian in high school."

The room erupted in applause as the conversation switched back to Italian. Sara struggled to make sense of the flurry of questions that followed.

"Mass," one of the aunts repeated when Sara failed to answer her in Italian. "You and Paul go to Mass every Sunday?"

"Um, no, not *every* Sunday." Sara hoped her misleading statement might be enough. But Marianna wasn't fooled.

"But you are Catholic, no?"

Sara hesitated. She hadn't attended a church service since moving away from Lubec, and she wasn't Catholic. She steeled herself for rejection. "Um, no."

Luisa interceded, took Sara by the arm and guided her to a plate. "Not to worry, Sara. I sure you convert for Paul." Sara started to laugh, but quickly realized Paul's mother wasn't kidding.

Paul shot her another pleading look, and she grinned and nodded.

*It's not as if we're engaged.*

*-Let it go.*

Dinner was a feast of lasagna, gnocchi, veal parmesan, romaine salad, fresh bread, and endless wine. Luisa was an amazing cook. The meats had been roasted slowly for hours, and the combinations of scents, flavors, and textures were heavenly. Sara ate so much her stomach was stretched tight. But every time she managed to finish, Paul's mother slipped another impossibly large serving onto her plate.

"How do I ask her to stop?" she whispered to Paul. "I don't want to offend her, but I can't eat another bite."

"Don't finish it. If you finish, she'll assume you're still hungry." Paul, Sara noticed, had a little bit of everything left on his plate. Sara nodded and did the same.

But moments later Luisa appeared at her elbow wailing, "Oh, Sara, I so sorry you no like. What else I can make for you?"

"I love everything. It's wonderful." Sara shoved more gnocchi into her mouth and grinned as she chewed. This, of course, resulted in a much happier Luisa and another gargantuan serving of gnocchi.

"They think you're too thin," Paul whispered. "Try to stick your stomach out. It might help."

Sara slipped half her gnocchi onto Paul's plate. His ability to make food disappear was astounding.

When the meal came to an end the questions began in earnest.

"How did you meet?"

"How many children you plan to have?"

"When you two getting married?"

*I'm getting dizzy.*

*-Run!*

The family moved to the kitchen, and Sara pulled Paul toward the front door. "Would it be rude if we took a short walk? I could use a few minutes to decompress."

"A bit much, eh?" Paul looked at her sympathetically. "Everyone's waiting for my uncle to call from Trieste. He expects to talk to me, but..."

"Perfect. Can I duck out for maybe five minutes? If they're all waiting for the phone to ring, no one will miss me." Sara grinned and glanced toward the kitchen. "Just tell them I'm in the bathroom. I'm sure your mother would appreciate some time alone with you so she can ask all the questions she was afraid to ask me."

Paul groaned in reply.

Sara slipped out the door, grateful for a few minutes of peace.

*-They're crackers. Like him.*

*Cut it out. They're wonderful.*

*-Then why are you out here?*

*Shut up.*

She took a long look at the rose-colored Victorian and formed a mental picture. Then she checked her watch and headed north. In a few minutes she would turn back.

She barely reached the end of the block when a car pulled up beside her. Five people leaned out the windows, their faces drawn. "Sara, are not safe here to walk alone. Come back inside."

Sara stared in disbelief. Three of Paul's aunts and two uncles had come looking for her, and it couldn't have been more than a minute.

"It's okay. I just need a short walk. So much food," she added, rubbing her belly.

"Please, Sara. We don't want to lose you." Their distress was palpable, and Sara knew she had no choice.

"Okay, take me back," she laughed as she hopped into the front seat. Despite the inconvenience, their concern made her feel tingly and warm. Suddenly Paul's honesty made sense. He hadn't been raised to mislead and manipulate the way she had. What would it be like to be part of such a loving and happy family?

She knew it was far too soon to be picturing a future with Paul, and she put the thought from her mind. Aunt Marianna clasped Sara's hand, her brow furrowed as she searched for the right words. "Paul finally find nice girl," she said, "and we no want to lose."

Uncle Salvo looked grave as he explained, "Paul lived with that Adam fellow so long, we think maybe he a little funny, you know?"

Sara's mouth fell open as Salvo's words became clear. She tried not to laugh, snorted, and dissolved into giggles. "No, Paul isn't funny," she said, wiping her eyes. "He's just fine."

"Really? You know?" Everyone looked at each other, mouths open.

*Aw, shit. Here comes the premarital sex lecture.*

*-Slut, slut, slut, slut-*

Instead every face broke into a grin. "These are very good news!" Suddenly Sara was slapped on the back and applauded by a car full of enormously relieved and exceedingly happy Italians. She couldn't stop laughing.

When they returned to the house, Paul hurried to her side. "I'm sorry. I couldn't stop them. They banged on the bathroom door for about thirty seconds and then ran for the car."

Sara started to reply, but the whispered news of Paul's conquest traveled in excited shrieks from one end of the house to the other. She doubled over, laughing so hard she could barely speak. Finally, Luisa screeched from the kitchen, ran to the hallway and squashed Sara against her breasts, shouting, "So, when you two give me some grandchildren?"

Paul looked as if he wanted to crawl under the couch, but Sara threw herself into his arms, still laughing harder than she'd thought possible. "Your secret is out, Paul. They know you're not saving yourself for marriage."

Paul held her close. Sara breathed the scent of his new shirt, and for a moment she forgot they weren't alone. He bent down and kissed her, then whispered in her ear, "I was saving myself for you."

# Chapter Twenty-One

On the following afternoon, Sara headed for Brett Foster's farm with Harlee in tow. As a new working student with no history or standing, she knew her weekend would be spent mucking stalls, grooming and tacking up horses for Brett to ride. Then she would receive a much coveted riding lesson from Brett himself before heading home on Sunday afternoon. As she drove up Brett's private road, her heart raced.

*Me! Riding with an Olympian!*

*-You'll blow it.*

*Will not.*

The driveway was lined with acres of pasture surrounded by well-maintained white PVC fencing. Sara passed a simple but charming ranch house with a mowed lawn, fruit trees and neat flower beds. At the top of a gentle hill stood a stately barn, bordered by traditional post-and-rail paddocks. Horses whinnied from the fields as she pulled into a generous parking area. Brett waved from the barn doorway.

"Get a saddle on that mare, and meet me in the arena," he called out as soon as she parked the trailer. "Let's see what you two can do."

Sara felt the blood drain from her face, but in the rush to get ready, she had little time to give in to nervousness. Following a cursory grooming of her already-clean horse, she tacked up and jogged to the oversized indoor arena. Minutes later, she and Harlee were hard at work performing a complicated exercise designed to improve her already good dressage scores.

Harlee floated across shredded rubber footing, each stride magnified by the bounce of the springy surface. She glided through a shoulder-in, transitioned smoothly to canter, and bounded through a clean flying lead change. Sara kept the mare in counter-canter through the corner, then came gracefully back to a balanced walk.

"Good job!" Brett called out. "Do it again! But use a little less hand, if you please, and carry your ribcage. I want to see more lift in that canter."

Sara nodded and repeated the exercise, fractionally changing her posture to free the mare's shoulder. Harlee lowered her haunches and raised her withers. The resultant lofty gait seemed hardly to touch the ground.

"Wow! That is one nice mare. Well ridden, too." Brett glanced at his watch. "Want to hop over a few fences?"

"Yes, please," Sara's answering nod was abbreviated, hiding a surge of enthusiasm. "I can practice dressage at home, but cross-country courses are few and far between."

Brett swung up onto an elegant bay gelding and led the way to a grassy expanse surrounded by mature forest. Three hills sprawled over a dozen acres, filled with a variety of solid cross-country obstacles. Harlee grew taller, her eyes bright, ears pricked at the distant jumps. Brett watched her and laughed.

"She sure does love her job," he said, beaming. "A horse like that gives a rider courage." He caught Sara's eye. "And a brave rider makes a bold horse. I'm not sure which of you came first, but you're one hell of a team."

Sara murmured a thank you and gathered her reins in readiness. Brett scanned the course, all business. But when he turned back to Sara, a smile pulled at the corners of his lips.

"I'd like to see you gallop down to that bank complex," he said. "Then come up over the offset coops. Turn left down the hill over the picture frame, and finish with the white gate. Got it?"

Sara nodded and started to ride off. Brett stopped her.

"And," he said, his eyes conveying the dare, "I want it done at five hundred and seventy meters per minute. Advanced speed. I've already measured that stretch, and I'll time it. You just feel it."

Sara's stomach did an excited cartwheel. She pressed Harlee to a gallop and described a wide arc around the perimeter of the field. Gradually, she brought the pinto up to speed and leveled her out. As she began the course, she melted into Harlee's back and allowed exhilaration to merge with careful planning.

Together they soared up onto the bank and launched themselves down the other side. Sara nailed the striding on both coops. Harlee sailed through the picture frame and flew toward the gate. Rather than make a wide, time-consuming arc to approach the last fence head-on, Sara raced toward it at a nearly impossible angle. She and Harlee flew the very corner, finishing close, she hoped, to the time allowed.

Brett whooped and shouted, "Good decision on that gate! I couldn't have done better myself." He pointed to his watch. "You were too fast, about six fifty. Very good, but in the real world we'll have to work on that."

Sara felt like jumping up and down, but she focused on Brett's advice for improvement and hung on to a serious expression.

"I'm afraid I have to call it a day," Brett said, a trace of regret in his tone. "Shall we say eight o'clock tomorrow and same time Sunday?"

"That would be wonderful," Sara said, hardly daring to believe she'd receive three sessions with Brett. "And I'll be here every weekend, except for competitions."

Brett tipped his head in agreement. "I'd like you to school some horses for me tomorrow," he said, enthusiasm dancing in his eyes. "I'm not wasting your talent mucking stalls." Sara gasped and he chuckled in response. "It's high time you realize just how good you are, Sara Morgan. Mark my words. You and Harlee are going places."

Sara threw her arms around Harlee's neck, letting happy tears wet her horse's mane. For the first time in her life, everything was coming together. She was on track for Rolex. She had Paul. She might have a chance to run her own barn. She was meeting challenges head-on and reaching for her dreams.

"You and me, Harlee," she said, stroking the gleaming neck. "You heard the man. We're going places."

# Chapter Twenty-Two

Buoyed by memories of her weekend with Brett, Sara sprinted from her truck to Sylvia Green's office. She took the stairs two at a time, cell phone pressed to her ear. Cassie's excited shriek blasted across the line.

"It's ours! They accepted our offer!"

"The inn?" Sara skidded to a stop outside Sylvia's door and hopped in place, too excited to stand still. "That's great! I can't believe you found an investor so soon."

"Isn't it amazing?" Cassie giggled like a middle-schooler. "If everything goes according to plan, we'll close at the end of September and open for business a month later. It needs paint and paper and some new furnishings, but nothing we can't do ourselves. And I have a marketing plan all worked out."

"Of course you do." Sara glanced at her watch. She was already a few minutes late. "Look, I have an appointment. Can we talk later?"

"Is it Wednesday already?" Cassie's usual I-don't-trust-shrinks comment didn't follow. "Give Dr. Green hell for me."

"I'll do my best." Sara ended the call and pocketed the phone, then knocked once before letting herself inside. Sylvia was already seated and looked up, face pensive despite a welcoming smile. Sara ignored a cautionary whisper from within and hurried to her place on the couch.

"Sorry to keep you waiting." She flopped onto the cushion and kicked off her shoes, ready to dive into a hypnosis session. "Cassie called. They got the inn."

Sylvia's smile broadened. "That's wonderful news. Will you be able to work there?"

"I didn't ask, but it sounds promising." She dove back against the pillow as her usual misgivings gave way to optimism. "Honestly, everything is going so well, I can hardly believe it. And today's the day I'm going to remember what happened to me at Round Lake. I can feel it."

*-You'll quit again.*

*No I won't.*

*-You always do.*

*Not this time.*

"Let's put that on hold for a bit, shall we?" Sylvia perched on the front half of her chair, her face half hidden behind the notepad in her hands. "We've come close. You remember everything that happened up until the actual attack, but then, nothing." As she set the notepad on the coffee table, she spoke softly, but her voice had an unusual edge. "To be honest, I'm not at all sure that memory exists."

"What do you mean?" Sara picked her head up off the pillow and pulled herself to a sitting position.

"It may be a false memory." Sylvia placed her notepad in her lap and stared at it as she spoke. "When I suggested we look for an instance of betrayal, it's possible your mind invented the memory in order to satisfy my expectations."

"You think I made it up?" Sara shrank back, feeling a hundred fingers pointed in her direction.

"Not on purpose," Sylvia assured her. "I blame myself. It was a mistake, one I shouldn't have made."

*-Incompetent pretender.*

*-Stupid, stupid, stupid, stupid-*

"But it seems so real."

*If nothing happened to me, why am I broken?*

*-Sick, like your grandfather.*

*-Never normal. No hope.*

Sylvia peered over her reading glasses. "Real or not, it remains beyond our reach. I think it's time we try another approach."

-*Useless psychobabble. Nothing works.*

-*Nothing will ever work.*

"But that's not fair." Sara kicked the leg of the coffee table in frustration and clasped her hands to keep from pinching her thigh. "What if you're wrong? What if it is real?"

"Even so, I think there are things we need to discuss before we go back to the lake." Sylvia was maddeningly calm. Sara ground her teeth and tried not to shout.

"What could possibly be more important?"

"Your marriage to Mark."

The air went out of the room. *What's with her today? She's changing everything.*

-*Useless, useless, useless, useless-*

"Why do we have to talk about Mark?"

"Well, for starters, I want you to understand your mistakes so you have a better chance of avoiding them in the future."

A lump rose in Sara's throat. *I really don't want to talk about Mark.*

-*That should tell you something.*

"I think there's still a lot to be learned from your relationship. For example, can you explain to me again why you married him?"

Sara looked at the floor. "But we went over that. I told you he was pathetic. No one wanted either of us. My father thought he'd be good for me. What else is there?"

"You tell me."

Sara rolled her eyes. *Now she's using shrink-speak.*

-*She's trying to help.*

*I know.*

Sara's chest felt as if it had shrunk several sizes, as if her lungs were squashed into a sandwich bag. She gave up her attempts to breathe into her belly and settled for a shallow sigh. "I've thought a lot about it, and all I can say is I was seriously mixed up." She tried to be completely honest, to find the best words, even though saying them hurt in ways she couldn't explain. "My mother looked after the world. She worked at the soup kitchen, did crafts with the elderly, all that stuff. And I helped. She raised me to look after the needy, and Mark was in need."

"But why marry him? Couldn't you help without walking down the aisle?"

Again, Sara saw fingers pointing at her mistakes. She winced and looked away.

*It's like it happened to someone else.*

*-You were someone else.*

Sara tried to focus on the progress she'd made, but it was difficult to be positive with her nose buried in her worst failure. "I didn't know what a loving relationship was," she said between clenched teeth. "I'd never seen one."

Sylvia's words nudged her gently. "What about your friends? Didn't their parents behave differently than yours?"

"What friends?" Sara dipped her head and let her hair shield her eyes. "Do you know what my father did every September? He stood up in front of my whole school and told them I was sick, and they had to be careful of me." Her hands curled into fists at the memory of sitting at the back of the auditorium, wishing the floor might open up and let her dive through. "He tried to help, but he scared the crap out of everybody."

"Dr. Morgan did that?" The look on Sylvia's face more closely resembled betrayal than shock. "What an awful thing to do to a child."

Sylvia's response surprised Sara. No one ever questioned her father's actions, not where his daughter's safety was concerned. Dr. Green was quiet for a moment, her eyes empty as a china doll. Sara watched as she pulled in an over-deep breath and her face transformed to her usual expression of detached interest. "I imagine he had his reasons." She said the words, but her lips pursed.

"It wasn't so bad." Sara tried to sit straighter, to act stronger than she felt. "I didn't blame anyone for being afraid of me. Besides, I could always go to the stable and hug a horse."

"Horses." Sylvia said the word as if she'd discovered the missing piece of a puzzle. "I imagine they gave you the acceptance you needed so very badly."

Sara nodded. "I guess so. And when I came back from college, Mark was part of that world. And he was pathetic. It was a match made in heaven, right?"

"And where was Cassie?" The question sounded like an accusation. "Weren't you two still friends?"

Even now the memory was painful. Add Dr. Green's finger-pointing, and Sara's chest began to ache. "Cassie was in Boston with a brand new career. I was hundreds of miles away in Lubec, living with my folks and getting paid minimum wage for mucking stalls in Mark's barn." Sara folded her arms across her chest, feeling the rise and fall of her ribs, the rhythm quick and refusing to slow. "We tried to keep in touch, but we were too far apart, in every way."

Sylvia continued in a gentler tone. "So you bonded with the most wretched, needy person you could find, and you married him. And this would somehow make you whole?" Her eyes pushed for more. "Is there anything I'm missing?"

"Yes." Sara felt sick to her stomach as she forced a confession. "There was a moment before the wedding when I almost turned back. I knew it was a terrible mistake, and I decided to end it."

"What stopped you?"

"Mark was broke, and he was losing the farm." Sara stopped and pressed her lips together, determined not to cry. "My dad is well off. I knew he'd give Mark money if he were family, so I went ahead with the marriage." She stared at the table and shuddered, too ashamed to cry. "I couldn't bear to lose the horses, and Mark was my coach, my mentor. If the stable folded, I'd lose everything."

"Were the voices involved?"

Sara shook her head. She pressed her knuckles against her eyes until they hurt, but still her throat felt thick, and her nose clogged. "How could I have done something so *wrong*?"

Sylvia straightened to a more formal posture. "It sounds like an idea that formed at a very early age. Your parents manipulated one another, so you learned the pattern."

Sara nodded once. What more was there to say?

"What finally gave you the courage to leave?" Sylvia's voice was low and husky.

"Mark was coming closer and closer to really hurting me. He almost crossed the line, but he always pulled back just shy of doing serious damage." Sara paused and swallowed hard. "But I knew it was only a matter of time, and I deserved it."

"That's the victim talking. You didn't deserve any of it."

"I'm not so sure." Sara shivered in memory as the emptiness inside her darkened and grew. "I was dying. When I looked in the mirror there was nothing there. No spark, no hope. I was killing myself bit by bit, and I was the only one who could save me." Sara's voice cracked, and she stopped to swallow.

"Don't you see? I was still rescuing someone, still saving the most pathetic person in the room. But this time it wasn't Mark. It was me."

She slumped forward and let tears roll down her face. "Nothing changed. I never did grow the hell up. I only left because I had to. It was the only way I could stay alive."

Sara pulled her knees up against her chest, wrapped her arms around them and rocked. "I lied to Mark, told him I cared for him. And then I ran away like a coward." The room spiraled around her. Sylvia's hand touched her shoulder, followed by a firm embrace. Sara leaned into the comfort, breathed in the subtle scent of roses, and cried.

Minutes passed before she was able to open her eyes. The voices still filled her mind, but they were softer. Sylvia slipped her arms from Sara's shoulders and sat beside her.

"Sara," she began, her voice soft, eyes filled with encouragement, "I understand your mother's influence, and your own needs. But I think there may be something you're missing."

Sara sucked in a breath and lifted her eyes. "What?"

"Fear. Fear of the alternative. Mark was safe for you, emotionally. Maybe you aimed low so you couldn't be disappointed."

Sara cringed as the words added to the weight of guilt she already carried. The explanation made perfect sense. *I am my mother's daughter.* Joanie seemed to spend her life in perpetual compromise and disappointment.

"It wasn't my mother's fault." The words had to be said out loud. "I made my own choices."

Sylvia's voice was gentle. "*Fault* isn't a word I'd use, but your mother's influence was strong. We all behave according to beliefs formed through our experiences. Our actions are, in many ways, beyond our control." Sylvia's face hardened as she whispered, "We are who we are." Her words sounded like a confession.

Sylvia glanced at her watch, and her expression moved from sincerity to regret. "I think this is great work for today, Sara. But I need to leave you with one more thought. It's about Paul."

"Paul? What about Paul?" The edges of Sara's vision shimmered in warning. "When I'm with him, I feel completely safe. Most of the time, I don't even hear the voices."

Sylvia seemed to shrink, as if the words were as difficult for her to say as they were for Sara to hear. "I have no doubt he's a wonderful person. But you just told me nothing changed, and you left Mark only to save yourself."

"Uh-huh." *Paul doesn't need saving. Being with Paul is breaking the pattern, isn't it?*

"Just be sure you aren't expecting Paul to rescue you. More importantly, follow your own dreams before you risk tying yourself to someone else's."

*-Love is a trap.*

The voices snickered as Sara considered Dr. Green's warning. She already worried she was taking advantage of Paul's good nature, despite his reassurances. Now her therapist's echoed concerns brought her fears to the forefront.

"But Paul doesn't stand in my way at all. He doesn't even mind that I'm spending weekends away from him in Vermont."

*-He lies!*

*Shut up!*

Sylvia gave an odd, dismissive laugh. "Of course he minds. But perhaps he cares enough about you to give up what he needs. At least, for now." Sylvia fixed Sara with a sympathetic gaze. "You can't live separate lives forever. Someday soon you'll have to choose, his dreams or yours."

The floor tilted beneath Sara's feet. "What do I do?"

"Learn to take care of yourself first." Sylvia placed a cold hand on her shoulder. "Don't get serious about anyone until you're certain you can stand on your own two feet."

The air thickened as the room spun. Sara pitched forward and shoved her head between her knees.

*I must be misunderstanding.*

*-You're not ready.*

*-Never ready.*

Sara squeezed her knees against her chest and hoped for a different answer, one that lifted the black fog and gave her hope. "You, you think I should stop seeing Paul?" Her throat closed.

"It's a good idea, Sara," Sylvia said gently. "A clean break is best in these cases. It will be easier for both of you if you don't communicate with him at all."

# Chapter Twenty-Three

Twenty minutes passed before Sara rose from the couch and shuffled into the slanted rays of a dying sun. She felt detached from her feet, as if gliding or swimming through clotted air. Only half aware she was driving home, she couldn't remember walking from the office to her truck. Her head throbbed, the voices screamed, and she didn't care enough to fight the storm massing behind her eyes.

*This can't be real.*

*-You're sick.*

*-Crazy, crazy, crazy, crazy-*

She coasted to a stop in the middle of the driveway and stared at nothing.

*-Pitiful, useless girl.*

*-Just die, die, die, die-*

Her feet tingled with each step as she walked to her front door, cell phone in her palm, fingers punching out Paul's number. *I'll ask him to come over,* she told herself. *We'll figure something out.*

The phone rang three times, long enough to let herself through the door and walk to the kitchen. Eyes shut tight, she leaned against the wall. *There has to be another way.*

*-Do you want to get better?*

*Yes.*

*-What would you give?*

The warm timbre of Paul's voice simultaneously wrapped her in comfort and took away the last of her control. She hung up the phone, slid to the floor, and cried.

Paul heard a sob just before the line went dead. "Sara? Is that you?" He checked the caller ID. Cold with apprehension, he dialed her number. She didn't answer.

*What could be wrong?* He wavered for an instant before bolting out the door. Her cottage was fifteen minutes away. He could make it in ten.

Paul drove as fast as he dared. When he rounded the corner to the gravel drive he nearly cried with relief. Panting, he jumped from the car and jogged to her door. He pounded harder than he'd intended. When she didn't answer, he twisted the knob and found it open.

"Sara?" The door groaned as he pushed it aside. "Are you here?"

He'd barely crossed the threshold when he saw her. She glanced up and scrubbed at her face with the back of her hand. "Paul. I didn't expect to see you." Her voice was toneless, without a glimmer of its usual light.

"What happened? What are you doing on the floor?" She'd been so looking forward to working with Brett, hoping for a job with Adam and Cassie. "Oh, my God. Is it Harlee?" He rushed forward.

Sara shook her head, her face pinched.

"Then what is it?" Paul knelt beside her and slipped his arms around her. She fell against him and pressed her face into his shirt. Cupping her chin, he tried to turn her face up to his. "How can I help?" She twisted away, her shoulders shaking, something unintelligible drowning in sobs.

Her crying showed no sign of slowing down, and Paul waited, unnerved by her distress. Occasionally she seemed to regain control, but when she tried to speak, she came apart, crying so hard that he wondered how she managed to breathe. Minutes passed before she was finally spent, collapsed in his arms, clutching his shirt and sniffling against his shoulder.

"Whatever it is, we'll figure it out. Just tell me."

Her voice was hoarse, more a croak than a whisper. "I can't see you anymore."

"What? Why? What have I done? What can I do?" He gripped her shoulders, trying to see through her hair to her face. "Is it your father?"

"It's Dr. Green." She was near sobbing again, her breath wet and quivering past her throat. "She says I'm not ready to be in a relationship. She says I have to learn to be on my own first."

Paul put his arms back around her, trying to comfort her even as the words made him feel as if he'd stepped off a cliff. "Maybe you misunderstood. We'll go tomorrow and talk to her together."

"She thinks you're a crutch. She says I'm using you."

"Go ahead. Use me. I'm fine with that."

Sara exhaled on a whimper. Paul held her tighter than usual, afraid she might pull away given the smallest opening. "Is it temporary?"

She didn't answer, but she trembled against him. He tried to keep his frustration in check, but he couldn't stop resentment from creeping into his voice. "I thought Dr. Green said forming relationships was a sign of health. What changed her mind?"

Sara answered in a small voice. "I don't know. She said I have to learn to stand on my own two feet before I can be with someone else."

Paul clamped his mouth shut, wanting to kick something, hard. Instead he did his best to be practical. He had to think things through, try to see Dr. Green's side, form a plan, reach a compromise. "Can we can keep in touch? Stay friends?" Paul realized his voice had sunk to the same beaten tone as Sara's.

"She said I shouldn't see you at all."

*What the hell?* Paul stared with his mouth open. "And you think this is what you need?"

She pushed against his chest. He knew he ought to let go, but he held on and waited for her to stop struggling. When she finally went limp, her words came out in a squeak. "I don't know."

Paul didn't dare meet her eyes, afraid she would see the anger. "But I love you." His voice was soft, barely hiding the bitter edge.

She burrowed into his shirt and snuffled. "I know. I love you, too."

Her body sagged against him like something dead, as if her spirit had already left. As he held her, his irritation expanded until it was all he could do to remain silent. *Why isn't she fighting back? What the hell is Dr. Green thinking?*

"Maybe we can try it. Being just friends." Her words were spoken in a murmur, as if she didn't trust them.

For a moment Paul's irritation gave way to hope. Sara's doctor would come around. She'd realize Sara needed him as much as he'd come to need her. *But what if?*

He couldn't help thinking of Sara's nightmares, her terrified screams, the chanting - *She's been in a mental hospital, and she tried to kill herself. What if Dr. Green is right? What if she has another break because I'm too stubborn to let her go?*

The thought was devastating. What if she did need to be on her own? How could he live with himself if he kept her from getting well? Impossible as it seemed, maybe he did need to step aside.

"We'd better not."

Sara went rigid a moment before she tried to rip away from him, sobbing, "I won't tell Dr. Green. She doesn't need to know."

"Sara, listen to me," Paul pleaded, not letting her go. "Maybe she's right."

She screamed and swung at him, her fists pounding against his chest. He tried again. "I don't want to keep you from getting better." But she seemed beyond reason, fighting him like a wild thing.

He let go. She ran to her room and slammed the door, her sobs carrying into the hallway. He paused long enough to make a phone call, and he waited until Cassie arrived. Then he did the only thing he could. He walked away.

Paul got out of the car, stomped down the driveway, and kicked the *For Sale* sign at the edge of his lawn. Adam stuck his head out the door, his face flushed. "What's up? We barely got in the door when Cassie left like a bat outta hell."

"None of your business." Paul glared. He walked to the house, pushed past Adam, strode to the living room and threw himself on the sofa. Adam followed and stood in the doorway.

"Geez, Paul, you look like crap."

"Thanks. That's very helpful. Now please take your perfect self down the hall and leave me the hell alone." Paul's outburst was met with shock.

"Shit. Did she dump you?"

Paul turned and faced the wall.

"Was it her father?"

Paul shook his head.

"Your mother, then. She scares the crap out of me."

Paul bristled. "No, it was not my mother."

"What about our plans? What about Vermont?"

*Trust Adam to make it about him.* Paul ground his teeth. "A deal's a deal. I'm in."

Adam's relief was palpable. He flopped down next to Paul and awkwardly touched his shoulder. "It's bad, then." "The worst." Paul swallowed hard, determined to stay in control. "It's her illness. Her therapist doesn't want her in a serious relationship until she's well."

Adam let out a low whistle. "Wow, I did not see that coming." He raked his fingers through thick blond hair, illustrating yet another injustice and making Paul want to kick the *For Sale* sign a few more times.

"But you're holding out for a miracle," Adam said. "Right?"

Paul sighed. "Maybe I'm being an idiot, but I have to believe we can fix this. She'll get well, and we'll get back together."

He risked a glance in Adam's direction. "I've spent my whole life looking for someone like Sara, ever since I was old enough to notice girls. I know it sounds dumb, but she's the one." He shut his mouth, knowing Adam would never let him hear the end of it if he said she was his other half, the only girl he'd ever love. Instead he settled on a more logical argument.

"I've known her for months, and I don't understand why she has to have a guardian. She's completely competent. Look at everything she's dealt with already."

Paul glanced at Adam. For once his friend wasn't making jokes at his expense.

"She's got so much courage," Paul said, buoyed by his own words. "Have you *seen* the jumps she and Harlee go over? And the *speed!* She works really hard for everything she wants. She's honest and she's smart. And, damn it, she's *short.*"

Adam chuckled as Paul plunged onward.

"I know she'll make it. I don't care how long it takes."
Paul made a pickle face. "Okay, I hope it doesn't take too
long. But in any case I'll be here when she's ready."

"So, you're gonna wait for her."

"Hell, yes."

Adam patted Paul's shoulder before heading for the
storage rooms. "Sit tight," he said as he bounded up the
stairs. "I'll break out the comic books."

# Chapter Twenty-Four

Sara curled into a ball on the couch and tried not to start crying again. The look on Cassie's face was more demanding than sympathetic, and Sara knew her friend wouldn't quit until she had answers.

"What happened? Why in the world did Paul dump you?"

Sara rolled from the couch and headed for the back door. "I can't talk right now. It's time to feed the horses."

*He said he wouldn't be just friends.*

*-He only wanted one thing.*

Cassie tucked her chin into her scarf and followed Sara out onto the lawn, shivering in a business suit and heels. "Fine," she said. "Let me freeze my ass off. But don't think you're gonna get out of talking."

Sara clamped her mouth shut and tried to ignore the sadness that seemed part of her clothing, her skin, her hair.

*-No one will ever love you.*

*I thought he did.*

*-Stupid little girl, always the fool.*

"Did Paul say why he broke up with you?" Cassie's heels sank into the grass. She swore, but she didn't slow down. "It doesn't make sense. He adores you."

Sara tried for a breezy tone, but her voice wouldn't stop shaking. "I broke up with him."

"What? Why?" Cassie's tone shifted to accusatory in the space of a breath. "That's bizarre, Sara, even for you."

*-Bizarre!*

*-Crazy, crazy, crazy, crazy-*

"I had no choice." Sara pulled the barn door open and stepped into the aisle. The horses galloped in from the field, skidded through their back doors into clean stalls, and waited, ears pricked toward the feed room. Sara paused to give Harlee's forehead a scratch, and she spoke more to her horse than to Cassie. "Dr. Green said I have to be on my own before I can get well."

"Is she out of her mind?" Cassie gripped Sara's shoulder. "We all depend on each other. Do you have to dump me, too, or just poor Paul?"

"I don't know." Sara pushed Cassie's hand away and ducked into the feed room. "Dr. Green has been really helpful. Of all the therapists I've ever had, she's the only one who really gets me." Sara lifted an armload of hay and made her way down the aisle, tossing a substantial helping into every stall. "I have to trust her. She thinks I can be completely well, and I need to believe her."

As Sara reached the end of the aisle, a high-pitched hum invaded her head. Her vision blurred, and she grabbed the wall, determined not to faint.

*Not again.*

*-Pathetic.*

*-Useless, useless, useless, useless-*

Cassie held out a hand. "C'mon. The horses can wait a few more minutes for their supper."

Sara accepted Cassie's help, feeling even more damaged. Cassie helped her to the bench, and Sara sat, head between her knees, waiting for the dizziness to pass.

"You must get sick of me." Sara closed her eyes as the world spun around her. "Sometimes it seems all we do is sit on this bench."

"My fault." Cassie sat beside her and slung an arm across her shoulders. "I shouldn't have gone off on you like that. But dumping Paul. I don't get it."

"I don't either. Not really." Sara tried to lift her head, but a wave of sickness forced it back down. "I'd do anything to be well. You don't know what it's like, Cassie. Even now, they're all shouting at me. I can hardly hear myself think."

-*Give up!*

-*Take the drugs.*

-*Die, die, die, die-*

"And it's not just the voices." Sara put her hands over her ears and shut her eyes. "I never know when I might *break* again, do awful things I can't remember." She let out a long, shuddering breath. "Don't you see? I'm not fit to be with someone else, not like this."

Cassie moved closer, her hip resting against Sara's. "You're right. I don't know what it's like. And of course you'll get better." She hesitated, her breath still quick and uneven. "But I don't understand why you have to do it alone. I thought Dr. Green was supportive of your relationship with Paul. What changed all of a sudden?"

Sara leaned against her, still too lightheaded to sit upright. "I don't know. She thinks I'm using him. She says I'll have to give up my dreams for his." She pulled in a breath and held it until her chest begged for air.

-*Selfish bitch!*

*Can you all please shut up!*

-*Shut up, shut up, shut up, shut up-*

A wave of anger swept over her. "I deserve to get well. Paul deserves someone who doesn't talk to voices, someone who's not *crazy*. And if he can't wait around for that, it's his damn loss."

Cassie said nothing, but Sara heard a low chuckle making its way up from her belly. A moment later Cassie knocked her off balance with a shove. "I know what he's doing."

Sara bristled. "He's looking out for himself."

"Not even close. I swear, Sara, you can be so dense sometimes."

"He's running away from the crazy person."

"No, he isn't. He's giving you what you asked for."

*He ran, first chance he got.*

*-You pushed him away.*

*But he left.*

*-You told him to go.*

*He should have stayed. He should have fought for me.*

"Maybe he's been hoping for a chance to dump me. Maybe he was relieved when I handed it to him." Sara sat up slowly. Her ears still hummed, but her vision was clearing. The first thing she saw was Cassie, looking at her with a stupid grin on her face. "What's so damn funny?"

Cassie didn't stop smirking. "I spend a lot of time with Adam at Paul's house," she said. "I hear things. And you have to believe me, Paul is in it for the long haul."

Sara looked sharply at her friend. "What are you talking about?"

"Trust me, Paul may keep his distance, but he'll wait for you." Cassie held up her hand and caught the light with her diamond. "He's very much in love."

Sara stared at the ring. "He didn't, I mean, he wouldn't. We've never talked about—What do you know? Tell me."

"Nope, and I'm done dropping hints." Cassie folded her hands and hid her ring from view. "But believe me, Paul loves you, maybe a little too much."

Sara began to tremble. *What if she's right?*

*-You don't deserve him.*

*But what if?*

"Oh, Cassie, I said terrible things to him. He tried to explain, and I, I *hit* him."

"He understands. He's not going anywhere." Cassie backed away and poked a finger in Sara's ribs. "The question is, what are you going to do about it?"

"What *can* I do?" Sara stood slowly, testing her balance. "If I don't trust my doctor, what hope do I have?"

"What about a second opinion?"

-*They'll lock you up again.*

-*Make you take the drugs.*

-*Leave you there until you die.*

"NO!"

Cassie's eyes widened, and Sara turned and headed for the feed room. "You still don't get it. A new doctor would just delay things. I'd have to start all over again." The voices screamed. Her head pounded. She groped for words as she grabbed feed buckets from shelves and tried to explain. "I *need* to trust Dr. Green. I *have* to try it her way. My dad says Dr. Green is the best."

Cassie groaned. "Well, I guess that's your answer. Anything Daddy says is fine by you."

Sara bit her lip. *Cassie hates my father.*

-*She has reason.*

*It's time she let it go.*

-*Bitch, bitch, bitch, bitch-*

"Cassie, it was years ago. Cut him some slack."

Cassie's face pinched in hurt, but she held her ground. "I don't trust him, Sara, not since that stunt he pulled in college."

Sara said nothing, but she stomped her way down the aisle and slammed the buckets harder than necessary as she fed the rest of the horses.

Cassie's voice wavered. "But you're right. He's your dad, and I need to get over myself." She let out a drawn-out sigh. "I'm sorry. I'll try harder."

Sara's anger evaporated, and she looked sheepishly at her friend. "It would help if you got past it, but to be honest I was angry with him, too. He had no right going behind my back like that. I felt like a mental patient."

"And I felt like an ethically ambiguous little trollop, someone he thought would do something questionable for money." Cassie stifled a giggle. "When he asked me to look out for you and be your friend, that was one thing. But he thought I'd be his snitch, and he was dead wrong."

"He never made that mistake again." For a moment the memory lifted Sara's spirits. "You know, Cassie, that was the day I knew I could trust you. You told me what my father had done, what you had done. That meant everything."

Cassie grinned back. "I'll always tell you the truth, even if it hurts. And right now I think you're making a mistake."

"But I have to."

Cassie shushed her. "It's your mistake to make. Paul is crazy about you." She lowered her voice and spoke earnestly. "But you can't expect him to wait forever. I just hope when you get things worked out, it's not too late."

"Well, at least we agree on something." Sara spoke with a confidence she couldn't begin to feel. "I just have to get better. And I have to do it now."


Paul sat uncomfortably in a butt-sized depression that didn't quite accommodate all of him. Directly across from him was Dr. Peter Daly. Hands in his lap, sweaty forehead reflecting the glare of the cheap ceiling light, the psychiatrist moistened his lips for the third time and spoke for the fourth time.

"I'll ask again, Mr. Emerson." He leaned forward, poised, Paul thought, like a spider waiting to pounce upon an unsuspecting fly. And here came the question again. Paul could hardly believe his ears.

"This friend of yours who hears voices, is it you?"

Paul rolled his eyes skyward, once more reminding himself he was paying for the privilege of this third degree. "No, it's not me. It's a girl I'm dating. Or I was dating her until yesterday."

How many times would he have to repeat himself, he wondered, before this moron would take him at his word? It was no wonder Dr. Daly was the only psychiatrist within fifty miles with an immediate opening. Every nut job in the county must bloody well know to go elsewhere.

"I just want more information," Paul tried to explain. "If someone has a mental illness, why might it be damaging for them to be in a relationship?"

Dr. Daly frowned as an *Ah-ha* blossomed in his eyes. He began making little tsking sounds with his tongue, and his expression changed from challenge to sympathy.

"Well, Mr. Emerson, it would depend on the mental illness, and on the relationship."

Paul folded his hands in his lap. He felt like an errant child and wondered what he might have done to mess things up. "Well, um, we've been together since March, and we were getting along really well," he explained. "She was happy. I was happy. And then, out of the blue, her therapist told her to break it off."

Dr. Daly laughed, caught Paul's eye, and coughed into his hand. "Are you sure things were going well?" He folded his arms across his chest, adopting the posture of a disapproving parent. "Could she have used her therapist as an excuse to break up with you in order to spare your feelings?"

Heat crept up Paul's neck and warmed his face. It wasn't as if he hadn't asked himself the same question. Of course it was possible, but he didn't think so. "I doubt it," he said. "She was pretty torn up."

"Really."

Paul tried to read the psychiatrist's expression. Did he think Sara might have pretended to be upset? "She was a mess. I found her on the floor crying. She could hardly talk." The memory made his stomach hurt.

Dr. Daly pressed his fist against his chin and Paul wondered if he was thinking or pretending to think. "It's possible she was having an increase in symptoms. Did she appear less present? More distracted? Could the stress of maintaining a relationship have exacerbated her condition?"

"No, nothing like that," Paul replied, frustrated. "Her only symptom is that she hears voices. She does have nightmares, and if she gets really upset about something, sometimes she gets dizzy. Other than that she's normal, and she's the most honest person I know." Paul realized he sounded irritated, and he tried to slow his words and make his voice calm and reasonable.

"She said the voices were better when she was with me, not so angry, more like people she could reason with. She thought they might even go away." Paul's voice trailed off as he remembered that conversation. He'd felt special, a part of Sara's life. A good part.

Dr. Daly's expression shifted to pity. "Do you think she might be distancing herself for your benefit? Offering you a chance to be free of her? Maybe she hoped you'd talk her out of it."

"Oh, shit."

"So you went along with her? No argument?"

"I didn't even tell her how upset I was. And when she asked me to try being just friends, I said I wouldn't."

Dr. Daly looked at him as if he'd sprouted a second head. "Why was that?"

"I thought if her therapist wanted her to be on her own then she had to be on her own. And if I was with her, she'd just be pretending to be alone." Paul stared. "Oh, God. She thinks I don't love her. She thinks I took the easy way out."

"She may." The doctor pressed his lips together, eyes narrowed. "Honestly, Paul, not having spoken to her, I can only guess. But there is one thing you have to understand."

"At the risk of sounding like even more of an idiot, what?"

"We're not gods." Dr. Daly held his hands in supplication as an odd little smile played at his lips. "I'm sure your girlfriend's therapist is doing her best, and the recommendation that you step back from the relationship may be sound. But it's hardly the final word."

Paul felt a tingle of hope, and he forced himself to think before plunging forward. "So if I let Sara know I'll be there for her, it might not get in the way of her treatment?"

The doctor shrugged. "As I said, I don't know the situation, not from her point of view, nor from her therapist's. But it seems reasonable you can assure her of your support." He paused a moment, eyeing Paul in a way that made him want to squirm out of the chair. "There is one more thing."

"What?"

"Stop lying to her."

"What?" Paul gaped. "I've never lied to her. I..."

"Oh, yes, you have." Dr. Daly held up a hand to silence Paul's sputtering. "You told her you wouldn't be just her friend. Yet it appears you have no intention of moving on. Your heart was in the right place, but you didn't tell her the truth. This woman needs the truth."

"But what was I supposed to do? Demand she ignore her doctor and give me what I wanted instead?"

"Exactly." Dr. Daly's face was triumphant. Paul stared in disbelief.

"You're serious. I should expect her to jeopardize her recovery for me."

"Not exactly." The doctor looked at the ceiling, and Paul held his breath. "But when you're upset, don't hide it. If you're disappointed, let her know. Don't spare her feelings. You must be completely, unequivocally honest. In short, be someone she can always trust, even when the truth is painful."

Dr. Daly folded his arms across his chest. "You've told me she's the most honest person you know. That makes perfect sense." He shifted forward and locked onto Paul's gaze. "This is important, Paul. Listen carefully. Truth is everything to this girl. Honesty, even brutal honesty, is necessary."

"But what about common courtesy? What about hurt feelings?"

"You're not listening. She's been a mental patient most of her life. People treat her like a child. She's always been mollified and managed, and you can be sure she hates every last bit of it." Dr. Daly shook his head. "Lies are the one thing this girl cannot handle, the one thing she will never forgive. Do you want her trust?"

"Of course I do."

"If you want a chance with her, you must learn to be honest even when it's not nice. Can you do that?"

Paul stared. "I'm not sure I could bring myself to hurt her, not on purpose."

"You have to take that risk, Paul." Dr. Daly sighed, his frustration evident. "If you disagree with her, tell her. If she hurts your feelings, let her know." He shrugged, glanced at his watch and looked toward the door. "If you can't do that, Paul, then I'm afraid it's time to let her go."

# Chapter Twenty-Five

Even though she knew it would do no good, Sara glared at Dr. Green. "We've wasted half this session on nothing. When are we going to get somewhere?"

*-Patience.*

*No one asked you.*

Sylvia removed her reading glasses and placed them on the coffee table. Her eyes were puffy, her face unusually worn. Sara immediately regretted her outburst.

*-Impudent little girl!*

*-Biting the hand.*

*But she's not helping at all.*

"We are getting somewhere," Sylvia replied. "You have a much better understanding of your parents' relationship, of your motivations in marrying Mark, and of the reasons you were able to connect with Paul. You understand the voices better, and you're learning new ways to cope."

"Maybe if the voices weren't getting worse, I wouldn't have to learn new ways to cope." Sara hated that she couldn't keep from whining.

"It's an adjustment period, Sara. Give it time."

"But I'm in a hurry."

"Then it's my job to ask you to slow down." Sylvia was the picture of calm acceptance while Sara boiled inside. *I need to get better before Paul gives up on me.*

*-Dirty girl, wanting the sex.*

*Shut up.*

"What's the point in slowing down? I just want to *get* somewhere." Sara repositioned herself. The arm rest was prickly, the cushions hard, the weight of her hair irksome. Even her skin felt abnormally tight.

"Pretend you and Harlee are jumping downhill," Sylvia said. "You always tell me how important it is to get her hindquarters underneath her so you don't somersault and break your necks."

-*Die! Die, die, die, die-*

"Yes, fine, I get it." Sara itched in places she couldn't reach. She ground her back against the cushions and huffed. "But what are we going to do? The voices are much worse now that Paul is gone."

-*You'll never get better.*

-*Your grandfather's curse.*

-*Never better. Never, never, never, never-*

"Well, that should prove to you, Paul was a crutch."

"Or maybe I'm better when I'm happy." Sara radiated defiance, but Sylvia sidestepped her easily.

"How did he take it?"

"A little too well."

"I'm sure he was more upset than he seemed," Sylvia said. "He's probably putting on a good face, trying to make things easier on you."

"I hope so." Sara caught herself and snorted. "What am I saying? I don't want him suffering. That would be cruel."

-*Vicious girl.*

"He'll be fine," Sylvia replied. "As for you, try to focus on riding and competing, the things that made you happy before you met Paul."

"It's different now. I've had something special and lost it. That leaves a hole." Sara stared at her therapist for a long moment, waiting for a reply.

-*Sucking, dirty, empty hole.*

"Damn it, Sylvia! I want to get better now." Sara's hands went to her ears and ground themselves into her scalp. "I want to get rid of this noise. I'm sick to death of fighting so hard just to hear my own voice." Tears filled her eyes, and she blinked them back. "I've had it. I did what you wanted. It's not helping. What do we try next? Do you even have a plan?"

Every pore of Sylvia's face seemed to tighten, and Sara could almost hear her choosing her words. When she spoke, each syllable was enunciated separately.

"Even mentally healthy people have trouble moving forward." Sylvia rose from her chair and walked to the window. In the warm sunlight she looked thin and pale. "You won't get better overnight," she said. "This is a marathon, not a sprint. You'll get there when you're ready."

"But I'm ready now." Sara grabbed fistfuls of hair and pulled. "I want to sprint."

Sylvia turned away from the window and padded across the room. "We still have a lot of ground to cover. Today I'd like to talk about your guardianship. Exactly how did that come about?"

Sara clamped down on her annoyance and tried to appear cooperative and rational. "Which time?"

"I'd forgotten about the first time." Sylvia returned to her chair and eased herself down, sitting straight-backed and stiff. "Can you tell me about it?"

*Another waste of time.* Sara heaved a sigh. "I was my father's ward for four years." She frowned as Sylvia held up a hand.

"Four years? I thought you said the actual break lasted less than two months."

"It did." Sara felt sick to her stomach, wondering if she should have thought to question the length of the arrangement. Her father had been overprotective; that's what her mother said. She sneaked a peek at her watch. The session was nearly over, and they hadn't done anything useful.

*-Bitch, bitch, bitch, bitch-*
*She has her reasons.*
*-Don't trust her.*
*What choice do I have?*

Resigned, Sara thought back to the first time her mind broke. She remembered feeling giddy with anticipation, excited to meet people who didn't know about the voices. Her memories ended there.

"It was June," she began. "I'd just turned eighteen, and I was looking forward to going away to college in the fall."

"That must have been a wonderful time for you. What happened next?"

"I don't know. I'm told I jumped out my bedroom window. Sprained both ankles and broke my leg." Sara paused and shut her eyes, feeling damaged and worthless. No matter how hard she pushed, there was nothing, not even the smallest fragment of memory to latch onto. She slipped her hands into her pockets, dug her thumb into her thigh and winced. "After that I was a loony toon from June to August."

Sylvia raised her eyebrows at the word choice, and Sara wanted to scream. Instead she continued in a more reasonable tone. "That's when my father set up the guardianship. He was afraid I might never recover enough to leave the hospital."

"But why wasn't the arrangement dismissed or modified once you were released?"

The question was troubling. Her father had always acted in her best interests, hadn't he? Much as she disliked being under his rule, she realized constant vigilance was necessary. "My dad's a control freak," she said in a dismissive tone. "He wanted to keep a close eye on me while I was in college. To be honest, I sort of forgot about it."

"Can you tell me why you jumped out the window?"

"Who knows?" Sara stared at her hands, folded in her lap. "I don't remember much, but I do know I was looking forward to college. Lubec is a small town. The thought of starting fresh…" Sara's voice trailed off. That was a long time ago, and a lot had happened since.

"And then?"

"And then, nothing. The next thing I knew, I was locked up in the Machias Psychiatric Hospital." She glanced at her therapist, surprised to find shock and compassion in her eyes. "I still don't understand what happened. My dad says the police found me wandering and incoherent. They brought me home, and five minutes later I threw myself out a window."

Dr. Green's calm expression wavered. "You spent two months hospitalized after you jumped?"

"So I'm told. My dad monitored my treatment, and my mom visited every day, but I don't remember anything. My next memory is of my mother, crying and hugging me and saying she couldn't believe I'd finally come out of it. I thought it was still June. But it was August."

"What happened this time?"

"Same thing," Sara muttered, enveloped in a slick coat of shame. "I'm told I was a babbling nut job, wandering the streets of Lubec. I lost another six weeks in my father's hospital, and now he's my guardian again."

Sylvia's face was a mask of calm, but her fingers were white against her notepad. "Were you on any medications before this started?"

"Nope. My dad said I acted like a junkie on PCP. But he ran the samples to the lab himself, both times, and there was nothing."

"Have you ever taken recreational drugs?"

Sara shook her head. "Dr. Franklin asked the same thing. Drugs scare me. Even prescription medications mess me up."

"Perhaps you've not hit on the best combination yet."

"And I'm not going to." Sara turned a fierce expression toward her doctor. "Do you *see* what I do for a living? I can't afford to have my reflexes slowed or my mind dulled. I'll get killed."

"I see your point."

Sara took in her doctor's wavering expression and pressed. "So maybe we can try using hypnosis to figure out what set off that psychotic break."

Sylvia didn't answer and Sara pressed on. "Can we take off the kid gloves and push? Please?"

"No, we can't take off the kid gloves and push," Sylvia said with finality. "Not now."

"Why not?"

"Sara, you've had two breaks, and both occurred when you were under a great deal of stress. You're at a crossroads now, too. We need to be careful, take our time."

Sara fumed. The walls seemed to press in, the voices screamed, and she stayed seated with difficulty. "Then what *can* we do?"

For a moment Sylvia said nothing, but a light slowly came to her eyes, and her usual challenge returned. "Do you still have nightmares?"

-*Waking up screaming.*

-*Drowning in sweat.*

*Shut up.*

"Yes, but I can't remember them once I wake up. I've tried."

"You might be able to learn to recall a bit more, with practice."

Sara tensed as a shiver rushed over her. "How?"

"Can you leave a notebook and pen by your bedside? Every time you wake up, jot down anything you remember from your dreams. Over time, maybe we'll see a pattern."

"Over *time*? How long is this going to take?"
-*Until you rot and die.*
"Hopefully not long." Sylvia's determination was obvious in the resolute line of her lips. "I'm excited to see what you come up with over the next week."
-*Impossible. You forget everything.*
-*Stupid, stupid, stupid, stupid-*
Sara cringed as she thought of the many times she'd tried to remember her dreams. But that had been hours after waking. Perhaps in the moments immediately following, there might be something left. She sat straighter and looked Sylvia in the eye. "If it doesn't work, I want to go back to hypnosis." She dug a thumb into her thigh, spurring herself on. "And if you aren't willing to do that, maybe it's time I go somewhere else."


On the following morning, Sara slid open the barn doors and hurried into the aisle. Hugging herself, she shivered in the late September chill. Once the horses were fed and turned out for the day, she grabbed a wheelbarrow and reached for her manure fork and broom. As she pulled the tools from their hangers on the wall, something small and papery plopped to the floor.
Confused, she stared at the little gift bag.
*Is it for me?*
-*No one cares for you.*
-*Maybe Cassie.*
With a tingle of anticipation, she bent down and picked it up. Inside she found a pair of insulated work gloves, a tube of peppermint lip balm, a knit hat and a sticky note. Neat printing said, "Waiting patiently," followed by a smiley face.
*Paul.*

*-He's breaking the rules.*
*The rules suck, and he's only stretching them a teeny bit.*
Sara looked around, half expecting Paul to materialize from the shadows.

"Don't be silly," she said to the empty corners. "He won't come to see me, not unless Dr. Green says it's okay."

She pulled the hat over her head and tucked her hands into the gloves. The silk lining caressed her, and she closed her eyes as a shiver of hope tickled its way from her fingers to her toes.

*Does he know how much this means to me?*
*-You're hopeless.*
*No, I'm hopeful.*
*-You're weak.*
*No, this helps me be strong.*

Whistling, she pocketed the lip balm, picked up her tools and went to work.

*As soon as I finish, I'm going to the store for a new notebook.*

The day flew by in a haze of hard work, horses, and the purchase of a new notebook, now placed carefully on her nightstand. Filled with renewed hope, she set out two new pens and slipped into bed far earlier than usual. Reluctantly, she removed the hat she'd worn all day, stuffed the gloves inside it, hugged it close and snuggled against her pillow.

After an hour of sighing and repositioning and staring at the ceiling, she curled into a ball and pulled the blankets over her head. The thought of sleep had become increasingly disturbing. Every time she started to drift off, she jerked suddenly awake.

*-It's the notebook.*
*Why should that be a problem?*
*-Some things are better left alone.*

The warning did nothing to calm her nerves. As the

clock ticked past midnight she got up and paced the hall-way. Finally she climbed onto a kitchen chair and pulled a bottle of cough medicine from the uppermost cupboard.

*Just this once.* She poured a double dose and gulped it down, wincing as the thick liquid burned her throat. Feeling marginally more relaxed, she stumbled back to bed, hugged her hat and gloves, and fell into a fitful sleep.

*It was still early but already hot, even for July. Washed in sunlight she stood at the water's edge. Her shoulders prickled in the heat while her toes curled around smooth pebbles. Water lapped her ankles as she bent down to scrub at a small wound left by a bloodsucker.*

*A birch canoe bumped rhythmically against the submerged branch of a fallen tree, and something, no, someone, floated in the shallows. From behind her a man whispered, "It's all your fault."*

*She took a step away from the voice, toward the person in the water.*

*"But I didn't do anything." Her voice came back to her, thin and quavering, a little girl. The man's voice shifted to the sharp syllables of petulance.*

*"You screamed."*

*She winced, and her whole body folded in on itself, convulsed in silent sobs. She hadn't meant to scream.*

*"I'm sorry." Her words came out in a murmur, so quiet even the bull frogs didn't pause in their morning threnody. The other voice moved to a wheedling banter.*

*"It's okay. We won't tell anyone. It will be our secret."*

*Tears poured down her face as she walked into the water, hands stretched out in front of her. With trembling fingers she touched the man in the water.*

*"I didn't mean to. Please, don't be dead."*

Sara opened her eyes and flicked on the desk lamp, groping for the spiral notebook and a pen. Already the dream was fading, leaving behind a familiar emptiness and longing.

She stared into the shadowed corner of the room and tried to remember. "Someone drowned," she said, speaking the words out loud as she wrote. The image of a silent form face-down in the water clung to her consciousness for an instant before fading away. "There was more, but it's gone now."

She shut off the light and closed her eyes. Morning would come early, and she needed to rest more than she needed to remember. Just as sleep overtook her, the vision returned, and she sat up quickly and wrote one more word in the darkness, not bothering with the light.

"Bloodsucker."

# Chapter Twenty-Six

Sitting in a window booth beneath an elaborate paper dragon, Sara was overcome by a feeling of déjà vu. Through rain-spattered glass, she watched as razor-thin droplets pelted down on running shoppers. Beside her, a waitress rushed past, balancing celery-green tumblers atop a red tray. Cassie sat on the bench across from her and picked at baked salmon and broccoli florets. Sara looked up at the dragon with an uncertain smile, her cheeks bulging with scallion pancakes.

"It's been forever since we came here. I think the last time was the day I met Paul." A warm caress rippled through her at the memory. Sara dropped her chin to her hand and sighed. "He was so sweet, willing to lend a hand to a complete stranger. Even though he probably knew I was a fraud."

-*Liar, liar, liar, liar*-

Cassie snorted. "He helped out a pretty girl. Let's not make him out to be some sort of paragon."

-*Ass, ass, ass, ass*-

"But he *is* a paragon," Sara insisted. "Did you know he's been leaving me presents?"

"Seriously?" Cassie paused in mid-chew. "Isn't that a problem for your shrink?"

"I didn't tell her." Sara lowered her eyes and nudged a pot sticker across her plate. "It's not as if I've seen him or talked to him. It's more like having a secret admirer."

Cassie stared. "Wow. Good for you. I can't believe you're standing up to Dr. Green, even if you *are* doing it behind her back." She paused to wipe the corners of her mouth with a cloth napkin. "But you're not exactly a rule breaker. Neither is Paul. I'm surprised you haven't cleared this with your therapist."

Sara poked the pot sticker with her fork and popped it into her mouth. "Well, I thought about it, but—" She risked a peek at Cassie's face. Some of her uncertainty faded when she saw amusement in her friend's eyes. "Dr. Green might say no, and, well, it makes me feel better knowing Paul hasn't given up on me."

Cassie grinned. "Speaking of the good doctor, how's the hypnosis going? Making progress?"

Sara speared a piece of chicken and twirled it against a mound of rice sticks. "No, she's given up on hypnosis. Now she's all excited about dream analysis." Sara dropped her fork and groaned when it clattered to the floor. "It's a pain in the ass."

Cassie swallowed a laugh. "Do you think it's helping?"

"Not so much." Sara ducked under the table and retrieved her fork. Then she twisted around and stole napkin-wrapped silverware from the empty booth behind them.

"To be honest, the voices are getting worse," she said as she turned back to her plate. "They even scream at me while I'm riding now. Thanks to them, I messed up a fence last weekend at Millbrook." Her throat pinched. "It knocked me out of second place, all the way to ninth."

Cassie patted Sara's hand and spoke in a mollifying tone. "There, there, I'm sure the third place rider appreciated you taking a dive."

"Very funny." Sara tried to smile, but it felt more like baring her teeth. "Brett wasn't at all happy, and I don't blame him. If I don't get my act together, he'll probably dump me for someone with more promise."

"Ouch. He'd do that?" Cassie wrinkled her nose.

"Of course he would. It's a miracle I got the chance to work with him in the first place."

*-Undeserving, wretched, useless -*

*Shut up, please?*

*-Loser, loser, loser, loser-*

Cassie's voice interrupted the bickering. "So, explain this dream analysis your therapist is so hot on. Are you getting anywhere with it?"

"I don't know." Sara took another bite of chicken and looked out the window. Dark clouds rolled across a louring sky, and condensation blurred the glass. She sighed again. Then she slipped her hand under the napkin on her lap and pinched herself for sighing too much. "Dr. Green wants me to write down everything I remember about my dreams. We look for patterns." She touched a finger to the window pane and resisted the urge to write Paul's name across the glass. "It's taking fricking forever."

"And?"

"And nothing. I've had a few dreams about someone drowning, and once I think there was a voice saying it was my fault."

Cassie paled and Sara answered with a quick nod. "Yes, it's probably the same dream you listened to a million times. Only now there's someone behind me, blaming me. And I'm saying I didn't do anything wrong."

*-All your fault.*

*-Give up.*

*-Die, die, die, die-*

*Shut up!*

Sara dug her fingers deeper into her thigh, hoping the pain might anchor her thoughts. "Dr. Green says most dreams are metaphorical, not memories. So I shouldn't take it literally."

"What else do you dream about?"

"Paul." Sara picked up her fork and chased the last of her chicken into her Lo Mein. "Sometimes he's just staring at me. You know the look, like I'm important." She drew in a shaky breath and held it for several seconds before letting it out in a whoosh. "I want him so much, I can hardly stand it. But I walk away." Sara picked up her rumpled napkin and scrubbed at a drop of soy sauce. Paul's face faded from her mind, and for a moment she could breathe.

"And once I dreamed someone held me down and gave me a shot." The inside of Sara's elbow prickled, and she stopped to rub it with her fingers. "I suppose that might have happened in the hospital, but it felt like I was outdoors."

"Anything else?" Cassie's expression was difficult to read, and Sara considered keeping the rest to herself. But the last dream made no sense. Maybe Cassie could help figure it out.

"Two nights ago I dreamed I was in the water, holding onto a canoe paddle, swimming for shore. I was way out in the middle of the lake, and I was crying." Sara took a long, deep breath and kinked a lock of hair between her fingers. "My mom is a terrible swimmer, and she never let me go out that far, even with a kickboard."

"Weird." Cassie pursed her lips. "Isn't it sort of coincidental that so many of your dreams are on the lake? It's not like you spent your life there, just vacations when you were a kid, right?" She lowered her voice. "Didn't your grandfather drown? Maybe you're remembering that."

"I thought about that, but I don't think I was even there."

"You don't know?" Cassie nudged Sara's toe.

"My folks don't like to talk about it." Sara moved her foot away from Cassie's. "You know how my dad is."

Cassie kicked Sara's other foot. "Ask your mom."

Sara turned back to the rain, frowning to hide her apprehension. "I guess it can't hurt. I have to make sure my dad doesn't overhear, though."

"Why?"

"I don't know. My mom says he never really got over it." Anxiety caused her throat to burn. Her misgivings made no sense.

*Could I have seen something?*

*-You forget everything.*

*-Useless, useless, useless, useless-*

Cassie's nudge pulled her back. "Why wait? Call her now before you chicken out."

"What's the hurry?"

"Coward." Cassie folded her arms across her chest.

"But…"

"Do it now."

"Fine. Whatever." Annoyance competed with dread as Sara pulled her cell phone from her pocket. The voices, already chanting, increased in volume.

*-Coward, coward, coward, coward-*

The phone rang twice before her father answered. Flustered, she made a wincing face at Cassie and struggled to keep her voice cheerful.

"Hi, Daddy. Is Mom there?"

"No, she left an hour ago for Round Lake. She'll be back sometime tomorrow." His voice was surprisingly approachable, almost kind. Again Sara wondered at the transformation in her parents.

"Seriously? By herself?" Worry pricked at her like kittens' claws. "What about testing and insulin? Who's gonna do that for her?"

Her father laughed and continued in an amused tone. "Believe it or not, she's finally doing most of it herself. I guess having her independence cramped finally got to be too much for her."

"Really?" Sara's heart lifted at the unexpected news. "I wondered how she was going to manage her foliage outings. That's wonderf-"

"Sara, I hate to cut you off, but I have to head into Machais to check on a few things. Do you want me to have her call you when she gets back? She doesn't get cell service up there."

"No, that's okay. I'll try back tomor-"

The line went dead. She stared at the phone. "That was weird."

"What?"

"We were disconnected." Sara rested a finger on the redial button for a moment before shrugging and tucking the phone back into her pocket. She pushed her plate away and frowned. "I think it was on purpose."


Carl heard footsteps outside the door and hung up quickly. He hoped Sara wouldn't think they'd been cut off by accident. If she called back, it would complicate matters.

"Did I hear the phone?" Joanie hurried through the door as Carl replaced the handset and turned to meet her.

"Just a political survey. Elections are right around the corner." He smiled and took his wife's hand. "Ready to go?"

# Chapter Twenty-Seven

Joanie stood in late-afternoon sun, one side of her face bathed in a warm ginger glow, the other already cast in shadow. As she nudged blue driveway stones with the toes of her new boat shoes she appeared childlike and uncertain. "Are you sure you want to come along?" she asked. "I'll be fine by myself."

"I know," Carl replied, "but I'd worry too much." A soft sigh escaped as he took in her radiance. In the years of estrangement, he'd forgotten how lovely she was.

"Oh, that's so sweet." Joanie's eyes sparkled in the sloping rays of sun, and for a moment Carl felt a pang of guilt.

"I'll take the truck," he said brusquely. "You drive the Camry. That way I can go straight to work in the morning, and you can take your time." He planted a wet kiss on Joanie's forehead. Why women liked that sort of thing he couldn't fathom, but it brought a smile to her face, so who was he to argue?

"That's a wonderful idea," Joanie replied. "Are you sure you don't mind?"

"Not at all," he said, "but we'd better hurry. We don't want to lose the light."

They made the half-hour drive to Round Lake in tandem. Joanie parked the Camry on firm gravel just off the main road. Then she joined Carl in the truck for the final mile over a rough dirt track. They pulled into a grass clearing next to the old cabin, and Carl hurried to open the passenger door. Joanie stepped out into the sunshine and twirled around, face tipped to the sky.

"Oh, Carl, you were right. It's beautiful! The leaves are already turning." She skipped to the shed behind the hunting cabin, unlocked the door, and riffled through the contents. A moment later she emerged grinning, holding two life jackets and two paddles.

"Shall we? We can head for the mouth of the river. The maples should be stunning against the fir." She bounced down the wooden steps and shrugged into her life jacket, then unfastened the tie rope and pulled the birch canoe into the shallows. "Paddle or steer?"

"I'll steer," he said, feeding on his wife's enthusiasm and reflecting it back. "But first let's check your blood sugar."

Joanie rolled her eyes. "Oh, come on, Carl. It's just a canoe ride."

"And I don't want you passing out at the other end of the lake," he insisted. "Give me a finger."

Joanie looked away as Carl drew a drop of blood and waited for the beep. "It's on the high side," he said, frowning. "Good thing I brought insulin." He walked back to the car while Joanie hopped in place.

"C'mon, Carl! Let's get out there while it's still light. I feel fine."

Carl watched the little bubbles float upward as he injected air into the insulin bottle, then pulled back to fill the syringe. "It'll just take a minute," he said. "One of us has to look out for you."

He palmed the syringe and stepped deliberately down the wooden stairs. Sunlight pooled on Joanie's cheeks and shoulders, and he paused on the last step, drinking in the vision. She was exquisite, with dazzling green eyes so much like her daughter's blue ones.

*Her* daughter. He emphasized the word in his head. For so many years he'd believed he was in some way defective.

"Let's use the front of the thigh this time."

He glanced up before rolling the syringe from his palm.

Joanie was looking skyward. For the first time, her fear of needles was helpful rather than irritating. There was no chance she'd look, no chance she'd see the full syringe.

*Not my child.* The words lifted his heart in unexpected ways. He'd forced himself to keep the girl at arm's length, afraid he might slip again. But now he knew the truth; his feelings for Sara were not aberrant or repugnant at all.

He was careful to hold the syringe just so, approximating the angle she would use if she were brave enough to inject herself.

"Ow! It doesn't usually hurt."

"Sorry. I won't let it happen again." Carl caught hold of the chuckle that welled in his throat. Instead he grinned, and it wasn't forced or unnatural at all. The smile stretched his face in unaccustomed ways, and he let it.

Joanie rubbed her thigh for a moment before climbing into the bow. Carl took the stern, and before long the light craft cut through the water, heading for the opposite shore. Sunlight danced over the yellow birch trees that surrounded the lake, and ripples of golden light flickered across Joanie's life jacket. He watched the way his wife handled the paddle, watched the little whirlpools spin away. Her stroke was perfect. Everything was perfect.

Joanie deserved what was coming, of course; that alone was reason to celebrate. The lying whore had kept him in the dark since before Sara was born. Imagine his delight when she finally came clean, finally told him the truth about his so-called daughter. His relief had been difficult to hide, but he'd done it. He'd swallowed his overwhelming delight and put forth an expression of profound understanding and forgiveness.

"Hey! Quit watching me and paddle a little yourself."

Carl jerked to the present. *Why not?* He dipped his paddle into the water and watched it pierce the surface in a perfect J-stroke. Little ripples spread out and fragmented reflections of the first crimson blush on the western horizon. Beautiful. The lake was a fitting place for his resurrection, exactly right. Life had come full circle, and soon there would be no need to pretend, no reason to resort to lies.

"I love September. I think it's my favorite month." Joanie smiled as she spoke, her face filled with contentment.

Delight washed over Carl as well. He thought ahead to the cruise, warm water and clear skies. Mexico was beautiful in October.

They paused in the center of the lake. Joanie snapped a dozen pictures of Carl, then climbed awkwardly to the stern and snuggled against him. She held the camera at arm's length and took a few close-ups of both of them.

"Having fun?" It was obvious she was, and he was glad. The end would be painless; he'd seen to that. And if he said all the right things, it would be peaceful.

Happiness bubbled in her voice as she spoke. "Yes. It's been a long time since we did this, not since we lost your dad."

The smile slunk from his face. Why had she said that? Why had she rubbed his nose in his misdeed, as if he were a puppy who'd piddled on the floor? He looked down at the water, black and thick beneath the surface. They were over the deepest part now.

Joanie's voice reached him, but it was distant and soft. "I'm sorry. I know you don't like to talk about it. I still can't imagine what he was doing out here all alone that day."

He shouldn't tell her, should he? It might ruin her peace of mind. But someone should know the truth, even if only for a little while.

Carl gazed down at his wife, still nestled in his arms. Telltale sweat glistened across her brow. Her blood sugar was falling fast. Soon she wouldn't hear him at all. And people did say confession was a good thing, good for the soul?

The words tumbled forth without his participation. "Well, it's a funny thing." Carl paused, fighting back a grin. "Sara and I were with him."

Joanie looked up, confusion marring her features. "What?"

Carl molded his face into his best aw-shucks expression. "He caught us together, and you know he was incapable of keeping secrets. In his lucid moments he was quite rational. Someone might have believed him, and thanks to you, well, I thought I was doing something . . . unsavory."

He locked his eyes on the little puddle shifting across the floor of the canoe. There was no need to see her face. He could imagine the look of disapproval. Hadn't he seen it before?

"What are you talking about, Carl?"

He risked a look, and there it was, shock and revulsion. That was uncalled for. This sort of thing happened all the time. Look at Woody Allen. He'd married his stepdaughter, hadn't he? And what about those Mormon sects who married off their minor daughters, against their will, to wrinkled old men who already had several wives? What about the child brides of India and Afghanistan? The world was full of enlightened cultures, uncorrupted by this ridiculous western so-called morality.

He dismissed her. She was incapable of understanding. "What did you do, Carl?"

"I think you know."

Joanie scrambled to the bow and spun the canoe toward shore. There were tears in her eyes. Damn. Now she was all upset, and for what? There was nothing she could do. He watched as she pulled at the paddle, her arms turning rubber, legs jerking as fear replaced shock. She swung the paddle at him, and he ducked it.

"Just relax, Joan. You're upsetting yourself for no reason. It won't do a bit of good."

She was sobbing now. How he hated that sound, despised the preternatural gurgling. He waited until the paddle fell from her hands and she listed to one side, swatting the air as if attacked by mosquitoes.

Balancing carefully, he climbed to the bow. He had to finish while she still breathed. Water in her lungs would point to accidental drowning, the needle mark in her thigh the result of self-administered medication. She'd be unconscious momentarily, and soon after that her heart would stop. Between those moments was a window of reduced suffering for her and necessary forensic evidence for him. Time was running short.

He unclipped her life vest.

"Silly of you to come out here without a life preserver. Canoes are so unstable."

Eyes on the shore, he estimated the distance. This was the place, the spot where they'd flipped the boat containing his father's corpse. Carl remembered the old man flailing and gurgling as he held him beneath the surface just a few yards from shore. He thought of little Sara, medicated, but starting to bounce back. If only the damn drug had lasted longer she wouldn't have remembered anything.

"It's too bad Sara isn't along this time. She could have helped with the extra paddle." He smiled at the memory. Even after the midazolam wore off she was easily manipulated to silence. If not for the nightmares and the things she called out in her sleep, he could have left it at that.

He unfolded from his crouch and stood over Joanie's silent form. She looked even smaller, elfin, so much like the day they'd met. *Ah well, that was a long time ago.*

Straddling the boat he rocked back and forth, harder and harder. A vast sense of freedom expanded inside him, like a boy on a swing set finally managing his first loop-the-loop. The canoe reared like a serpent, hesitated, then plunged and smacked the water's surface, coming to rest upended.

The water was a shock when he hit it, nothing like that hot summer morning two decades ago. He shivered as he swam to Joanie's side, watched her arms flail like a newborn giraffe, clumsy and useless. It was easy to control the motion, to guide her downward until the movement ceased. The end was anticlimactic in its simplicity.

Once again he regretted Sara's absence. She was a good little swimmer even then, and she'd been a great help. She'd had a hell of a time though, what with all the crying.

Oh well, there was nothing for it. He'd have to carry everything. While inconvenient, acting alone did have advantages. There'd be no one to silence, no one to monitor and control.

He waited for the crushing remorse he'd felt at his father's death. But there was nothing, just a growing sense of rightness and ease. He'd only done what needed to be done, removed the girl's safety net and therefore the greatest threat to his happiness.

With arms spread wide he gave himself over to the water's embrace, allowing the feeling of release to flow through him as he hung suspended in the fading light. The cold water had a bracing effect, energizing and clean. As shadows crept across Round Lake, he took a last look at the overturned canoe and the dark shape bobbing just beneath the surface. With a lighter heart, he slung Joanie's life preserver over his shoulder, grabbed his paddle, and kicked toward shore.

# Chapter Twenty-Eight

With a playful smirk, Cassie pushed Paul off-balance, and he stumbled into the sale rack outside JCPenney. He shot her a thanks-a-lot glance and went back to reading the care tag on a cashmere sweater.

"You could help me out, you know." He replaced the sweater and picked up a quilted turtle-neck. It looked as if it would be warm, but...

"That's hideous, Paul. Put it back."

"She needs something for cold weather, but these all have to be hand-washed." Paul hung the turtleneck with the other sweaters, then carefully spaced the hangers and tidied the sleeves so they lined up in a neat row. "If she's gonna wear it shoveling crap, it needs to be machine washable."

Cassie shot him a you're-pathetic look as she took his sleeve and tugged him across the polished floor.

"Where are we going?"

"Athletic wear. Sara sweats a lot. Get her something that breathes."

Paul broke free of her grasp and pushed his way between clothing racks. Feigning nonchalance, he asked, "So, did Sara and Harlee compete at Millbrook?"

"Mmmm hmmm. They ended up ninth." Cassie pulled a brushed denim jacket from a display and held it up with a questioning look.

Paul shook his head. "Hay will stick to those fleece cuffs."

"But it's adorable." Cassie held the jacket against her chest and pouted for a moment before returning it to the rack. "Brett was disappointed," she added. "Sara messed up, and you know how she hates to let him down."

Paul couldn't help the twinge of jealousy. Brett, the Olympian, was at the center of Sara's world now. Even without Dr. Green's interference, how could he compete? Bristling, he turned his back to Cassie and sorted through cardigans. "So, how is the Ken doll these days? Is he still practically perfect in every way?"

Cassie giggled. "Brett's gay. I thought you knew that."

"Oh."

"And Sara's already in love. A Ken doll, no matter how motivated or anatomically correct, won't change that."

Paul opened his mouth for a clever retort, but in that instant he saw the perfect gift. With a rush of triumph, he dove across the aisle, grabbed a light jacket by its hanger, and dangled it in Cassie's face. "What do you think?"

"Perfect! It has horses and everything. How'd you spot it?"

Paul tucked the gift protectively under his arm. "I looked up, and for a moment I thought I saw Sara."

*Nope, that's not pathetic*, he told himself as he headed for the checkout. Aloud he said, "I may have lost the girl, but I have her jacket."

Cassie fell in step beside him and poked him in the ribs. "Hang tough. You haven't lost her yet."

Paul walked faster, avoiding Cassie's elbow. "Sometimes I can't help but be angry with her. I mean, we had something great. She just threw it away."

"Yup." Cassie's heels clicked louder as she hurried to keep up. "But we can't know what it's like to be in her shoes. Sara has the legal rights of a child. Her father decides where she lives and who she sees. She can't do anything without his permission."

Cassie glanced at Paul, and he shrunk from the reproach in her eyes. "She hears voices in her head, all the time," Cassie said. "Can you imagine?"

Paul slowed his pace and looked guiltily at the jacket. "Do you think I should back off? I'm trying to be support-ive, but is it too much?"

"I wish I knew." Cassie's face was wistful. "Personally, I think her therapist is an ass for breaking you two up. Sara's a different person with you, more confident, happier." She sighed. "But what do I know? It's just..."

"What?" Paul placed the jacket on the checkout belt and smiled at the clerk.

"Oh, I don't know."

Startled by the plaintive tone of Cassie's voice, Paul turned to face her. Until now, he'd never seen her ill at ease.

"I just wish she'd been able to choose her own thera-pist," Cassie said. "I know she likes Dr. Green, but why not a different perspective? It's always a hand-picked, daddy-approved, rubber-stamped shrink."

Paul slid his credit card through the reader and thanked the cashier. "Her dad seemed a little odd to me. He's nice enough, but sort of insincere."

"Like he's faking it?" Cassie's eyes flashed. "Thank God I'm not the only one to think so. He totally creeps me out." Her voice took on an apprehensive quality. "There's something not quite right about that man. I know Sara has problems, and I'm sure he worries about her. But he acts more like a jealous lover than a dad."

Paul picked up his shopping bag and turned toward the exit, trying to ignore the worry creeping into his gut. "In what way?"

"Do you know he *paid* me to room with her in college?"

Paul stopped and gaped. "He what? You what?"

"Don't look at me like that. I didn't know." Cassie turned her back to him and picked up a bottle of perfume from a display table. She seemed to have to work up to whatever she was about to say, so he waited, not sure whether to rest a hand on her shoulder or jab an elbow into her ribs.

"He contacted me," she finally said. There was a tremble in her voice, and her body stiffened. "I was on a list of students looking for work, and he offered to pay all my expenses if I roomed with his mentally ill daughter…" she swallowed. "…and pretended to be her friend."

"And?" Paul tried to soften his tone, but even he could hear the accusation.

"And I did." She set down the perfume and stood silently. Paul waited for her to continue, but when she said nothing he touched her shoulder. She jumped and turned toward him.

"I don't know, Paul. Maybe it was all on the up and up. He told me Sara needed someone to look out for her and smooth her way."

"But?"

"Then he wanted to know stuff."

"What sort of stuff?"

"He asked me if she had nightmares." Cassie sucked in a breath before she continued in a halting voice. "That seemed reasonable, actually. And for a while, I listened to her when she talked in her sleep." Cassie wrapped her arms around her chest and shuddered. Paul suspected which dream she remembered, and his own skin prickled.

"Then what happened?" Paul was relieved to hear his voice return to a more reasonable tone. If only his heart would stop racing.

"Carl wanted to know everything Sara said, in detail. And there was something creepy about the way he asked."

"It does seem logical, though." Paul made an effort to consider all sides and reach a compromise. "I mean, he's a psychiatrist. Don't they analyze dreams?"

"I guess, but it didn't end there." Cassie's voice dropped to a low hiss. "After that, he asked if she was going out with anyone. And if she was, he wanted me to bust it up."

"What?" A jolt shot through him. "Why?"

"He said she wasn't capable of any sort of adult relationship, that if anyone got too close to her she might..." Cassie dropped her head and played with a faux diamond necklace bolted to the display.

"She might what?"

"Hurt herself." Cassie didn't look up. "She did jump out a window, you know. She is capable of..."

"I know." Paul's chest tightened as he remembered Sara's words. *This stuff happens. It's part of the package.*

"But she seemed so . . . normal." Guilt covered Cassie's face, and her voice caught as she spoke. "I did warn people away from her. At first. I thought I was doing the right thing."

"Oh, Cassie." Paul's stomach squirmed. *How could Cassie lie to her like that? But what if her father was right?* "No wonder she doesn't trust anyone." He pinched the bridge of his nose and groaned. "Her dad's been doing this to her all her life."

"I think he has." Cassie's lips trembled. "Sara and I, well, we became friends. For real. And I came clean, told her everything I'd done."

"She must have been devastated."

"She was." Cassie looked as if she might cry. "But she forgave me. She said her father was just looking out for her, being a good dad."

"But you don't think so."

"I don't know." Cassie started to walk toward the exit, and Paul followed. "There was something weird about him. It was nothing I could put my finger on, but he's a bit off, you know?"

Paul stopped, creating a minor traffic jam at the exit. As people dodged around him he stared at Cassie, open-mouthed. "Dr. Green told Sara to break up with me right after I met her father. You don't think..."

Cassie shook her head. "I don't much care for shrinks, but they do have ethics." She paused, brow furrowed. "Sara's dad is in a position to help or hinder a psychologist's career. Even so, I doubt Dr. Green would risk her license by colluding with the man."

"You're right. I'm being dumb." Paul sighed and walked toward the parking lot. Part of him agreed with Cassie's assessment, but part of him hung on to the doubt. He knew nothing about Dr. Green. Perhaps he should find out more.

Cassie's words reflected his inner dialogue. "You're gonna google her, right?"

Paul chuckled and risked a sideways glance. "Ah, Cassie. You've been hanging around programmers too long."

"Jeezus, Paul." She shoved him again, and he narrowly missed a potted palm. "I'm shocked you haven't done it already."

"You don't think it's weird?" Paul made his way to a bench and fumbled his phone from his pocket. "I don't know, Cassie. It feels like an invasion of privacy."

Cassie sat beside him. "Just check to see if she has a website. I don't think there's anything wrong with that."

Paul punched in Sylvia's name, followed by "Psychologist," and watched as his screen filled with hits. He opened the first, but it was a different Sylvia Green, one with a practice in Minnesota. He looked at the length of the list, felt creepy, and snapped his phone shut.

"Later," he said, getting to his feet. "If I'm gonna be a stalker, I'm gonna do it in private."


Later that evening, Paul sat with his feet on the coffee table, laptop across his knees. He wanted to search for testimonies from patients who'd had bad experiences with

Dr. Green. Maybe there was something he could use to discredit Sylvia, make Sara reconsider her trust.

*Nope. That's not pathetic.* He set the computer on the couch, went to the kitchen, and rummaged through the refrigerator. *Be honest,* he reminded himself. *Be someone she can trust. Quit acting like her father.*

Diet soda in hand, he flopped onto the couch, deleted his original search criteria and instead looked for success stories. Google found nothing, no mention of Dr. Green at all. Feeling useless, Paul shut off his laptop and went to bed.

# Chapter Twenty-Nine

"Shit! Shit! Shit! Shit!" Sara tried to correct her mistake, but it was too late. Harlee crashed into the practice fence and sent rails and standards flying. The pinto scrambled through the debris, barely avoiding a fall.

"What the hell is wrong with you?" Brett shouted for the fifth time that day. "If that had been a solid fence, you could have been killed!"

Sara ran an apologetic hand down Harlee's neck. Her riding was in free fall, and she'd been unable to pull herself together.

"Who died?" Brett stood in the center of the jumping arena, fingers raking his hair. If he'd worn a hat, Sara had no doubt he'd be stomping on it by now.

She pulled up in front of him, feeling like a whipped puppy. "I think maybe I did."

*-Incompetent idiot.*

*-Worthless, worthless, worthless, worthless-*

Relentless chanting joined with a crackling hum, swelling until sounds of the outside world faded to little more than a dream. Finding her voice amid the increasing din was a constant, exhausting effort.

"I have personal issues," she said, hoping Brett wouldn't ask for details. "I've been letting them get to me." The words didn't begin to describe the nightmare in which she found herself. Her mind was a battleground, and she was losing. "I'll do better," she promised, but she knew it was a lie. She was floundering. Asking Harlee to take up the slack was unfair.

237

*-Selfish, selfish, selfish, selfish-*

As if reading her thoughts, Brett took Harlee's bridle in his hands. "You're going to ruin this mare. Get off before you do any more damage." The words were harsh, but Sara could hear concern in his tone. He must know she was shattered inside, broken beyond repair.

She dismounted without a word. *Brett deals with enough prima donnas. I'm not going to make a scene.*

*-Failure! Idiot! Useless!*

*-Quitter, quitter, quitter, quitter-*

Brett placed a hand on her shoulder, his sympathy enough to bring tears to her eyes.

"Look, Sara, it's not safe to compete at this level if you're not a hundred percent. You know that." Brett's gaze shifted to Harlee, and disappointment enveloped his normally cheerful features. "Fix whatever's bothering you. Come back once you've worked things out."

*-You can't come back.*

*-Dreams are for other people.*

Sara forced back the inner chaos, turned to Brett, and focused.

"Maybe it's best if I take the rest of the season off." The words stung. She knew she was doing the right thing, but the thought of giving up left her bleeding inside. Quitting was a choice someone else might make, someone without dreams or goals. Someone with the fight taken out of them.

Brett hesitated a moment longer, then handed the reins back to her. "Good decision," he said. "If there's anything I can do to help, let me know." Then he turned to rejoin his other students. Sara watched him go, knowing her dream of riding at Rolex was on hold, at least for now, maybe forever. The thought should have crippled her. Instead she felt an all-consuming apathy, as if something inside her had turned to dust.

As she drove home, Sara ran over the day's events in her head. *I don't understand why I'm getting worse. Why did Dr. Green give up on hypnosis?*

*-Sicker now.*

*-Afraid you'll break.*

*-Sick, sick, sick, sick-*

Tears rolled down her cheeks. She backhanded them away and turned all of her attention to watching the road. As she pulled into the driveway, Janet came out the barn door and walked toward her. Seeing her employer only deepened Sara's feelings of worthlessness. *Janet has been so supportive of me, and I've let her down, too.*

*-Useless, useless, useless, useless-*

"What are you doing home so early?" Janet called out, radiating concern. "Is Harlee okay?"

"She's fine. I decided to take a break from competing." Sara unloaded Harlee and shuffled toward the barn, keeping her back to her employer and shielding her face behind her hair.

Janet didn't press. "Well, it's good to have you back. The kids have been dying to go for a ride with you."

Sara managed a smile, but even thoughts of kids and ponies brought her no joy. She was numb. Nothing mattered.

*I'll never be okay.*

*-Crazy, like your grandfather.*

*-Crazy, crazy, crazy, crazy-*

The analogy hit home. Maybe she was destined to end up like her grandfather, old and confused. She'd be selfish to marry, foolish to think of having a family and passing on her taint. How could she think of raising children, being alone with them? What if she broke and hurt someone she loved?

*It's a good thing Paul got out while he could.*
*-Better off alone.*

As she hung her saddle on its rack, she spotted a gift bag. Paul's gestures of support normally lifted her spirits, but today his present chafed at an open wound. She pinched herself as hard as she could, hoping it might leave a bruise.

*I'm useless. I'm not being fair to Paul, letting him think there's hope.*

*-Worthless, worthless, worthless, worthless-*

As she pushed the bag aside, a jacket fell to the floor. The bright pattern of jumping horses caught her eye, and she bent down and picked it up. Her fingers sunk into a soft sheepskin lining, and she smiled as she read the tag, *Machine Wash, Regular.*

*-He knows you well.*

*That he does.*

Sara draped the jacket over her shoulders, and it enveloped her like a warm hug. As tears swelled against her eyes, she cautiously tried out a new thought.

*Maybe Dr. Green is wrong.* The words sprawled awkwardly in her mind, but they had a ring of truth. For a moment there was a break in the cacophony, but the voices returned immediately, louder.

She tried again. *Maybe I should ask my dad if I can see a different therapist.*

A tiny voice of rebellion took root inside her as she led Harlee to the pasture and turned her loose. *Maybe Cassie's right. I should find a lawyer and get out from under this guardianship. My mom will help.*

The thought sparked a little fire in the empty place, warming her from within. The voices shrieked. The din grew louder. But she clenched her fists and held firm. *I'll call Paul. I need to know if there's still a chance for us.*

The voices snickered and told her to give up. She ignored them and stuffed her mind full of thoughts of a life of her own. Her ringing cell phone sounded far away, but she reached for it with a tingle of hope.

*Maybe it's Paul.*

*-Idiot.*

Her father's voice was anxious, muddled by the din. She pressed the phone more tightly to her ear. "What did you say?" Her head pounded as the voices chanted, *Worthless girl! Just die, die, die, die* . . . louder and louder. She could barely think, let alone hear.

"You need to come home, Sara. Your mother is missing."

Her father's voice broke, and so did she.

# Chapter Thirty

*–She's dead.*

*No, she's not.*

The drive to Lubec seemed to take days rather than hours, Sara's frantic call to Paul a plea for help rather than the hoped-for invitation back into her life.

"I have to go to Maine. Can you please help Janet with the barn?" was all she could manage. He'd been understandably confused, but willing, and she'd hung up, unable to say more without crying.

Now she huddled in her mother's sitting room and stared at the opposite wall, twisting a child's toy in her lap. Her father pried the stuffed mouse from her hands and replaced it with a mug of hot chocolate.

"Drink. You'll feel better."

"No, I won't." The dark liquid swirled before her eyes, and she tried to block out an image of her mother suspended in black. Police, she'd been told, had found Joanie's truck and the overturned canoe, but nothing more. Sara had searched the trails along the shore of Round Lake until she'd nearly collapsed from exhaustion. Her father had dragged her to the car and driven her home while she screamed in protest. Now guilt held her down, bound her to the chair, left her unable to think, unable to feel, unable to move.

*If I hadn't moved away, I would have been with her, like always.*

*–It's all your fault.*

242

*-All your fault, all your fault, all your fault-*
*I didn't mean to. Please, don't be dead.*

The words were familiar, attached to the dead man in her dreams. She stretched out her mind and almost touched him.

"Drink. That's an order." Her father tipped the cup to her mouth and forced a trickle between her lips. She coughed against it.

"No, thank you. Not now."

*-He drugs it.*

*He wouldn't do that, not without telling me.*

There was a knock at the door, and her father stepped away. A policeman entered the hallway, his voice cutting through the din as he asked to talk with her. Carl refused. She heard the usual words, "My daughter is delicate. We have to be careful not to upset her."

She'd been grateful for his protection in the past. He'd stood by her side when they'd been questioned by an officer at the lake; he'd explained that Joanie was there alone, that she was diabetic, that canoes were easily tipped. *Perhaps she was so engrossed in her photography that she leaned too far—*

Sara shuddered. *No, I won't go there.*

*-Dead, dead, dead, dead-*

Her father's shoulders slumped in defeat. He and the police officer both turned toward her. Sara's heart pounded. Even when she'd *hit* a police officer, her father hadn't allowed anyone to question her directly, and she hadn't been required to appear in person for the hearing. Her father had warned her to avoid the police. They knew she was mentally ill, he'd told her. They'd treat her differently.

She sank deeper into her chair, hiding. Surely there was nothing she could tell him that would help.

*But what if there is?*

*-You are nothing.*

*-Useless, useless, useless, useless-*

She studied the man with a sideways gaze. His expression was grave, carried over a square face with eyes that lacked the expected condescension. The bulky uniform swished as he moved, and the sound sent dread prickling through her. She shook herself.

*I have to try.* With a steadying breath she forced her fear away and turned toward him. "How can I help?"

Her father looked angry; his face contorted as his sputtered warning was brushed aside. She barely heard him, couldn't see past the police officer striding toward her. He stopped several feet away and stood slightly off to one side, relaxed, not quite facing her.

*The way my grandfather taught me to approach a stray dog.*

*-Vicious girl, dangerous girl.*

*-Crazy, crazy, crazy, crazy-*

His expression was kind, and the lack of contempt left Sara more disoriented than comforted. In the small community of Lubec she was still known as the crazy girl, yet his face betrayed not a hint of prejudgment. Even so she felt the need to break the tension, if only for herself.

"I don't bite, despite what you may have been told. And I haven't hit anyone in almost a year."

He stepped closer. A quick smile acknowledged her joke, while his overall demeanor remained appropriate to the gravity of the circumstances. "I'm Officer Bradley. I'm very sorry about your mother."

"She's fine," Sara said with a conviction at odds with the evidence. "We'll find her. Maybe she went for a hike and got lost. Or maybe she met up with a friend."

"Do you know of anyone who may have been with her?"

"No." Sara stared miserably at the carpet, sorting through memories, searching for a clue. A thought tugged at her, and she closed her eyes and followed.

*Was there someone? Anyone?*
*-The letter.*
She opened her eyes, still considering.

"Did you remember something?" The officer faced her, wind-chapped lips slightly apart.

"Nothing useful." She knew she was snatching at air. But perhaps air was better than nothing. "My mother knows someone in Massachusetts, Samuel something. I don't know the address, but I know she wrote to him."

Her father's hand dropped to her shoulder. "She wrote to someone in Massachusetts?"

*-She lied!*
*Everyone lies.*

Sara shifted beneath her father's hand, looked up at the police officer and spoke in a rush. "I mailed a letter for her in April. It was addressed to a post office box in Boxford, Massachusetts. I think the last name was Reynolds, or maybe Randall.

Officer Bradley wrote in a notebook and moved toward the door, taking out his phone as he walked. "We'll check it out. And we'll keep searching the lake."

Sara smiled a thank you, buoyed by an unrealistic flicker of hope. "My mother isn't in the lake. She wouldn't go out without her life jacket, and it's still in the shed."

The officer's smile was too rigid. She peeked up at her father's face, thin-lipped, eyes cold and distant. His gaze met hers, and the anger vanished behind a veil of concern.

*-He didn't know about the man in Massachusetts.*
*Maybe it's part of the secret.*
*-A part she didn't tell him.*

She didn't look up as she asked, "Are you okay?"

"I'm holding up. You?" His fingers dug into her shoulder.

"Not so much." She drew in a shuddering breath.

He pulled a folding chair close, sat beside her and pulled her into an embrace. His voice was husky, his cologne cloying in the small room. "Everything will be okay. I'm here."

She crumpled into his arms and sobbed against his shirt. He squeezed her so tightly she could hardly breathe, touched his lips to her hair and reached past her. The scrape of china was followed by steam against her lips, and the smell of chocolate momentarily obscured the cologne.

"Just a sip, Sara. I promise you'll feel better."


Morning came by inches. A dull glow warmed the horizon as Sara stared past Sail Rock over the Bay of Fundy. She willed the sky to lighten as she said a silent prayer, then slipped into her truck and drove toward Round Lake.

When she reached the cabin, a knot of people stood in the clearing, shivering in pink sunglow. They looked up at her approach and immediately turned away, flocking together, shuffling toward parked cars. A deputy from the Washington County Sheriff's office hurried over.

"I'm terribly sorry, Sara. We found your mother." He swallowed the words, "She's dead."

Sara didn't feel herself falling. One moment she was on her feet. Then the ground struck her knees and would have reached up to smack her face if not for the arms that caught her. The sound coming from her throat was as unnatural to her as it was to the dismal group of rescuers, but she couldn't stop.

"We've called your father," the deputy said, but his words barely registered. The light dimmed as pain hooked into the empty places and the world receded from her conscious mind.

# Chapter Thirty-One

Paul whistled as he forked manure from the very last stall. He was thrilled to be back in Sara's world, even if she wasn't there. At least she'd finally asked him for help, a step in the right direction and a reason for optimism. Filled with confidence, he pushed the wheelbarrow out the door and nearly ran into Janet as she came up the path. They both skidded to a stop.

"Aren't you going to Lubec?" Janet asked. "I can handle the stalls."

"Lubec? Why?"

"Sara's mom. I thought you knew."

Paul set the wheelbarrow down. "All I know is Sara needed someone to help with the barn. What's going on?"

Janet's eyes welled up. "Joanie was missing for two days. They found her yesterday. She drowned." Janet closed the distance between them and touched Paul's shoulder. "I'm so sorry. I assumed Sara told you."

The air left his body in a groan. Sara had already been through so much, how could she be expected to handle more? "When's the funeral?"

"Tomorrow, Thursday." Janet sniffed. "Are you going?"

"I need to be in Vermont for the real estate closing Friday morning," Paul said, planning quickly. "But yes, I want to be there for her tomorrow. Can someone look after the horses?"

"Not to worry," Janet replied. "We're leaving for Vermont ourselves first thing in the morning. I can ask a friend to look after Harlee and Frosty for as long as you need."

Once again Paul deflated. With all that had happened, he'd forgotten the family's plans to spend October in Vermont. It would have been the month he proposed, the month he gave Sara his engagement gift, if things had gone differently.

"Don't give up on her, Paul. You two are great together, and her therapist is an ass."

Paul smiled despite the pain. "Thanks. I think so too, on both counts."

He dumped the wheelbarrow and watched as manure balls tumbled to earth amid a swarm of flies. It seemed everyone thought he and Sara belonged together. If only Sara felt the same.


On the following afternoon, Sara stood beside her father, a black veil hiding vacant eyes. The voices chanted -*Dead is dead, dead is dead, dead is dead*- in relentless rhythm at the edge of her consciousness. A waking dream replayed the morning her mother first said those words.

Sara was five years old when Mikey the hamster swallowed a rubber band and died. She cradled the tiny body in her hands, crying and pleading with her mother to bring him to the vet. She pledged her allowance toward the bill. But Joanie knelt down, looked directly into her daughter's eyes and said those three words that carried all the finality in the world. And Sara understood. There is no coming back from death.

-*Dead is dead, dead is dead, dead is dead*-

The words had returned, along with the finality. Her mother was gone. Sara would never see her again. Her father cremated the body so quickly, she'd hardly had a chance to say goodbye.

Instead she clutched the little mouse her mom had made, turning it over and over in her palm. It was hand-sewn felt, stuffed with cotton batting, and it had thread whiskers, a pink hand-knit sweater and a matching ruffled skirt. Tiny felt ice skates with runners made from paper clips hung from her flat felt hands. She was perfect, like everything Joanie did, perfect and beautiful and now wet with tears.

"Are you okay?" It was her father's voice, and she reached for his hand.

"No. Dizzy." Sara's speech was thick and slow, her throat sore, eyes and nose swollen from crying.

"Just a little longer. I'm right beside you." Sara wondered why she didn't take comfort in his words. She felt nothing; even her feet seemed disconnected from the floor. She floated like a balloon, her father's hand the only thing keeping her earthbound.

Well-wishers paraded past them. As time went by, Sara slipped farther away. She wondered why they were here. Had something happened? It looked like a funeral, but why?

The task of shaking hands, uttering thanks, and occasionally pausing to give or receive a polite hug, seemed to wear on and on. In time, even the numbness faded, and her mind longed for sleep. There was nothing beyond this moment, nothing beyond her father's hand. She held on, a kite on a string, longing to let go and fly.

Someone took her hand. The touch was warm and comforting, and she fought to bring his face into focus. Her little sob sounded strange, and at first she didn't recognize her own voice. She fell into an oasis of peace, a grounding embrace. It only lasted a heartbeat. Carl spun her around and shook Paul's hand with unexpected enthusiasm.

"Good to see you, Paul. Thank you so much for coming."

Paul released Sara and shook her father's hand, murmuring condolences. Cassie moved in and Sara crumpled against her.

"Say, 'thank you,'" her father's voice whispered against her ear. She said the words. They came out flat and cold, and the bubble of warmth and safety scuttled away.

Paul said, "I'm so sorry for your loss. If there's anything I can do. . . ." and moved down the line. He hovered at the edge of the buffet, waiting. She was drawn to him, but she couldn't remember why.

As if in a dream, Sara disengaged herself from the well-wishers and crossed the room. She took Paul's hand and tried to focus on his face. "I know you," she said softly.

His eyes were wide, mouth open, and she wondered why he looked afraid. Had she done something wrong? Why didn't he tell her what to do? She'd be happy to comply.

"Are you okay?" His voice came out in a gasp.

"No. Dizzy."

Arms wrapped possessively around her. She shivered as the feeling of recognition faded and Carl smiled down at her.

"Come back to the line, sweetheart. Your Aunt Marion wants to see you. Don't be rude."

Carl nodded curtly to Paul as he steered Sara away. The next time she looked across the room, he was gone.

Somewhere, deep inside, a piece of her broke. But it was small and distant, and she barely noticed. She turned back to her father, took his hand and asked, "What do you want me to do now?"

# Chapter Thirty-Two

Sara dozed on the front seat and dreamed of Paul. Her breath quickened when she saw him, slowed and deepened when he held her, wavered when he walked away. Then she was alone with weirdly clouded voices. Carl's fingers drilled into her arm and her heart pulsed in an erratic rhythm. Cassie's eyes met hers, wild with concern. What was she saying? It was all strange and distorted and difficult to comprehend.

Her father had given her something; of that she was certain. She should have known, should have believed the voices' warnings. But until now he'd never drugged her in secret. By the time she realized what he'd done, it was too late.

As they pulled into the yard the familiar crunch of gravel startled her awake. Her mind was clearing, and the weight of her mother's death grew more difficult to bear. Sara trudged into the house and sat at the kitchen table. The room slipped into focus as the veil lifted from her mind.

Carl took a tea kettle from the stove and reached for the sugar bowl. "Empty," he said, his jaw tightening even as he smiled and shrugged. "I guess we used the last of it this morning." He glanced at Sara. She knew the light had returned to her eyes, and she stared back at him, matching his gaze until he looked away. His voice sounded as if his throat had fallen in on itself. "I'll run to the store. Sit tight."

She started to tell him not to bother; bitter tea would be welcome. But then it hit her.

*He wants to hide the taste of the sedative.*

A flash of anger swept over her. But she pushed it aside and reminded herself he was not just an overprotective father, but also a physician and her guardian. If she hoped to stay medication-free, she needed to gain his respect, and she had to do it now. Arms folded across her chest, she settled herself and spoke calmly.

"Daddy, I know you're medicating me, and I want you to stop." She trembled as the voices, too, came more fully awake, chanting and shouting and competing with her thoughts. She tried to focus on her words, say the right thing. Her mother would have been furious that Carl had medicated her against her will. But her mother was gone.

Indignation settled across her father's face. There was a sharp edge to his voice, and his fingers tightened on the kettle. "Sara, I'd never do such a thing without your permiss..."

She silenced him with a glare. "I understand what you're doing. You think I can't handle the stress, and you're trying to help." She squared her shoulders and looked directly into his eyes. "Mom is gone, and it hurts. But it's supposed to. Please don't take that away."

He stared at her. She held his gaze, determined not to give in. Finally he turned his back to her and walked to the hallway.

"I'd like you to reconsider. Did the medication help with the voices?"

Sara's shoulders crept upward, and she continued to watch her father as he rummaged through the hall closet and pulled his coat from its hanger. "Yes, they were much quieter. But I barely knew where I was. That's not okay with me." She pulled her feet into the chair, drew her knees to her chest, pretended to close her eyes and continued to watch him through her lashes.

"How much do you remember?" He didn't look at her, and the question sent prickles down her spine.

"I hardly remember anything about the funeral." She tried to think, but everything was fragmented. Dreams and reality blurred into a confused jumble. "Was Paul there? Was Cassie? I know she and Adam are closing on the inn tomorrow. I doubt they would have had time to come."

"You saw Cassie. You spoke to her." Carl shrugged into his coat. "She and her fiancé were both there."

*Not Paul.*

*-He gave up.*

*-Too much trouble, nothing in return.*

Sara laid her head on the table and let her eyes fully close. Paul still cared, didn't he? Or had she waited too long, expected too much?

"We need a few things," her father said. "Are you okay alone for a half hour or so? I'll be right back."

In response to her abbreviated nod, he stepped out the door. The lock clicked behind him, and her stomach pinched in response. She jumped up and crept to the door, watched the tail lights recede into the black.

Heart pounding, she twisted the lock and tried the knob. It turned easily. He hadn't locked her in, not this time. But knowing he could sent a shudder through her.

As she stared out the square windowpane in the center of the old wooden door, a shadow fell across the porch. Cassie's face appeared behind the glass, followed by a soft knock.

With a cry held in check for far too long, Sara threw the door open, grabbed Cassie and held on. Cassie hugged her hard, and they clung to one another under a dim circle of light.

"What are you doing here? Don't you have to get back for the closing?"

Cassie tightened her grip. "We were worried about you. You seemed so out of it at the funeral." She stepped back and looked into Sara's eyes, her expression guarded.

Embarrassed, Sara turned away. "I *was* out of it. My father sedated me. I hardly remember being there at all." She covered her face and peeked through her fingers. "Did I do anything stupid?"

"No, of course not." Cassie's shoulders were tight with worry as she glanced toward the road and back to Sara. "How long will he be gone?"

"My father?" Sara shrugged. "Maybe a half hour. Why?"

"We, well, we wanted to let you know, if you want, you can ride back with us. Adam can drive your truck, and you can ride with me." Cassie startled as a car passed the end of the driveway.

Sara waved to Adam before she pulled Cassie through the door and closed it behind her. "I'd love to go home, but I should stay here for a few days and make sure my dad is okay."

"What if he drugs you again?" Cassie blurted the words. She clapped her hand over her mouth.

"I asked him not to." Sara laughed, a short, nervous little chuckle. "He's overprotective and controlling, but he's not a monster. Give him some credit."

Cassie's eyes wandered over Sara in a quick assessment. "You do seem to be back to yourself. It was just a shock to see you like that." Her anxious expression softened. "I'm sorry. We thought your dad had medicated you against your wishes. We all know how you feel about drugs."

"He did, actually," Sara admitted. "But I spoke to him about it. I told him it wasn't right to take away the pain, and I think he agreed." Her voice broke as the last of her composure crumbled and tears burst free. "It was just so sudden. And it makes no sense. My mom would never go out in a canoe without her life vest. She's not a good swimmer and she's always really careful."

"Could someone have done this to her?"

"On purpose?" Sara sat heavily on the carpeted stairs, her thoughts tumbling. "The police ruled it an accident. Besides, who would want to hurt her? Everyone loved my mother." As tears slid past her lashes, she hid her face in her hands. "My poor dad. He's all alone now. He's devastated."

Cassie sat next to her and draped an arm around her. "I'm sure he's had quite a shock, and I understand your need to support him, but don't become his babysitter, okay? You have a life."

Sara nodded. Cassie was right. Already she felt an acute sense of responsibility toward her bereaved father. He needed her, but if she stayed too long, she could easily fall more deeply under his control. Without her mother's support, she'd have to be vigilant in protecting her remaining rights.

"Thank Adam for me," she said, her voice thick with grief. "It was a kind offer."

Cassie hesitated, then spoke in a rush. "Paul's with us, too. Is there anything you want to say to him?"

"Paul? He's here?"

"You don't remember?"

"No! Did he come to the funeral?"

Worry lined Cassie's face. "You spoke to him."

Sara scrambled from the stairs, bolted through the door and ran over the gravel. Paul jumped from the car. She threw herself against him, knocked him onto the hood, and clung to him, crying and stammering and gulping back tears.

"I'm so sorry! Dr. Green's an idiot. So am I." Paul said nothing, and her chest pinched. "Is it too late? Do you still want me?"

His voice was low and hoarse as he wrapped his arms around her. "Do you have to ask?"

She buried her face in his jacket and breathed the unfamiliar smell of his new suit.

"Come with us, Sara." Paul's voice was pleading.

"Mmmm. I wish I could." She hung in his embrace, and a little bubble of happiness stood between her and the grief. "I'll be along in a day or two. I can't leave my dad all alone just yet. He doesn't have anybody."

She reached up and kissed him, then wound her arms around his neck and held on.

*How could I have ever doubted him?*

*-Stupid, stupid, stupid, stupid-*

Headlights flooded the driveway. Cassie stepped closer to Adam. Paul moved to stand in front of Sara, still holding her snug against him. Sara peered into the glare, squinted, and called, "Daddy! Look who's here!"


*What the fuck? What are they doing here?*

Carl drove up to the close little group. He shut off the engine and wiped sweat from his hands. *Twenty minutes. I left her twenty minutes, and already the vultures are massing for their share.*

Barely hiding the scowl behind a smile, he stuffed a white pharmacy bag under the car seat and paused to consider. His customary expression of unrestrained welcome wouldn't do. Now it had to be tempered by grief. He really should have tried to cry on the way home. It simply hadn't occurred to him until now.

He drew a deep breath and stepped from the car.

"Paul! Cassie! It's kind of you to stop by." He stepped forward and offered his hand. Cassie wore her usual tight-lipped expression of disapproval. So much like Joanie, that one. She was trouble; always had been. And Paul, the little troll, why was he still hanging around? Carl extended his hand to the man beside Cassie, the one he'd met at the funeral. What was his name?

"Adam, good of you to come." Carl glanced about, maintaining his puffy-eyed half-smile with difficulty. "Sara, where are your manners? Invite your friends inside."

Carl reached for her, but Paul stepped into his path. "We were just discussing the possibility of Sara riding back with us. She'd be safer with friends than she will be traveling alone. One of us can drive her truck for her."

*Fucking ass. Where does he get off?*

"I'll be fine. I'm sure my dad would prefer I stay here for a few days." Sara moved out from behind Paul and stretched out a hand. Carl caught it, wanting to pull her against him. Instead he released her and turned toward the house. He tried to keep his tone welcoming, but he croaked the words, "Come on in. I'll make tea."

# Chapter Thirty-Three

The evening crawled like a three-legged spider, and Carl writhed beneath the unreasonable scrutiny of Sara's so-called friends. Who knew they would overstay their welcome by such lengths, ignoring the fact that their hosts had suffered a terrible loss? Did they think Sara would leave with them? Idiots. She couldn't walk away from someone in need.

His performance in the kitchen was some of his best work. Clutching the countertop, squeezing tears from his eyes, sliding to the floor, wracked with sobs. That damn Cassie wasn't fooled. He could see it in her eyes and the tight line of her lips. But she knew enough to choose her battles. And Paul, so goofy in love. He couldn't see anything but Sara. Carl could have enjoyed the spectacle if only it hadn't stolen his time with her.

Finally they were gone. The thought of being alone with Sara had blood pooling in his groin. But he couldn't risk revealing himself to her, not now and not here. He'd have to be patient for a little while longer.

She sat on the couch across from him, still clutching that ugly felt thing Joanie had made for the church fair. The attachment was fast becoming irksome.

Carl cleared his throat. "We need to talk."

She rolled the stuffed mouse into her sleeve and looked up. "What is it?"

He puffed out an exaggerated sigh, hoping to convey inner conflict without being melodramatic. "It's about the cruise. Would you think me terrible if I went?"

Sara was silent, and Carl used his sleeve to swab at the dampness accumulating on his forehead. "I think it would be good to get away from here. . . ." He let his voice trail off, feigning contemplation.

"I think it's a good idea."

Did he detect relief in her voice? Ah, she thought he'd be far away, no longer a bother. He let his head fall forward, and he stared at the ugly carpet his late wife had picked out, a mass of muted colors that hid the dirt and allowed Joanie to decorate in multiple palettes. He heaved another sigh. It worked the first time.

"What's wrong?" There was concern in Sara's voice. Was it sympathy for him? Or was she afraid he might ask too much of her? He'd have to proceed with caution and make sure she understood exactly what was required.

"I just hate to go alone. None of my friends can come on such short notice." Carl paused, giving her a chance to make the offer. Sara looked at her hands with her damn hair hiding her face. He sighed again.

"I remember you telling your *mother*." He choked on the word rather convincingly, he thought. "You said that you have October free. I wondered if you might be willing to come with me."

She didn't answer. He listened to her breathing, slow and deep with a little catch. She was struggling with the request, wanting to please him, of course, but also probably thinking of Paul. He could fix that.

"Paul loves you. But if he can't understand your responsibility toward your family in a time of crisis…" He left the rest unsaid. She was a smart girl.

"When is it?"

Carl locked onto the change in pitch. She was leaning. The slightest push would shift her balance. "We'd leave a week from tomorrow." He let the words lie between them and waited to see if she picked them up or stepped around them. When she didn't answer, he pressed.

"I don't want to make this mandatory, Sara. But you do realize I don't have to ask."

"You wouldn't force me to go?"

Carl risked a glance and found Sara's eyes wide with surprise and a touch of anger. Surely she'd seen this coming. There were precedents.

"I feel very strongly about this, Sara. I can't risk leaving you alone." He couldn't look at her. What if something of her mother's derision gazed back through her eyes? The *Joanie* look would ruin everything.

But she sighed, and her exaggerated swallow filled the silence. "I'd rather go home. I want to patch things up with Paul and get my life back together. What if you come with me instead? We could look after each other."

It was a very sane, rational, considered offer, but not the one Carl wanted. He pinched the skin of his wrist, allowed a fingernail to sink in, and closed his eyes against the slow burn. When finally his fingertip was warm and sticky, a few stubborn tears spilled down his face. It would be enough.

"I just want to get away. I need you. You're the only family I have. Please don't make me force you."

When Sara looked at him with shock and compassion, Carl knew he had her. Everything had been timed with the utmost care, each step scrutinized and found infallible. He knew her witch of a mother had planned to circumvent the guardianship, had planted the seed of rebellion in her daughter's mind. But Sara couldn't do it alone. Not in mere days, not with a grief-stricken father to support, not with her friends hundreds of miles away.

Her best option was to comply, perhaps planning to begin the legal process upon her return. The thought threatened to transform Carl's ragged mouth to a smile, and he struggled to hold on to the expression of bereavement.

Sara swallowed hard, took in an irregular breath, and faced him. "I guess I could find someone to look after Harlee." She lowered her head. Her hair, once again, covered her face. "Dad, I need to tell you, Mom told me why you keep me at arm's length."

The feeling of a punch to the ribs surprised him. There wasn't time to construct an appropriate response. Something unintelligible tumbled from his mouth as he dug for meaningful words to say. How could Joanie have guessed his secret? Why would she tell Sara how he felt about her? The filthy, disloyal bitch!

Sara continued, her voice soft and unexpectedly calm.

"I understand why you've always been so distant with me. The guilt. Mom said you always wondered if you could have helped, if only you'd noticed I was sick sooner. She said you blamed yourself for my illness."

Carl bit back the words of denial he'd been assembling. The girl knew nothing.

Sara's chin quivered, and her eyes were wide with compassion. Carl turned away, afraid too much of his intention might peek through. Not trusting his voice he ground his lips together and waited.

"Maybe this trip can be a new beginning," she said softly in the silence. "Maybe we can finally get to know each other. As adults."

A warm flush crept over Carl's skin as a smile stretched his face of its own volition. Once again he marveled at the feeling of cheeks and lips rearranging themselves without conscious effort. Sara's words exactly echoed his thoughts. Perhaps she would give herself to him more easily than he'd hoped.

"I'll make all the arrangements." Carl's heart beat so loudly, he was afraid Sara might hear it. "You won't be sorry."

While he suspected he might be pushing his luck, there was one more thing he needed to ask. If he could cut Sara off from Cassie and Paul, she'd be less likely to change her mind. He could compel her, but first he'd frame his demand as a request. Perhaps she would simply agree.

"I'd like you to stay here until the cruise. I've barely seen you in so very long, and I don't think either one of us ought to be alone."

Her whimper was all the answer he needed. She might resist, but she'd give in. He'd raised her to be compliant, and truthfully, she had no choice.

"You've no idea what it means to me to have you here," he said, hiding an impulsive smirk. "No idea at all."

# Chapter Thirty-Four

"What do we do now?" Cassie fumed as Adam drove across the bridge into Bucksport. Paul used his phone to google State of Maine laws regarding guardianship. He was completely focused and oblivious to Cassie's ongoing tirade.

"Paul! Listen to me!"

Cassie's piercing tone cut through his concentration. He tore his eyes from the screen and fixed her with a frown. "We can't know what to do until we understand our choices. I'm researching choices."

"How can you be so calm?"

Paul turned back to Google, relieved Cassie couldn't see past his skin. If his heart beat any faster he might pass out, and he doubted he'd ever eat again.

Carl had seemed . . . hard to describe, really. One moment he played the worried parent, the next, concerned doctor. Then grieving widower. Something was wrong, off kilter, but what?

Paul had nothing on which to base his fears. Sara was back to normal. Probably her odd behavior at her mother's funeral had been due to nothing more than an *appropriate* sedative, administered to help her through the ordeal. And she had chosen to stay behind. Carl hadn't forced her, or even pressured.

And then it hit him. "Crap. That's it."

Cassie paused in mid-sentence. "You haven't heard a word I've said, have you? Put that stupid phone down and listen to me."

"No, wait!" Paul replayed the events of the evening, letting images of Carl flash through his mind. "Sara's father, he only does one emotion at a time. Did you notice?"

Cassie slapped his shoulder. "We've been over that. He's a fake. Everything he says or does is smoke and mirrors. Nothing is real."

"But why?" Paul asked, completely bewildered. "His wife just died. How could he be…"

"Methodical? Calculating?" Cassie's voice rose in frustration. "I don't know, but he's always been that way. There's something not right with him and Sara doesn't see it. She never has."

Adam, silent until now, butted in. "She grew up with him. To her, he's normal." He paused, staring at the road. "Besides, when he looks at her the smile is real. He cares about her. It's obvious."

"She does have a mental illness, and he is a psychiatrist," Paul said, rubbing his forehead. He twisted in his seat and faced Cassie. "And Sara did have two psychotic breaks. Isn't it responsible for her father to keep her close while she deals with her mother's death?"

Cassie leaned between the seats and rested her chin on his shoulder. "Paul," she said, her voice remarkably calm, "you're an ass."

He swatted her away. "I'm trying to be reasonable. It's normal for family to stick together when someone dies. I understand Sara wanting to stay behind and make sure he's okay."

Cassie punched Adam's arm. "What do you think? Am I being silly?"

Adam's eyes remained glued to the road. "You've known Sara and her father a lot longer than either of us. I trust your judgment."

"Way to back me up, Adam." Paul elbowed his friend in the ribs before hissing, "Whipped."

"Sorry, pal, you're on your own." Adam shot Paul an apologetic look, then looked adoringly at Cassie in the rearview mirror.

She leaned forward and kissed Adam's neck, then bounced back and kicked Paul's seat. With a growl, she wrapped her fingers around his head rest. He could feel her silent glare heating up the back of his neck.

"Fine," Cassie said. "You've explained Carl's side. What about mine? Have you found anything we can use to get her out of there?"

Paul shook his head. "We don't have much. He gave her a sedative. He's a doctor. He can do that."

"But he's so controlling and manipulative," Cassie argued. "Sara's vulnerable right now. She just lost her mom, right after Brett let her go…"

"Brett what?" Paul jerked away from his phone. "When did that happen?"

"A few days ago. I talked to her when she was driving back from Vermont, just before she got the call from her dad."

Paul clamped his mouth shut, went back to reading and tried to quiet the pain throbbing in his chest. He'd been angry with Sara, hurt that she'd taken her doctor's advice and cut him loose. But she'd had to deal with much, much more. "It's a wonder she's still standing."

Cassie kicked his seat again. "She's tough. It takes a lot to get her down."

"This *is* a lot." Paul focused on the Board of Health page, then clicked to a site that advertised legal assistance. He read a moment longer before he sighed and flipped the phone shut. "I'll make some calls in the morning and figure out what we can do to keep an eye on her. Meanwhile, I suggest we change course and drive straight to Vermont for the closing, save time."

Adam picked up the GPS and tossed it to Cassie. "Good idea. We can catch a few hours of sleep at a hotel and pick this up first thing in the morning."

"But someone needs to keep an eye on Sara! Check on her!" Cassie's voice rose to pitches Paul had never heard before. He was reminded of fingernails on chalkboards and nuns with rulers.

"Crap!" Paul sat upright. "That's it! Why didn't I think of it sooner?"

"What?" Cassie and Adam spoke in unison.

"We contact Joanie's church! We tell the pastor that Carl's been acting strangely, and with Sara's illness, perhaps it would be best to arrange visitations for a few days." For the first time since leaving Lubec, Paul grinned. "We'll have Joanie's friends arriving at the house all day, bringing casseroles and offering support. Sara won't be alone for a minute."

"Except at night." Cassie's worry surrounded her in frizzy hair and chewed fingernails. Paul had never seen her so disarrayed.

"Call her," he said. "Call her at random times, right up to midnight. Make sure there's no pattern so Carl doesn't know what to expect. We'll take turns."

"Not a bad idea." Cassie gave Paul's shoulder a much friendlier squeeze before settling into the backseat. "I just wish she'd come home with us. I fucking hate that man."

"We know." Paul's head pounded in time with his chest. He understood Cassie's frustration. Something about Carl made him nervous, too. Leaving Sara alone with him had his nerves on edge and his temper ready to snap. He linked his fingers behind his neck and pulled, hoping for a moment's relief.

"Carl decides where Sara goes and who she sees," he reminded himself. "Unless she asks for help, our hands are tied. And for all we know, her father is doing the right thing."

Cassie glared at him, and he frowned back. "Look, Cassie, I don't like it any more than you do. As soon as we get through the closing, I'll get in touch with Dr. Green. She needs to know what's happening. Maybe she'll have a suggestion. It's a start."

Cassie lunged forward and swatted Paul's shoulder one last time before settling back and pulling out her cell phone. "I'm calling Dr. Green right now," she said. She finished dialing and went back to chewing her fingernails. "I just hope she answers."

# Chapter Thirty-Five

Carl reached into his top drawer, pushed aside neatly folded boxers, and withdrew a brown glass bottle with a bright orange cap. Cool and slick, it settled against the contours of his hand, its smooth surface conveying a sense of rightness. He carried it to the bathroom and grinned at the mirror. His reflection leered back.

The continued role playing was a burden, and he chafed at the necessity of donning today's grieving-widower disguise. But he mustn't stray from his plan, not with success so close at hand. So he painstakingly refined his features to an expression appropriate to the circumstances. This took twenty-three seconds. He congratulated himself for increased efficiency and cunning.

He'd been clever, hiding his medications at the church so he could experiment at Joanie's funeral. Sara, still as gullible as ever, had avoided his offers of apple juice. But not for a moment did she suspect the finger sandwich he'd given her moments before mourners began to arrive.

"You have to keep up your strength," he'd told her. "Eat something." And she'd complied. The dose would need adjustment, though. As time passed and the drug increased its hold, Sara's lack of awareness had become obvious. People noticed.

Today he would use a lower dose, keep her awake and responsive, and perhaps he would add something to prolong the effect. The beauty of the drug was, of course, its ability to produce amnesia. She would remember nothing, as if he'd never touched her at all.

The system had worked well when Sara was little, although she'd been less present than he would have preferred. No one suspected, not even Sara, not until the day his father caught him with her at Round Lake.

The old man's threats were unacceptable. Carl did what had to be done. But Sara's injection began to wear off before he'd had time to dispose of the remains, and a few unfortunate memories had been allowed to take root.

*Damn the old fart for his interference! He ruined everything.* Carl spat in the sink as he recalled his father's disgust, as if the demented old fondler had any claim to moral high ground. He'd had his hands all over the girl, grabbed her and tickled her until she couldn't breathe, and all he got was a pat on his addled old head.

Carl pocketed the medication and headed for the hallway. This was no time to relive the past. He and Sara were alone, as they were meant to be, and apple juice would hide the taste of this morning's experiment.

His cheer was interrupted by the doorbell. Cursing, he hurried down the stairs. As he rounded the corner, he collided with Sara in the hallway.

"Who the hell would be here at this hour?" he muttered, forgetting to hide his irritation. Sara ducked ahead of him and peered through the glass.

"I don't know who they are, but they have breakfast."

"It's barely seven o'clock. What are they thinking?"

Sara turned to him, one eyebrow raised, and Carl searched for a more appropriate expression. While she greeted the two elderly visitors, he managed to sculpt a convincing smile of welcome over his annoyance.

"Pastor Judy asked us to stop by and make sure you two have somethin' for breakfast," Trudi Marsh explained as she pushed past him to the kitchen. "These blueberry pancakes were made fresh this morning. I can warm them in the oven while I scramble some eggs." Her husband Joe placed a covered platter on the kitchen table. Sara set out plates and silverware while Carl silently seethed.

They sat down to pancakes and sausages with scrambled eggs and toast. Trudi clutched Sara's hand and offered words of reassurance and support. Carl's smile hardened with frustration at yet another delay.

"You have your mother's eyes, Sara," Trudi said. "Hers were green, of course, but they had the same sparkle."

Carl swallowed bile as Sara smiled at the comparison. She appeared comforted, as if it were a good thing to resemble that over-critical, complaining bitch of a mother. Of course Trudi would remember his wife fondly. Joanie had cooked countless meals for those moth-eaten old Bible-thumping battleaxes.

But why did the old woman have to hold Sara's hand like that? Trudi's gnarled, translucent fingers didn't belong anywhere near Sara's smooth skin. And what was she saying? "It's gonna hurt for a long time, dear. But it gets easier, eventually."

Sara looked doubtful. Well, he wanted to make her forget, and he hoped to. Hypnosis, augmented by a few pharmaceuticals, might do the trick. He'd managed to bury those few memories of her grandfather's death, and with time and privacy he intended to develop a more effective protocol.

Now what was Sara saying to the old biddy? "It's just so hard, knowing I'll never see her again."

"But, of course you will." The wrinkled crone pulled Sara to her feet, towed her to the mirror in the hallway, and stabbed a stubby finger against the glass. "Just look right there, Joanie's nose. And like I said, those eyes! The expression is so like your mother's." She patted Sara's shoulder and played with her hair. Carl managed not to throw up.

"So whenever you find yourself missing her too much, you just look in the mirror. She'll be there."

Sara's eyes misted. Trudi led her back to the table and placed a mug of hot cocoa in her hands. "Drink up. There's nothing like chocolate to make you feel better."

Carl stepped aside as the old bag reached past him and poured herself another cup of coffee. She sat back down in an attitude of permanence. Sara glanced at her father, and the tentative smile fell from her lips.

*Damn*, he needed to play along. How did one appear grateful? Another fucking smile was the only thing he could come up with, and he doubted his face could take much more.

Joe and Trudi said their goodbyes at eleven o'clock. Trudi's last words were, "Donna Whitley is making lunch. She'll be along soon. And I expect Pastor Judy will stop by for a while this afternoon."

Carl longed to punch the wall, but he knew from experience he'd only bruise his knuckles. Shaking with the effort, he resorted to quiet simmering.

The day dragged interminably. Donna's chicken spinach roll and scalloped potatoes were followed by a two-hour visit from Joanie's pastor. By the time she and her words of comfort trundled out the door it was nearly dinner time, and Paula Shapiro arrived with a boiled dinner. Paula stayed and stayed until even Sara looked as if she might prefer some solitude.

Finally the last do-gooder left, and it was only seven o'clock. The day was gone, but the evening beckoned. Carl hurried to the kitchen and poured the juice. He touched fingers to the bottle sequestered in his pants pocket. Finally.

The phone rang. He ignored it. Sara would answer. But when he stepped into the sitting room, apple juice in hand, he found her deep in conversation. She turned to him and mouthed, "Cassie," before waving him away.

An hour later Sara finished her conversation and hung up. Carl handed her the glass, and she took it with a guilty smile, saying, "Sorry, Daddy, I know we haven't had much time together." She touched her lips to the edge of the glass, wrinkled her nose, and set it on the counter, still recounting her conversation with Cassie. "They closed on the inn today. Isn't that wonderful?"

Carl grunted a reply.

Sara prattled on. "Cassie said everything went smoothly, and they finished by noon. They might take a drive up here this weekend and hang out with me for a day or two."

Something caustic frothed in Carl's chest, swelling until he felt he might explode. He calmed himself with one thought. *There will be time.* Tonight belonged to him, and knowing this, he turned to Sara with renewed cheer. "Can I get you anything? A snack?"

The doorbell rang and expletives cascaded from Carl's mouth. *Are the church ladies sending after-dinner mints now?*

Even Sara seemed reluctant. But she put on a smile and strode to the foyer. Her shriek of delight startled Carl, but not nearly as much as her words.

"Paul! What are you doing here?"

# Chapter Thirty-Six

The first rays of morning light fell across the flowered sofa and cast a lacy pattern over the top of Paul's head. Wrapped in a thick blanket, Sara sat in the armchair facing him. She'd been there since four o'clock, watching and waiting.

He'd murmured a few words in his sleep, but the only one that made sense was her name. She'd kissed his forehead the first time he'd said it, but now she only listened, her brow puckered in reflection.

The evening had been odd. Her father was livid when Paul arrived. She'd watched him as he tried to hide his rage, his lips pulled back in a smile that more closely resembled constipation. She could understand his need to explode after putting on a brave face for the succession of supportive seniors. Perhaps his anger was due to pent-up grief. In any case, she appreciated his efforts, and theirs.

But the look in her father's eyes, and in Paul's, was unexpected. They'd hit it off so well on Paul's first visit, yet last night they faced off almost as adversaries. After a brief skirmish in which neither said anything of substance, Carl excused himself and went to bed.

Paul's explanation, too, was abridged. He'd driven with Adam and Cassie to Vermont so they could close on the inn. Then he'd rented a car, he said, with every intention of returning home. Instead he'd been drawn back to Lubec.

"I just had a feeling," he'd said, stammering. "I thought maybe you needed me. But probably it was the other way around, me needing you."

He seemed so unsure, so ill at ease, she wanted to believe him. But she knew he was holding back. There'd been fear in his eyes when he came to visit after the funeral, and that fear hadn't left. Cassie must have voiced her opinions of Carl, and Paul had listened.

*-She hates your father.*

*-Turned Paul against him.*

*-Bitch, bitch, bitch, bitch-*

Sara listened to the voices, but their words left her even more conflicted. Her father had given her a strong sedative without her permission, and that was unacceptable. True, the circumstances were extreme. Between her mother's death and her own collapse at the lake, he probably feared for her sanity. Sara's first psychotic break had occurred when she was faced with a simple high school graduation. Maybe he did have reason to be both protective and proactive.

But she'd also survived a stressful divorce with no pharmaceutical help at all. In any case, he should have been honest with her. Because now she and her father had a greater problem. She couldn't trust him.

She looked at Paul, just beginning to stir, and she wavered. He was holding back, too. His lack of candor, however well-intentioned, meant her faith in him must also be uncertain.

*Everyone lies.*

*-Trust no one.*

*-Better alone.*

Paul loved her. That much was given. But her father loved her, too.

"Penny for your thoughts?"

She startled. Lost in her internal debate, she hadn't realized Paul was awake and watching her. He pushed himself into a sitting position, and she locked onto his eyes. There was the usual humor, but a shadow veiled the rest. As disappointment rose from her heart to her face, she saw Paul's cheerful façade break. He lowered his head.

"I suppose you want to know what I'm really doing here."

"Mmm hmm." She held her breath. Did Paul suspect how important his honesty was? His voice was hesitant, but as he spoke, he met her gaze.

"I was worried about you," he said. "I thought your father might give you something against your will or without you knowing. I'm probably being a jerk, but I thought if someone were here with you, he'd have to be more up front."

He looked away again. "Cassie spoke to Dr. Green."

"She what?"

*-Told her your secrets.*

*-Stripped you naked.*

"Your doctor didn't say much, just that you might want to have us close." He reached for her hand. "Would you rather I left? I'll do whatever you think is best."

"Stay." The word shot from her mouth, and she continued in a rush. "You're right. My father . . . I'm afraid he's so overcome with grief, his judgment might be affected." She paused, ashamed at her lack of faith. But her own inner voice pushed her forward.

"He means well, but he's acting like a psychiatrist. He thinks drugs are the answer to everything."

"And you still think you're better off without?"

Paul's question threw her. She hadn't expected to have to defend herself, not to him. "Yes," she said, irritated and anxious. "Medications have never helped with the voices. They just make me slow and clumsy and forgetful." She watched Paul's face and worried her lip, trying to stay calm.

*Please let him be on my side.*
*-Don't trust him.*
*-Run away!*

She allowed defiance to creep into her gaze. "I'm doing fine. I'm shaken, but that's normal, isn't it?"

"After all you've been through? It's more than normal. It's bordering on heroic."

Sara blushed. Paul's praise came as a surprise, and some of the tension slackened as she realized he still believed in her. "It's going to be harder now. My mom always ran interference for me. She hated drugs as much as I do. But my dad is on his own now, and he manages my medical care." She shivered as the full realization of her predicament settled over her. "Cassie was right. I should have contested this guardianship the moment I got out of the hospital. I have very little say."

Paul moved closer and sat on the carpet at her feet. "When would you be comfortable coming home? Once you're out from under your father's immediate control, I can get the ball rolling. I'll find a lawyer and see what we have to do."

Paul's offer of help warmed her, but... "I can't come home. He won't let me."

"What? Why?"

"He wants me to go on a cruise with him. He's insisting, not asking. And he wants me to stay here until then."

Paul looked at her in shock. "But that's not right. You're an adult. You should get to choose."

"I'm his ward," she reminded him. "If I don't go willingly, he can force me."

"How?"

"How could he make me?"

Paul nodded, and Sara realized she'd never asked.

"I don't know. I guess he could involve the police."

"Would he risk alienating you like that?"

"Maybe." Her father's temper had been difficult to predict.

A corner of Paul's lip twitched upward. "Let's find out."

"What?" Her heart plunged at the thought of Paul taking such a risk. "I don't know. You could get arrested."

Paul got to his feet. "I very much doubt that. And anyway, you're worth it."

"What about your car?"

"I'll have the rental agency pick it up." Paul held out his hand. Sara wavered.

*-He'll come after you, lock you up forever!*

*-Put Paul in jail!*

Sara held her breath as she sorted through the din. A spark of rebellion kindled inside her. Her words sounded bolder than she felt.

"Let's go."


The old house had thin walls, and Carl knew where best to place an ear. Conversations from the sitting room carried easily through the heating vent to his room, directly above. From the comfort of his bed, he could make out most of the words, and recognize their implications.

Sara's decision to leave was a slap to the face. For a moment he'd considered storming down the stairs, making it clear who was in charge. But such an act could lead Paul to secure legal counsel, and Sara would find out how effortlessly she might sidestep the guardianship. Temporary measures were all too easy to put in place.

There was wisdom in holding one's tongue, much as it galled him to watch through his window as the pair drove away without so much as a goodbye. He would have to support Sara's decision, allow her to enjoy her adventure. His plans would need only minor alterations, and everything would work out to the good.

He dressed in an appropriately morose gray suit and made his way down the stairs. Sara had left a note, of course, written in a predictably unsteady hand and apologetic tone. *Poor, silly girl, intent on her escape.* She was so unsure of herself, so lacking in any real conviction. Within an hour she'd be calling, swollen with guilt and needing to be sure he was okay. With a tight laugh, he turned off his cell phone and stepped out into a perfect autumn day.

The breakfast sedan pulled into the yard as he drove out with a wave and a smile, leaving Pastor Judy with a plastic-wrapped bowl in her hands and egg on her face. Well, why not? It wasn't as if he'd asked for breakfast or sympathy, and the endless presumption had already worn thin.

Following a bagel and coffee in Machias, he picked up a swimsuit and an assortment of girls' shorts and shirts from the junior section at Sears. Sara was a tiny thing, and she'd be lovely wearing his purchases, stretched out in the sun at poolside. The thought gave him a needed boost, and he hurried on to the travel agency.

The cruise and flights would need to be changed. A Manchester departure would be swapped for Bangor, and Sara's name would replace Joanie's. As he left the office, he had a sudden thought. *What if Paul tries to come along? How can I best divert him?*

Amused by his cleverness, Carl returned to the travel agency and dropped into the seat he'd only just vacated.

"I wonder if you might show me another cruise. Something leaving the same day, from the same port."

The agent gave him a questioning look. "Problems? You do understand the trip we booked for you is non-refundable at such a late date."

"It's not for me," Carl assured her. "But my daughter's ex has been stalking her and might try to follow us. I'd prefer not to share our cruise."

"I understand." She flashed a conspiratorial grin and handed him a printout. "This one parallels yours until you reach the Panama Canal. Then it circles back to Ft. Lauderdale while you continue to San Diego. Make sure you don't mix them up and try to board the wrong ship."

Carl laughed at the joke.

At one o'clock he lunched at his favorite diner. He pulled out his cell phone, wondering if he'd waited long enough. By now Sara would be concerned, would have called several times.

Carl pocketed the phone. Another hour would have her frantic and considering turning back. She'd drive the little nerd batty with her vacillating.

A hospital visit was in order. One must keep up appearances, and Saturdays were no exception. Carl made a pretense of checking on patients while listening to condolences from members of his staff. Finally the parade of support came to an end, and he closed his door and picked up the phone.

"Eeny, meeny, miny, moe. Which one do I call first?"

Carl went through several versions of the children's rhyme and finally dialed Sara's number. The sound of her voice had his heart racing, his throat dry. This proved his love for her, he told himself, and supported the rightness of his actions.

"Daddy! Are you okay?"

He winced at the name. *Patience*, he reminded himself. *She doesn't know any better.*

"I'm fine, sweetheart," he said in his most jovial tone. "I see you decided to head home after all." There was a moment of silence before her voice returned, small and uncertain.

"You're not mad?"

"Why would I be angry? I'm proud of you for taking a stand." Carl listened to the stunned silence. Then he spoke quickly, careful not to give her time to recover.

"We'll have to talk soon. I'm at work, and there's quite a bit of catching up to do. Think about the cruise and let me know what you decide." He clicked the phone off and set it on his desk. Then he dialed 0 on his internal line and waited for the lobby receptionist to answer.

The voice was bright and perky. "Front desk. How can I help you?"

"Hello, Sylvia." His voice was smug, more self-satisfied than he'd intended. "I know you spoke to Cassie, and I know what you told her." When she didn't reply, he tsk'd into the phone and lightened his tone.

"I'll overlook it this once," he said, smooth as butter. "But thanks to your interference, I'll need you to meet with Sara this week after all."

"Why?" Sylvia's voice was even smaller than Sara's. "You said she wouldn't need to see me anymore."

"That was before her mother died." He let his voice catch on the last word. "She shouldn't be on her own right now, so you'll need to convince her to accompany me on that cruise." He paused for effect before he said, "Make her think it's her idea."

# Chapter Thirty-Seven

Sara sat beside Paul in the office of Attorney Craig M. Driscoll, a lawyer Cassie had recommended. "Don't let those baby browns fool you," Cassie had told her. "He's been my family's lawyer for as long as I can remember. He may look like a kindly old grandpa, but he's a viper. He's exactly the sort of lawyer you want on your side."

Paul did the talking, but Craig's relentless scrutiny was aimed at Sara. As she sat in the straight-backed chair, listened to Paul's explanation of her circumstances, and struggled to meet the lawyer's persistent gaze, the word *viper* seemed fitting. Finally Craig stroked his neatly trimmed beard, raised his free hand to silence Paul, and addressed her.

"I think it's time you told me how *you* feel about this." Craig's unwavering gaze dared her to speak candidly. "What exactly do you hope to gain?"

"My freedom." The longing that rushed through her was painful in its intensity, and Sara swallowed hard before plowing onward. "I want the right to make my own choices without pressure and without force. I want to decide where I live, to choose my friends, and to determine my medical care, on my own."

Craig's eyes were slits beneath stubbly brows, and Sara fought the urge to look away. Finally his steely expression softened.

"I like you," he said. "You were quiet when you came in, and I wondered how coherent you'd be. But you come across as smart and very much in control." He folded his arms across a barrel chest and expanded into his chair. "To be completely honest, if everything Paul says is true, I see no reason why you should have been subjected to a guardianship in the first place. How did it come about?"

Sara glanced at Paul. His encouraging smile helped to cement her conviction as she gathered her thoughts.

*-Mowed down your husband.*

*-Hit a policeman.*

*Shut up. I don't want your help.*

Shaking off the voices, she faced Craig with a mixture of hope and dread. "I've had two psychotic breaks," she began, "one when I turned eighteen, and one almost a year ago." The lawyer didn't smile, and once again Sara felt as if she were being dissected. But Craig's brusque nod urged her to continue. "I don't remember either episode at all, but everyone agreed I was incapable of looking after myself."

"She's been fine otherwise," Paul was quick to add.

"Not fine," Sara said, reaching across the arm of her chair to hold his hand. "But coping." She turned back to Craig and spoke in her most matter-of-fact tone. "I hear voices. I know they aren't real, and I don't do as they say. I treat them the same way another person might treat their thoughts. But I do hear them out loud and I can't make them go away. I realize that's not normal."

Craig's eyes crinkled in humor. "I suppose not entirely normal," he said. "But seriously, how many of us are?"

Sara and Paul both laughed, but Sara's optimism faded as she thought back to the night she'd left Mark. Leaving the scene of an accident wouldn't look good for her. She took a deep breath. "When I left my husband, there was an incident."

"What sort of incident?"

Sara leaned closer to Paul, and he squeezed her hand. "Mark was abusive, and I was afraid he might really hurt me. When I tried to run away, he jumped out in front of the truck. I don't remember what happened, but I'm told I hit him and kept going."

Her hopes dimmed as the lawyer's expression darkened. "Was there a police report?"

Sara shook her head, wanting to look away, but determined to maintain eye contact. "No, my father talked to Mark and convinced him not to go to the police. He gave him money."

Craig pursed his lips. "So your father kept the incident in the family. Took care of his own."

"Yes, but that's when I ended up in the hospital again. I'm told I attacked a police officer who tried to help me."

"How long were you hospitalized?"

"About a month and a half." Sara reached up to rub her temples, caught herself and folded her hands in her lap. "My father was afraid I might not come out of it, so he set up the guardianship for my protection."

"And now?"

"He wants to keep it in effect in case I have a relapse. And I think he wants to put me on prescription medications. That's not what I want."

Craig stared at Sara, a look of intense concentration on his face. "Have you spoken to him about terminating the arrangement?"

Again, Sara shook her head. "Not really. My mother said she'd talk to him, but..." Sara's eyes welled up, and Paul jumped in.

"Sara's mom passed away last week," Paul explained. "So now there's no one in her corner. Her father will do as he sees fit."

"Why do you oppose medication?" Craig's eyes were on Sara, and she knew he disapproved. *Why does everyone assume I should be on drugs when they've never helped me at all?*

"When my father medicates me, it's as if I'm sleepwalking." She tried to emulate Cassie, to hang onto an appearance of poise. But her head bowed and her shoulders crept toward her ears. She gave up her pretense of courage and spoke softly. "At my mom's funeral, he gave me something. He didn't ask, or even warn me. I don't remember being there. I didn't get a chance to say goodbye."

Paul wrapped an arm protectively around Sara's shoulders. "Her father is sort of a control freak."

Craig said nothing, but he continued to watch Sara, and she tried not to fidget. At length he rose from his chair and paced, his footsteps punctuating his words. "You have the right to the least restrictive arrangement that meets the needs of your condition," he said. "On that point alone, it appears we can petition the courts to set aside, or at least modify the terms of the guardianship. Your competence should seal the deal."

Sara's hopes rose with his words and she looked excitedly at Paul. His answering grin buoyed her, and for a moment she dared to hope.

"That's the good news," Craig continued. "Your father is an expert in his field. The judge may agree to prolong the guardianship based on his recommendations. If that happens, we'll have a fight on our hands. It won't be cheap."

Sara stared at the table. *I don't have money.*

*-Trapped, trapped, trapped, trapped –*

"What do you suggest?" Her voice came out smaller than she'd hoped.

Craig resumed his pacing. The steady thud of his shoes against the hardwood floor echoed the rhythm of the chanting in her head. "The thing is, you come across as capable. But you've been deemed mentally disabled. That changes things." He paused a moment, eyes locked with Sara's. "I know this isn't what you want to hear, but your best bet is to get your father on your side. Talk to him. Convince him to recommend the arrangement be terminated. That's your least expensive option."

*He'll never agree.*

*-Fight back!*

*-Give up.*

*-Quitter, quitter, quitter, quitter-*

"Sara, look at me."

Sara hadn't realized she'd looked away, and she flinched at the lawyer's gruff tone. She looked up slowly. His expression was kind, but serious.

"What sort of relationship do you have with your father? Is he someone you can talk to?"

She shook her head. "He never has been. But he did ask me to go with him on a cruise, and I thought it might be a chance for us to get to know each other better."

"Are you going?" Craig's expression told her he thought the cruise was a good idea. In the silence that followed even the voices softened, as if holding a collective breath.

Paul cut in. "I'd rather she didn't. Her father makes me nervous."

Anxiety surged through her like electricity. She forced it down and tried to think logically. "I've never spent time alone with him," she said, biting the inside of her lip. "My mother was always with us, and they were always fighting. I guess when you come right down to it, I barely know him at all."

Paul's arm tightened across her shoulders, and his words came out tight and clipped. "I'm trying to be completely honest here, Sara. Your father gives me the creeps." His face was apologetic, but he didn't back down.

Sara laughed. She knew it was a nervous reaction to Paul's concerns, not a reflection of how she felt. "I know he's sort of odd, but he's always been there for me. I talked to Dr. Green about it yesterday, and she seemed to think I should go."

Craig caught her eye. "I would have to agree with your therapist. It would be a good idea for you to find a way to work things out with your father. We can always take action, but you'd be surprised how many problems can be solved if people simply talk to one another."

Sara looked from Paul's anxious face to Craig's confident gaze. She concentrated on her breathing and tried to relax. "He was going to make me go with him, but now he's letting me choose," she said, wondering why she felt as if she might cry. "But you never know with my father. He could change his mind again."

Craig gave her an encouraging smile. "If you decide not to go, call me. We can put something temporary in place to prevent him forcing you."

Paul's grin seemed misplaced as he stood to leave. "You see? It will all work out. You have options."

Weighed down with the probability of an expensive fight, Sara got up more slowly. "I don't know, Paul. I don't have much money, not unless I sell Harlee." Her voice trembled, but she stood straight and leveled her gaze. "That'll be my last resort."

Paul looked at her with a mixture of shock and sympathy. "My money's tied up, but I think I can get a loan. I'll help."

His offer warmed her from the inside, but she knew she couldn't accept, not when she had choices. "You're wonderful and generous," she said, "but I do have the means. I just have to decide which dream is more important. Harlee, or my freedom."

As they walked to the door Sara let herself consider the cruise. It was only for two weeks. How bad could it be? "Maybe I do have to get closer to my father," she mused.

"Maybe I can get him on my side."

Craig smiled as he ushered them outside. "Well, if you ask me, it's a very good sign that he's no longer insisting. Perhaps he's already coming around."

Sara nodded, wondering at the jumpiness of her heart. She looked at Paul, took in his unease. "I know you think I shouldn't go," she said, "but the lawyer thinks it's my best option, and we are paying for his opinion. Besides," she said as the door closed behind them, "that's what Dr. Green said, too."

Sara woke in Paul's arms, feeling safe and cherished. Her mother's death was still a crushing weight, but the feelings of loss and loneliness seemed less immediate, softened and distanced by the warmth that surrounded her.

She left him sleeping and ran to the barn. It felt empty with only two horses. Harlee's welcoming nicker and the dull thud of Frosty's hooves echoed in the vast space. Sara buried her face in Harlee's coat and let the scent of horses and pine shavings lift her up. With a spring in her step she fed both horses and cleaned stalls while they ate. Then she tacked up Harlee and rode out into the crisp fall air.

*Harlee is magic,* she told herself as she rode along wooded trails to her favorite galloping lane. *An hour on her back always helps me to see through the weeds.*

She coaxed the mare into a canter, thrilling to the sensation of frosty air whipping against her face. Harlee threw a buck before settling into a ground-covering gallop, and Sara followed the movement easily. They arced through the air, landing in a rush of feet and a burst of speed. She laughed at her horse's enthusiasm as her own spirits rose.

*She's my heart. For someone else, she'd be a means to an end. I can't let her go.*

*-You'll have to face him.*
*Maybe he'll listen.*
*-He'll give you drugs.*
Sara crouched lower in the saddle. *He said he wouldn't give me anything without asking me first.*
*-He lies.*
*Everyone lies.*
*-Not everyone.*
Sara brought Harlee back to a trot and followed the trail. On a whim, she tied her reins in a knot and rode with no hands, throwing her arms wide, soaring toward home.

*It's two weeks out of my life, two weeks to be support-ive and help him with his grief.* She sat deeper in the saddle and shifted her balance, asking for a walk. *Maybe we can reach an understanding. Maybe I really can get him on my side.* Harlee snorted, and Sara bent forward to bury her face in the mare's soft mane. *If not, I'll have to consider alternatives.*


Once Harlee was cool and dry, her autumn coat plush and soft from vigorous grooming, Sara hurried back to the house. Paul was up, his laptop humming on the kitchen table. The cruise itinerary lay open across his keyboard.

"I figured you'd decide to go," he said sheepishly, "and I thought maybe I could come along." He flipped through screens, and Sara leaned over his shoulder, hardly daring to breathe.

"Can you get a reservation this late? We leave tomor-row morning."

"I've put in a request." Paul's voice echoed Sara's doubt. "The cruise is booked, but there's always the possibility of a last-minute cancellation."

Sara slipped her arms around his neck and kissed him.

Then she went to the refrigerator and pulled out eggs and bacon. "Hungry?"

"You have to ask?"

She giggled as she cracked eggs into sizzling butter and laid strips of bacon on the griddle. Her mind wandered to her father's unexpected anger the last time Paul had arrived unannounced.

*Why was he so upset?*

*-Stole his time with you.*

*Shit.*

If Paul came along, Carl would spend the cruise sulking. The trip would be a waste of time. She tried to keep her tone casual as she spoke to the back of Paul's head. "To be honest, I'd rather you stayed here and looked after Harlee."

Paul spun around, a mixture of shock and concern spreading across his face. He covered his worry with a smile. "You'd rather I shoveled shit when I could be rubbing suntan lotion on your thighs?"

Sara blushed and turned back to the bacon. "I want you to come along, but I need you to stay. If this is going to work, I have to convince my father on my own. I have to stand on my own two feet like Dr. Green said."

Paul was at her side in an instant. He took her arm and turned her to face him. Sara stepped back in surprise.

"Please do one thing for me." Paul hesitated, gave Sara's shoulders a squeeze, then released her. "Please, the moment you get on board, go see the ship's doctor. Introduce yourself. Tell him about the voices. Tell him you're not on any medications. Make sure he hears you."

"Why would I do that?" Sara scrunched her face in confusion. "I spend my life trying to fit in. That would put me on his radar. He'd be watching me."

"Exactly." Paul's smile was small, but genuine. "Promise me. Please."

Sara tried to keep the tremor from her voice, but her words came out soft and thready. "You think he might drug me again?"

Paul let out a groan. "I don't know what to think. But he makes you nervous, and he makes me nervous, and I want you to have someone you can go to on that ship, someone you can trust." He looked as worried as he had the day she and Harlee nearly fell at the coffin. The memory still caused Sara's toes to bunch up.

"He's my dad," she said, turning her back on Paul and focusing her attention on the eggs. "He may be overprotective, and he may not agree with my choices, but he's always done what he thought was best."

"I know." Paul rested his hands on her shoulders, and his lips caressed her ear. "Humor me anyway. Please?"

Sara giggled as she flipped the bacon. Paul rarely asked her for anything, but he sure was persuasive when he did. She slid his eggs onto a plate, pressed two strips of bacon between paper towels and turned to face him. "If it'll make you feel better," she said, leaning against him and settling into his warmth, "I promise."

# Chapter Thirty-Eight

Sylvia looked peaceful lying among the trees and moss and fallen leaves. Her silence was a welcome change from the gaping terror when she'd run, bleating like an orphaned fawn, and found her legs unable to sustain her desperate attempt to survive. The last of Joanie's insulin had done its job more quickly than Carl had expected. A sign of rightness.

He took a moment to close her eyes before walking the short distance back to the rest stop at mile post 245. He paused to scan the dirt parking area, relieved to find it still empty save his car. Stretching his arms over his head, he leaned left, then right, until his back rewarded him with a resounding crack.

The first rays of sun struck Mount Katadin as he turned his back on the brightening horizon. It was a magnificent sight, *the most beautiful scenic rest area on I-95,* he'd told her when they'd jumped from the car and searched the murky horizon.

The view lifted Carl's heart almost as much as his deed lightened his concerns. The mountain really *was* purple, bathed in an unnatural but stunning yellow glow. He wouldn't mind spending eternity here, when it was his time.

He stripped off his jogging suit and vinyl gloves along with the knockoff muck boots from Walmart. Each item was then bagged separately, to be discarded methodically in rest area dumpsters along the route to Sara's house. Shivering in his underwear was unpleasant, and he quickly dressed in the insulated jeans and sweatshirt he'd stored in the trunk.

The cold made his fingers clumsy. Thin vinyl had been no help in that respect, and it took him two tries to tie his new laces. Swearing softly and stamping his feet against the chill, he checked his watch—still an hour ahead of schedule. The little detour north on I-95 had taken less time than he'd dared hope. Dumping Sylvia on the northbound side was a stroke of genius, since he was, of course, heading south.

She'd been easy to lure. *Sara decided not to go, and I have an extra ticket. I want to thank you for all your help.* Her faith in him was a given. He'd spent over a decade cultivating just the right mixture of gratitude, hope and dependence. Today represented the culmination of careful planning, nothing more.

Despite his certainty, he frowned as he closed and locked the trunk. *Damn that Sylvia.* She was easily molded, easily duped, yes. But even so, she'd gone a long way in undermining his assiduous planning. The silly girl hadn't realized he wanted her to fail, not until he spelled it out. Even then, a spark of rebellion had swelled into mutiny. And after all he'd done to ensure otherwise.

Ah well. His heartfelt apology and sincere offer to set things right had reassured her, had convinced her to make the trip with him. And he'd only done what had to be done. Collateral damage was unavoidable, a fact of life.

Preoccupied with his bundles, he stepped in mud and cursed the filth coating the soles of his new Nikes. He couldn't wait to rid himself of this upper corner of New England, to move on to sandy beaches and skies unsullied by pissing-down rain and swirling fog. With one last look at the distant mountain he bid a long overdue goodbye to the state of Maine, grateful he would never have to see it again.

Paul shivered, not from the cold. Sara hugged Harlee a full five minutes, four and a half minutes longer than she'd hugged him. Carl would arrive momentarily, and Paul hadn't said enough, hadn't done enough, to ensure she'd be okay.

"I love you."

Sara looked up. "Me too."

She seemed comfortable with her decision, confident and at peace. Paul's heart still beat way too quickly, and his shoulders ached right up into his head. But the choice was hers. He'd already expressed his concerns. To do more would make him no better than Carl.

He reminded himself he had nothing concrete, no obvious reason to distrust the man. There was just a nagging suspicion, as if something were askew, sideways.

"Make sure she and Frosty always have water and hay." Sara's voice floated across the aisle in endless repetition. "And use bug spray. The flies are gone, but we still have ticks."

"I will." Paul held up the seven pages of instructions she'd left him. "I'll brush her every day. I'll soak a bucket of alfalfa pellets morning and night, and I'll feed them to her while they're still warm."

Sara kissed Harlee's nose and stepped back, blinking. "It's only two weeks. I'll be back before you have time to miss me."

Paul cleared his throat. "I miss you already, so I assume you're talking to Harlee."

"I'm talking to both of you." She smiled, but sadness dulled her eyes.

"I programmed my cell and work numbers into your phone," Paul said. "Don't try my home phone. It's out of order. Check in once in a while, okay? Let me know how it's going."

Sara ran her hand across Harlee's forehead and traced her fingers down the mare's face to her sensitive muzzle. Then she closed the stall door and linked arms with Paul. "I'll be fine. You worry too much."

They walked together to the driveway and waited, hunched and shivering. Paul reached into his pocket, withdrew a tiny gold bag and slipped it into her hand.

"It's not much," he said, his words thick and slow, "but I saw this and thought of you."

When Sara turned to him, Paul was reminded of the balloon ride. She'd worked hard to face her fears, and she'd won. He could see she was struggling now, but unwilling to voice her concerns. Instead she reached into the bag and withdrew the tiny pendant he'd bought the previous day. The woven gold chain caught the rising sun and glowed warmly beside a delicate porcelain iris set in gold filigree. Her breathing paused, then resumed, ragged and slow.

"It wasn't expensive," he said, apology creeping into his tone, "but the iris is symbolic of courage and hope. And I thought maybe it would help."

She grabbed him and held on. He whispered into her hair. "You don't have to go. I can pay for the lawyer. You have options."

She buried her face in his sweater and shook her head. "I can't always let you rescue me."

Her face looked older when Carl pulled into the yard and parked beside them. But she heaved a sigh and straightened her shoulders, once again radiating strength. "Dr. Green was right. I do need to learn to stand on my own two feet." She reached up to kiss Paul's cheek before giving him a final hug. "This is my chance," she said. "This is where I take back everything that's mine."

Paul pulled her close, torn between admiration and unease. "Good luck." The words were inadequate, like everything else he'd said or done.

Carl waved and grinned as Sara stepped away and moved to join him. Paul lifted her suitcases into the trunk, then held out his hand to Carl. His eyes were drawn to a splotch of blood, clotted just above Carl's collar, at the fold of his chin.

"Cut yourself shaving?"

Carl's confident manner evaporated as he touched a fingertip to the blood. "I must have. Got up early, you know."

Paul rummaged through a pocket and produced an antiseptic wipe and a plastic sandwich bag stuffed with an assortment of adhesive bandages. "Better get something on it."

"I'm sure it's fine."

Sara appeared at Paul's elbow, grinning. "His pockets are like Mary Poppins' purse. He has everything in there."

Paul shot her a self-conscious smile. "More like Batman's tool belt." He let Carl wipe the spot clean, then handed him the bandage. "Safe trip," he said. "Take good care of her."

"Of course," Carl replied. "I always have."

Paul waved as the car rolled down the driveway. Sara waved back. Paul couldn't help but notice, Carl's smile was as phony as his own.

# Chapter Thirty-Nine

They boarded the ship late that afternoon. Carl's eyes were overly bright and a broad grin slashed his face. He bounded up the gangway, grabbed Sara and hugged her. She pushed away from him as he swung her like a rag doll, laughing out loud.

*How can he be so happy? Mom just died.*

*-It's the shock.*

*I've been through a shock, too, and I'm not being an ass.*

Counting her steps, glancing left and right, she followed him to their cabin. An efficient bathroom stood open to her left as they entered the short hallway, and there was a shallow closet to her right. The combination living and sleeping area had two twin beds, and opened onto a narrow veranda overlooking the sea. The steep drop beyond the rail made her toes hurt, but when she leaned over the railing, she found an identical stateroom immediately below theirs.

*We're stacked on top of each other, like cages.*

*-Trapped, trapped, trapped, trapped-*

*Shut up.*

As Sara put her things away she thought of Paul and chuckled. He would never approve of the haphazard way she stuffed her clothing into drawers. She spent only a few minutes, while he would have taken an hour to unpack and re-fold. Despite her speed, Carl paced endlessly from the doorway, past the bathroom, between the twin beds, then back to the door. He glanced at his watch and cleared his throat. She pretended not to notice.

Finally he stopped in front of her, close enough that his breath raised gooseflesh on her arms. "Sara, leave that for later. We don't want to be late for the tour."

"Hang on, Daddy. I just need to grab one thing." She reached deep into her suitcase and pulled out her mother's stuffed mouse. "I thought it would be nice if a part of Mom came along. She looked forward to this vacation."

Carl's grin vanished behind a glare of disapproval. But a moment later the smile resurfaced, tender as a painting. Sara felt his impatience growing behind his mask, and she tried to keep her wariness from showing as she hurried out the door.

Together they jogged down the hallway and up the companionway stairs. Sara carefully noted every emergency exit and memorized locations of life jackets and lifeboats. Just as the first tour began, they burst onto the deck, fell in step and followed.

Despite her misgivings, Sara had to admit the ship was amazing, a floating city. It would travel while they slept and arrive in a different port every morning. On board there were theaters and restaurants, a ballroom, a heated pool, and best of all, a well-equipped workout area.

She ran her fingers over the treadmills, and some of her tension drained away. Finally she'd found something familiar, something normal. She studied the control panel. The belts went up to ten miles per hour. What would it be like to run while the deck rolled beneath her feet?

When the tour ended it was time to dress for the Welcome Aboard Dinner. Carl donned a suit and tie while Sara wrapped herself in a black evening gown. She'd found the elegant dress at a thrift shop, and it was meant to be tea-length. On her it reached the floor, and she had to wear her highest heels to keep from tripping.

"How do I look?" She twirled before the full-length

mirror, feeling pretty and exotic in the warm Florida air. "It's like summer here. I could get used to this."

"Could you?" Carl's voice was plaintive, and Sara was thrown by the wistful note. "I've spent quite a bit of time at medical conferences in Mexico. Sometimes I think about moving there." His voice trailed off.

"But you've lived your whole life in Lubec. Why would you leave?"

His answering shrug seemed lonely, and his eyes were puffy and red. Sara's heart pulled toward him as he spoke. "Too many memories, I guess. It would be good to start fresh . . . somewhere else."

It wasn't often her father showed any real emotion, and Sara felt closer as she looped her arm through his. He towered over her, his arm muscular, his hand cold against hers. From somewhere deep inside a warning hissed.

*Why am I always so nervous around him?*
*-He's a fake.*
*-Fucking idiot!*
*That's enough!*

She threw a mental scowl at the voices and did her best to shut out their noise. Her father's long stride was difficult to match in her dress shoes. A life with horses rarely required her to wear heels, and she worked hard to keep up.

At the entrance to the formal dining room they were greeted by a line of ship personnel. As they moved from handshake to handshake, Sara was reminded of her mother's funeral. She tried to wall off the weight of sorrow and to pay attention as her father introduced her to the Captain and crew. His repeated introduction, "I'm Dr. Carl Morgan, and this is Sara," sounded rehearsed, as if he'd practiced it in front of a mirror. The inflection never changed as they moved down the line.

Finally they reached the end, and Sara shook hands with an older man. He was moderately overweight and balding with an agreeable expression that spoke of cleverness and wit. Sara was drawn to him even before he introduced himself as the ship's doctor, Gavin McNeel.

She pulled him off to the side, remembering Paul's advice, but already wavering. Should she tell him about her illness? The plan made sense, but now she wondered if Paul might have been a bit melodramatic. Why become the center of unwanted attention?

But what if she had an episode? Or what if her father felt the need to sedate her again? Perhaps the ship doctor should be forewarned; maybe he could help. She made her decision, organized her thoughts, and spoke in a rush.

"I'm Sara Morgan, and I'm schizophrenic. I wondered if we could keep in touch while I'm here."

He flashed a cordial smile and tipped his head. "Stop by my office any time. If I'm not there, the nurse will page me."

Carl swooped in, nudged Sara aside and offered his hand to Dr. McNeel. Uncertainty flashed across the doctor's face as Carl repeated his introduction. Dr. McNeel looked from Sara to Carl and back to Sara.

"It was lovely meeting you and your husband, Sara. Like I said, come see me any time."

Sara laughed and opened her mouth to correct him, but Carl interrupted. "We enjoyed meeting you as well. Thank you for your kind offer. If we need your services, you'll be the first to know."

"Daddy! He thinks I'm your wife." Sara pulled her father back toward the line, but Dr. McNeel was already talking to someone else. Bewildered, she let Carl steer her away. "What was that all about?"

"Sorry, I should have said something." Carl reached over and tousled her hair. "I didn't want to embarrass the man. What's the harm?"

Dinner and dancing lasted well into the night, but despite her exhaustion, Sara slept lightly. Every time she drifted off, she came suddenly awake, holding her breath. The voices screamed to be heard above the roaring in her ears and she strained to sort the warnings from the endless babble.

*-Nowhere to run.*

*-Caged, caged, caged, caged -*

*Can't you all please shut up?*

She almost said it aloud. But even with eyes wide open, the feeling was there, creepy, as if someone were watching. She could sense eyes leering, could feel unwelcome kisses trailing across her bare shoulders while rough hands pulled the covers down.

*Mark. That dream again.*

*-Run!*

Her heart raced. She focused on her breathing, took charge of the frantic rhythm and asked it to slow.

*All of that happened a long time ago. It's over.*

*-It's not.*

*I'm fine.*

*-You're not.*

Sara pushed the voices to the farthest corners of her mind and willed them silent. They chanted louder. She repeated her well-rehearsed relaxation ritual over and over, molded her head to her pillow and forced her eyes shut. Still the voices screamed. She pulled the covers over her shoulders and tucked them under her chin. A moment later she pulled the blankets over her head.

*I'll be home in thirteen days.*

*-Too late.*

Her father seemed to be asleep, his breath slow and deep. She squeezed her eyelids tighter and tried to follow his example, but it was no use. She lay awake, gripped by an unreasonable sense of foreboding. Tired and cranky, she crept from the bed just as the sky warmed to pink.

Shorts and a tank top lay on the floor where she'd left them. She pulled them on, picked up her discarded running shoes and ducked through the door. Once outside, she pulled on her sneakers and laced them up.

She took the stairs two at a time. Intent on her destination, she nearly ran into a complete stranger, a man about her age who appeared startled at the sight of her. Averting her eyes and mumbling an apology, she bounded up four flights to the top deck where the treadmills stood empty and waiting. The sea was calm, the deck steady beneath her feet. It was a perfect time for a run. She could go fast if she wanted to. Fast sounded good.

Allowing her body time to wake up and prepare, Sara started with an easy jog. Carl's odd behavior puzzled her while thoughts of her mother's death drove her on. She pushed the treadmill to eight miles per hour, wondering if it might be possible to outdistance the confusion and pain.

The voices chanted a warning. She ran faster, goading them as they taunted her.

*Try to keep up.*

They screamed at her. She ignored them.

*Eat my dust.*

Heart racing, she kicked the treadmill to ten miles per hour, pushing hard. A wind came up, and the deck heaved beneath her feet. She flew, running faster and faster toward freedom, determined to leave the voices behind. At last, they fell silent, drowned by the whirring of the treadmill and an endless high-pitched wailing in her head.

She ran in slow motion now. The walls shimmered and moved like wraiths as lightning bursts sparkled in her eyes. She was alone. She had won. The only voice she heard was her own.

For a moment she basked in the silence. Then everything went black.


Sara became aware of voices, and she moaned her frustration. But gradually she realized the words came from outside her head, through her ears, as they should. Cautiously, she opened one eye and squinted at the light. A boyish face with bright blue eyes surrounded by unruly brown hair stared back at her.

"Welcome back, speed demon." He appeared far too happy for the circumstances, grinning like Christmas morning as he said, "Have you achieved your exercise goals for the day?"

Sara was still dazed, but her cheek stung and throbbed. She reached up and felt something warm and sticky.

"Not to worry. You scraped your face on the belt when you passed out." He laughed and held up a short cable with a red plastic clip. "You know, you're supposed to attach this to yourself so the treadmill stops automatically if you fall."

"How bad does it look?" She didn't care, but it seemed polite to say something.

His smile widened. "I was right beside you, and I shut the belt off as quickly as I could. I don't think you'll have a scar, but it'll be butt ugly for a week."

Taken aback, Sara stared at his eyes. They were as blue as her own. "Who are you?" she said, her voice still wobbly.

"I'm Jonah," he replied. "Are you, by any chance, Sara?"

# Chapter Forty

"How do you know my name?" Still lightheaded, Sara was unsure if she should trust her ears.

Jonah's grin hadn't faded, but now it shone with sympathy as well as humor. "I'm sorry," he said. "You're hurt, and all I've done is laugh at you. Can you stand?" He glanced toward the stairway. "There's something I'd like to show you, that is, if you have a few minutes." He held out his hand, but it was too late. A swarm of uniformed ship personnel appeared out of nowhere, shepherded by Dr. McNeel.

"Oh, shit. I've made an ass of myself." Sara tried to rise, but Jonah placed his hand on her shoulder. She flinched at his touch, and he quickly withdrew.

"Someone must have called for help when you fell." He glanced at Sara's face and scrunched his nose. "You do look a bit like an assault victim. Better let them check you out."

Sara opened her mouth to protest, but a booming voice cut her off.

"What happened here?" The words sounded more like a command than a question, and Sara shuddered as she peeked in the doctor's direction.

"I guess I overdid it." She spoke cautiously, glancing from Jonah to the doctor to the group of gathering onlookers. "I was running too fast for too long. I have a little bitty heart murmur." She looked at the door, twenty-three steps away. "Once in a while, I faint."

*I need to sound like I'm in control.*

*-Idiot! Running yourself unconscious.*

*-Stupid, stupid, stupid, stupid-*

Dr. McNeel hurried forward, slapped a blood pressure cuff on her arm and pressed a stethoscope against her chest. "Have you had an ultrasound?"

"About a year ago. They said it was nothing to worry about." Sara shrugged and tried to emulate Cassie's dismissive air. "It's not a problem as long as I'm not a complete idiot about it." She let her hair hide her face from the crowd, wishing she could vanish. When she glanced up at Dr. McNeel, he looked more approachable, his face hinting at the warmth she'd seen the previous evening.

"I'd like to take you to my office for observation, if that's okay with you." Sara shook her head, but the doctor pressed.

"It's just a precaution. I'm covering my butt and the cruise line's butt all at the same time." He glanced behind him before leaning close and speaking in a whisper. "And I'd like to continue our discussion from last night. Your husband seemed to prefer I not involve myself."

"He's not my husband," she whispered. "He's my father." Sara watched the doctor's face, and was relieved to see a flash of surprise and concern. "My mom passed away recently," she said as softly as she could, "and he's been keeping me a little too close, as if he's afraid I might fall apart."

Dr. McNeel hushed her with a look. "Let's get you taken care of. We'll talk in private." His attitude was all business as he supervised Sara's transfer to a gurney. Gesturing to Jonah, he asked, "Do you want your friend to come along?"

"My what?"

Jonah was still there, hovering. "I'll be right behind you," he answered for her. Without another word, he followed the procession to the lower deck and the cramped medical facility below. Once there, Sara was transferred to a hospital bed. Jonah waited outside while Dr. McNeel cleaned the scrape and applied a bandage. When he finished, the doctor closed the door and pulled up a chair.

"Returning to our discussion, is there a reason your father should be concerned about you?"

Sara made sure to look him in the eye when she answered. "I hear voices. I've had two psychotic breaks, one six years ago and one almost a year ago. Other than those two instances, I've been stable."

"Except for the voices."

It was a statement, but Sara nodded in reply. "Yes, but I can cope. I know what's real and what isn't."

"And how can I be of help to you while you're on board?"

Sara took a deep breath and swallowed before speaking in a matter-of-fact tone. "My father is a psychiatrist. He favors medication, and he sometimes gives me drugs without asking." Dr. McNeel's face darkened as Sara spoke, but he gestured for her to continue.

"Meds have never worked for me. They make me worse." Sara knew she was blotchy-faced with embarrassment, but the doctor listened to her with interest and concern. He took a moment to enter information into a computer on a desk beside him, then turned the screen away from her.

"I'd like you to check in with me twice daily," he said, his insistent tone backed by the rigid set of his jaw. "And I'll speak to your father and make it clear that any medical decisions will be made by me for as long as you're on this cruise."

Relief poured through her, leaving Sara giddy with a sense of freedom. "I can't thank you enough," she said, trying to put all her emotion into words. "My father means well, but since my mom passed away, I think he's having trouble dealing with it all."

Dr. McNeel rose from his chair. "I'll help in any way I can. If I have you under observation, he'll be unlikely to medicate you." He reached for the door. "I'll let your friend in now. He seems anxious to see you."

"He's not my friend," Sara said, bewildered. "I just met him."

"Would you prefer he not come in?"

"No, that's okay. I want to thank him for helping me."

The doctor hesitated before opening the hallway door. "I'll give you a few minutes. If you need anything, just call."

Jonah entered quietly. His face was far less buoyant than it had been earlier. Eyes downcast, he stood beside her. "I heard what you said about losing your mom. I'm sorry. I know how hard that is."

Sara nodded as the ever-present lump rose in her throat. "Thank you."

"I know this isn't the best time," he said, "but can we talk? I mean, are you up for it?" His confidence seemed to abandon him, and he looked less and less comfortable. "I can come back later."

"Do I know you?" she said. "You do seem familiar."

"We've never met," Jonah replied. "But I know *of* you."

He was interrupted by a commotion in the hallway, and a moment later Carl burst into the room. His eyes were wild as he shouted, "Are you okay?"

"I'm fine, Daddy." Sara turned away to hide the bandage, but it was too late. Carl's shocked expression told her he'd seen her face. She braced herself for a tirade of fatherly concern. Instead, she saw only disappointment.

His voice was cold and flat, and he leaned close as he spoke. "That's not very attractive, Sara. You need to be more careful." His tone hurt worse than the words, and Sara blinked in surprise.

Jonah's voice came from behind him. "A woman as

beautiful as Sara can get away with a few flaws. It would take a lot more than a scrape to make her unattractive."

Carl took a step back, eyes narrowed to a squint. "Who the hell are you?" he demanded. "And how do you know Sara?"

Sara quickly interceded. "This is Jonah, Daddy. He helped me when I fell. He's been nothing but kind." She fixed Carl with an icy stare of her own.

*-He's acting like a child.*

*-Ass, ass, ass, ass, ass-*

"Daddy, I think you owe Jonah an apology."

For a moment Carl's eyes filled with resentment. But conflicting emotions crossed his face in quick succession until finally his smile returned. "I guess I owe everyone an apology," he said in a conciliatory tone. "It's just that I was so worried when I heard Sara had been hurt. I'm afraid I lost it." He looked at Jonah with a stiff-lipped expression of contrition. "I'm sorry for my behavior, Jonah. It's very nice to meet you."

"Not a problem." Jonah glanced at Sara. "I'll catch up with you later." He left quickly, and Sara watched him, perplexed.

"Do you know him?" she asked her father. "He thinks he knows me."

"Oldest pickup line in the book," Carl said, frowning at the doorway. "Watch out for him."

*He seemed nice.*

*-Stupid, stupid, stupid, stupid-*

Dr. McNeel returned and held out his hand. "Ah, Dr. Morgan, we need to talk."


The incident with the treadmill ruined everything.

The first evening aboard had been heaven, a hurdle

cleared, a milestone met. At the Welcome Aboard Dance, Carl had reveled in the feel of Sara draped across his arm, basked in the envy of his fellow passengers. It had been a perfect moment in his life, a satisfying foretaste of things to come.

But now, the dream evaporated. The damn doctor demanded that he see Sara twice a day! What was he thinking? Sara's injury was unattractive, yes, but otherwise minor. There was no need to monitor her so closely.

He couldn't risk medicating the girl; the doctor would know. She was, once again, just beyond his reach. His best option was to bide his time, pretend to enjoy the cruise, play the part of doting parent, even though the absurdity of the role caused him to twitch.

Even his harmless fantasy was gone. In the days following the accident, everyone crowded around Sara asking what happened to her face. And she told them, which he supposed was the right thing to do. But then she introduced him, saying, "This is my *father*, Dr. Carl Morgan."

She had to know it wasn't true. If only she'd give in, admit she wanted him every bit as much as he wanted her. Instead she'd avoided him, ruined his day at the floating markets of Aruba, taken away the thrill of crossing the Panama Canal. The Pacific ports would be no better. Each would offer its own version of rip-offs and dysentery while the little whore paraded about in her low-rise shorts and halter tops, scanning the crowds for that boy toy she'd met when she fell. Keeping those two apart had eaten up far too much time.

She should know better, almost certainly did know better. But she'd always been coy, forever pretending to think of him as her father and nothing more. Her childish charade was cute when she was small, but the ongoing pretense was tiresome.

Fine. He could play along with her games. This morning, for example, he'd pretended to discuss her guardianship. He'd dangled her freedom in front of her and allowed her to hope while she nibbled at tamales and gazed over Puerto Caldera. It was enough to know she wasn't fooling him, probably not fooling anyone else either.

The years of existing in that rundown little house at the ass end of Maine were finally over. Socking his money away, never allowing himself or Joanie a single extravagance; it had been difficult but worth the effort. He briefly wondered how Sara would like the villa he'd purchased, but it didn't matter. In rural Mexico she wouldn't have a say in her accommodations, not when he had money with which to bribe and enough chemical persuasion to ensure her willing compliance.

Once he had her safely off the ship, beyond the reach of that damn nosy doctor, she'd have no one.

Giggling, he withdrew her cell phone from his pocket and flicked it into the sea. She was a clever girl, adept at surrounding herself with protectors. But they wouldn't come ashore with her in Tijuana, and one thing was certain. Sara would not be going home.

Five days had passed since Sara's last phone call, and Paul's concern transitioned to worry. He'd left messages and sent email, but she hadn't replied. He calmed himself with the knowledge that the cruise was nearly over, and in just two days she'd be home.

Today he'd left work early, and now he soaked warmth from the fading rays of sun as he curried dust from Harlee's coat. The mare pinned her ears and gave Paul a nip as he ran a brush under her belly. "Too hard?" he asked. "Or is it the wrong brush?"

Harlee flicked an ear in his direction, then drew her nostrils back in a snort. Paul laughed and scratched her withers with his fingernails. She stretched forward and closed her eyes.

"Not too spoiled, are you?" Paul handed the horse a peppermint and started putting the brushes away when a truck and horse trailer drove into the yard. A tall, dark-haired man got out and walked toward them. The swagger in his step accentuated the uncompromising angle of his jaw.

"Can I help you?" Paul couldn't imagine who would be here with a trailer. Perhaps he was lost? More likely it was a friend of Janet and Marty, someone who didn't realize they were spending the month in Vermont. The man came to a stop and looked past him at Harlee. A smile plucked at his lips.

"I'm Mark Dalton," he said. He looked Paul up and down with an expression that said he'd been evaluated and found wanting. "I'm here to pick up my horse."

# Chapter Forty-One

"What did you say your name was?" Warning bells sounded in Paul's head. "Are you Sara's ex? Are you *that* Mark?"

Paul took in the size and power of the man facing him. He was of average height, but lean and hard-muscled with a sullen twist to his mouth. Next to Sara, the man was a giant. Paul rarely thought of hitting anyone, but if this were Sara's Mark...

Mark swore and dropped his eyes before he answered. "Yes, I'm *that* Mark. And yes, I was an ass." He kicked the dirt at his feet. "I'm a fucking idiot when I'm drunk, and back then, I was drunk a lot."

Paul relaxed as the other man acted in a reasonable manner. Sara's ex sounded as if he might be sorry for the way he'd treated her. But a moment later Mark's gaze latched onto Harlee, and his expression looked a lot like pride.

Paul closed his fist around the lead rope. "So what do you mean, your horse? Harlee belongs to Sara."

Mark snickered, and the swagger returned to his eyes. "Yes, I let Sara have her in the divorce settlement. But Carl controls Sara's assets, and he called last night and said I could come and get her."

"Why would he do that?"

"We had a deal." Mark's grin showed an excess of teeth. "Sara got the mare until she and her father moved to Mexico. Now ownership reverts back to me."

"What?" Paul planted himself between Mark and Harlee. "They're not moving. They're just on vacation."

Mark reached past him for Harlee's halter. "That's not what Carl said and none of my business. I'm just here for my horse."

Paul spun Harlee toward the barn, letting the mare's rump swing into Mark's face. "Look, I don't know what's going on here, but this is Sara's horse, and I'm responsible for her. Do you have proof of ownership? A signed bill of sale?"

Mark laid a hand on Harlee's rump and worked his way toward her head. "No, we're going to pass papers by mail once Carl and Sara are settled. Why?"

Paul placed his feet shoulder-width apart. "No proof, no horse."

Mark hesitated. Paul gripped Harlee's lead rope with one hand while the other closed around his cell phone. "Do I need to call the police?"

Mark stared a moment longer, then rolled his eyes and scowled. "What are you, her new boyfriend?" He sneered at Paul's nod of assent. "Take some friendly advice from someone who's been in your shoes. The money isn't worth it."

"What are you talking about?"

"What do you think I'm talking about?" Mark spat on the ground. "You'll want to help her, but Carl will never let her go. How much is he paying you, anyway?"

"Paying me? He's not paying me."

A trace of doubt flickered in Mark's eyes. "What's in it for you, then? We both know it's not the sex."

The words turned Paul's stomach. "Carl paid you to do what, exactly?"

"Look after her, keep her quiet." He caught Paul's eye and smirked. "Don't play stupid."

It was all Paul could do to keep his fists at his side. "What the hell is wrong with you? How could you do that to her?" Fury pushed aside his better judgment, and he advanced on the taller man.

"Hey, take it easy." Mark held his palms out in front of him as if trying to calm an unruly horse. "Whatever you might think, she was better off with me than she was with him."

Paul locked his arms to his sides, but his fingernails bit into his palms. The man was an ass. It was hard not to smack the smirk off his face, even though he doubted he'd succeed.

"But you were horrible to her." Paul shouted louder than he'd meant to. "You choked her! She still has nightmares."

Mark shook his head. "I did things I'm not proud of, but she came with those nightmares, and they don't have a damn thing to do with me." Some of the smugness left his face, and he flinched as he said, "Something bad happened to that girl. If you ask me it's something Carl would do almost anything to keep secret."

Paul's knees went weak. He knew Sara's nightmares had started as a child, but what about the rest? Cassie had never trusted Carl. He'd paid her to watch Sara in college, and this prick had been hired, too?

"Why didn't you tell her what her father did? Why didn't you warn her?"

"I *tried!*" The remorse on Mark's face was instantly covered by belligerence. "Sara passed out and crashed the truck. I called Carl, and he came right over and got her. Next thing I knew she was in the loony bin and Carl slapped me with a restraining order."

"What? Didn't Sara hit you with the truck?"

"Are you shittin' me?" Mark looked at Paul as if he'd sprouted wings. "Sara can't even swat a mosquito. That's probably why she crashed, turning herself inside-out in order to miss me."

Paul's mouth fell open. "So Carl didn't pay you not to go to the police?"

"Pay me? Fuck, no. You're as gullible as she is." He laughed, but it was a humorless sound that turned Paul's stomach. "Carl threatened me with a lot worse than a restraining order if I didn't stay out of Sara's life. All the way out."

*What the hell is going on?* Paul fixed Mark with an icy glare. "Leave. Now. Don't come near this horse without a signed bill of sale." Mark hesitated. Too angry to give in to Mark's size and strength, Paul flipped open his phone and scrolled to his pre-programmed 9-1-1. The man was a bully, but would he risk assaulting someone who wasn't afraid to press charges? "I said NOW!"

"ALL RIGHT!" Mark slouched back toward his truck, shouting over his shoulder. "I'm coming back with the papers. Make sure Harlee is here when I do."

Paul watched until the truck turned onto the main road, his mind galloping to put the pieces together. He closed his eyes and calmed himself. In order to make sense of Mark's claims, he needed to focus, to prioritize, to organize one thing at a time. He cleared the phone, dialed, and crossed his fingers.

"Janet!" He blew out a grateful sigh. "I'm glad you're there. I need a favor."

Sara hardly noticed the passage of time. Her father had been distant since she'd hurt her face. A blessing, she supposed, though his disapproval was clear. He still kept her close when they went ashore, insisting the various ports were no place for a young woman to walk about unescorted. But on the ship, she could often find a few minutes to herself. The cut was almost healed, barely visible, and she wondered if she ought to scrape the other cheek.

The voices had been more subdued since she ran them to the ground, and despite the outcome she was proud. Like her mother, she'd never been one to take a risk. It was silly, but she felt a sense of accomplishment. She let the sea breeze cool her face, took in the brilliant blue of the Pacific Ocean, and pretended she was looking out over the Bay of Fundy, Paul by her side.

"Hey."

Sara jumped and spun around to find Jonah striding toward her. "Hello," was all she could think to say.

*-Stalker, stalker, stalker, stalker –*

*Shut up!*

"Look," she said, irritation crowding her usual politeness, "could you drop the mystery and tell me who you are?"

Jonah reached for her hand, and she snatched it away and folded her arms. He shrugged. "I'd rather show you. Got a few minutes?"

"What do you want to show me?" Sara glanced along the deck until she spotted the white uniform of a crew member. His nearness reassured her.

"I've been trying to get you alone ever since we met." Jonah glanced behind him. "Come with me before your father sees us together."

Jonah's words came with a pang of guilt, and Sara looked anxiously for a sign of Carl. She'd managed to lose him, but she often spotted him watching from a distance. "Come with you where?"

"This way." Jonah stepped toward the companionway, and she started to follow.

"Where are we going?"

"My cabin."

Sara ground to a stop. "I don't think so."

Jonah laughed. "You don't need to come inside. Just wait in the hallway. I have something you need to see."

His sincere manner told her she was probably safe with him, but she knew better than to trust her instincts; they'd betrayed her so many times before. She hesitated a moment longer, reminding herself that the corridors were well lit and rarely empty.

*Oh, why not?*

*-Stalker, stalker, stalker, stalker-*

With a nervous sigh, she followed him down two flights of stairs to the cabins below. Jonah's face lost its cheer as he let himself through his door and pulled a duffel bag from the closet. Sara watched from the doorway as his shoulders rose and fell with a calming breath. He extracted a photo album and ran a hand over the cover. "Are you ready?"

"Uh-huh." Her stomach pinched. She leaned into the door frame and swallowed, wondering why her throat had gone dry.

Jonah held out a photograph, dog-eared and cracked from age and frequent handling. Sara let out a cry when she saw her mother's face, young and beautiful. A man stood beside her, his hand draped carelessly over her shoulder, smile wide, eyes clear blue.

"My father," Jonah said softly.

Sara cradled the photograph. She'd never seen her mother so blissfully happy. "Your father and my mother, they were friends?"

"More than friends." He placed the leather-bound photo album into her hands. "See for yourself."

She opened the album, turning each page as if it were made of ash, ready to crumble if she so much as breathed. It was filled with pictures, not of her mother, but of her.

"Look at this one." Jonah reached past her hands and turned to the front page, where Joanie sat cradling a newborn baby. The caption said, "Your daughter, Sara."

She snapped the album shut and stood rigid, staring at the monogrammed cover. Her fingers traced the letters, "S. A. R."

*The first three letters of my name.*

"What's your father's name?"

"Sam Randall."

*The letter.*

Lightheaded, Sara let herself slide down the wall until she sat on the floor. Guilt washed over her as she wrapped her head around Jonah's suspicions and realized she hoped he might be right. She didn't look up as she spoke. "You think Carl isn't my father."

"What do you think?"

*-The secret!*

*But this would make my father furious, wouldn't it? The secret brought them together.*

*-He lies.*

"I don't know what to think. It's a lot to take in all at once."

At first Jonah seemed at a loss for words. But he settled onto the carpet beside her, just far enough away that not even his clothing touched her. "My folks were killed in an accident two years ago," he said. "That's when I first found the pictures." He rubbed at his eyes for a moment before he continued.

"The letters kept coming, every two or three months. They were always postmarked from somewhere in Maine, but never with a return address." Jonah glanced sideways and caught Sara's eye. "Six months ago your mother sent a letter asking my father to meet her on this cruise." His lopsided smile carried a trace of apology. "I had no way to reach her, didn't even know her last name. So I came in his place. I couldn't find her, but I recognized you."

Sara shivered in memory. "I think I mailed that letter. Was it postmarked Bangor?"

Jonah nodded. "Want to know more?"

"I'm not sure I can take more."

Jonah held out his hand, and Sara nodded her approval. His fingers laced with hers, soft and earnest as his voice. "When I went away to school, my father told me about his college sweetheart. He said she was pretty and sweet with a huge smile and the most amazing green eyes. They were crazy about each other, but they broke up over something silly, a misunderstanding. He said he never got over her."

Sara smiled, imagining her mother as a young woman. "We always think of our parents as old. It's weird knowing they were dumb kids."

Jonah chuckled. "My dad said they got together a few years later when they ran into each other at a conference. After that he never saw her again." He cleared his throat several times before he spoke again, his voice husky. "Her name was Joan. I'm named after her."

A shiver crawled up Sara's spine as the pieces fell into place. "My mom was a photojournalist. She traveled a lot before I was born."

Jonah looked away. "That would fit." He peeked at her again and Sara saw herself reflected in his eyes.

Buoyed by a sudden sense of kinship, she forced a smile. "Wanna find out? I mean, when we get to San Diego, do you want to get tested? See if we really are related?"

Jonah hunched his shoulders in an exaggerated shudder. "I don't know. The thought of having a sister is…"

"What?"

He gave her sneaker a little shove and laughed when she pushed him back. "I don't have any family left. Except maybe you."

"Oh, shit."

"What's wrong?" Jonah's hand was on her shoulder, warm, like Paul's.

"Please don't tell Carl. He just lost his wife and I don't want him to feel like he's losing his daughter."

"Of course," Jonah reassured her. "Whatever you want. For all we know, this could be a huge mistake. I might be nothing to you." He frowned for a moment, but brightened immediately. "If that's the case, I'd love to get to know you anyway, ask you out."

"Yuck!" Sara laughed then, a real honest laugh. It came out of nowhere, and it surprised and embarrassed her. "Don't make me laugh," she said, ducking her head. "My mom just died. I'm not supposed to be laughing."

"Not supposed to be laughing? Why ever not?" Jonah smiled broadly and squeezed her hand. "You can't put off happiness until everything's perfect. You'd never laugh again."

"I suppose." Sara wondered at the feeling of belonging, wished she could stay hidden in the doorway until they reached California. But it was almost time for dinner, and Carl would be waiting. Reluctantly, she got to her feet.

"I need to get back. My fath . . . Carl. He'll be angry if I'm late."

"Can we get together after dinner?" Jonah's expression was hopeful, and Sara realized how lonely he must be.

"I should spend some time with Carl. But do you want to meet up once he's in bed? I'll be up most of the night anyway." She stepped out into the open hallway, feeling suddenly exposed in the stark glow of the overhead fluorescents.

Jonah stood and moved into the light. "It's a date," he said, his words echoing along the passage. "Can I hug you goodbye?"

She nodded. He held her briefly, released her immediately, but she still stiffened. He stepped back, seeming to understand her need for space. "I'll wait for you on the deck below yours so Carl won't see me. Does that work?"

She wasn't sure what to say. "I really do have to go. Carl is . . . he's sort of strict." She turned and hurried toward the stairs, calling over her shoulder, "Once he's asleep, I'll come and find you. But it might be late."

"I'll be there."

Jonah's words felt like a promise, warm and safe. She bounded up the stairs, so wrapped up in her discovery that at first she didn't notice the sudden chill. Rubbing goose bumps from her arms, she paused to search the corners where shadows had begun to fall. She saw nothing, but the chill persisted. And though she knew her fears were silly, she couldn't shake the feeling that someone was watching.

# Chapter Forty-Two

Sara hummed to herself as she bounded up the companionway, a tentative smile easing its way to her lips. Feeling defiant and daring she took the long way back, stealing a few moments to stroll along the deck and let the sea air cool the flush of optimism. Her hand slid along the rail, and the nubby texture of paint tingled against her palm. Its sensation was exhilarating, and she laughed into the waves, wishing she hadn't lost her cell phone so she could share her news with Paul.

*Can this be real?*

*-Don't get your hopes up.*

*Shut up. You sound like Carl.*

As she crossed the final yards to her father's state room she slowed to a shuffle. Her happiness slunk away, replaced by a hollow sense of longing.

*I'm not being fair, hoping he's not my father. And I shouldn't keep secrets from him, like my mother.*

*-Cheating slut!*

*She made a mistake.*

*-Whore!*

The door flew open as Sara reached for her key card. Carl's icy glare snuffed out the last of her light.

"Where the hell have you been?" A scowl deepened his customary frown. His fingertip tapped his watch. "You'll make us late for dinner."

Ducking past him, Sara grabbed a skirt from the closet and closed herself in the bathroom. Carl was still her guardian and the only father she'd ever known. She wanted, *needed* him on her side. Her tone was important. It must be bouncy.

"Don't worry, Daddy. We'll make it in plenty of time." She slipped out of her shorts and into the filmy skirt, let her hair loose from its ponytail and fluffed it around her shoulders. Pushing the door open, she gave Carl her prettiest smile and was relieved to see a barely perceptible softening of his perpetual glower.

"Your face looks better." He touched her cheek, letting his fingers trace the pale depression where the cut had been. "I can't even see it with your hair down."

"It was just a scrape, Daddy. I don't know why you made such a big deal out of it." Sara heard the censure in her voice and scolded herself.

*I sound like my mother.*

*-Bastard daughter of a lying whore! You are nothing.*

Sara reached for Carl's arm, and he pulled her into a hug. A wave of anxiety ripped through her, and she pushed away, heart pounding. With a forced smile of apology she took his hand and allowed him to lead her toward the dining hall. Questions swam in her head.

*Why is he always so short with me? Why the hostility toward Paul? None of it makes sense.*

Still thinking of Paul, she caught a glimpse of Carl's cell phone, just visible in his shirt pocket. She smiled up at him, keeping her voice bright. "Hey, Dad, can I borrow your phone? I still can't find mine, and I haven't checked on Harlee for days." She knew better than to mention Paul. His name would only light Carl's fuse.

"There's no signal here, and don't even think about using the cabin phone. It's way too expensive. You can call from Mexico tomorrow."

Disappointed, Sara searched for alternatives. Paul

would be worried by now. But she also longed to hear his voice, to tell him about Jonah and to let him know everything was okay.

"What about the Internet Café? Can I stop and send an email?"

Carl's jaw tightened; his eyes stared straight ahead as he walked briskly toward the dining hall. "Not now. There might be time after dinner."

"After dinner, it is," she said. But as they walked past the rows of computers behind a glass window, a plan formed in her mind.

The Internet Café was right next to the ladies' room.


Harlee and Frosty munched hay as Paul hauled them up Route 89 toward the Vermont inn. Brett Foster had sent a working student to ready the barn, and Janet had loaned Frosty as company for Harlee. Paul didn't know what to think about Mark's visit, but it seemed prudent to hide the mare until her ownership was settled.

He drove Sara's truck and trailer with one hand. The other pressed his cell phone to his ear. The lawyer wasn't making sense. Nothing was making sense.

"What do you mean you can't find Dr. Green?" Paul asked, incredulous. "I thought you went to her office today."

There was a heavy sigh, and Craig Driscoll repeated himself. "I did. The office belongs to a massage therapist. She said Sylvia sublets the space on Wednesdays. The rest of the time she lives in Machias, Maine."

"That's insane," Paul said. "Is she driving all the way to Amherst every week just to see Sara?"

"It would seem so. And that's not all."

"What?" Paul's head ached, pounding in rhythm with

his heart. What more could there be?

"Sylvia Green is not licensed to perform psychotherapy in the state of New Hampshire or in the state of Maine. I've searched everywhere, contacted all the relevant licensing boards. Near as anyone can tell she's not a doctor at all."

Paul tried to swallow against a sudden ache. "There must be a mistake." Even as he spoke, he knew it was true. He'd googled Sylvia himself, and he, too, had come up empty. At the time it had seemed like a good thing.

"What about the hospital in Machias?" Paul asked, hopeful Carl's workplace could clear up the misunderstanding. "Didn't she used to work there with Carl?"

Craig's voice was calm, but there was a frustrated edge. "I called there, too. The only Sylvia Green who's ever worked for them is a receptionist. And get this. She's been missing for over a week."

Paul nearly dropped the phone. What the hell was going on?

"Can you please call the police?" Paul said, fighting panic. "Something's wrong, and it sounds like Carl's in the middle of it. Call Cassie with updates. I'll be there soon."

He hung up and immediately dialed. The line only rang once before Cassie's shriek caused him to hold the phone at arm's length.

"Where are you? What's happening?"

"I'm fifteen minutes away." Paul wiped sweat from his forehead and tried to keep the dread from reaching his voice. "Are you ready for the horses?"

"Yes, everything's set up," Cassie replied. "Brett's student will look after both of them for as long as we need."

"Great. I need one more favor."

"Anything."

"Call the Burlington airport. See what's available for flights to Mexico."

"Where in Mexico?"

Paul knew Sara's itinerary by heart. "Acapulco. The next flight out."

Carl wished this evening could go on forever. Sara was radiant. Her voice bubbled, and her eyes sparkled with a thousand lights. True, her happiness was probably directed at that boy she'd met. He'd watched her at *his* doorway, overheard their plans to meet *once he was asleep*.

"Be right back. I need to hit the ladies' room." Sara darted away, and he watched the supple swing of her hips, the mass of curls rippling down her back. She glanced back and smiled shyly before ducking out the door to the hallway, leaving him alone with his ever-evolving plans.

Medicating Sara tomorrow would be easy, safe. Once they left the ship the meddling doctor would no longer pose a problem. But a sedative tonight would ensure she didn't sneak off to meet her new beau. Like Paul, the boy was an unwanted distraction, another of her power plays.

Sara did so enjoy her games. She paraded men before him, hoping to make him jealous, even though, deep down, she knew she was his. But the chase was amusing, and it would only make their inevitable union that much sweeter.

His thoughts strayed to Sara's childhood. Even then, she'd been easily duped; her general mistrust had never extended to him. He'd worked hard to stay away from her, believing her to be his flesh and blood. His father's censure had disturbed him greatly, reminded him the girl was off limits. Since that day, he'd kept her close, but not too close. Her nearness plucked and pulled at him until he thought he might again relinquish control. But he'd held fast. Now he counted himself lucky he'd had the strength to resist her, and she hadn't caused him to lose his mind.

His efforts to avoid her had been exactly right, and now worked to his advantage. By staying just beyond Sara's reach, he'd become an enigma, the one person she wanted desperately to please. A good thing.

Carl raised his glass to the couple seated at the table beside him and said, "To Mexico." They smiled back, but in his mind the room erupted in applause, and he took a bow.

Sara hiked her skirt up above her knees and ran. The Internet café was just around the corner, a few yards past the ladies' room. She could take a minute to send an email, and Carl would be none the wiser.

"Sara!" She slid to a stop at the sound of Jonah's voice. "Are you trying to pass out again? Slow down."

She giggled at the joke but dashed away as soon as he caught up. "I want to send an email before Carl notices I'm missing."

Jonah fell into step beside her. "Why do you have to sneak around?"

"It's a long story. Let's just say Carl likes to be in control."

"That doesn't sound good." Jonah was already panting, and Sara hid a chuckle.

"It's not good. But I'm working on getting out from under his thumb."

She skidded through the doorway, grabbed the first available computer, spun the chair down to her height and punched in her room number. When she logged on to Gmail, a dozen messages came up.

"Looks like Paul's worried," she said. "Most of these are dated today."

"Are you gonna read them?" Jonah slid into the chair next to her, still breathing hard.

"No time. Carl will come looking if I'm gone too long." Sara clicked on *Compose mail* and wrote quickly.

*Everything's fine. We dock at Tijuana tomorrow and I fly home from San Diego the next day. Lost my phone. Love you. See you soon!*

"Who's Paul?"

"My boyfriend. Carl likes to pretend he doesn't exist."

Jonah nodded, but a frown puckered his forehead. "Is everything okay with you and Carl? He seems odd, possessive."

"That he is," Sara agreed. "But he means well. I hoped to get closer to him on this trip, but..." She glanced at her watch. "Gotta run."

With a sigh, she looked away from the unread messages, logged off and headed for the door. She paused and looked back. "Don't forget to wait for me."

Jonah's answering smile lifted her spirits as she sprinted back to Carl.


Cassie met Paul with a grim expression when he pulled into the driveway, horses in tow. "Craig Driscoll called. He spoke to the Maine State Police. They're looking for Carl."

"What? Why?"

"They found some new evidence. They want to question him about Sara's mom." Cassie's eyes filled with tears, and she grabbed Paul's hand. "Craig says he checked with a friend in law enforcement, and it's a murder investigation now."

Paul's legs buckled, and he leaned against the truck for support. "Is Carl a suspect?"

"I don't know. I just know they want to talk to him."

"Do they know he's on a cruise with Sara?"

Cassie nodded, tears forming tracks on her cheeks. "Yes, but they checked the itinerary you gave to Craig. Carl and Sara aren't on that ship."

"What?" Paul staggered as the pieces came together and realization landed like a punch to the gut. "That piece of shit! Carl gave me the wrong itinerary!" He barely caught Cassie as she toppled against him, sobbing uncontrollably. "Shhhhh," Paul said, trying to console her. "Calm down. They'll find her."

Paul's phone chirped, and a mixture of relief, hope and fear shot through him when he saw Sara's name across the display. "It's Sara! She sent an email!" Cassie tried to rip the phone from his hands, and he ducked away, reading quickly. "Tijuana! Their next stop is Tijuana!"

Paul handed his phone to Cassie. "I'll put the horses in the barn and get them settled. You call the police. Let them know where Carl and Sara are going. Then get Adam out here. I need a ride to the airport."

Cassie ran toward the house, phone held tightly against her ear. Paul untied Harlee and backed her down the ramp. The mare looked around, eyes wide and anxious.

"I know just how you feel, girl." Paul stroked the horse's neck and rubbed her forehead before leading her toward the barn. Harlee pranced and snorted, then whinnied to Frosty, still waiting patiently in the trailer.

"Don't worry, girl. We'll find her. We'll bring her home."

He was grateful for the dim light that hid his tears. Sara was heading for foreign soil with a man who might have been involved in her mother's death. Carl had hired Sylvia Green to pose as Sara's psychologist, and now she was missing. And if Mark were to be believed, Carl had paid him to marry Sara and keep an eye on her.

*Why?*

Mark's words came back to him. *Something bad happened to that girl, and if you ask me, it's something Carl would do most anything to keep secret.* Paul wondered if Joanie might have known the secret, too.

# Chapter Forty-Three

Sara stepped onto the veranda and curled up on a chaise lounge. As usual, her head came to rest just south of the pillowed cushion. The chair, like everything else in life, was made with a larger person in mind, someone stronger, braver and more capable than she. Here she was, the cruise nearly over, and she'd accomplished nothing.

Carl had sidestepped her every effort to discuss the guardianship. Meanwhile he exercised his authority with an air of entitlement; clearly he would never willingly relinquish control. The cruise had been an eye opener and a waste of time. She would have to fight for her independence and give up one dream in favor of the other.

Which dream was never in question. She would trade Harlee and Rolex to buy her freedom. The thought was crushing. Perhaps instead Harlee could be leased for a year. Surely one of Brett's students would pay generously for the privilege of riding such a competitive mare. Could that bring in enough to cover legal fees? Was it possible to hold on to Harlee and still be free?

The bathroom door was open a crack, and puffs of steam breathed into the narrow hallway. Carl was in the shower, his clothes just visible atop the vanity, reflected back to Sara in the mirror's haze.

-*Do it!*

*He'll catch me.*

-*Coward.*

-*Quitter, quitter, quitter, quitter-*

*The hell I am.*

With a flicker of daring that she barely recognized as her own, Sara rolled off the lounger. She crept thirteen steps, through the slider, between the twin beds and down the short hallway. Closet to her left, exit straight ahead, bathroom to her right, she crouched low and nudged the door open. The hinges' drawn-out groan carried over the spitting hiss of the water-saver shower spray, and caused her to wince and duck. Carl's palm-tree shirt lay near the door, reeking of talc and a long day in the sun. One sleeve trailed into the sink, and his cell phone bulged from the vest pocket.

Sara reprimanded herself for childish misgivings as she reached through the opening and felt her way across the slick Formica. Half expecting Carl's hand to material-ize from the steam and grab her, she darted a glance at the shower door. Her glasses fogged, and she took them off and slipped them into her shirt pocket. A shadow blurred the frosted glass. She touched the shirt, but her eyes lingered on Carl.

Was it possible he might laugh the way he used to when she was little? They'd been close once, before her grandfa-ther had drowned, before the nightmares and the hospital and the voices.

The memories softened her fear, and she reached boldly. Her fingers closed over the phone, and she silently with-drew. Dashing away, giddy with insolence, she laughed at the unease that attached itself like a puzzle piece wedged into the wrong corner. She bounced onto her bed, willed away the odd little sense of warning, turned her back to the bathroom and dialed.

Her excitement dimmed with every unanswered ring. When Paul's voice mail finally played, she considered hang-ing up and returning the phone quickly before Carl noticed it was missing.

*It's okay to make a call, isn't it?*

*-He hates Paul.*

*How could anyone hate Paul?*

She sighed as the recording asked her to leave a message. There was only one thing she wanted to say.

"I love you..."

"What . . . the . . . hell . . . are . . . you . . . doing?"

A shout would have been better. The quiet hiss of Carl's voice sent a shiver down her spine. The phone tumbled to the floor, and she sat rigid, eyes to the wall, jarred by ghosts of memories just beyond her reach.

"I told you to wait until we got to Mexico. Who do you think you are, stealing my phone while my back is turned?"

"Stealing? Are you nuts?" Sara spun around, stunned as the memories and the feeling of foreboding fled. Carl stood at the foot of her bed, a towel around his hips, anger perverting his features.

"I just wanted to check in. I'm asking a lot of Paul and it's only polite to keep in touch." Sara's sense of justice pushed her forward. She swung to the floor and ducked past Carl. "If you want to be an ass, you can be an ass by yourself. I'll be back when you've cooled off."

The words felt good. It wasn't as if he were going to help her anyway. She might as well let him know she would no longer be his sock puppet. Head held high, she stomped into her sandals and reached for the door.

Her head struck the wall before she realized he'd grabbed her. Something smashed into her ribs with a crunch, spinning her as she fell. The pain was delayed for a split second before it ripped through her in a frenzy of white heat. She retched on the floor, every part of her on fire. When he dragged her to her feet and threw her to the bed she choked on a scream, landing in a tangle, gasping.

Sara's first thought was a once-familiar question, one

she hadn't asked herself in months. *What did I do wrong this time?*

Carl answered.

"You wicked little cunt, running off to your new boyfriend. I won't allow it."

Sara forced aside the black haze that clouded her eyes, and rolled her head toward the door, just eleven steps away. Carl followed her gaze and snickered.

"It's no use, Sara. We've done this before."

He clicked on the television, turned up the volume, and lowered himself to the bed.

"Can't you go any faster?" Paul was beside himself as Adam wove in and out of rush hour traffic.

"Take it easy, buddy. Carl isn't going to hurt his own daughter." Adam pulled into the breakdown lane, avoided a knot of traffic, and gained fifty yards.

"You don't know that." Paul tried to calm himself by googling Sylvia. He'd found an article written by her co-workers at the hospital. There was a photo, and underneath, a caption: *I owe Dr. Morgan my life.*

"Shit, Adam, listen to this. *Sylvia Green is our poster girl for hope. An inpatient for twelve years, she was discharged in March and now works at the hospital as a receptionist. She credits her doctor, Carl Morgan, with her complete recovery.*"

Paul grabbed the door handle as Adam swerved past a slow-moving VW Beetle. Adam's brow was creased in concentration, his hands draped loosely over the wheel. "So Carl was Sylvia's doctor and he discharged her in March? Is that when she started posing as Sara's therapist?"

Paul nodded. "It looks like Sylvia replaced Mark as Sara's keeper."

"And now Sylvia's missing? I'll bet he paid her off." Adam punched the steering wheel and accidentally blew the horn. The driver ahead of him extended his middle finger. Adam seemed not to notice. "But why? They're just an ordinary family from Maine. They're not the Mansons."

Paul stared out the windshield, heart pounding. "I don't know, but maybe Mark is right. Maybe there is something Carl doesn't want Sara to remember. He wanted Cassie to listen to her dreams. And Sylvia broke us up right after I met Carl, when he saw how happy she was, and..."

Stomach already in knots, Paul went rigid. "Sara told him she was close to finding out what caused the voices. What if something did happen at Round Lake? What if he doesn't want her to remember?"

Adam glanced sideways at Paul. "You don't think it was Carl who attacked her, do you?"

Paul took off his glasses and wiped them on his shirt, the clean chamois in his pocket forgotten. "I don't know, but I'm calling the police again. They might think I'm nuts, but maybe this is the missing piece they need." He stared at the road and willed the car to go faster. "I have to help her."

"How? She's in the middle of the ocean."

"I know." Paul groaned, put fists to forehead and shut his eyes. "I can't get to her until they dock. But maybe the police can put something in motion to keep her safe until then." Sweat beading on his forehead, Paul speed-dialed the non-emergency number for the Maine State Police. Just as a harried dispatcher answered, Paul's phone beeped to announce that an incoming call had gone to voice mail. He hoped it wasn't important.

Sara felt as if a part of her split off and watched while Carl held her down, his weight crushing her, his knee between her thighs, hands choking her down. The room shimmered and spun. Her head throbbed, her eyes burned, and each breath set off waves of searing pain.

-*Fight!*

She tried to push him away, but he pinned her arms and rested his elbow across her throat.

*I can't*

-*You can.*

Carl's face was close to hers, and she gagged against the lingering scent of champagne. He'd been so excited about Mexico. A dozen toasts, a dozen sips of sparkle. His eyes had been just a little too bright, his voice too rhythmic. She'd noticed his imbalance, wondered if he was okay. If only she'd understood.

Something sticky and warm trickled over her forehead and into her eyes. She opened her mouth to scream, but couldn't manage more than a moan.

"Shut up. Don't think I won't do to you what I did to Sylvia." Carl let go with one hand and cupped Sara's chin. He turned it right, then left, and finally released her with a smirk. "There's not a mark on your face. We can still get off the ship tomorrow with no one the wiser."

"I'm not going anywhere with you." The words sent a stabbing burn through Sara's chest, and she whimpered. He covered her mouth and bent closer.

"Oh, but you are. And don't worry, sweetheart. You won't remember any of this . . . unpleasantness."

Carl withdrew a pre-filled syringe from a drawer in the bedside table, held it to the light and giggled. "This won't hurt a bit. It'll be just like those camping trips at Round Lake."

An icy shudder swept through her. *Impossible.*

"Was it you?"

"Was what me?"

"At the lake." Sara ran out of air and pulled in a shallow breath. "The man who raped me."

Carl faltered. He rocked back to eye her quizzically, then shook his head and tsked. "Sara, darling, it was never rape."

He leaned over her and pressed his thumb into the crease of her elbow. Sara felt the prick of the needle a moment before she lunged forward and slammed her forehead into the base of Carl's nose.

The full syringe flew from his hands before he could press the plunger. Carl's blood spattered her face. Wild with fury and fear Sara threw herself forward and gouged his eyes. Pain exploded as his fists struck her face and belly, and she doubled over and shut her eyes against bursts of red and white. She knew she couldn't win, didn't have the breath to scream. And if she tried he'd only hit her harder.

"Look what you made me do! You bitch! Whore! Just like your mother! I made sure she'd never lie again, and I'll do the same to you."

*My mother?* Everything inside her shattered. She pulled her knees to her chest and folded both arms over her face. Her vision clouded, and little pops of light pulsed as her heart broke.

*-He's sick.*

*-Sick, sick, sick, sick-*

"And now it's just us! You and me, the way it should be."

"There is no you and me." The pain of her mother's death rose like a wave and broke over her. "You're sick, Daddy. You need help."

Carl's tittering laughter brought an involuntary whimper from somewhere deep within her. He gripped her chin, forced her mouth shut.

"I'm not sick, but you are," he said, his voice cadenced as a song. "Oh, Sara, you're so stupid sometimes, so easy to bend." He wound his fingers into her hair and pulled her close.

"Do you remember when you were seven? Your stay at *my* hospital?"

Sara nodded, lips pushed tightly together as she swallowed blood.

Carl grinned. "I only wanted to help you forget what we did to my father. I had to put an end to those awful nightmares and the *things* you called out in your sleep. Terrible things, and much too accurate." He pressed his lips against her ear, his breath sticky. "But I had access to so many wonderful medications, how could I resist? And when your grandfather's death was finally buried deep enough, the voices took its place."

*Daddy, Daddy, make them stop!* The voice of a child shrilled in her memory, followed by her father's face, his voice masking a sense of triumph.

*Who, sweetie? Make who stop?* Smirking.

*All of them!*

He dropped her and walked to the bathroom. His reflection looked back as he rummaged through a drawer. "Can you imagine my relief? Here you were, just seven years old, and already I could label you schizophrenic, even though you weren't. After that, even if you did remember, no one would listen to the *crazy girl*."

He plunged a needle into a bottle, filled a syringe, and wiped blood from his face. "There's no way out, Sara. Just cooperate. Don't make me throw you out another window."


Paul thanked the dispatcher and ended the call. His screen flashed. "Shit! I have a message!"

He pressed the phone to his ear. "Oh, thank God! It's Sara! She sounds okay." He listened to the three words, 'I love you,' and the tangle inside him began to unwind. His respite was brief. The rest of the message was filled with sounds that could only mean one thing.

*She's in trouble.*

"Adam, give me your phone." He called the police one last time, played his message to them and listened as he came apart inside. When he hung up, the words stuck to his tongue.

"The FBI is involved. They know where she is. They're sending the ship's security to check on the cabin." He stared straight ahead and listened to his breath as it shuddered in and out.

"All we can do is wait."


*-Do it!*

*He'll kill me.*

*-He'll kill you anyway.*

Sara held her breath. It was eight steps to the bathroom, another three steps to the door. Carl would have no trouble stopping her.

*There's only one way out.*

She rolled from the bed. Her legs ran on their own, searing pain compartmentalized, eyes fixed on the rail. She touched its smooth surface and swung into the night, trusting her memory and her instincts.

There was another state room directly below, another veranda, another rail. She had studied it carefully, just as she studied every exit, had practiced it over and over in her mind. With luck, she might succeed.

Hands on the rail, she arced up, over and down until she hung by her fingertips. Her belly rested against the side of the ship; her toes pointed toward the waves. In that moment she heard Carl's bellow.

She let go.

The wind lifted her hair, cool and soothing. The coppery smell of sea spray cleared her senses enough to see the glint of the rail below, to reach out, grasp it. Her shoulders felt as if they ripped from her body as she slammed face-first against the ship. Pain tore through her. The world twisted and blurred.

She pulled herself up, tumbled over the rail, and plunged through the sliders to the empty cabin. Past the queen-sized bed, toward the hallway, she focused on her goal.

The door stopped her with an agonizing shock. She threw herself against it, grasping for the handle, crying when her hands seemed unable to grip and pull. Finally it gave way, and she spilled through, fell to her knees, shrieking.

Blood dripped to the carpet, and for a moment she was seven, sitting in the shallows at Round Lake, lost and alone. Carl lifted her from the water, kissed her forehead and pushed the hair from her eyes. She saw the sunlight glint off the needle, felt it slip beneath her skin. She screamed and cried and punched him as hard as she could.

He held her gently, close, told her everything was okay. He was here now. She was safe. The tone was soothing, not Carl's voice at all. She opened her eyes. Dr. McNeel rushed toward her amid a panorama of white uniforms. She peeked up into vivid blue eyes amid swirling shadows. Her voice was far away, drowned by an insistent storm.

"Jonah?"

A whirling haze dimmed his answering smile an instant before blackness spun out the light.

# Chapter Forty-Four

Sara bobbed in and out of consciousness, aware of the roar of the helicopter, the heaving air currents, the edge of pain and the hand holding hers.

"Paul?"

She thought someone answered, "Yes."

His touch comforted her as the world pitched and whined. Images of Carl whirled behind her eyes. The voice didn't sound like Paul. Was it Jonah? How did he get here? Where was here? She tried to hold on, but her fingers slackened as she dipped below the reach of touch and sound.

She woke briefly as the helicopter bumped, then came to rest. White fabric surrounded her with antiseptic scent. It lifted, dropped and clattered down a bare hallway. Square fluorescent lights flicked past. She counted three lights, five, eight, then darkness. Voices told someone to step back, and the warm hand abandoned her cold one.

"Paul?"

There was no answer. A beam of light flashed in her eyes, and a new voice told her everything would be okay. The room came into focus and she arched upward, screamed and struck out at needles and tubes. Gentle hands pressed her down, and again darkness swarmed into her eyes and ears. Even the table beneath her faded to a distant chill, then nothing.

Sara was in surgery when Paul called Cassie from Chicago O'Hare. She'd been med-flighted from the ship directly to Chula Vista, just north of the Mexican border in California. Paul changed his connecting flight from Tijuana to San Diego as he rode the moving walkway from Terminal Two to Terminal One.

Paul spent the four-hour flight staring at the seat in front of him. The woman beside him prattled about her granddaughter and her aging beagle with bladder problems. Paul smiled and nodded while visions of Sara, fighting for her life, swirled through his head.

By the time he touched down and taxied to Gate Thirteen, Sara was in recovery. When he hailed a cab for the fifteen-minute drive to Chula Vista she was still unconscious. Her condition was *guarded*. What the hell did that mean?

Traffic in Chula Vista slowed to a crawl and Paul abandoned the cab several blocks from the hospital. Running through crowds of tourists was a welcome release from his state of leashed panic. He dialed as he ran. The receptionist at the hospital, obviously blessed with caller-ID, now answered with, "Hi, Paul, still no change."

He panted his way into the main lobby, shouted for directions, dashed down a hallway and finally skidded to a stop outside the ICU. A volunteer led him to Sara's room as he wiped sweat from his forehead. In the sudden hush his footsteps echoed. A man stepped forward and flashed a badge, FBI, and spoke to him as he walked to Sara's door. Someone sat at her bedside, a man about her age. He looked up with eyes that hadn't slept in a long time.

"Are you Paul?"

"Yes."

"She was asking for you."

"She's awake?" Relief flooded through him as he hurried toward her.

"No, she's not." Apology swept across the man's eyes. "She asked for you on the way here, in the helicopter."

Paul stopped and swallowed as cold fingers wound back into his chest. "Oh."

"I'm Jonah Randall." The man placed Sara's hand over the covers. His fingers lingered on hers, then slid free as he rose from the chair. "We can't both be in here at once, so I'll head for the waiting area. She's moving, and her eyelids are fluttering. The nurse says it's a good sign."

Paul nodded and stared at the silent form, almost blotted out by bandages and tubes and monitors. Jonah put his hands on Paul's shoulders and guided him to the chair, placed Sara's hand in his, and spoke quietly.

"It's okay to hold her hand, and you should talk to her. Don't hug her."

Paul's gaze locked onto Sara's bruised and swollen face. She'd never looked so small. He cradled her hand and glanced at Jonah. "Do you work for the cruise line?"

"No, I met Sara on the ship. It's a long story." He gave Paul's shoulder a final squeeze and walked from the room. Paul looked after him for a moment, then turned his attention to Sara.

She was alive. He should feel a sense of relief, but he shook with fear and guilt, wishing he'd been able to keep her safe, certain he'd let her down.

For the first hour Paul sat rigid. He cupped her hand, afraid to squeeze it. Her every movement startled him, gave him hope and simultaneously dashed it. In the slack hours before dawn he let his head rest on the bedside. The frantic drive with Harlee, the airports and changes and constant fear had all taken their toll. He dozed, jerked awake, stroked her fingers, and drifted off again.

As the first rays of sun pierced the window, Paul woke with a start. Sara looked back at him. Her brow wrinkled in pain as she opened her mouth. Soft and hoarse, she spoke slowly but clearly.

"You . . . look . . . like . . . hell."

Paul laughed so hard, the nurse glared and shushed him. He squeezed Sara's hand and said, "You're beautiful." Tears spilled down her cheeks as she faced him and struggled for words.

"The man . . . at the . . . lake . . . it was Carl."


The surgeon finished his exam and Sara shuddered as she tried to tug the sheet over her knees. Her initial relief at finding herself alive and in the hospital faded as memories returned and brought with them a creeping sense of danger. She focused on the doctor's words while fear burrowed into her throat. *Concussion*, she told herself by way of distraction, *ribs cracked but not displaced, surgery to stop internal bleeding. . . .*

And bruises, lots of bruises. To her lungs, to her liver, to everything. She tried not to think of the horror of being powerless and alone. The last thing she remembered was running for the rail.

*Did I make the jump, or did they fish me out of the sea?* She thought hard, but everything beyond that point was a jumble of images, like actors flickering beneath a strobe light.

Paul hurried to help her. He tucked the blanket and adjusted her pillows until she was as comfortable as possible. Her jaw was too swollen to move more than a fraction of an inch, but it was enough to allow her to speak. There were things she needed to know.

Fear stood between her and the most important of her questions. What if *he* were here, waiting? What if they gave her back to *him*? How long would it be before she could run? As the minutes passed, her need to know overcame the terror.

"Where's Carl?" She held her breath and tried to fade into the sheets the moment the words left her mouth. Saying the name out loud terrified her, as if the word might cause him to burst through the door.

"I don't know," Paul replied. "I was told he was detained, but I don't know if he's still in Mexico or on the ship or here in California."

Sara swallowed back queasiness and hugged herself as she spoke in a thready voice. "Can you find out?"

Paul touched her shoulder. His hand rested there for an instant before he crossed the room and opened the door. "There's an FBI agent outside," he said. "Agent Lange, I think. I'll see if he's still waiting."

"FBI! Why the FBI?"

Paul motioned to someone outside, then returned to Sara's bedside and took her hand. "It's okay. He told me they have jurisdiction over crimes committed on cruise ships." Paul's confident smile did nothing to mitigate Sara's dread. "The agent seemed very nice," Paul said. "He was waiting for the doctor's okay before talking to you."

Sara flattened herself against her pillow as a wave of dizziness broke over her. If only she could disappear until everything was over. But she was too weak to run away, and her helplessness only increased her dread.

"You don't get it," she said, shaking. "The FBI agent, he won't believe a word I say."

Paul stroked her hair. She felt him pull back with a start when he brushed against the neat line of stitches that ran in an oblique line across her head. As she reached up and touched the shaved section of scalp she thought of Frankenstein. An assemblage of pieces cobbled together, broken inside. A monster.

Paul's hand returned to the safety of hers. "Why wouldn't he believe you?" He looked honestly perplexed, and Sara couldn't help but wonder why he didn't understand.

*-He never saw you as anything but sane.*

*-He's an idiot.*

She winced at the pain and spoke in small breaths. "You've obviously never been a mental patient."

Paul closed his eyes before he kissed Sara's hand. His touch was sympathetic but firm. "Look," he said. "There's a lot happening. You have to trust me. Agent Lange will listen to you."

"But I'm *mentally disabled*. Carl's a doctor. They'll believe *him*." Sara clutched her side as the pain increased with her anxiety. "He'll tell them I tried to kill myself. He'll say he did what he had to do, to stop me. They'll give me back to him."

Paul shook his head. "No, they won't. Just trust me."

Sara blinked back tears, determined not to cry. *They'll just think I'm crazy if I fall apart. I have to keep myself together.*

Paul hovered. "I know you're afraid, but I think you'll feel better once you talk to this guy. I'll be right here with you. Just give him a chance."

Special Agent Lange tapped on the door before he stepped through. Sara could feel the man's eyes appraising her, dismissing her. "Ms. Morgan? Are you up for answering a few questions?"

She shuddered and squeaked a "No," tucked her hands beneath the blankets and bit into her lip until it bled.

"Can I stay and hold her hand? I won't say a word." Paul moved to stand between them. Sara gulped back a sob.

"That's fine, Paul." Lange turned to Sara. "Normally I'd prefer to have you interviewed by a woman. But you're stuck with me, so I've asked a member of the hospital staff to sit in."

A nurse entered behind him. She took a seat in a corner and folded her hands in her lap.

Sara turned her head just enough to steal a look through her hair. The agent's gaze was steady as he pulled up a chair and settled into it. His tone seemed genuine when he spoke. "Can you tell me what happened between you and your father? Take all the time you need. Don't leave anything out."

Sara listened and could find no patronization or disdain. She took in Agent Lange's open expression, reached for Paul's hand and closed her fingers around his comforting warmth. Her voice broke when she tried to speak. She cleared her throat, swallowed, and tried again.

"He's not my father. He's a monster." She spat the words with a vehemence that surprised her. Eyes closed, she breathed for a moment before gathering her courage to speak again.

"Where do you want me to start?"

# Chapter Forty-Five

"Hello, Dr. Morgan. I'm Special Agent Jonathan Lange."
The FBI agent rose from a vast chair behind an expansive mahogany desk. He shook Carl's hand and gestured to a leather captain's chair. "You've been apprised of your rights." It was a statement rather than a question, and Carl nodded as he took a seat.

He'd expected an interrogation room; stark, hot and bright with the screech of metal chairs jammed against commercial flooring. This comfort was unexpected, a welcome retreat from the unreasonable demands of the utilitarian space beyond. But it also caught him by surprise, put him off balance and set his teeth on edge. He chose a straight-backed posture of confidence and poised to defend himself against the coming accusations.

Agent Lange returned to his seat behind the desk and smiled. "This conversation is monitored and recorded in order to cover both our asses. It'll help us remember what was said in the event of a disagreement."

Carl inclined his head in acknowledgement and studied the man. Lange appeared confident. Well, why not? He was tall and attractive, probably had his share of women. These things tended to increase a man's sense of worth. His close-cropped shit-brown hair was unremarkable but neat, and Carl had to admit it showed off the square jaw.

Lange's relaxed manner and tendency to under dress, combined with a touch of humor, pegged him as trustworthy and approachable. Probably a junior agent, anxious to prove himself, none too experienced, and likely borrowed the executive office from someone further up the food chain.

Lange cemented Carl's impressions when he leaned forward, pursed his lips and spoke in a compassionate tone. "You must be devastated by this business with your daughter." The agent shuddered and riffled through a neat stack of papers on his desk. "I have several reports to complete and I wonder if you might be able to shed some light on the events leading up to Sara's injuries."

Carl began to relax. He'd expected to be accused of a host of misdeeds. Instead it seemed his *help* was required. The Bureau needed someone to explain what had happened so they could fill out their reports and put the incident to rest. They'd assigned an inexperienced agent who seemed interested in efficiently completing his task.

This was good. Very good.

Carl's breath escaped in a prolonged hiss as he eased into the chair and reflected the agent's look of concern and interest. He formed words in his head and spoke them in his mind, listened to the cadence and timbre, judged them suitable, modulated his voice to one of intense concern, and finally spoke aloud.

"I suspect my daughter had a psychotic break," Carl began, allowing a clinical demeanor to overtake his features. "I believe it was similar to the episode she suffered eleven months ago. She wasn't making sense, talking gibberish. Then she threatened to kill herself, and she ran for the rail."

Agent Lange's expression registered an appropriate level of shock. Carl continued, his confidence swelling. "I was able to restrain her and pull her back into the cabin, and I attempted to administer a dose of midazolam to calm her. She's small but extremely fit and strong, and I wasn't certain I could control her long enough to call Dr. McNeel and wait for his assistance, per his request."

Lange nodded again and lifted an eyebrow, indicating Carl should continue. Carl took a breath and tried to show a suitable level of anguish in wide eyes and parted lips. "That's when she attacked me." He folded his arms across his chest and dug his thumb deep into the space between his ribs until he was certain an appropriate level of distress had settled across his face. "She broke my nose and gouged my eyes. I was blinded by blood. Look what she did to me!"

Carl gestured to the deep scratches running across his cheek, the purple swelling of his crooked nose. He allowed his eyes to bulge in horror. With an exaggerated sigh, he swallowed twice. That ought to convey shock.

"I tried to defend myself, tried to stop her. But she got away from me, and . . . she must have gone over the rail." He bowed his head and shuddered. "You can't imagine my relief when I learned she was alive. I thought I'd lost her."

Lange stared, unblinking, for what seemed like a very long time. His expression shifted to an attitude of sympathy. "That must have been horrible for you, watching your daughter come apart like that." He placed his hand over Carl's. It was comforting, warm, and Carl scrunched his eyebrows together and tried to force a tear.

Lange released Carl's hand. He tapped his fingers on his desk as he asked, "But can you tell me, as a professional, why someone would make such a jump if she didn't intend to harm herself? Sara jumped to the balcony below yours and ran for help. It appears she had no intention of falling to her death."

The room tilted and came out of focus, but Carl recovered quickly and molded his features into a patronizing gaze. "It is not unusual for a suicide victim to change her mind once she's committed to the jump. Sara is more athletic than most. She was able to save herself."

"Ah, that makes sense." Lange wrote something across an official-looking document, and Carl smiled to himself.

The man was easily led. In fact, this interview was far easier than he'd anticipated.

Hoping the gesture of anxiety would be recognized as such, Carl pressed fingers to his temple and rubbed. It was imperative he see Sara soon, make certain she understood that she had no options beyond her complete cooperation. He rubbed his eyes and tried to put a bit of entreaty into his voice. "I'd like to see my daughter. I can only imagine how confused she must be. She desperately needs my guidance."

Lange grunted and shook his head. "We still have ground to cover here. Is there anything you might want to revise in your statement thus far?"

Carl shook his head. To re-examine might introduce inconsistencies. Did Lange think him a fool? He watched as the agent placed a digital recorder on the desk top and pressed *play*. Moments later Sara's voice filled the room.

"I love you."

Carl's involuntary gasp was followed by his own words coming from the recording, softer than Sara, but clear as air. "What the hell do you think you're doing?" There was a clatter, and Carl's voice continued, more distant, but distinct. "I told you to wait until we got to Mexico. Who do you think you are, stealing my phone while my back is turned?"

"Stealing? Are you nuts? I just wanted to check in. I'm asking a lot of Paul, and it's only polite to keep in touch. If you want to be an ass, you can be an ass by yourself. I'll be back when you've cooled off."

A sickening smack followed, and a cry of shock and pain. Lange placed his elbows on the desk and looked Carl in the eye.

"I'll ask again, Dr. Morgan. Is there any part of your statement you'd care to amend?"

Carl clamped his mouth shut and ground his teeth. "No. Nothing. And I'd like to call my lawyer. Now."

Lange switched off the player. "That's up to you, Carl. May I call you Carl?" He paused a moment, then continued when Carl remained mute. "But to be honest, while your attack on Sara is troubling, we have more important things to discuss."

Carl darted a glance. Did Lange know about Joanie or Sylvia? No, that wasn't likely. He'd been far too careful. The man was trolling, hoping to snag a bit of information and reel it in.

"Police detectives recovered your wife's camera, Carl. Do you remember the last pictures she took? The camera leaves a time and date stamp. Did you know that?"

A prickle of fear crept up Carl's neck. He looked down at his hands, folded one on top of the other in his lap. The pale depression of his absent wedding band caught his eye as he cast about for a clever solution. There'd be a way around this. The camera must have been submerged for days. The date couldn't be trusted. A decent lawyer would make certain it was inadmissible as evidence.

"And then there's Sylvia Green. Poor woman was near death when they found her. You'd think a physician would be more thorough."

"What?" This time Carl couldn't keep the shock from his voice. "Sylvia? What's this about Sylvia?"

"She's alive, Carl. She's in a coma. According to her neurologist, she's showing signs of coming around." Lange's voice took on an unnatural quality, as if the room were humming. His words seemed to produce eddies in the air. "I wonder what she'll have to say about the person who left her for dead on the side of I-95. Can you imagine?"

Carl hastened to assemble an appropriate expression of injustice. "You can't think I'd do something like that! Sylvia was my patient. I worked with her for over a decade when others gave up on her. I saved her."

Lange's lips curled into a strange little smile. "Odd, then, that we'd find a tire track at the crime scene that matches your Camry, right down to the patch plug you purchased at Sears Automotive three months ago. We also have a clear left footprint that matches your new Nikes from Sports Authority. Would you care to see a copy of the receipt? And the mud from your shoes has been sent to the lab along with dirt from the scene."

Carl's anger rose like bile. "That means nothing. How many people have those tires? Hundreds? Thousands? How many people have those sneakers?" He pounded the desk for emphasis. "And what would I be doing on the north-bound side of the highway? I was going south that day."

Lange remained maddeningly calm. "I didn't mention she was on the northbound side."

Carl clamped his mouth shut as the distant humming rose to a roar.

"Don't be too hard on yourself, Carl. It's your DNA under Sylvia's fingernails that will hang you." Lange fixed him with a sympathetic stare. "Sara tells me your neck was bleeding when you arrived to pick her up. Paul corroborates. We're running the samples. Care to predict the results?"

Carl's fury boiled forth in a gallimaufry of justification. "Sylvia would have exposed me. After all I've done for her! And that adulterous witch of a wife deserved everything she got. Sara's not even my child!"

Silence hung thick in the air. Agent Lange said nothing for a moment, but his features relaxed, and he pushed his chair back from his desk and smiled. "That lovely, brave young woman is not your child? Why am I not surprised?"

As Carl sat in stunned silence, Lange walked to the door and summoned a guard. "Blanchard, would you take Dr. Morgan to a holding cell in the general population, please?"

"General?" The guard sounded surprised. "Isn't he accused of child molesting?"

"Nope, just a homicide." Lange turned to face Carl, but he spoke to the guard. "If he were charged with assaulting a little girl, then yes, we'd have to put him in protective custody."

"But the other detainees know," Blanchard said. "It doesn't matter whether he's been charged. They'll rip him apart."

"Will they?" Lange's gaze locked with Carl's. "Well, there's not much I can do about the rumor mill, is there?"

# Chapter Forty-Six

"No horses for two months. You heard the doctor." Paul risked a sideways glance before returning his attention to the road. Sara sat in the passenger seat, brow furrowed, her face a study in determination.

"I'm not going to get on. I'm just going to visit." Her expression left no room for discussion as she faced him, arms folded, unflinching and obstinate. "Will you come with me, or do I have to go alone?"

"You've changed," he said, trying not to laugh. "You're a real bitch."

She giggled, and immediately yelped in pain. Paul gripped the steering wheel and coasted to the shoulder.

"Stop laughing. You're not ready," he said, wincing along with her.

"Jonah says you should never put off laughing. Just do it and suffer the consequences."

"And your new brother is an authority on broken ribs?"

"Nope, but he does know how to laugh." Sara clutched her side, grinning despite the pain. "Why are we stopping? We're not there yet."

"For this." Paul leaned across the seat and kissed her forehead. He'd been tied in knots since picking Sara up from the hospital and driving straight to the airport. But once they'd landed in Vermont, he'd felt lighter. He couldn't remember when he'd spent this much time smiling.

"You're amazing, you know." He brushed the hair from

her eyes, avoiding the bruises that covered her face. "You are incredibly strong."

"I had to be." Sara's smile went slack. "It's still hard to believe Carl engineered both breaks. He drugged me, lied to me, made me believe I'd tried to hurt people." As she spoke she drew her shoulders back and lifted her chin. Paul marveled at her resilience as the serious expression fell away and challenge filled her voice.

"Now, about Harlee…"

"You do have a one-track mind." Paul tried for a stern tone, but he couldn't help laughing. "The doctor said no, not until your ribs are healed. What if Harlee bumps into you?"

Sara batted her lashes, and he realized it was pointless to argue. "Fine," he said. "I'll go with you, just as soon as we have you settled."

Sara dropped against her seat with a minimum of cringing and flashed a victorious grin. "Hurry up. It's almost dark."

They drove the rest of the way in silence. Sara dozed while Paul's thoughts strayed to the future. With Carl behind bars awaiting trial and the guardianship officially set aside, Sara's life and decisions were finally her own. Not wanting to pressure her, he hadn't told her he'd invested in the inn. She knew only that he'd taken a six-week leave of absence, and those weeks belonged to her.

"It was awfully generous of Cassie and Adam to let us stay here," Sara said as they drove the last mile up the winding road. "I can't thank them enough for taking in Harlee and Frosty. I owe them."

Paul's answering chuckle rumbled all the way up from his belly. "Oh, I'm sure they'll find something useful for you to do in return," he said, teasing. "They have more laundry than they know what to do with."

"Great. You'll have to teach me to fold."

"I have tried." Paul's voice trailed off as they reached the packed parking area. "Do you think these are all guests? I know tonight is the grand opening, but this." He gestured to the parking lot, filled to capacity, with more cars spilling onto the grass. "This is unbelievable."

Sara looked past him toward the inn. Music carried over the evening air, and crowds of people were visible through the windows. "It looks awfully busy. How 'bout we check out the stables first?" She jumped from the car, cried out, swore and grabbed her side. "I keep forgetting how much this hurts."

"Let's get you and your things inside," Paul said, taking charge. "Then we'll go see Harlee together." He opened the trunk and bent low to pull out Sara's suitcases. When he stood up, the barn lights were already on. He dropped the luggage and ran, shouting, "Crap, Sara! Wait up!"

By the time he reached the barn Sara was in Harlee's stall cradling the big black head and tousling the mare's forelock. At his approach she wiped tears from her cheeks and turned toward him. "They're happy tears," she said. "Don't look so worried."

Paul realized he'd gone white, partly due to Sara's tears, and partly her proximity to a thousand pounds of enthusiasm. He flinched as the mare gave Sara a playful nudge.

"There'll be plenty of time for Harlee tomorrow," he said. "How 'bout we get you unpacked?"

Sara kissed Harlee's muzzle and gave the wide forehead a final rub before she left the stall. "I can't believe I almost lost her. What if you hadn't been there?"

"But I was there, and she's fine," Paul reassured her. "Carl and Mark have no claim to her now. And you'll be back in the saddle before you know it."

Sara wiped her eyes with the back of her hand. Then she

closed the stall door and leaned against Paul for a moment before taking his hand and following him back to the car.

Paul lugged her suitcases up the back staircase in order to avoid the crowds. He felt as if he'd carried a great weight for weeks. All he wanted was a soft bed and a chance to finally let the fear and worry drain away. He knew without asking that Sara, too, was near exhaustion. After making sure she had everything she needed, he kissed her goodnight.

"I thought it might be better if I stayed in the room next door," he said. "I set up the pillows the way you had them at the hospital."

"Are you nuts?" Sara pulled him inside and closed the door. "Haven't you learned anything? Never put off happiness." Her boldness fell away, and she drew back. "Besides, I'm gonna need help getting undressed."

A wave of dizziness swept through him at the sight of her injuries, with bruises spreading in dusky rainbows across her ribs and belly. He draped a flannel nightshirt over her shoulders, tugged her arms through the sleeves and helped her under the covers.

"You coming?" She lifted the blanket and tipped her chin to the space beside her.

"I can sleep in the chair." Paul gestured to a recliner against the window. "I don't want to roll over and crush you."

"You won't, and I refuse to spend another night without you."

Paul undressed and slipped between the cool sheets. Sara molded herself to him, pulled his arms around her and held on so tightly that he wondered if her fingers might snap. At first, she breathed evenly. But as time passed, her little mouthfuls of air became increasingly ragged and wet, her body quaking against his.

Paul lay awake, afraid to move, until finally she relaxed

into a peaceful snore. When he kissed her goodnight there was a wisp of a smile on her lips.

Paul woke to the smell of bacon. Rubbing sleep from his eyes, he made his way to the dining area and came to an abrupt stop in the doorway. The room was filled with guests.

He hurried to the kitchen and found Adam cooking eggs benedict, pumpkin pancakes, bacon, and sausages. Sara toasted sweet cardamom bread and sliced fresh strawberries and pineapple. Cassie filled orders and brought heaping platters out to the tables.

"What can I do to help?" Standing in the doorway, watching the industry before him, Paul felt useless.

"Paul!" Adam's face lit up. "Can you start another pot of coffee? And refill these pitchers with orange juice. Sara shouldn't lift them." Adam flipped a dozen pancakes in rapid succession. The smell of sizzling batter and melted butter filled the room. "And when you're done, can you toss more wood on the fire?"

Paul joined in, awkwardly at first, but soon he caught up to the frantic pace. "How did you manage all of this?" he asked Adam as he sprinted past, arms laden with wood for the fire. "I mean, this is amazing. All these people. So soon."

"Blame Cassie's marketing expertise," Adam replied. "All I do is cook and write checks."

Cassie hip-checked Adam as she hurried by, a platter of home fried potatoes and maple bacon balanced on her shoulder. "What good is an inn if no one knows it exists? It'll take us a while to recoup what I spent, but I think we've put this place on the map."

"I'll say. Man, Cassie, you've outdone yourself." Paul followed Cassie into the dining area and stoked the fire while she delivered side dishes. He checked to be sure Sara was still in the kitchen before taking Cassie's arm. "Did Brett have any luck finding boarders for the stable?"

"Oh, that worked out better than I could have imagined," she said, beaming. "We have a group of horses moving in on December first, and the owners plan to run it as a co-op. They do all the work in exchange for a reduced rate. We just collect the checks, do repairs and stay out of their way."

"Wow. Sara will love that."

Cassie tossed him a warning frown. "Don't get ahead of yourself again. We don't know what she'll decide. It's here for her when and *if* she wants it."

Paul nodded in agreement. After everything Sara had been through, she would need time to heal. He'd have to be patient, give her the space she needed, no matter how strong she appeared on the surface.

A light snow was falling, and though it had little chance of lasting in late fall, everyone talked of snowshoeing and cross-country skiing. A few people settled into overstuffed chairs before the fire, noses buried in books from the well-stocked library. Couples held hands and sat by wide windows, watching the snow come down. It was a happy place, filled with possibilities.

"Isn't this the best?" Sara appeared at Paul's elbow, a dish towel slung over her shoulder. "I had no idea it would be so much fun here." She looked around and whispered, "Do you know if they've found someone to run the stables?"

Paul molded his face into a mask of nonchalance and kept his tone casual. "Cassie was hoping you might ask. I think they'd be willing to wait until you're ready."

Sara's eyes lit up. "Seriously? I'd love that. Why didn't they say something?"

"They probably figured you'd want to stay with Janet and Marty." Paul winced inwardly at the disappointment that flickered across Sara's face.

"You know Janet couldn't hold my job for me, not for another two months. Didn't you tell Cassie?" She rolled her eyes and ducked into the kitchen. Moments later she emerged and gave him a thumbs-up. "They're running the barn as a co-op! I can start a lesson program any time I want. But that's not the best part." Her eyes glowed with excitement. "They said I could live in the house by the barn!"

Paul couldn't help grinning. "That's great," he said, buoyed by the light in her eyes. "You can focus on the things you want to do. No more mucking."

"I wish I could start now." Sara's eyes were on the stable, just visible through the bay window. "But at least I know where I'll be in a couple of months."

As Sara disappeared into the kitchen, Paul closed his eyes and breathed a silent thank you.


A week later, Sara returned from her first visit with her new therapist. As she walked up the stone steps and let herself inside the inn's front door, she rehearsed the words. She still had trouble believing them and wondered if she ever would.

Paul was on his knees, scrubbing the dining room floor. The scent of oil soap was heavy in the air, mixed with the smell of fresh blueberry cobbler. Cassie's voice carried from the kitchen. She was on the phone, taking a reservation. Eyes closed, Sara pushed away the distractions and forced the words out.

"I'm not schizophrenic."

The statement felt awkward, no matter how many times she said it, no matter how vehemently her new doctor insisted it was true. She'd repeated it over and over during the short drive home, and every time she said it, suspicion welled in her throat and pushed the smile from her face.

The doubt was familiar, the same as the feeling that wormed its way into her gut when she reminded herself, *Carl isn't my father*, and *I have a half-brother*. With so much of her life built on lies, she found it difficult to trust anything she *knew* to be true. Even Cassie had been paid to be her friend, Sylvia was a fraud, and Mark had been hired to—

"You always seemed normal to me." Paul set down his sponge and walked toward her, rubbing his hands dry on a clean towel. Some of the tension in Sara's shoulders eased as she slipped into his arms. Paul, she could trust.

"I may be stuck with the voices," she said, letting the feeling of safety wrap around her. "But Dr. Brenner thinks there's a good chance someday they'll be gone."

*-Never.*

*You'll go away when I'm ready.*

"That's great news." Paul looked at her the way he always did, as if she were special. She burrowed against his shirt and inhaled. He smelled like bar soap, simple and direct.

"At least I know I'm stable. I won't break. I can have a life."

"You and Sylvia, both." Paul hugged her tighter. "She called while you were gone. She's leaving the hospital today, heading for rehab." He backed away, far enough to meet her gaze. "The charges against her might be dropped in exchange for her testimony, and she wondered if you'd be okay with that."

"Really?" Sara paused as conflicting emotions swept through her. "I think that's the right thing to do. I mean, I know what she did was wrong, but she did try to help me. She believed Carl. We all did."

"Except me," Cassie called from the kitchen. Sara snorted, and Cassie giggled back.

Sara gave Paul a quick kiss before she turned away, picked up a cleaning rag and sprayed it with lemon-scented polish. With wide strokes she wiped the surface of the maple breakfront. "I love it here," she mused. "The only drawback is, it's too far from you." She glanced at Paul. *Maybe he'll stay.*

*-He doesn't belong here.*

Paul wrung out a sponge, added a dollop of oil soap, and rubbed at a sticky spot beneath the oak table. "I'm hoping I can telecommute part of the time. But even if they say no, I'll be here weekends, and I'll call every day."

Sara hid a twinge of disappointment. She'd hoped Paul might stay and work at the inn, but he seemed determined to return to New Hampshire. Sylvia had been right. The time would come when she had to decide: mold herself to Paul's world, or create a life without him.

*Or perhaps I can mold him to mine.*

*-Fat chance.*

*-You're not worth it.*

*Maybe I am.*


On their last day together, Sara rose early. She wiggled out from under Paul's arm, sneaked outside, and padded quietly to the stables. The horses nickered as she crept down the aisle, and she gave them each a bit of hay to tide them over until the boarders arrived to feed breakfast.

"What do you think, Harlee?" She shoved a carrot between the mare's greedy lips and stroked the whorl between her eyes. "Is it fair to ask him?"

*-He'll say no.*

*I'm not asking you, and he won't.*

*-You haven't exactly planned this.*
*It's more romantic this way.*

Eyes closed, she leaned against Harlee's shoulder, breathed the smell of clean coat and fresh pine shavings, and whispered a prayer. Then she gave the pinto a final scratch and jogged back to the cottage. Her ribs were nearly healed, and while she couldn't yet run without pain, a slow jog was doable. In a few weeks she'd be riding, making up for lost time, mapping out the road to

Rolex. The thought had her grinning as she wiped her feet at the door and slipped inside. Paul was already up, brewing coffee.

She crossed the room with a bounce in her step, wound her arms around his neck and kissed him. His hands rested against the small of her back, and their comfort seemed to seep through her skin, warming her from the inside out. She tipped her face up and spoke over a contented sigh. "Hey, can I talk to you about something?"

Paul's face went from welcoming to concerned. Sara stifled a giggle and smoothed her features into a more serious expression. "You leave tomorrow morning, and I need to know something before you go."

"What is it?" His voice was higher than usual, almost a tenor.

*-Quit scaring the poor guy.*
*-What a dweeb.*
*Shut up.*

She took his hand and pulled him to the cozy living room. "I'm not trying to make you nervous, but I think you should probably sit down."

Paul planted himself on the edge of the couch, his face broadcasting dread. She knelt on the braided rug, reached into a pocket, and removed a cigar band she'd found in an outdoor ashtray. Eyes closed, she sucked in a breath and spoke quickly over an exhale.

"Paul Emerson, will you marry me?"

"What?" Paul's mouth fell open.

*-Is he breathing?*

*-Check his pulse.*

*He's fine. Give him a minute.*

Paul stammered, "Are you serious? Are you kidding? Are you sure?"

Sara held out the cigar band. "Is that a yes? I think I've proven I can stand on my own two feet."

"You always have." He grabbed her hand and kissed it.

Sara slipped the makeshift ring around his finger and launched herself against him. His arms slipped around her, warm and undemanding, and she covered his face in kisses, finally plucking at his lips with her teeth before covering his mouth with hers. She wrapped her fingers around his belt buckle and gave it a speculative tug.

He whispered against her ear, "Hold on a minute." With a quick roll to one side, he deposited her on the cushion beside him and got to his feet. "I'll be right back."

*What the hell?*

*-Gay, gay, gay, gay-*

*He is not!*

Paul headed for the bedroom, and Sara listened to the sound of his desk drawer being pulled open, then pushed back in place. He returned holding a small velvet box and a large manila envelope. "I bought this for you months ago," he said. "But I wasn't sure I'd ever be able to give it to you."

Sara held her breath. Paul knelt before her, held out the plush little box and opened the lid. She gulped at the sight of a diamond set on a simple gold band.

"It's way prettier than yours," she said as Paul slipped the ring onto her finger, "and it doesn't smell at all of tobacco."

"I'm not done yet." There was mischief in his eyes as he held out the envelope. "I have something else for you."

*Now what?*

*-He's been planning.*

*-Way better than you.*

*Shut up.*

Sara took the envelope from his hands, wondering at his obvious delight.

"What's in it?"

He raised an eyebrow. "It's an engagement gift."

Sara reached inside, tingling with curiosity. But when she withdrew the deed to the house and stables, she couldn't say a word.

*-He kept secrets.*

*Gifts are supposed to be secret, so shut up. I'm not listening.*

"How did you afford it?" Sara wiped tears from her cheeks. "You already have one mortgage."

"I sold the house in Hollis," he said. "I decided I'd rather be with you than live in a fancy neighborhood. We own the house and stables outright, and we have a share of the inn."

"But why?" Sara stared at him as realization settled over her. He'd bought the house and stable while they were apart. It didn't make sense. "Why take the risk when you weren't sure we could ever be together?"

He cupped her chin in his hands, turned her face upward and answered her with a kiss that left her quivering, aching for more. As she snuggled against him, he scooped her into his arms and carried her to the bedroom. His eyes were moist as he touched her. His gentle embrace reminded her she could easily pull away, could always be herself, would forever be free. For the first time in her life she felt completely safe.

She waited for the voices to disagree, to tell her she was stupid and naïve, to warn her that Paul would hurt and betray her. But as she wrapped herself around him and surrendered to the warmth of his caress, her mind was still. Her thoughts were her own.

The voices had nothing to say.

# About the Author

*Author Nancy DeMarco and Miss Louise*
*Photo courtesy of Tammy McCracken*

*From the author, Nancy DeMarco:*

All I ever wanted was to spend my life in the company of horses. Like the character in this book, I had no social skills. The only place I belonged was on the back of a horse.

My mother was the writer in the family, though she didn't have the confidence to pursue her gift. She did all my high school writing assignments, not that I couldn't do them myself. But she had a burning need to write, a hunger that I lacked.

When I began putting stories on paper, for the first time, my passion for horses took a back seat to something new. I realized a part of me had always wanted to write, and it deserved a chance to breathe.

I still have my horses, though I'm less of a rider than I once was. And I'm married to the most wonderful man in the world, the inspiration for one of the characters in this book. But now, when the roosters crow me awake, my mind skips past the barn and goes straight to the stories I will tell.

I write for myself but also for my mom, who may have become a writer herself, if only she'd known she could.

CPSIA information can be obtained at www.ICGtesting.com
Printed in the USA
LVOW041729210812

295315LV00005B/66/P